an Offer from the Marquess

SADIE BOSQUE

Copyright © 2022 by Sadie Bosque

All rights reserved. No part of this publication may be reproduced, stored or transmitted in any form or by any means, electronic, mechanical, photocopying, recording, scanning, or otherwise without written permission from the publisher. It is illegal to copy this book, post it to a website, or distribute it by any other means without permission.

First edition

*This book was professionally typeset on Reedsy.
Find out more at reedsy.com*

To all the mothers on earth and in heaven.

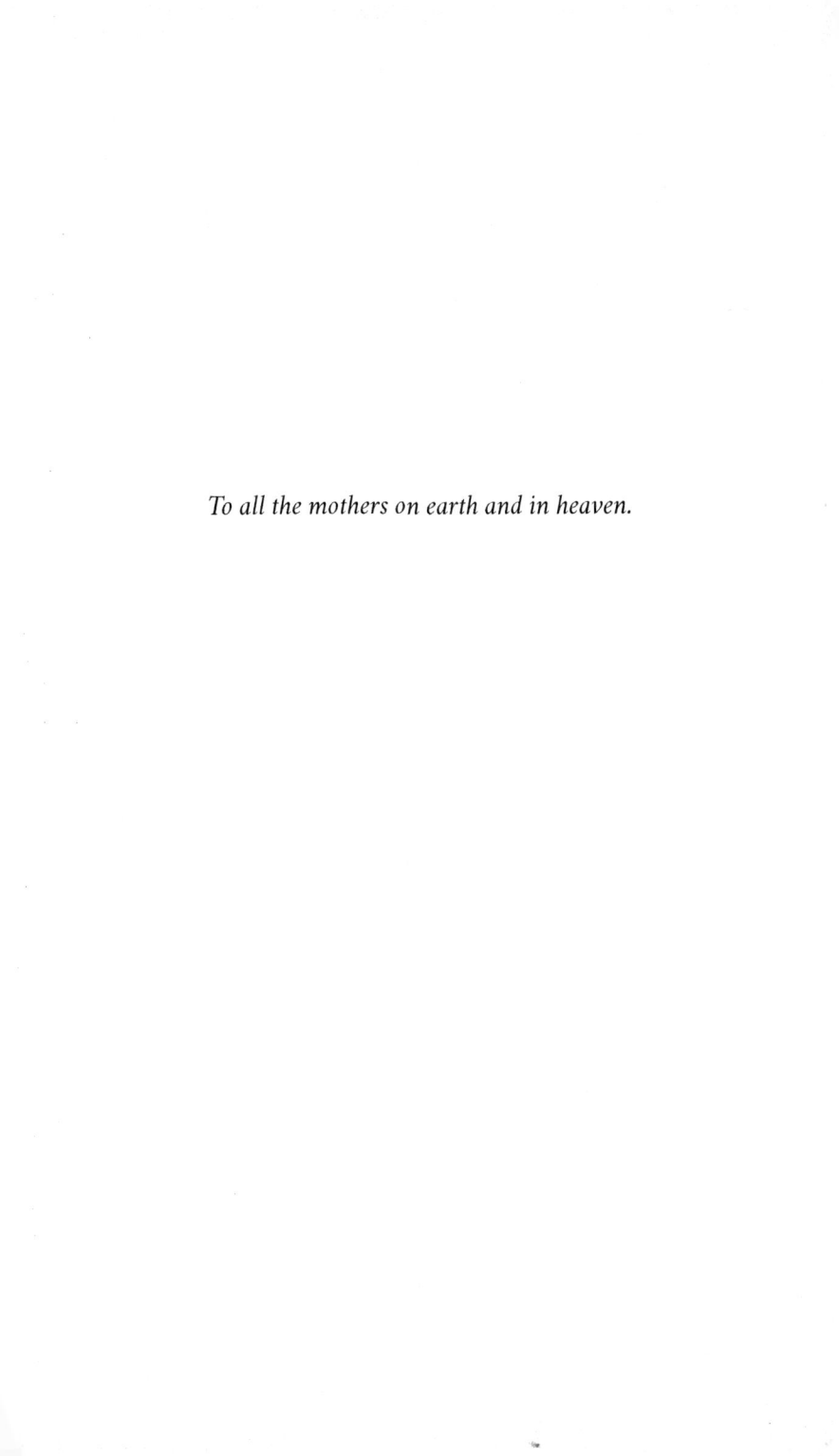

Contents

Acknowledgement	iii
Author's note	iv
Chapter 1	1
Chapter 2	14
Chapter 3	24
Chapter 4	41
Chapter 5	48
Chapter 6	62
Chapter 7	73
Chapter 8	81
Chapter 9	94
Chapter 10	106
Chapter 11	115
Chapter 12	124
Chapter 13	132
Chapter 14	140
Chapter 15	152
Chapter 16	162
Chapter 17	170
Chapter 18	181
Chapter 19	192
Chapter 20	204
Chapter 21	216
Chapter 22	228

Chapter 23	233
Chapter 24	239
Chapter 25	250
Chapter 26	260
Chapter 27	270
Chapter 28	281
Chapter 29	292
Chapter 30	305
Chapter 31	317
Chapter 32	325
Chapter 33	334
Chapter 34	348
After The End	353
Epilogue	355
Salted Almonds	358

Acknowledgement

Writing a book is never a solo effort. My book wouldn't be the same without my friends, my biggest supporters. So the hugest of thanks to the following people:

My trusted beta reader, who is also my biggest cheerleader and helper, Nicole Yost. She is also a bookstagrammer with plenty of books to recommend. Follow her @happily_after_heas

My amazing editor, who is lightning fast and super thorough. I would never meet a deadline without you, Tracy Liebchen.

My friend and Regency romance authors Fenna Edgewood and Cara Maxwell. Thank you, for your friendship, advice and support.

Author's note

This work of fiction contains adult content, strong language, violence, off page death, bullying, child abuse, infertility issues and other content that might be triggering to some.

Chapter 1

Every mistake is precious.

I remember you telling me those words, dear Mother, as clearly as though you whispered them to me yesterday.

Every little, insignificant mistake we make teaches us truths about the world, truths that are necessary for building our character. And the more mistakes we make, the more equipped we shall be in our future life.

However, what you failed to mention was something I had to learn on my own. Not only do we learn from our mistakes, sometimes we have to pay for them, too.

For me, payment came during the dreadful night of the Duchess of Somerset's ball...

The Honorable Isabel Lewis sat in the corner of the room, flanked by Lady Crosby and the Dowager Marchioness of Somerville. The older ladies were discussing some mishap or another, which Isabel was not terribly interested in. At least not at the moment.

An Offer from the Marquess

She was preoccupied with watching the servants fill the food trays and pour the punch.

Isabel enjoyed balls, but ever since the death of her parents, she had always attended them with one goal in mind: to learn from others and become a better hostess.

Everything was running like a well-oiled machine in the Duchess of Somerset's ballroom. The decorations were wonderful, the food was lovely, and the music was pleasant. There weren't too many guests in the ballroom. At least, not so many that people were suffocating in the heat. The windows were open, allowing for a fresh breeze.

The ice had melted in one of the bowls by the banister. Someone needed to—the footman quickly stepped in and refilled it.

Isabel sniffed. *Not a flaw in sight.*

Well, maybe there was something that Isabel would consider a flaw. But it had nothing to do with Evie's hosting abilities.

There was a man present in the room whom Isabel did not particularly find pleasant to see. It was her former betrothed, the Earl of Stanhope.

Stanhope and Isabel were hopelessly in love once upon a time, or at least that's what Isabel had thought. But he proved rather quickly that he was not the man she had thought him to be. He had abandoned her during the most difficult time of Isabel's life, the time when she needed all the love and support she could get.

That summer, Isabel's family had received a missive that her brother Ben had died in action. Unable to cope with her grief, her mother had soon left this world, too. And right after her mother's death, Stanhope had disappeared without

Chapter 1

a trace.

This would not have been the worst thing if Isabel had not found out that he had eloped with another lady shortly after. Only weeks after the tragedy at the Lewis household.

Isabel had never properly moved on from the pain of his betrayal.

How was she supposed to move on when the person she relied upon most left her during the most trying time of her life without so much as a word?

She tried to ignore the gaping ache in her heart, but every time she saw him, the raw injury bled a little more inside.

It didn't matter that she didn't want him anymore. It did not matter that so many years had passed. The memory of first love and first betrayal was difficult to shake off.

Isabel often fantasized about seeing Stanhope crawl on his hands and knees, begging for her forgiveness.

She did not want him, no. Besides, he was a married man, an entanglement she neither needed nor wanted. But fantasy wasn't rational. It was just that—a fantasy. And there was something extremely satisfying about imagining a man who had abandoned her admitting to his mistake.

With a wistful sigh, Isabel got up, excused herself from her companions, and headed for the ladies' necessary.

She wasn't going to be invited to dance. She almost never was. Isabel was headed toward spinsterhood with sure steps, and she did not mind it one bit.

Her brothers were the only people who ever asked for her hand in dance, but they were currently occupied, discussing some gentlemanly business with a group of other men. This meant that Isabel was practically invisible and bored out of her wits.

She was looking forward to the next part of her life when she'd finally be able to happily retire to one of her brother's numerous estates.

Soon, when Richard—Viscount Gage and the oldest of her brothers—finally married, she would not need to perform hostess duties for him. He'd have his wife by his side, and Isabel would be free to do as she pleased.

She already had a plan in mind. First, she'd go and visit her little sister, Samantha. Sam had gotten married last season and birthed a healthy babe a couple of months ago. Isabel had gone to visit her for a few weeks back then, but she had to return because of Gage's upcoming betrothal ball. But once this business with his wedding was finished, she would spend a few months in the loving bosom of her sister's family.

And then she would settle down at one of Gage's quiet estates.

So lost was Isabel in pleasant thoughts of the future that she hadn't heard the steps slowly approaching until someone grabbed her by the arms and shoved her into the nearest alcove.

Isabel took a breath to scream, but a hand covered her mouth.

"Shh, it's just me." The hand slowly lifted off her face. "Please, do not scream."

Isabel squinted in the dim alcove only to recognize Stanhope, her former betrothed, as he stood a few inches away from her.

"Oh, Lord, you frightened me out of my wits!" Isabel said in a hushed tone.

"Apologies, but I had to be circumspect. I've been meaning to speak to you all evening."

Chapter 1

"Why?" Isabel smoothed her skirts, while inside, her turmoil raged. "Why not just approach me in the ballroom?"

"Because what I am about to say to you is not for anyone else's ears. I-I needed to speak to you privately."

Isabel looked around the curtain-shielded alcove and crossed her arms over her chest. She felt vulnerable alone with the man who'd broken her heart and wished to be out of the confined space as soon as she could. "Well, we are certainly alone now. What do you wish to speak to me about?"

"Isabel... I know that we haven't spoken for a long time, and I know that I am to blame, but I wanted to apologize for the way I behaved when your mother passed on."

Isabel was taken aback for a moment, but she quickly composed herself and scoffed. "Please, this is unnecessary. It was a long time ago and best left forgotten."

"But it's not," Stanhope said vehemently. "My mother pressured me to get married. With her health issues, she was worried I'd be left without a mistress of the estate, and you know she was all about doing one's duty."

Isabel and Stanhope had been betrothed for over a year, and his mother had not been vehement about them marrying. So Isabel doubted she'd suddenly pushed him into marriage in a span of two weeks. Unless, of course, she'd taken the opportunity to get him married to someone more suitable than a viscount's daughter. She decided not to voice her thoughts, however.

"I wanted to wait for you, but with your mourning, I knew I couldn't wed you soon. And I couldn't go against my mother's insistence... I know it is a poor excuse," he hastened to continue when he saw Isabel was about to interject, "but I was young and a fool. Please, I do hope that you can find it in your heart to forgive me."

Isabel stood frozen, listening to the overdue apology. How many nights had she cried, wishing for Stanhope to call on her after their family tragedy? How many times had she wished to be enveloped in his comforting embrace? But it had been years ago. Stanhope had ignored her and hadn't made any attempts to speak to her since. What had changed, and more importantly, why now?

"Very well," Isabel said slowly. "I forgive you."

She moved to leave, but Stanhope took her hands in his. A frisson of pleasure passed through her despite her better judgment.

"Truly?" His voice held a note of hope.

This was too much. Isabel's cheeks burned, and her heart rioted in her chest. She wished to leave. "Lord Stanhope, why are you insisting on it now?"

"Phillip. Please, call me by my first name."

"I don't—" Isabel started, but Stanhope cut her off.

"I think we are too familiar to be so formal. Or have you forgotten?"

"No. I have not forgotten, but it seems like you have. It's been years, Phillip!"

"I know. And I am a fool to have waited for so long. I know that now too. I tried to be a faithful husband, a good husband to my wife, and that is why I have not come to you sooner. But my marriage is not a happy one, Isabel." He tightened his fingers around hers. "You might even know that. Perhaps that is my fault because I have always been in love with you. That has never changed."

Isabel's mouth gaped open. Had she dozed off? Was this one

Chapter 1

of her flights of fancy? Because a man who had barely looked at her for the past eight or so years seemed to be currently confessing his love to her. Isabel had to blink to make certain she wasn't dreaming.

"I want us to be together, Isabel, dear." Stanhope raised his hand and cupped Isabel's cheek.

The contact jolted Isabel back into reality.

"But... how? You are married!"

"Yes, I am. But it isn't a happy marriage. You needn't worry. And I heard that you are not looking to marry either. We can be together. I shall set up a townhouse—"

Isabel reared back, freeing her hand from his grasp. "Are you propositioning me to become your mistress?"

"Yes... I-I thought it clear. I am a married man, but this shouldn't impact our relationship. You are a spinster now. You are free to do as you please."

Isabel scoffed and fought her way out of the alcove. Stanhope grabbed her by the arm and slammed her back against the wall. Dull pain originated in the back of her head and back. Isabel tried to wiggle out of his hold.

"Do not walk away without thinking it through. Without giving us a chance," he growled.

"You took our chance away when you walked away from our betrothal while I was the most vulnerable," Isabel sneered into his face.

"I know you are angry, but if you think about it a little, you will understand. We can still be happy."

Isabel found it difficult to breathe in the tiny alcove with Stanhope towering over her. Her face heated, and her breaths came out in short gulps. "Please unhand me."

"There's still passion between us. I know you feel it too."

An Offer from the Marquess

Stanhope's face descended toward her, and the next moment, his lips were on hers.

Isabel tried to twist away, but he took her face between his hands, opening his mouth over hers, and kissed her savagely. His mouth, wet and demanding, was moving over her lips, his tongue seeking entrance. Isabel whimpered in protest and shoved at his chest, but Stanhope didn't budge.

The next thing happened in a flash. Isabel barely registered herself move.

She had grown up with four brothers, and they had taught her a lot. Isabel knew how to climb trees, swim in the lake, and, most importantly, how to fend off an attack.

Isabel raised her leg and stepped on Stanhope's instep with the heel of her slipper. Stanhope yelped as he let her go, a grimace of pain and surprise on his face. Isabel didn't wait for him to retaliate or apologize. She took off in the opposite direction.

"Isabel, wait!" Stanhope called behind her, but she didn't even slow down.

Isabel picked up her skirts and hurried away from him. What a pompous cad! To kiss her—*forcibly*—when his wife was in the next room. His marriage might not be a happy one, but Isabel intended to be happily unattached to slimy lords.

There was a crash behind her as if someone hit the wall or a floor. Perhaps Stanhope had stumbled and fell. That would certainly teach him not to accost unsuspecting ladies in alcoves. Voices followed her, and Isabel hurried her steps. She was not about to be witnessed with Stanhope. That way lay an unpardonable scandal.

She was so adamant about getting away that she didn't pay attention to what she was running toward. Her mind was

Chapter 1

in complete disarray. And that was the reason that she only realized at the last moment that she was approaching the ballroom doors.

It wouldn't do to show up in the ballroom winded and out of breath. Her hair must be terribly disordered, too. Isabel made a sharp left turn into an adjoining corridor and... collided with the tall, broad form of a man.

The man didn't anticipate a tackle, so they both fell over in an undignified heap. Their limbs tangled as Isabel's skirts weighed them both down. Isabel sputtered, fighting to get off the floor.

"Miss, please stop moving. You are crushing my... the most valuable parts of male anatomy," the man beneath Isabel stated in the driest of tones.

"I am trying to get off you! I would appreciate a little help," Isabel answered irritably.

"Your hair is in my face, I can't even—" The man didn't finish his sentence, and whatever he was about to say would forever stay a mystery because, at that moment, the doors to the ballroom opened, and light footsteps alerted them that someone had stepped into the hall.

"For shame!" The voice of a withered old lady sounded like a whip to Isabel's ears. "During the ball and right in the hall!"

Isabel whimpered as she tried to get up. The gentleman beneath her took her by the waist and easily set her aside. Isabel scrubbed the hair away from her face, her neck growing more heated with every moment. Her legs were uncovered to her knees, and she hastily covered them with her skirts.

The Dowager Marchioness of Somerville was still sputtering offendedly with her companion, Lady Crosby. Evie appeared at their side, followed by her husband, the Viscount

An Offer from the Marquess

St. Clare.

Perfect. All she needed was more people to witness her disgrace.

St. Clare took in the tableau with raised brows, then whistled low.

"I suppose our work here is done, Vane," he said cheerfully. "Congratulations, we've just found you a wife."

* * *

Richard Lewis, Viscount Gage, paced the floor of the duchess's library like a tiger restlessly circling his cage. Only he wasn't circling the room. He was walking a straight line between the two camps that had formed in the library.

On the far side from the doors sat Isabel with her brother Adam, while on the other side of the hearth Evie, St. Clair, and the Marquess of Vane—the man Isabel had run into—discussed something in hushed tones.

Any moment now, Isabel expected Richard to erupt into a rage. Instead, he slowed his steps and halted right in front of her.

"You do not have to marry him. I hope you know that," he finally said.

Tears sprung to the corner of Isabel's eyes. She could withstand rage and anger, but she was unprepared for kindness. "Don't I?"

"We married Sam off to Ashbury because of a scandal, and you know how that turned out," he said with a grimace. Richard did not like Sam's husband one bit.

Isabel wiped at her eyes and suppressed a chuckle. "With Sam happily married and a beautiful babe on her lap?"

Chapter 1

"He almost killed her!" Richard growled.

"Please, do not be overdramatic," Isabel said quietly.

Richard ran a hand through his hair. "I am glad Sam is happy, but I do not trust Ashbury, and I shall be keeping an eye on him at all times. Despite that, Sam is in love with him for reasons I shall never understand. You, on the other hand, do not even know Vane. Hell, I don't even know Vane. Adam?"

Adam shook his head. "He's a recluse. He's been hiding for over a decade at his estate. Who knows what he's been up to there." He turned toward Isabel with his brows furrowed. "What do you want to do?"

"What do you mean, what do I want?" Isabel played with the folds of her skirt, not meeting her brother's searching eyes. "You know what I want, what I've always wanted."

"Isabel, it is because I know of your wishes I am asking you this. If you showed any desire for a family, I would be challenging Vane to a duel."

Richard scoffed.

"Very well, perhaps Rich here would be doing the challenging, but I wouldn't be far behind."

"Oh, for heaven's sake! A duel? For running into me in the hall? Perhaps you'd be better off challenging Mrs. Busybody Crosby for tittering false testimonies about what happened to everyone at the ball."

Adam took a deep breath. "Either way, since you don't want a marriage... Then perhaps it's best ignored altogether. We shall support you in any decision, shan't we?" He cocked a brow toward his brother.

Richard shifted from one foot to another.

"Shan't we?" Adam repeated louder.

An Offer from the Marquess

"Adam is right," Richard agreed reluctantly. "We do not have any more sisters to marry… And it will be years before Sam's children make their debut. Perhaps this scandal will be forgotten."

"And what of your aspirations in Parliament? Wouldn't a ruined sister spoil your chances at respectability in the House of Lords?" Isabel protested.

"The *ton* doesn't look at a lord with a ruined sister with the same contempt as it does a ruined lady herself," Richard said.

Adam nodded. "We shall make do. And by the time Sam's child grows up, the scandal should be forgotten."

"Oh my God!" Isabel covered her mouth with her hand, just remembering Richard's bride. "What about Lady Aurora Bainbridge? Her father despises scandal. He was hesitant about the match as it is!"

"The pompous marquess didn't think a viscount was suitable enough for his daughter," Adam confirmed, grumbling under his breath.

"See? He is not going to let her marry you after this. Or even if he is, he is within his right to forbid your wife—your children—from seeing me."

"That is not going to happen," Richard boomed.

Isabel didn't pay him any heed. "I am fairly certain the Bainbridges shall not accept me as part of their family, and I am not certain I would fault them for that. I can't jeopardize your future."

Richard waved a dismissive hand. "Let me worry about my wife, dear sister."

"I am afraid I cannot." Isabel stood and smoothed her skirts. "And perhaps you, as a lord, can afford the risk, but what about Adam?"

Chapter 1

Adam scoffed. "Please, do not fret about me."

"And Alan? Once he returns from the Continent, he shall have to look for a respectable career." Isabel shook her head, resolute to do what was right. "No. I shall not let you carry the brunt of my failure. It was not my fault, or anybody's, but I am the one to pay for it."

"I am not about to let you martyr yourself for the sake of the family," Richard protested.

"It is not your choice to make," Isabel said stonily. She thought for a moment before continuing. "Besides, it does not all have to be bad. I might get children out of this unfortunate situation."

Her brothers shifted uncomfortably, not quite meeting her eyes.

"Yes," Isabel said with a nod, more confident in her decision. "I have made up my mind. I shall marry him."

Chapter 2

Rhys, the Marquess of Vane, sat opposite his friend Viscount St. Clare and his wife, the Duchess of Somerset, in the library. The couple talked between themselves in hushed tones, letting Rhys stew in his thoughts, and he was grateful for it.

When Rhys came to the Duchess of Somerset's ball, he did so with the sole purpose of finding a wife. He knew exactly the kind of woman he wanted to marry.

He needed a seasoned woman who knew how to deal with children and run his estates. Perhaps a widow with a child or two in tow.

He needed a proper woman. Someone who was free of scandal and could demonstrate all the rules of proper decorum and never sully the Vane title. His title had suffered enough. He needed to bring it back into the world with grace.

He didn't need the lady to be attractive. The less appealing she was to other men, the better. And as for him, after years of abstinence, he was certain he'd be able to conjure up the

Chapter 2

need long enough to try and conceive an heir.

After all, he had managed to bed his former wife for almost two years. He couldn't imagine the nights with his next wife to be more daunting than that.

In short, he needed a mother for his daughter, a hostess for his estates, and a perfectly proper lady to carry his title.

And Miss Isabel Lewis was absolutely wrong for all his purposes.

"Well," St. Clare said, as he took his wife's hand and played with her fingers, "at least it was quick."

"Only you could see something good from this atrocious situation," Rhys noted drily.

"You did say you didn't want to linger among the *ton*," the duchess pointed out.

"No." Rhys let out a pained breath. "No, I did not want to linger among the *ton*, but what I wanted more was to avoid scandal."

"Pft!" St. Clare waved the issue away. "This little thing? It will be forgotten by noon on the morrow."

The duchess chuckled. She looked at her husband with bright eyes and a clear expression of adoration on her face. They were absolutely in love, damn them. Rhys felt a slight pang in his chest. He had given up on love a long time ago and was prepared to spend his life without it. But something about watching the couple before him called to the young boy that Rhys had once been—the boy who'd yearned for love.

Rhys cleared his throat. "I doubt that. And Miss Lewis is not exactly the proper lady I was looking for. I do not need a scandalous woman for a wife."

"Scandalous?" The duchess dragged her attention from her adoring husband long enough to raise a brow at Rhys. "I hardly think you know Isabel well enough to make such an assessment of her character."

Rhys was afraid he did know Miss Lewis well enough to make such a statement. He was prepared to wager that he knew her a lot better than the duchess did. After all, he had known her when they were a lot younger. Before he had even married.

After all, he had thought himself in love with her once upon a time.

Rhys shook the memory away.

"With all due respect, you married St. Clare. So I think your threshold for the word *scandalous* might be a lot higher than mine," Rhys said.

St. Clare laughed, and his wife directed a stern glance his way.

"My debauched husband aside, I do not associate myself with scandalous people," she said with all the haughtiness of a duchess.

St. Clare raised a brow. "You ran away in the middle of the night, accosted me in my bedchamber, and demanded I marry you. I do not think we could find a lady more scandalous than you if we tried. So, of course, in comparison, every other lady seems quite proper."

The duchess started protesting, but the viscount took her face between his hands and planted a demanding kiss on her mouth.

Rhys directed his eyes heavenward before looking away. He did not want to witness the improper behavior of his scandalous friend.

However, St. Clare could afford it. He was the most notorious rake in London, and he'd managed to marry the

Chapter 2

most influential woman in England aside from the Queen.

Rhys had no such luck. He would have to make do with the unscrupulous sister of a rakehell viscount.

"Gabriel, please!" The duchess twisted away from her husband with a chuckle. "I think you proved your scandalous reputation quite enough." Her cheeks were cherry red from embarrassment.

"Very well, I'll wait a few moments until we're done here," her husband said in a low voice.

"My apologies for keeping you here with my unremarkable problems," Rhys said drily.

St. Clare sent him a charming smile. "I do sympathize with your plight, my friend. You shall have to marry a beautiful lady with a sizable dowry. The horror!"

"You cannot possibly understand the quandary I am in. You court scandal; I try to avoid it. And I have to think thrice about the choices I make. Once for myself, once for my title, and once again for my daughter."

"If you want, I can go out there with my wife and create another scandal that will eclipse yours in a trice."

The already red face of the duchess turned the color of vermilion. She swatted at him playfully and pursed her lips, trying to remain composed. "Nothing you can do will ever surprise the *ton*, my dear."

St. Clare caught her hand and placed a lingering kiss on her knuckles.

Footsteps sounded from the other side of the room, and Rhys was actually relieved to be joined by the Lewis family, whom he did not particularly like. But he could not be more grateful for the interruption. His friend was not helpful at all, and Rhys didn't think he'd be able to spend another moment in the company of the two lovebirds.

Miss Lewis was flanked by her brothers, forcing Rhys, St. Clare, and the duchess to get up and greet them.

"Have you come to a decision?" Viscount Gage, Miss Lewis's brother, asked.

Rhys gave a slight nod, although his insides tightened with apprehension. "I do not feel like I have a choice in the matter."

"Don't you?" Gage raised his brow.

Rhys shook his head. "I need a respectable marriage. Your family is anything but respectable—"

"Vane!" the duchess and St. Clare exclaimed in unison.

Rhys frowned. "Well, it's true. Gage is a libertine and a rake. Their younger sister married out of scandal, and now you want me shackled to the most scandalous of you all!"

Everyone turned to Miss Lewis, their expressions confused. She frowned. "I am the most scandalous?"

She looked straight at him, but it was obvious that she did not recognize him at all. None of them did. And while Rhys had not spent much time in the company of the men of the family, he had spent quite a few summers following Miss Lewis around.

He had been in love with her, for heaven's sake. Yet there was not even a glimmer of recognition in her eyes. And that hurt him more than this entire situation. And perhaps it was the reason for Rhys's brusqueness.

"But if I refuse to marry you," he continued, "the scandal will follow my name, too. It is better we marry, and soon."

Miss Lewis stood as still as a statue as if shocked by his words. Why was she shocked? Had she not expected a proposal?

She blinked, looked at her brothers, then squared her

Chapter 2

shoulders. "Absolutely not!"

Her brothers looked at her in surprise. Apparently, they did not expect her refusal either. Was she mad? She had no choice but to accept. Unless, of course, she was immune to scandal.

"Pardon me?" Rhys scowled.

Her brothers stepped closer to her and crossed their arms over their chests. Both Viscount St. Clare and the Duchess of Somerset were pursing their lips, holding on to their laughter.

"I am afraid you've been rejected, my friend," St. Clare clarified helpfully with a wide smile.

Rhys just shook his head. The impetuous woman was ruining her future and his as well. "Well, I do not accept your rejection. Have you no thought for your future at all? I should have realized that considering the past, but—"

"What past?" she cried. "I don't even know you!"

Rhys's heart sank at the confirmation of his assumptions. She did not remember him at all. He cleared his throat. "You have no choice but to marry me. Otherwise, you're courting scandal."

"I do not care," Miss Lewis said calmly. "I'd rather eat maggots right off the ground of our northernmost estate than marry you."

St. Clare gave a low whistle, and Gage patted her approvingly on the back.

Rhys just stared at them blankly. *What is going on?*

He had not anticipated a rejection. While sitting across from the scandalous St. Clare and his wife, all Rhys's thoughts had been occupied by his misfortune. He was upset that he'd have to marry a woman he did not want.

Not even once had he considered that she would give him

a clean way out. But now that she had, he felt oddly bereft.

"You heard her, Vane. She is not marrying you, and that's that," came Gage's steady voice.

Rhys did not understand her brothers' support. Their name would be associated with a ruined sister forever. "Surely, you know this is a mistake. You are a peer, Gage. Your reputation will be in tatters after this scandal."

"And so will yours," Gage said calmly.

And don't I know it! "So why would you agree to this madness? Your sister clearly has no regard for you or anyone else in this room!"

"Careful," Gage growled and stepped forward. "Or you might earn yourself a spot at dawn."

"Perhaps some tea is in order?" the duchess intervened cheerfully.

"No, I am not in a dining mood. Thank you." Rhys turned on his heel and stalked away before the scandalous family dragged him into a duel. *A duel!* That's the last thing he needed.

* * *

Isabel stood shaking in the library, watching the marquess stalk away.

Her hands were clammy, and her heart was rioting inside her chest. What had just happened?

"I better follow him," St. Clare said. He bent down and placed a lingering kiss on his wife's cheek.

Isabel barely paid attention to her surroundings. She was in a state of shock.

"Where in the world did that come from?" Evie exclaimed

Chapter 2

as soon as the door closed after her husband. "I thought you were the most sensible in your family." She came toward Isabel with a puzzled frown on her face.

Adam wrapped a protective arm around Isabel's shoulders.

"I thought you were going to accept him," Richard said.

"I-I do not know what came over me," Isabel stammered out. "But after what probably constitutes as a proposal in his addled mind, I imagined my entire life with him. I imagined looking at his disapproving frown every time he saw me, and I just could not accept. I am so sorry, Richard."

"Do not apologize, sister. We stand by you without question."

"I shall be honest. I am puzzled by his behavior," Evie said. "He was very adamant against marrying you and the way he approached it... He said something about your past. Did you ever cross paths? Perhaps you offended him without noticing?"

"I—" Isabel shook off Adam's arm. She was getting overwarm and a bit unsettled. "I-I don't think I've ever met him in my entire life. I heard he married young, right around the time our... when—" *When our brother died.* And then their mother.

Isabel couldn't finish the sentence aloud. There was too much grief in the Lewis household around the time of Samantha's debut. Add to that Isabel's broken betrothal to Stanhope, and Isabel had spent most of her years out of society's eyes.

"And then when I returned to society, he was already widowed, living at his estate, a hermit. I don't believe we have crossed paths."

Evie frowned and looked at the door. "He was nothing

but gracious toward me when we visited his estate. I cannot explain the change of attitude."

"Well, it does not matter anymore," Richard said. "We are not to be connected to the arrogant arse by marriage. You did well, sister. Let us go home now."

"Yes, please. I believe I've had enough excitement for one day," Isabel said, still shaken by the experience.

"Perhaps you'd want to leave through the servants' exit to avoid all eyes on you?" Evie offered solicitously.

"No." Richard's voice was stony, confident. "We shall not hide out. Neither of us has done anything shameful."

Isabel smiled. She could use the vote of confidence.

"Oh, wait. I asked for this to be brought for you." Evie walked over to the settee and picked up a beautiful emerald green shawl. "To go with your gown," she said with a smile.

"Oh, no, it's not necessary—" Isabel began, but Evie was already cloaking Isabel in the shawl.

"You have a rip in your bodice. This should cover it," she whispered in her ear.

A rip in my bodice? Was it from the fall or her struggle with Stanhope? Isabel's cheeks heated in embarrassment. How long had she been walking around with the rip and had not known?

"Thank you," she whispered back.

They walked out of the library a moment later. A few people lingered in the hall, staring at them and whispering behind their fans. Gentlemen leaned their heads toward their companions to hear what was being said about the Lewis family.

"Maybe we should have used the servants' exit after all," Isabel said with a tight smile.

Chapter 2

"Hold your head high, sister," Richard said. "Hold your head high."

* * *

Rhys entered his home, still bristling in anger. He was not easily irritable. On the contrary. Usually, he could not conjure enough emotion to care. But this girl—this woman—Miss Isabel Lewis seemed to pull at his strings.

He didn't want to marry her, he reminded himself. So then why did her rejection sting?

Rhys took off his coat and hat and handed them to his butler. Then he slowly made his way up the stairs.

He walked silently toward the farthest door on the right and cracked it open. The light from the crack between the curtains illuminated his peacefully sleeping daughter's face.

Rhys smiled, studying her innocent features.

No, his daughter deserved far better than a fallen woman for a mother. She'd already had one egotistical wanton for a mother, and that had not ended well at all. The next woman he married would be a perfect lady for his treasure.

Far more suitable than Miss Isabel Lewis.

Chapter 3

A rejection to Gage's upcoming betrothal ball came early the next day. And then another, and another. Some even openly stated in their notes that they would not have their daughters associate with a fallen woman.

As it turned out, polite society was not so polite once one of its members fell from grace. Or just fell.

Nobody cared for the truth. Nobody had even seen Isabel and Vane outside of that ballroom except for the two dreadful old women who had tattled to everyone the inflated tale of what they thought they saw.

There was no explaining what had truly happened. There was no saving Isabel's reputation. She had ruined the good name of her family by simply falling onto the wrong man.

If she had just accepted the dreadful marquess's proposal, she could have avoided more scorn. But it was too late.

Was it too late?

Isabel tapped her foot nervously by her brother's study. Richard and Adam were having a heated discussion about

Chapter 3

their uncertain future. They were arguing about what to do with Isabel since she was now unwelcome in most society homes.

Isabel knew what she wanted to do. She'd go to Sam's house and hide away there for the rest of the season. The scandal would be forgotten by the next year, or at least, people would pretend to have forgotten about the unfortunate Lewis sister and would only whisper about it behind their fans.

Next year, everything would be better. Isabel would be leading the quiet, peaceful life she had always wanted, and her brothers would continue their political aspirations.

"The Marquess of Bainbridge sent a note," Richard said, a little quieter.

"What? What does it say?"

"He rejects my suit. The bastard didn't even have the guts to say it to my face. Coward." There was a loud thump as if something had been thrown against the wall, or possibly Richard's fist crashing onto his desk.

Isabel jumped.

Richard had just lost his bride. And it was all because of her. Isabel swallowed, turned, and quietly left the hall. She didn't have the strength to look into her brothers' eyes. She'd ruined everything.

Next year, everything will be better. But what about this year?

There was only one person who could fix everything. And if there was any way she could salvage the vestiges of their tattered reputations, she'd have to swallow her pride and beg him to do it.

* * *

Isabel stood on the doorstep of the loathsome Marquess of Vane's house, cursing herself inwardly. She would have to scrounge up all her tact to have this dreadful conversation with the awful man. She took a deep breath for the third time and raised her hand to the knocker, only to freeze an inch from the door.

"Do you want me to do it, Miss?" her lady's maid, Anthea, asked behind her.

"No, Anthea, I am quite capable of doing it myself," Isabel said resolutely and then added in a barely audible whisper, "I think."

She raised the knocker and let it fall, praying under her breath. Isabel was not certain what she was praying for. Patience, perhaps, to deal with the marquess and his enormous ego.

A thin, tall, graying old man opened the door and looked at Isabel down his long nose as if she were a bug he wanted to squash.

"Miss Isabel Lewis, for the Marquess of Vane," she said.

The butler glanced around the street as if looking for someone. Then his gaze fell on Isabel's maid, and he raised his brow. "I shall inquire whether his lordship is at home," he said and closed the door in Isabel's face.

Well, the butler was just as arrogant and rude as his master! Isabel dusted her skirt irritably. She was standing like a beggar or a wanton outside of a bachelor's home. She doubted, however, that this trip would land her in a bigger scandal than the one she had already courted. Her brothers might scold her—*would* scold her—but she did not care. She was doing it for them.

The door opened a few moments later, and the butler

Chapter 3

stepped aside, letting her in.

"Thank you," Isabel said with a tight smile.

She stepped into the hall and smoothed her skirts when loud footsteps—or rather a sound loud enough to qualify as the stomping of the bulls—descended from the stairs, echoing against the walls.

Isabel did not have time to look up before a huge, monstrous-looking animal tackled her to the floor. She squeaked before hitting the ground.

The animal sniffed her face and licked her nose.

Isabel didn't know which emotion hit her first. Was it the surprise of being tackled, the horror of a huge animal crushing her, or the disgust at being licked by the foul-smelling fiend?

It definitely took her a moment to realize she was even in pain. Her back felt as if it was on needles, and her head gave a dull ache. Then the monstrous animal got distracted and ran off.

There were more screams and a high-pitched shout as it doubtless tried to tackle more people.

Isabel struggled to get up when the butler finally came to her aid. She dusted off her skirt and cradled her aching head in her hands, thinking that she'd have a rather ugly bump there in a moment.

"Miss? Are you hurt, Miss?" Her terrified maid rushed toward her.

Two or three footmen ran off in pursuit of the beast, leaving the door open after them.

Loud steps sounded from the staircase again, only this time they seemed human.

"Why in the bloody hell is the door open, Monroe?" the

man growled, barely reaching the hall. "You know—" He halted in his tracks, his mouth slightly open, an unspoken syllable on his lips. He looked Isabel up and down with an unflattering gaze and sketched a shallow bow before turning to the butler. "Please, have Miss Lewis wait for me in the study. I need to chase after the bloody dog. And send a few footmen after him, too."

"Yes, my lord. Footmen are already in pursuit."

"Good. Get my coat and hat. I shall follow."

The butler hastened to obey as more steps sounded from the direction of the staircase. Was someone else coming to kick Isabel while she was down?

A small girl ran up to the stern marquess and grabbed him by his breeches. "Where did Button go?"

Button? Isabel raised a brow.

"He ran off. The door was open." The marquess scowled at Isabel. "I shall try to go fetch him, but will you call Mrs. Ainsworth and keep our nice guest company?"

The girl frowned at Isabel and hid behind the marquess's long legs. "Did she let Button free?"

Isabel opened her mouth to respond but was interrupted.

"Darling, you're supposed to greet our guest and curtsy," the marquess said softly.

"But she lost Button!" the girl protested, still not looking directly at Isabel.

"I did not lose him. He attacked me!" Isabel said, offended.

The marquess sent her a withering glance before turning back to the girl. "Button is not lost. I shall find him."

The marquess took his coat and hat from the butler's fingers, donned them, and turned to exit the house.

Isabel looked at the girl, who was now scowling at her. With

Chapter 3

that look on her face, she resembled the marquess immensely.

Isabel had no desire to be left in the house with a hostile little girl and a conceited old butler. Besides, that dog could be anywhere, and she could be stuck there forever.

She turned to the girl with a sweet smile. "I shall go and assist his lordship in looking for the dog," she said as the door closed behind the marquess. "Anthea, please, wait here."

With a nod toward her maid, she scurried out of the house.

Isabel saw the marquess disappearing in the direction of the park and hurried after him. "It is impolite to leave a guest alone in the house," she said as she matched his step.

"You were not alone," he answered, without even bothering to look at her.

"A five-year-old does not count as company in polite society."

He looked at her queerly. "She is six. And since it was your fault the dog has escaped, I do not think leaving you was the worst thing I could have done."

Isabel sputtered in indignation. Was that a threat? "How is that my fault?"

"If you hadn't come, he wouldn't have escaped."

"If it had been trained properly, it wouldn't have jumped on people and left the house at the first available opportunity. Or perhaps it was trying to escape your righteous presence."

The marquess didn't seem to pay attention to her words. He craned his neck, squinting into the alleyway. "He," he said in an offhand manner.

It took Isabel a couple of moments to realize he was addressing her. "Pardon me?"

"He is a he, not an it. And he has a name. *Button.*"

What an inappropriate name for a monstrous dog. Isabel

scoffed. "I have not been properly introduced to that dog, save for the fact that *he* tackled me to the floor. That does not earn one the familiarity to be called by one's first name."

The marquess scoffed. "It is odd to be listening to a lecture on proper decorum from a woman who tackled *me* at the ball and then came to a known bachelor's home without a proper chaperone. So calling a dog by his name might not be the most scandalous thing you have ever done. Besides, he was probably just avenging my honor after what happened at the ball."

"Firstly, spinsters do not need chaperones. And what happened at the ball is that you tackled me! And then insulted my family in what probably passes in your addled mind for a proposal. And after that, you are acting all righteous, as if I am the one in the wrong? At least your name reflects your high opinion of yourself, Lord *Vain*!"

The marquess threw her a withering gaze. "I might be vain, but at least it is not I who spends most of her time on the floor with her skirts tossed up."

Isabel's mouth fell open, but no sound emerged, so shocked she was.

"And since I've seen you this way more than once, then perhaps we should act familiar. You can drop the lord and call me Vane."

"You cad!" Isabel finally pushed past her lips.

"You seem to have trouble with names. It's Vane," he said, unperturbed, then his brows furrowed, and he dashed toward the entrance of the park.

Isabel would have been happy to leave the marquess at this moment, but she had no choice, so she followed him.

They had been walking briskly for a few minutes, and it

Chapter 3

was getting obvious that *Button* was nowhere to be found. Isabel stepped in some mud and cursed.

Vane raised his brow. "It should not come as a surprise that you curse too."

"Oh, would you stop with your righteous attitude? What have I ever done to you to deserve your scorn?" Isabel stopped, forcing the marquess to halt also.

He opened his mouth to say something, but she cut him off with a wave of her hand. "That was rhetorical. I do not need that answered."

"If you're worried about your slippers, you shouldn't have followed me out," he said drily.

"I need to speak with you, and lord only knows how long you will be running around looking for your monster of a dog."

Vane crossed his arms over his chest. "If you need to speak, then speak. And let us part right here."

"There will be no parting." Isabel squared her shoulders. "I came here to accept your insult of a proposal."

Vane didn't move a muscle. Didn't react in any way.

"Did you hear what I just said?"

"Yes. Perfectly. But what makes you think that I shall accept your acceptance of my proposal?"

"Pardon me?"

"You're scandalous, impetuous, and as it turns out, a menace around animals. What is the benefit for me to have you as my wife?"

Isabel was about to turn on her heel and walk away. She contemplated kicking some mud into the overbearing marquess's eyes as she did so, but she took a breath instead. Her brothers' future depended on her.

Then she remembered the spoilt little girl in the house. She might seem like an abomination to Isabel, but the marquess seemed to hold her in esteem.

"Because," she said, with a feigned smile, "the scandal we've created shall haunt every female under your care into their debut. That girl in the house shall not have a chance at a respectable marriage. Your title will be a laughingstock, and all respectable matrons will hide their daughters from you. As much as you might dislike me, marrying me shall solve most of your problems."

The marquess's brows twitched. Was that a reaction?

"All except for finding the damned dog," he said.

He looked away, distracted. He was too concerned with searching for his blasted dog and was not paying her any heed.

Isabel inwardly prayed for patience. "Very well," she said at last. "What if I find the dratted dog for you? Will you marry me then?"

The marquess turned to her, startled. He looked her up and down again with an unflattering gaze, and something of a smirk appeared on his face. "Find the dog first, then we shall talk."

* * *

"What an arrogant cad!" Isabel muttered to herself as she walked through the park, looking for the massive dog that had nearly killed her. Very well, perhaps she was exaggerating. That dog had been trying to be friendly when it tackled her. Or rather, when *he* tackled her, she corrected herself, mimicking marquess's self-important grimace.

Chapter 3

As a result, she was walking alone around the park, like a lunatic. She'd been seen in front of a bachelor's lodgings. She'd probably been observed arguing with Vane. Her already ruined reputation would be in tatters if he didn't marry her. And she'd better hide out in the remotest of estates or even commit to a nunnery.

And she didn't even *want* to marry the righteous marquess! What had she done to deserve such a fate?

Anything was better than becoming Stanhope's mistress, she supposed.

Isabel heaved a sigh and leaned against a tree. Tears burned at the back of her eyes.

What had become of her life? She had been a diamond of the *ton* when she made her come out. Every eligible gentleman bowed at her feet at the mere opportunity to escort her on a walk or to bring her a cup of ratafia.

Now she was fighting to marry a man she didn't like, so she could avoid becoming the mistress of a man she'd once loved.

Her gown was rumpled, her half-boots muddied, her hair disheveled, and she was looking for an enormous dog that had the power to knock her over with a flick of its paw.

And once she found it, what was she to do then?

Isabel flicked a lock of hair away from her face and pushed off the tree. She was not a simpering debutante. She would not be caught crying in the park alone. She was a strong, confident woman who had been taking care of her four siblings after the death of her parents. She'd single-handedly hosted balls and soirees for stuffy old lords and pretentious old matrons when her brother became a viscount.

She could handle one bloody dog!

Isabel put two fingers to her lips and whistled loudly.

Whistling was not something ladies did. But nobody would expect ladylike behavior from her anymore. Her reputation was already in shreds. The least she could do was secure herself a husband.

She whistled again, although she doubted the dog would even respond.

Either fate had finally smiled upon her, or the dratted dog actually paid some heed to the whistle, for at that moment, the monstrous animal galloped toward her. Isabel positioned herself in front of the tree so if the dog attacked her again, she would catch him and not tumble down in the process.

The dog ran full speed toward her, his ears flapping in the wind, his tail wagging happily, his tongue sticking out and slobbering everything on his way. Isabel fisted her hands at her sides and dug her heels into the ground so as not to take off running.

Once the dog was just a foot away, he stood on his back paws and planted his muddy, heavy front paws onto Isabel's chest.

Isabel screamed and covered her face with her hands. Forget being a strong, confident woman! She was not an animal handler. She had never seen such a large animal up close except for a horse, and if she were to die right then and there, she'd make certain to let everybody know that the Marquess of Vane was to blame.

But just as her tumultuous thoughts took on a dark turn, somebody dragged the dog away from her. Isabel opened her eyes to see Vane put a leash on the dog's collar.

"Sit!" he commanded sternly, and the dog obeyed.

Hell, Isabel was tempted to obey too. Her legs barely held her, and she would enjoy sitting down immensely.

Chapter 3

But now, as the dog sat quietly, she could see him clearly. He was truly large, although he didn't seem so sitting next to the tall marquess. He had white—albeit dirty—fur with black spots on his back, his rear, and his head. His dark eyes shone with kindness, and his tongue still stuck out as he studied Isabel.

"Rogers! Gerald!" the marquess shouted.

A few moments later, two liveried footmen appeared by his side.

"Take Button home," he said.

The footmen took the leash and led the animal away. Button barked in protest, although he had no choice but to follow the footmen.

The marquess looked at Isabel and shook his head as if in disapproval.

"I found him," she said as confidently as she could, but her voice shook.

Vane took a handkerchief out of his pocket and handed it to her. Isabel looked at it with a frown. What did she need the handkerchief for? She shrugged and wiped the sweat from her forehead.

The marquess's shoulders shook, and a moment later, he started wheezing. The cad was laughing at her!

Isabel scowled and threw the handkerchief back at him. "What could possibly cause you such amusement?"

Vane caught the handkerchief against his chest and took a step closer. "What causes me amusement is the fact that you're all covered in mud, but the only thing you think of wiping is sweat off your forehead."

Isabel looked down at herself and groaned. Her cloak was covered in paw-shaped mud, her skirts were dirty, and she was certain her face was muddy as well.

"I doubt your handkerchief would help," she grumbled.

"Here, let me." He stepped even closer and started wiping mud off her chest.

A strange feeling originated in the pit of her stomach at the contact. Then he touched her breast... Unintentionally, obviously.

Or was it so unintentional? He thought her loose, so perhaps he was testing how far she'd let him go with his ministrations.

Isabel brushed off his hand. "I am perfectly capable—"

"Hold still." The marquess folded his dirty handkerchief away and took out a clean one.

He put it to her cheek and gently wiped the mud away. He cradled her other cheek in his hand as he did so, his face just inches away. The warmth of his fingers sent shivers up and down her spine.

Isabel's breaths accelerated, her nipples hardened, and now chafed against her corset. She was getting a bit too warm. She swallowed, and the marquess's gaze followed the ripple in her throat.

What was happening?

Vane paused and looked into her eyes. His gaze was heated, and Isabel had a feeling she'd burn if she continued looking into his dark irises. All too soon, he stepped away, and Isabel had to brace her knees and lean against the tree lest she fell.

Isabel blinked and shook her head to collect her scattered thoughts. She started putting her clothing to rights, as she wasn't ready to meet his gaze again.

"I've found your dog," she repeated. "You said we'd talk after. It's after. Let's talk."

Chapter 3

"A public park is not the best place to discuss the scandal we're involved in. Perhaps we should adjourn back to my townhouse."

Isabel dug in her heels. "No. You keep prolonging the inevitable. I just want to know whether you'll marry me or not."

The marquess wrinkled his nose. "To be completely honest, I am not very enthusiastic about the prospect."

Isabel scoffed. "And you think I am? I am horrified by the idea that I might join your family of rude people and gigantic, unmannered dogs!"

"If you find my company so unpleasant and that of my dog, then why chase me *and* the dog around the park? Perhaps you should consider other prospects."

"I have no other prospects!" Isabel cried and squeezed her eyes shut.

She was willing to endure a lot for her family. She swallowed her pride and dignity by even conversing with this man. Her already unsavory reputation was getting dragged through the mud every second she argued with him outdoors. If she didn't marry him, it would be unsalvageable.

But if she did… Well, she'd certainly die.

"Last time we spoke, you said you'd rather eat maggots than marry me. What has changed?" the marquess asked. "Maggots were not to your liking?"

"If it were just about me and my wants, I'd never look your way, you arrogant cur."

"And if it were just about me and my wants, I'd never exchange a word with you, you ill-mannered old shrew."

Isabel gasped.

She wanted to kick him in the shins and leave him to suffer.

But they were still outdoors. And although the hour was not fashionable, there were still people about. So she took off her glove and threw it in his face.

The marquess blinked as if startled and caught the glove against his cheek. "Is this an invitation to a duel? That would be vastly preferable to marrying you."

"Take it as an expression of my disgust. Even the thought of being married to you, seeing your face every morning across the breakfast table, repulses me beyond your imagination."

"If we did marry, you wouldn't have to worry about that. I'd lock you up in my northernmost estate and make certain you'd eat nothing *but* maggots."

"Then you'd have to live without heirs. Not that I look forward to sharing a marital bed with you. Maggots would be a better—Oh!"

The marquess seized her by the waist and crushed her body to his.

Isabel's breath left her body as her hands instantly went to hold onto his wide shoulders. Her waist burned where he held her even through the layers of his gloves and her clothing. Her entire body trembled in either anticipation or trepidation.

She craned her neck to look at him and swallowed. He was so very tall. Her head barely reached his shoulders.

He held her tightly in his arms, his eyes roaming her face as he lowered his head. "I'd rather forfeit the marquessate than spend any time in bed with you," he growled, his face only inches away from hers.

"And I'd rather give birth to the spawn of the devil than to your heir. Please unhand me. I am about to cast up my accounts from the feel of your touch on my person."

Chapter 3

"A wanton like yourself?" he scoffed. "You are begging for my touch."

"As if!" she spat. "I'd rather touch a—"

She was rudely interrupted as Vane dipped his head and captured her mouth in a hard kiss.

His lips were unyielding and his kiss urgent, demanding. Isabel opened her lips and welcomed his heated embrace.

Her body went limp as he continued devouring her mouth, his hands roaming her body. It was so pleasant to be held so tightly, kissed so ardently after years of being so alone.

Lonely.

She felt his heat all along her length, and her body instantly arched against his.

Why was he kissing her? *Weren't we just arguing? Is this kiss meant as a punishment?*

Isabel put her arms between their bodies and thumped at his chest. She twisted her head away, and the marquess kissed her ear, her neck.

Isabel whimpered, confused and aroused. She wasn't supposed to feel that way. She was repulsed by the marquess, wasn't she?

He still held her tightly, and she could feel the evidence of his desire pressed against her thigh. The realization made her heat from the inside while her body itched, and she wished to crawl out of her skin.

All too soon, Vane let go of her and stepped away. Isabel reeled and caught herself against the tree.

"See?" the marquess croaked. "Wanton."

Isabel felt her neck and cheeks heat in anger and embarrassment. He'd just used her body's unconscious responses against her. He'd made her enjoy his kisses, only to prove a point! And the most dreadful part of it was that she did indeed enjoy his kisses.

She was so upset and confused she wanted to cry. More than that, she wanted to give him a piece of her mind. But her mind proved blank, so she picked up her skirts and turned on her heel.

"We marry on Sunday," he said to her back. "I'll get us a special license by then."

Isabel did not answer. She walked away, not looking back, and resolved to forget the entire encounter.

Chapter 4

Rhys walked back home, lost in deep thought. What devil had prompted him to kiss Miss Lewis? In daylight, in the middle of the park, no less.

He used to be rational and logical. He had rarely let his emotions get the best of him, yet this woman brought out the worst in him.

When he was close to her, he returned to that young boy, hurt by the girl he thought he loved. But that was so long ago. Harboring any ill will toward her was childish and irrational.

She might be a fallen woman—a wanton—but he did not need to stoop to her level.

He was a marquess. He had a daughter to think of. He had too much to lose, and he shouldn't let that woman get to him.

He entered the house to see the servants scurrying to clean up the hall.

"Where's Millie?" Rhys addressed his butler.

"She went to the blue salon with Button," the old man answered.

Rhys heaved a sigh. The blue salon was probably already ruined.

Button was a good and clever dog. But he was spoilt, and he enjoyed running around the house and jumping on furniture, especially in the company of his little mistress.

Rhys had bought him for his daughter as a puppy. He had never seen a Newfoundland dog before in his life, so he had no idea how large he would grow up to be. Luckily, Button was very friendly. Unluckily, being as huge as he was, he often didn't anticipate his weight would overpower the object of his affections.

The only person he was gentle with was Millie. And for that, Rhys was grateful. Button did not listen to his tiny mistress. But at least Rhys could be certain that the dog would never hurt her.

Rhys slowly made his way toward the blue salon. A loud crash came just before he opened the door and beheld Button rushing toward Millie with something in his mouth.

"Button! Stop!" Rhys yelled, terrified that he could have been wrong and the dog would hurt his little girl.

The dog came to a halt, his tail wagging, a candleholder in his mouth.

Millie giggled and ran toward Rhys. He caught her, picked her up, and approached the dog.

"Why does he have a candle holder in his mouth?" Rhys asked.

"We were playing fetch," Millie answered, unperturbed.

Rhys reached Button, took the candleholder, and placed it on the table.

"What did I say about playing fetch inside the house?"

Millie scrunched up her nose in thought. "Not to do it?"

Chapter 4

"Then why did you do it?"

"I thought we lost him and was so happy to get him back." Millie looked at Rhys with her wide, innocent eyes.

He could never be angry or upset with her. No matter how many times she disobeyed him. Rhys scratched Button's head, and the dog leaned into his touch.

"He is extremely dirty," Rhys said, looking at the dog. "Let us ask Mrs. Ainsworth to bathe him before you play with him further. But no fetch. At least not inside."

Millie wiggled out of Rhys's hold and hugged the dog. "But we do not have a yard here. Where am I to play with him in London?"

Rhys scratched his chin in thought. "You can run with him in the corridor. But please, do not break anything. And we can go for a walk with him in the evening before the sun goes down."

Millie clapped happily and bounced to the servants' bell. She pulled it, and a moment later, Mrs. Ainsworth appeared. Together with a couple of footmen, she took Button for a wash.

Millie was about to run and join them, but Rhys stopped her.

"I need to speak with you," he said, putting a hand on her shoulder.

"But I want to help wash Button!"

"You can help later. Come. Let us sit."

He settled on the sofa, propping his daughter on his lap.

"I have some excellent news," he said with a tight smile. "Soon, you will have a mother."

Millie scrunched up her nose. "But I don't want a mother."

Rhys heaved a sigh. Millie didn't take well to strangers, not that he blamed her. "You need one. And I need a marchioness. This is the way the world works."

"Well, I dislike how the world works. Can we make the world work differently?"

Rhys furrowed his brows, then scratched his jaw. "Perhaps... I hope we can. You will definitely change the world, darling girl. But not right now."

"Why not?" Millie pouted, bouncing her leg.

"Because it takes a long time to change the way the world works. And sometimes, we need immediate action. And at the moment, I need to marry Miss Lewis."

"Miss Lewis? The lady who lost Button?"

"Actually, she was the one who found him—"

"I don't want Miss Lewis to be my mother!" Millie scrambled from Rhys's lap and stomped her tiny foot. "I don't want a mother! Why can't we live like before?"

Rhys slid from the sofa and crouched before his daughter. "I promise you, nothing will change in this house. Nothing will change with us. She will just help us, that's all."

Tears slipped out of Millie's eyes. "I don't want anyone's help. Why do we need help?"

Rhys's heart squeezed at Millie's reaction. *My fault.* "You're growing up, and you need to know things... Things that I can't teach you. And I need to take up the reins of my responsibility in Parliament."

"Did I do something wrong? Is it because of me?" she whispered.

"No, my darling. Trust me. You are a perfect little angel. But you need education. You need to learn how to be a lady."

"I don't want to be a lady. Please, Papa!" Millie directed her liquid eyes toward him, and he almost relented. He could

Chapter 4

never refuse her anything.

But the situation with Miss Lewis was beyond his control. And for the first time in her entire life, he had to say no to his sweet daughter.

"I am sorry, darling girl. But it is done."

* * *

"You are not marrying that man, and that is that!" Richard roared into Isabel's face.

Isabel reared back, wisps of her hair moving from impact, then unhurriedly took out a handkerchief and wiped her face. "I am. He shall come to visit you on the morrow to sign the marriage contract."

"While you were out, running around and getting compromised all over again, I made some inquiries. Do you know that man is accused of murdering his own wife?" Richard scrubbed his face and started pacing restlessly.

Isabel frowned. "Accused? By whom?"

"Rumors, Isabel. There are rumors about this man and not the flattering kind." Richard irritably threw his hands.

"Since when do you put much stock in rumors?"

Richard halted. "Since they are about a man my sister is willing to marry!"

Isabel crossed her arms over her chest. "What do the rumors say, exactly?"

Richard waved a hand.

"No. You are not about to tell me he killed his wife and wave your hand at details."

Richard resumed his pacing. "Does it matter? Because to me, it does not. I have enough trouble worrying about Sam.

I am not about to hand you over to an abusive man."

Isabel crossed her arms over her chest. "I am not leaving until you tell me."

"Lord, why do you have to be so stubborn?" Richard threaded his fingers through his hair in frustration. He walked toward his side table, poured himself a drink, and downed it in one gulp.

Isabel stared at him, unblinking. He must have been truly beside himself to drink in the middle of the day, in front of Isabel no less. "Richard?"

He turned to her, his eyes wild. "Apparently, there was gossip around the *ton* that he mistreated his wife. After about a year of what everyone thought was a happy marriage, his wife started appearing at balls and other functions by herself. And she started telling people that he was cruel and unkind."

"She was walking around London spreading those rumors herself, and everyone believed her?" Isabel had a hard time believing that a cruel man would just let his wife spread those vile stories about him.

"Not at first. Everyone thought she just wanted sympathy and attention—things she probably did not get from her husband. But a year later, she ran off with her lover. That was enough reason to start the rumors, but when her ship was lost at sea, the rumors took a more ominous tone. Isabel, what woman would leave her husband and face ruin if he hadn't treated her badly?"

Isabel wrinkled her nose. Richard made some good points. A happily married woman would not spread vile rumors about her husband and then leave him alone to…

But she hadn't left him alone. She'd left her daughter with the man she called cruel and beastly. What woman would do

Chapter 4

that? There was more to the story, Isabel was certain. And she needed to know more before she retracted her decision. "Richard, I know you are worried—"

"No, don't take that mothering tone with me. You are not my mother, and even if you were, I would not allow you to sacrifice yourself for this family. How can our family prosper if you are in harm's way?"

There. And that was what solidified Isabel's belief that Vane's wife was not as innocent as she proclaimed. There was no better future for the person who left their loved ones in harm's way.

So either she'd lied about Vane's beastly nature to escape with her lover, or she'd left her daughter in the hands of a beast.

Perhaps there was a third option Isabel was not taking into account, but she wouldn't damn her family and drag them all to ruin based on a rumor. She needed to know more. And she knew exactly the person who could help her with that.

Chapter 5

The Duchess of Somerset's carriage rolled up in front of the Gage townhouse the next day. A groom opened the door and helped Isabel inside.

Evie smiled brightly as Isabel sat opposite her. "How happy I am to see you! And extremely glad you decided to marry the marquess, after all. I am certain you two will be a perfect couple."

Isabel smiled tightly. "I highly doubt it."

Evie laughed as the carriage jolted into a start. "So, let's talk about your trousseau!"

Isabel pursed her lips. A trousseau. *Her* trousseau.

Isabel had resigned herself to never even think of a trousseau for herself, let alone order it. She had helped her sister Sam with her needs when she had married, but now that it came to her, she was absolutely lost. And if she could have anyone help her in this matter, there was no one better than the most fashionable lady of the *ton*.

"I've made a list of things we need to order, and I am quite

Chapter 5

certain Madame Deville will be able to make most of it on time," Evie said. "When did you say the wedding will take place?"

Isabel swallowed. "Sunday."

She was suddenly feeling queasy.

"So soon! Well, I have all the faith in my favorite modiste." Evie nodded resolutely. "But before we get there, I'd love to know how you came to accept Vane's proposal. Has your heart changed regarding the marquess?"

Isabel bit on her lip. "It has. If it is possible, I dislike him even more."

Evie's mouth slacked open. "Oh, no! Why did you agree to marry him then?"

"I had little choice in the matter. The rumors became vicious, and people started declining invitations to Richard's betrothal ball—which we would have weathered. But then he lost his fiancée over it."

"I can't believe it!"

"Me either." Isabel shook her head. "But polite members of the *ton* refuse to socialize with fallen women. And by all definitions of the word, I did fall."

Evie let out a burst of laughter, then covered her mouth with her hand. "I am so sorry. I did not mean to laugh."

Isabel grinned. "No, please! Feel free to find joy in my misery. At least something good will come of it then."

Evie bit her lip. "I am so sorry. I feel like it's my fault—"

"Please, do not even think that. You are not at fault that I fell onto him at your ball. If anything, it was Stanhope's fault." She laughed nervously and picked at her fingertips.

"You do not have to worry about Stanhope. I do not presume to know what transpired between you two, but my husband threatened him good and well."

Isabel smiled faintly. She was grateful to Evie and her husband, but Stanhope was truly the least of her problems. He was not violent, even if too loose with his hands, but Isabel could fend off an attack from him. She didn't fear him.

Her betrothed was another thing altogether. Behind the closed doors of his familial estate, her husband could do to her as he wished, and nobody would be in a position to lend her a hand. And living in a house full of people who loathed her was not an enticing prospect either.

"Actually, my trousseau is not the only reason why I called you today." Isabel played with the pleats of her skirt.

"No?" Evie leaned forward.

Isabel shook her head. "There is… Well, you know Vane quite well, don't you?"

"No, I do not know him that well at all. I've met him only thrice. Gabriel is the one who knows him very well. They've been friends for years. Attended school together, I believe."

"Well… Do you know about the rumors about him?"

Evie grimaced, and Isabel immediately knew that she did. "About his wife?"

"Yes! Please, tell me everything you know!"

"Well…" Evie bit on her lip. "I do not know much, to be honest. Every time I attempted to ask more, Gabriel just became angry. He is very protective of Vane. He likes him immensely. I would go so far as to say he admires him."

"That's good to know, I suppose. He wouldn't be protective of a murderer, would he?"

Evie let out a chuckle. "A murderer? Did he become a murderer now, too? I've only heard people call him a cruel and unjust husband!"

Chapter 5

Isabel lifted her hands up in a shrug. "I do not know. And that's what's so frustrating. People won't tell me anything now that we're betrothed. I was hoping you would since you know him. But my brother fished out some rumors and now forbids me to marry him!"

Evie shook her head. "Did you see his daughter? Or his dog? They love him. And so do his servants. People are afraid of cruel people. They are not relaxed and comfortable like the people on his estates. And dogs... Well, you can tell a lot about a dog's owner by the way the dog treats them."

"The only time I met his dog, it tackled me and then ran off. So it does tell me a bit about him if his only dog tries to escape his household."

Evie laughed. "Oh, Button is adorable. He has a free spirit. Difficult to contain in a townhouse, I suppose."

The carriage drew to a halt at that moment, and they both exited the vehicle. Madam Deville was the most fashionable modiste in town. It was the only place Evie frequented, and as she was the belle of the *ton*, Isabel trusted her impeccable taste.

They were welcomed into a sitting area and offered some tea while they waited for Madame to finish up with other customers.

"What were you saying about Vane?" Evie asked as they each took a sip of the tea.

"Oh." Isabel pulled on a thoughtful grimace.

Her mind chose that exact moment to remember Vane's kisses in the park. Her neck started heating, and she was afraid Evie would guess why she was getting uncomfortable.

Isabel forced her mind back to the conversation. "Right. About the rumors, of course. Well, the issue with that is people won't tell me anything now that we're betrothed. And everything Richard has uncovered will be the last piece of gossip we hear."

"And that piece of gossip is?"

"Only that he married young, conceived a daughter, and then lost his wife all in the span of a few years. But, most importantly, that his wife went around parties and soirees blabbering to anyone who'd listen that he was a cruel and beastly husband."

Evie hid a smile behind a cup of tea. "You don't seem convinced."

Isabel shrugged. "Maybe I just prefer not to be convinced. I am to marry him. And if I don't marry him, I shall ruin our family's good name even further. But also I do not think a cruel husband would let his wife out of the house alone to tell everyone how cruel he's been to her. However, I've never been married, so who am I to make those conclusions?" Isabel placed the back of her hand on her warm forehead. She was starting to get a headache.

"I shall ask Gabriel to speak to your brothers and put their minds at ease… Although that truly should be Vane's responsibility."

Isabel scoffed. "I doubt he has any interest in easing anyone's mind. I had to beg him to marry me."

Evie almost spewed the tea from her mouth. She coughed and wiped her lips with the handkerchief. "You did what?"

Isabel waved a hand. "Well, not literally. But he was not enthusiastic about marrying me."

Evie's smile turned gentle, and she patted Isabel's hand. "He can seem slightly gruff and perhaps a bit surly, but he seems to have a heart of gold."

Chapter 5

Isabel smiled in turn. "You just refuse to see the bad in anyone. Or you are trying to put *my* mind at ease."

"I would never endorse anyone who I thought was violent or cruel. I would especially not encourage my dear friend to marry such a person. I do not know what transpired between Vane and his wife. I was also in mourning during that time. But Gabriel says that his wife was fanciful and unfaithful. She did run off with her lover, leaving not only her husband but her child. And I think we should let actions speak louder than words. No matter what she said, in the end, she left her little girl. And I could not imagine a good mother ever doing that." Evie placed a hand on her stomach as if she felt ill from the thought. "Especially not if she thought her husband a beast."

Isabel nodded. "Thank you. Thank you for rationalizing my thoughts back to me."

Evie smiled. "He retreated to his estate and hid there immediately after the wedding. And he didn't appear in high society for years after his wife's demise. That must have fanned the flames of gossip until it grew like wildfire. Were he an active member of the *ton*, nobody would dare. But I will have Gabriel speak to your brothers so they are not worried to give you away."

Isabel let out a chuckle. "I am not certain they will ever be calm about giving me away. But are you certain St. Clare will agree to speak to my brothers?"

Evie smirked. "I have ways of persuading him."

Isabel smiled widely. "It sounds like a wonderful marriage."

"It is." Evie's smile turned sour as she suddenly frowned and placed her hand on her abdomen. "Oh, lord, my stomach is extremely queasy today."

Isabel reached out to Evie and placed her hand against her

cool cheek. "Well, you are not feverish, but you look pale. Perhaps you should lie down. I shouldn't have dragged you here—"

Evie smiled again. "Isabel. Breathe. I am quite well. I've just been rolling around London for the better part of the week, and I detest riding in carriages. Makes me nauseous. But this shall pass. I just need some ginger root—"

"Well, you heard her!" Madame Deville entered the room at that moment and immediately addressed her staff. "Go bring her ginger root!"

One of the seamstresses jumped to her feet and ran to the back of the shop.

"No need to worry. We take care of our guests," Madame Deville said, her head raised proudly. "Would you accompany me to the pedestal?"

She gestured for Isabel to follow her, and the latter complied with a smile.

"What would you like to order today, Miss?" Madame asked as she surveyed Isabel from head to toe.

"Everything," Evie answered from her seat. "Eight of everything. Day gowns, evening gowns, riding habits, unmentionables. Everything."

"Eight?" Isabel craned her neck to look at Evie from behind the modiste.

"Yes. One for every day of the week and a spare."

"What would I need all of that for? I have a few gowns already—"

"Dear." Evie stood and walked toward her. "What you have is the clothing you prepared for spinsterhood. Now you're a marchioness, and you have to look the part. Am I wrong?" She addressed the last question to the modiste.

Chapter 5

"You are never wrong, Your Grace," Madame answered with a curtsy.

"And more importantly," Evie added with a smile. "We need a wedding gown!"

Isabel scrunched up her face. "Right, that."

The modiste's eyes lit up. "I shall take your measurements first, but do you know what design you prefer? Oh, I shall bring you some sketches. Marie! Go take the marchioness's measurements while I look for the sketches!" She hurried out of the room.

Isabel shifted uncomfortably as Marie came toward her, preparing to take her measurements. She didn't like being called the marchioness. She wasn't one yet, and she didn't know whether she'd get used to the title any time soon.

"See?" Evie directed her radiant smile toward Isabel. "No need to fret. Madame Deville will take care of everything. But I understand your uneasiness. The nerves must be knotting up your stomach."

Isabel tried for a smile, but she was afraid she failed abominably. "They truly are."

"I am sorry. I can't presume to know how you feel."

"Not everyone is so lucky as to marry the man they've been in love with for the past five years."

"Do you have someone else in mind? Because it's as easy as dragging one to Gretna Green." Evie smiled slyly. "Do you know that my cousin Julie also had a marriage of convenience? She was mightily unhappy with it."

Julie? Isabel frowned in thought. "Lady Clydesdale?"

Isabel knew Evie's cousin. But Lady Clydesdale was a happy young woman, a loving mother, and absolutely in love with her husband. Had she been married against her will? It was difficult to fathom.

"Oh, yes," Evie added with a nod. She walked toward the silks rack and ran her hand over the fabric. She picked one piece of cloth after another as she continued, "She was so unhappy she wanted the entire world to know about it."

"What did she do?" Isabel asked as she watched the duchess play with the fabric.

"She wanted to wear the most hideous gown there ever was to show just how unhappy she was with the arrangement."

"She did?"

"Yes, and she asked the most fashionable young lady of the *ton* to help her design it."

"Truly? Who did she ask?"

Evie raised her face to Isabel's, her eyes glinting with mischief. She pulled the hideous black cloth out of a glorious selection of silks and waved it in the air like a magician. "Me."

A real smile tugged at Isabel's lips. "Did you help her design a hideous gown? I have a hard time believing you could come up with anything hideous."

"Oh, I can. And I did." Evie nodded emphatically.

Isabel bit her lip. "Oh, no! I am certain her new family was not happy about it."

"No," Evie agreed. "Neither was her old family. Her father made the heinous arrangement and betrothed Julie to a man she did not know while Julie was in love with another."

Isabel's mouth dropped. "How did she escape the atrocious man she was supposed to wed?"

Evie smiled as she walked back toward Isabel. She shrugged as she placed the black cloth against Isabel's skin. "She didn't. She married him."

Isabel crinkled her nose. "But she is married to the Earl of

Chapter 5

Clydesdale. I am quite certain the couple is happily in love."

Evie pulled back the cloth. "The black does not suit you at all. Perhaps we should find another way to protest your wedding," she muttered. "And yes, Julie is happily in love now. But she wasn't at the beginning."

Isabel looked back at her reflection. She looked pale and rather confused.

Evie went back to sifting through the fabrics.

Lady Clydesdale had married out of convenience and ended up in love. *How strange.* Was there a possibility of happiness under those awful circumstances?

Perhaps for others. If Isabel had learned anything in her thirty one years of existence, it was that she was not an exception to the rule. She *was* the rule. And happiness with a man like the Marquess of Vane? *Impossible*.

"I do not want to protest the wedding," she finally said.

Evie turned and raised a questioning brow.

"No. I want the world to think that we are perfectly in love. I do not want more gossip surrounding my family. As it is, I've already brought shame upon my brothers. Richard's fiancée withdrew her hand because of my transgressions. I do not want the people around me to suffer. I want to be the perfect wife and hostess. I want everyone to point at us and whisper behind their fans that ours is the perfect union."

"Well, it is easily achievable if that's what you want."

"You truly think so?" Isabel watched Evie expectantly.

"Yes, but it means you shall have to smile from time to time," Evie pointed out. "But the rest, you leave to me. I shall make certain gossip is plentiful about the radiant bride and her fortunate groom. And do not fret about the trousseau. As soon as Madame Deville has your measurements, I shall order you everything you need."

Isabel exhaled a breath of relief. "Thank you," she said and reached a hand toward Evie, who took her palm and squeezed. "I am so grateful to have you here, Evie."

"I am always here for you and your family."

* * *

"You are cordially invited to a true celebration of love between Lord Vane and the Honorable Isabel Lewis," Gabriel, the Viscount St. Clare, read with a grand flourish, sitting across the desk from Rhys.

"A true celebration of love." Rhys scoffed.

"That should get people curious enough to attend your wedding," the viscount pointed out as he lounged in the chair.

"Will it?" Rhys scrubbed his face with his hand. "It seems to be a perfect cause for continued gossip."

"It is. But that's the entire point. Stir gossip prior to your wedding, collect the largest assembly of stuffy lords and ladies, and then have the most mundane wedding anyone ever attended, boring everyone out of their wits. That should kill their will to gossip any further. Or perhaps, lie your bottom off by telling the most extraordinary story of love, shocking the *ton* even more. That way, the gossip will not cease, but at least people will leave you alone and just whisper behind their fans when you show up at a ball."

"I do not want people to ignore me. Nor do I want them whispering about me behind anything."

"You do not?" St. Clare raised a brow.

"No. At least not for the sake of Millie. I need to make as many connections with members of the *ton* as I can to aid

Chapter 5

Millie with her debut."

"I'll say you are worrying too soon about that. By the time Millie makes a come-out, half the current *ton* will be dead."

Rhys let out a huff of laughter. "Those old dragons will live on forever, I am convinced."

"Well, you are in the good graces of the Duchess of Somerset. Who else do you truly need?"

Rhys heaved a sigh. "Someone with heirs of suitable age to my Millie. And even if the duchess birthed a son at this very moment, he'd be slightly young for Millie. Therefore, I need to make more connections."

"Don't say you want to arrange a marriage for her!"

"No, of course not." Rhys waved a careless hand. "But I want her to have options. I do not want her to be a wallflower because of my sins. I do not want her to be unmarriageable because of my mistakes. I want her to have choices. I want her to be able to marry anyone she wishes without society matrons calling her unsuitable. It is enough that she will forever be embarrassed by her mother." He paused and shook his head. "No, I shall not allow her to suffer because of my poor choices."

Gabriel grimaced. "Tumbling over Miss Lewis in the corridor was not exactly a choice. I'd say it was fate if anything."

"Well then, I'll have to fight fate if that's the case."

"Fighting fate... Doesn't seem to work out in most circumstances."

Rhys leaned heavily in his chair. Just this conversation made his insides tighten unpleasantly. "You do not understand. Being the biggest libertine in the world will not affect your children. People forgive men their indiscretions. But having a strumpet for a mother? That's different."

St. Clare shifted uncomfortably. "That isn't the only rumor going around. People still whisper the lies she spread about you."

Rhys waved a careless hand. "And yet people were eager to introduce their marriage-minded daughters to me this season. The *ton* forgives men. I am a walking example of that."

St. Clare scratched his jaw. "I don't know about others, but Gage is not too pleased with the prospect of giving his sister away."

"Give her away? She was the one who insisted we marry!"

"Yes, well, apparently her brothers were not thrilled with the idea," St. Clare said, stretching in his chair lazily.

"As long as they don't create another scandal, I shall be glad. It took me years to crawl out of my self-imposed banishment. And now that I have, I managed to entangle myself with another scandalous lady of the *ton*."

"You really should cease calling her that. Before you, she did not have a single scandal attached to her name," Gabriel protested.

"Well, that comes at a surprise considering—" Rhys clamped his lips shut. He wasn't about to air her dirty linen.

"Considering?"

"Let's just say I know a slightly more scandalous side of her than you do."

Gabriel let out a chuckle. "And isn't it the most perfect state of affairs? Nobody but me knows how scandalous *my* wife truly is. And I prefer to keep it that way."

Rhys raised his eyes heavenward. "I have no desire to tolerate her scandalous behavior."

"Perhaps not. But you might be able to keep that behavior

Chapter 5

inside the walls of your bedroom." With a wink, the viscount stood. "Well, I have to go. I need to keep my wife's scandalous impulses occupied. Call on us if you need anything. But you do not have to worry. If Evie is involved with the planning of the wedding, everything will go without a hitch."

Chapter 6

As you can see, Mother, my life might have changed drastically overnight. But I was building toward that overnight change my entire life. A series of unfortunate events led to this one moment. The moment that turned my life upside down.

Now, I have to marry a man I loathe, whose daughter detests me, and whose dog is adamant about killing me.

Today, my dear mother, is the worst day of my life. My wedding day.

Isabel wrung her hands as she surveyed her appearance in the looking glass. Part of her trousseau had arrived just the night before, including her wedding gown. Therefore, Isabel had not been able to try anything on until this morning. She was glad that the wedding gown had arrived at all since part of her trousseau was still to be finished.

As it was, Isabel wondered how Madame Deville had managed to finish half the wardrobe, including a wedding

Chapter 6

gown in such a short time.

Her gown was impeccable. Not that she'd thought it wouldn't be. Evie was in charge of it, after all. And anything Evie attempted came out perfect.

The deep emerald gown had a feathery bodice and bottom of the skirt. A thin satin bow adorned her waist.

Emerald suited Isabel wonderfully, and it contrasted perfectly with her pale skin. Isabel applied some rouge to her cheeks, too aware of her pale complexion. She would not usually use the rouge, but she wanted to appear as if she was glowing today.

With a soft knock, Evie entered the room. Isabel let out a sigh of relief upon seeing her friend. She needed a reassuring female presence in the absence of either her mother or sister.

Isabel was too nervous, and as much as her brothers loved her, she doubted they would understand the state of her nerves the same way a woman could.

"You look beautiful," Evie breathed as her gaze swept over Isabel's form. She looked as if she was about to tear up.

"Oh, Lord! Evie, you are not about to cry, are you?"

Evie's face scrunched up a little, and she fanned herself. "No," she said, her voice breaking.

Isabel chuckled and went to hug her friend. She'd never seen Evie so emotional.

Evie disengaged from Isabel with a small laugh as she wiped at her face. "I am supposed to be the one to comfort you, not the other way around!" She drew a shaky breath and fanned her face with her hands. "I am well, I promise."

Isabel bit her lip. "I never imagined this would be the way I got married."

"Comforting an overwrought duchess?"

"That too." Isabel smiled. "But mainly, without my sister by my side, without my parents, Alan away on the Continent… And marrying a man I do not know, a man I do not even like!"

"I am sorry Sam couldn't be here for you. I know she wishes she could, but with a young babe—"

"I know. And you will never know how grateful I am to have you here now."

Evie waved a dismissive hand. "Do not even mention it. You and Sam are like family to me. And I would do anything for my family."

Isabel smiled warmly, her affection for the young duchess seeping out of her.

"But how fun it would be for all three of us to be here now," Isabel said with a sigh.

"I am certain she will find an excuse to visit you as soon as she and the babe are strong enough to travel." There was a pause as they were both lost in their own thoughts. "Is your mind a bit more at ease now regarding this marriage?"

The quiet question and the way Evie asked it somehow almost made tears appear on Isabel's face. She wasn't certain how to answer.

Isabel had not seen her fiancé since the day of their betrothal, and the knot in her stomach grew bigger and bigger each day. "I am not certain," Isabel answered truthfully.

"Listen, Isabel…" Evie took Isabel's hands in hers and squeezed. "I do not believe those rumors about Vane for a moment. He is kind and thoughtful, and I adore the man. But I am not the one who has to marry him. So if you are having doubts, if you are afraid for your safety, or you are just not certain about him, you can just walk away. You do not need to marry him!"

Chapter 6

Isabel grimaced. She would be ruined.

More importantly, her brothers would be ruined. Walking away from this marriage once was enough to fuel the gossip. If she were to do it right before her wedding, the scandal would be impossible to overcome. And with the gossip surrounding the marquess, her last-minute defection would certainly fan the flames even further, destroying the marquess, too.

But was Isabel willing to bargain her life on it? She was not so certain.

Perhaps if the marquess frightened her or hurt her, she would have substantial cause for leaving him at the altar. However, aside from the wretched kiss, he had not done anything violent toward her. And she wouldn't exactly describe that kiss as violent either.

Isabel's body started heating like it did every time she thought of that dratted kiss. She still dreamed about that sometimes. And the dreams were rather pleasant…

She shook her head. That was not the point.

His wife had probably enjoyed his kisses as well, at least at first. Isabel frowned at her conflicting thoughts.

She knew *ton* gossip very well. They loved to exaggerate things and paint anyone they deemed necessary in the least flattering light. She supposed she'd have to marry the wretch to find out the truth. And if anything went wrong, she had powerful allies on her side.

She drew a shaky breath. "Thank you, dear. But I am afraid I cannot gamble my standing in society and the reputation of my brothers on gossip. You know how gossip is."

"I do," Evie said with a sad smile. "But you will write to me, won't you? Or I shall worry."

Isabel took Evie's hands in hers. "The last thing I need is for you to worry. I shall be certain to post a letter every day."

"And if you miss a day, I shall come and visit you immediately."

Isabel chuckled and embraced the duchess. She drew away and looked at the door. Soon, she'd have to exit, and then she'd become the Marchioness of Vane. She wanted to delay the moment as much as she could.

"In any case, as dreadful as this marriage may turn out to be, it will give me children. I truly hope that it will happen sooner rather than later. It might make the marriage more tolerable. I don't know how long it usually takes, but hopefully not too long. It didn't take Sam long to conceive, did it?"

Yes, but Sam is young, her traitorous mind whispered, *and you are not.*

Then she looked at Evie's thoughtful face and bit her lip.

"Oh, I am sorry. I am being insensitive, aren't I?" Evie had married a few months after Samantha did, and she was yet to start increasing. "I am certain it can take different amounts of time for everyone."

Evie raised a shoulder in a delicate shrug. "I wish I knew the answers to these things, but it's all part of a miracle. It happens when it happens."

"Evie…" Isabel paused, uncertain how to approach the subject that had been bothering her since the day of her betrothal. She sat on the bed, and Evie joined her. Isabel nervously played with the pleats of her skirts. "Can I ask you something?"

"Of course, you can ask me anything."

"It's about… This is entirely too embarrassing for me to ask, but there is truly no one else I can approach with this. Perhaps

Chapter 6

if Sam was here... Although even asking one's younger sibling is a little uncomfortable, to say the least—"

"Isabel." Evie softly put a hand on Isabel's, halting her nervous movements. "You can ask me anything. You know that."

"I wanted to ask you about marital duty," Isabel finally forced out, without looking up at her friend. She was absolutely mortified she had to bring up this subject. "Do you—How do you feel about it?"

Evie's face split into the biggest of smiles. "I enjoy it immensely. It's one of my favorite past times."

"Truly?" Isabel faced Evie fully, her mind full of questions. Isabel wasn't exactly a virgin. She had been young once and very much in love with Stanhope. They had tasted the forbidden fruit, but that had left Isabel with more questions than answers. It was quick, painful, and confusing. "But it doesn't seem like a pleasurable activity..."

"Trust me," Evie said, blushing. "It is very pleasurable. But I suppose if one has a former rake for a husband and is not enjoying it, well... then there is something extremely wrong."

Isabel frowned and turned to face Evie fully. "But why do you like it? I... Apologies. I don't want to intrude if it's very personal. I am just very nervous, and I want to know... Apologies, you do not have to answer."

Evie bit her lip. "It is personal. Very much so. But I do not want you to fret, Isabel. It is the most exciting activity. Every kiss, every touch, slowly builds up the anticipation of something grand and wonderful. And then the sweet taste of release... I apologize to be so frank, but being joined with the man you love is just the best feeling in the world." Evie met Isabel's gaze, and her blissful look vanished instantly. Her eyes rounded as she hastened to continue. "Oh, I apologize. I am such an idiot. You do not love Vane, but perhaps in time..."

Isabel grimaced and looked away. It just seemed like her luck. Of course, she would have to lie with a man she loathed. Of course, there would be nothing pleasurable about the marital bed for her. True, she'd felt a strange flutter in the pit of her belly when he had kissed her. She'd felt the licks of flame and tingles low in her body. But it was probably just the animal instinct to mate.

It was about time she felt that instinct. Without it, she doubted any woman would willingly agree to procreate. Unless she was in love.

Evie was married to an infamous rake. Surely he knew how to make a marriage bed exciting. She wasn't so certain a hermit and a rumored beast would do the same for her.

Evie bit on her lip in thought. "Well, if you are frightened about the prospect, I advise you to just tell him directly."

Isabel scoffed.

"No, truly. Ask him to not rush it and give you some time to get to know him out of bed. Unless, of course, you want children so badly."

The last thing Isabel wanted was to draw it out. She wanted children, and she was afraid her time was ticking. "I would rather get it over with."

Evie narrowed her eyes, her lips in a thoughtful pout. "Well, if you don't want to delay things... Just ask him to take his time and be gentle with you. And try to enjoy each other's kisses."

"Kisses?" Heat crept up Isabel's neck and to her cheeks.

"Yes. A kiss can tell you a lot about a man. If his kisses

Chapter 6

make you sag in his arms and flutters appear in your stomach, it is a sure way to conclude that the marriage bed will be pleasurable. But you have to give him a chance. Relax and try not to worry about anything. Try not to think about anything. Let yourself enjoy his kisses and touches… No matter how indecent."

Isabel's skin tingled in anticipation, and her breath came shallower than usual. The memories of Vane's kiss heated her body.

Still, she frowned. She remembered enjoying Stanhope's kisses, too, at least in the past. But she had not enjoyed the act. And perhaps the same fate waited for her in Vane's bed.

"Thank you, Evie," Isabel said with a smile. "But the truth is, it doesn't matter if I enjoy the act or not. It will bring me children. And they will be the light of my life."

Evie took Isabel's hand in hers. "I am certain you shall have a lot more light in your life than that."

* * *

The wedding passed in a blur. Isabel had been shaking like a leaf throughout the entire ceremony, and her nerves had been drawn so taut she wondered how she'd managed to stand upright.

The church had been filled to the brim with people. And more people had been standing outdoors waiting for the ceremony to be over so they could meet the bride and groom.

All morning, Isabel had concentrated on appearing happy and smiling so that now her cheeks hurt. But it wasn't over yet. She needed to live through the wedding breakfast, and after that, she, her husband, and the rest of his brood, would travel back to his country seat.

My husband.

The words sounded foreign to her ears. Well, she'd have a lifetime getting used to them. Now and for the rest of her days, she was to be the Marchioness of Vane.

Isabel took a deep breath and ventured out of the ladies' necessary. The moment she opened the door, the tall form of Stanhope appeared before her.

"Phillip?"

He grinned, visibly pleased that she'd addressed him by his first name.

"What are you doing here? I wasn't aware you were even invited!"

He sniffed. "Of course, you knew. Do not pretend to not want me here. You sought to hurt me. Well, it worked. Now cease your childish games and kiss me already."

He dipped his head, but Isabel turned away, squeezing her eyes shut. Stanhope kissed her cheek, then moved to her ear.

"Oh, stop! Or I'll scream!"

"And risk the scandal? I doubt it." He kissed her chin, and Isabel pushed at his chest.

"Stop it! Let go of me! I am a married woman now—"

"Exactly. And you are free to have your liaisons."

"What?" Isabel stared at him in shock.

Was he delusional? At what point since their last assignation did he think that she'd be amenable to that?

"It was clever of you to get married. But now we can be together again, and nobody will bother to gossip or pay attention to our relationship," Stanhope added hastily.

"Phillip," Isabel said softly. She wanted to make him understand that she would never welcome his advances. And

Chapter 6

obviously, fighting him, arguing, and even stepping on his instep hadn't helped him understand, so she'd have to try plain and calm words.

"Do not tell me you don't still think about me. I know I think about you," Stanhope interrupted.

She remembered all her dreams about him crawling back to her on his hands and knees, and she couldn't remember why. Perhaps it was her pride, certainly not her heart.

"Of course, I think about you—" *in revulsion*, she was about to add, but at this moment, a shadow appeared behind Stanhope, and a huge hand landed on his shoulder.

"Your tryst is over," boomed Vane's voice. "Now, get the hell out of this house."

Stanhope turned to face him and visibly shrunk. He was about a foot shorter than the marquess—which wasn't difficult since Vane was the tallest man Isabel ever knew—but Stanhope seemed feeble now, almost childlike. Nevertheless, he didn't scurry away.

"I believe this is not your home. And you cannot turn me out," he said somewhat calmly. Isabel gave him credit for not quivering out of his boots. Vane's presence was rather intimidating. "I shall see you at the table." Stanhope addressed the last to Isabel and walked away.

Isabel was left staring at Vane's chest.

"If you must cuckold me, couldn't you at least wait until *after* the wedding breakfast?" Vane's tone was as dry as a desert. He asked it as though he didn't doubt what he'd witnessed, more so, as if he'd expected it to happen.

"I did not cuckold you," Isabel said between her teeth.

"I do not expect you to be faithful, but the least you can do is be honest… And for the sake of both of us, circumspect."

"I did not—" Isabel started, her nostrils flaring. She took a deep breath to calm herself. "That was not what you think it was. He accosted me."

Vane just looked at her, boredom evident in his eyes. He did not believe her. Not only did he think her an adulteress, but also a liar. And he was not even angry about it. What kind of marriage did he expect them to have?

"Come," he said curtly. "Guests will start wondering where you disappeared to."

Isabel did not have the will or strength to argue just then. She'd address all her issues with him after they got back home.

Home.

Only her home would be a foreign place with strange people and huge, unmannered dogs…

She took a deep breath, squared her shoulders, and placed her hand on her husband's sleeve.

Chapter 7

They returned to the table just in time for the toasts to start. Isabel sat grinding her teeth, listening to the insincere wishes of good health, grand love, and a brood of children.

After every mention of children, old matrons and young ladies alike gave the customary once over along Isabel's length. They were clearly thinking that at her age, she'd be lucky to bear one child, let alone an entire brood.

Isabel kept her back straight and her smile wide. She pretended that those scathing looks didn't hurt; she pretended that the whispers didn't sting while she had all those doubts herself.

She knew there would be no grand love between her and her new husband. But what she did not know was whether she'd be able to perform her wifely duties.

She had been a hostess in Gage's house since she was three and twenty. She knew how to run that house, how to arrange balls and soirees. But she'd always had the supportive hands of her family at her back. Now, she'd be living with complete strangers and the husband who loathed her.

Still, she was determined to carve out a piece of heaven at his remote estate. But first, she'd need to give him an heir. And just like most of the guests present at her wedding breakfast table, she doubted very much she'd be able to perform this duty.

As the last toast rang, Isabel sagged against her chair, glad that this part was finally over. But her relief was short-lived. At that moment, a frail old lady—the same lady who was responsible for drawing too much attention to Isabel and Vane's plight in the corridor—the woman responsible for gossip that pushed the two to marry—stood from her chair.

Isabel hoped she'd thank the hosts and say it was time to leave. Instead, Lady Crosby looked from bride to groom a few times before saying, "We've spent the entire morning at your wedding breakfast, and yet, we're still to hear this grand love story of yours!"

Isabel blinked. *What?*

"I beg your pardon?" her husband asked in a low voice from the other side of the table.

"The invitation," the woman said loudly, waving said invitation in her hand. "It stated that we were invited to witness a celebration of true love. Yet nobody told us the story. I, for one, am dying to hear it."

"I don't doubt it," Isabel ground out between her teeth.

"Did you say something, dear?" Lady Crosby turned toward Isabel.

"No, my lady," Isabel answered sweetly. "Just that my husband tells the story so wonderfully. I would love to hear it again, too."

Chapter 7

She turned toward the Marquess of Vane, laughter in her eyes. She was certain he'd deflect it back to her and was already coming up with a story she could pass off as a *grand love story* when Vane stood.

"Very well," he said and pierced Isabel with an intent gaze.

Isabel started to regret her impetuous words. What could he possibly say that would sound romantic? Or was he determined to ruin her? Surely not! His reputation was on the line, too.

"Isabel," Richard murmured at her side and then tipped his head toward her glass.

She turned to look at her hand and realized she was squeezing the poor glass so tightly it was ready to break. She relaxed her hold and smiled at Richard.

He furrowed his brows and mouthed, "Are you well?"

Isabel nodded and turned back to her husband. He stood with a glass in his hand, his gaze still on her, a frown of concentration on his face.

"It was love from first sight," Vane finally said, then cleared his throat. Isabel almost groaned. This was going to be terrible. "Or at least for me, it was."

People around the table started chuckling, and Isabel looked around. Everybody's attention was riveted to her husband. *Good.* Nobody was paying her any heed. She turned back to Vane, biting on her lower lip.

"I was a young boy, visiting my uncle who happened to be neighbors with Viscount Gage," he continued, and Isabel frowned. *What is he on about?* "One day, I was walking through the forest and stopped for a rest by the stream. I was tired. I disliked my new lodgings, and I just wanted to go back to school. I was very young, you see." He paused.

Isabel wondered if he was concocting the story on the fly. But why would he start so far in the past? So many years before they'd actually met?

"Just then, I saw a beautiful young girl wade through the water, walking along the stream. She was barefoot, with her skirts hiked to her knees—scandalous—but we were too young for that yet. She raised her head toward the sun, scrubbed her face, and laughed. The sound of her laughter was the most beautiful melody I've ever heard. She waded through the water, a wood nymph, a siren, a Goddess." Vane shook his head as if waking up from a daze. He then turned and looked Isabel straight in the eyes. "And I was hopelessly in love."

"Oh, my!" "How romantic!" people started exclaiming from their seats.

Isabel's neck heated, and she found it hard to breathe. Vane's gaze was still trained on her, and she felt decidedly uncomfortable.

"She did not know I was watching her, of course, and I thought it indecent to keep watching her without her realizing it," Vane continued with a chuckle. "So I decided to make myself known. I stepped closer, not taking my eyes off her… then tripped and tumbled in an undignified heap."

The entire room boomed with laughter, and Isabel found herself chuckling too. But as Vane continued his story, Isabel frowned. It sounded familiar. Hadn't something similar happened to her in the past?

"I landed right at her feet," Vane continued. "But instead of cursing me or screaming, the girl helped me up and tended to my wounds. And that's the moment my love for her strengthened. Because not only was her visage beautiful, but

Chapter 7

her soul was also just as mesmerizing."

"Oh, what a beautiful story." A woman next to Isabel wept into her handkerchief.

"It is," Isabel breathed, lost in the fictional tale of their love.

"That was the day I fell in love with the beautiful Miss Isabel Lewis. And I vowed to make her my wife someday." A pause. "Of course, she did not reciprocate."

More laughter followed from the men and a few gasps from the women.

"I was a gangly youth. I was thin and uncoordinated. My arms were long and disproportionate to my body, adding to that the fact that the first time she saw me, I was covered in dirt and couldn't utter an intelligent word... I never had a chance with her."

Isabel doubted this perfect specimen of a man, tall, wide-shouldered, and yes—she had to be honest with herself—handsome was ever the uncoordinated, awkward youth he described.

But she did know a boy like that, she suddenly recalled. And if she remembered correctly, they'd met similarly to the way Vane described. He'd fallen at her feet and spent the entire summer following Isabel around. The only difference in the story was that she had not been walking alongside the stream; she had been bathing in a single chemise. And they were not extremely young either, or at least Isabel wasn't. She had been nineteen at the time, and the boy fifteen.

What was his name, again?

She frowned in thought. It was on the tip of her tongue.

Ah, right! Thomas. She wondered what had happened to him.

"Soon, she made her come out," Vane continued. "I went to

university, and our paths diverged. I didn't think I'd ever see her again. Until I ran into her—quite literally—at the Duchess of Somerset's ball."

"And accosted her right in the corridor?" The dowager marchioness of Somerville raised a brow.

"I decided not to let go of my chance for the second time," he said, and everyone laughed again.

Isabel huffed a laugh and shook her head. He could be quite charming, her husband, when he wished to be. She supposed she should be thankful that he'd expertly weaved them out of scandal.

When Vane concluded his speech, he walked toward Isabel and swept her away.

As they said their goodbyes and rode along the London streets in the carriage, Isabel looked at her husband. He was staring out the window, a familiar frown on his face.

"It was a lovely story you told," Isabel said. "How did you come up with it so quickly?"

Vane didn't turn to look at her. "I didn't."

"How interesting," Isabel said, watching Vane's face carefully. "Because I met a boy once in a similar fashion."

He didn't react. "Many young people meet at the stream, I imagine," he said in bored tones. "I met a girl when I was young, just the same way."

Isabel furrowed her brows. *A coincidence?* But she had no time to ask any more questions as at that moment, the carriage stopped, and the groom opened the door.

They'd arrived home.

* * *

Chapter 7

Isabel entered the Vane townhouse and looked around. The place was empty and quiet. That fact alone gave her unpleasant shivers. The last time Isabel had been there, the place was in chaos. Now it seemed like a tomb of the dead. Or perhaps it was just her gloomy mood finding reflection inside her new home.

"Monroe," Vane addressed the butler. "Please, tell Mrs. Ainsworth to collect the servants. We are ready to depart."

Isabel turned to Vane sharply. "Depart?"

"Yes, we are leaving straight for my country home."

"We are? But—"

"Did you have a reason to stay in London?" Vane asked as he moved farther inside.

"Well, yes." Isabel followed Vane's footsteps. "My brothers don't know I am leaving—"

"We shall post them a note."

"That's not enough. They will worry!"

"I am certain they will make do."

"My trousseau is not ready! Half of it is still at the modiste."

Vane turned then and looked her up and down, lingering slightly on her decolletage. Isabel drew the shawl closer to her body.

"Do you have enough clothes for a few days?"

"Yes, but—"

"Then the rest shall be sent straight to us. We do not have to wait for it here." He turned back and approached the stairs without waiting for her response.

"Vane!" Isabel said as loudly as she could without shouting. Or perhaps she did shout. She wasn't quite certain, but her hands were fisted at her sides, and it felt like her head was about to burst. "I do not like to be ordered about. Does my opinion count for nothing?"

Vane halted on the steps, then slowly and unhurriedly turned toward her. "Did you not just vow in front of God and men that you shall obey me for the rest of your life?"

"Well, you vowed to cherish me, and I do not see you keeping that vow."

"Miss Lewis—"

Isabel scoffed.

"My lady," Vane said drily. "I came to London for one reason and one reason only: to acquire a wife. Now that my task is completed, I would like to go home. It is too cramped in here, and I do not like town life. And to be quite honest, neither does my dog."

Isabel narrowed her eyes. *The dog?* The dog's preference was more important than hers? She was preparing him a proper set down, but he raised a hand, halting her before she had a chance to open her mouth.

"And it is advisable to leave before you set up more clandestine meetings with your precious Stanhope. So we are leaving for my country seat. Right now. And you are coming with us either willingly, or I shall tie you up to a horse."

Vane turned on his heel, leaving Isabel still standing there with her mouth wide open in astonishment. Nobody had ever talked to her so rudely. The steel in his voice sent an unpleasant shiver down her spine. His gaze was cold, his voice harsh. And for a moment, she started to believe the rumors.

Oh, Lord. What did I get myself into?

Chapter 8

The journey to the Vane estate was grueling and tedious at the same time. Vane was out on horseback, while Millie sat inside the carriage conversing with her nursemaid, Edith. She pointedly avoiding Isabel and not answering any of her questions.

They stopped a few times so that Millie could play with Button, who spent most of the journey in a separate carriage, and as a result, the journey dragged on longer than it should have.

With nothing to do, Isabel tried to read a few chapters of her book, but since Millie had spent most of the trip chattering away with Edith, Isabel found it difficult to concentrate on the page.

The next activity she tried was stitching. But after pricking her fingers with every bump and jolt, she gave up the idea after a few minutes. As a result, the rest of the trip was spent staring at the horizon and cataloging all the things she'd need to teach Millie. Because as bright as the girl seemed, she was mannerless and impolite.

Isabel was quite surprised the girl did not have a governess. She was six, and it was time to start her schooling. She was too old to roam around the woods with the dog, which Isabel supposed was exactly what she did most days based on the girl's behavior. And when Vane was busy running errands, he must have left her with the servants.

Millie was on a first-name basis with all the servants and regarded them all in a friendly manner. Isabel had a friendly household as well, and she loved all the servants as family. She even took her favorite footman, James, with her, along with her lady's maid.

But at six, she had been educated enough to hold a polite conversation with ladies of a similar station. Millie, on the other hand, conversed with everyone but Isabel. And when Isabel tried to address her, Millie just sat still and watched Isabel with distrust and hostility in her eyes.

Isabel would have to breach the subject of Millie's education to her husband somehow. And she wasn't looking forward to the conversation. Isabel would need to find a brilliant governess who would not alienate the girl, the way Isabel apparently did.

Isabel would have loved to bond with the girl and even teach her. After all, Isabel had learned almost everything from her mother. But she doubted she would be able to breach Millie's defenses, especially since her father showed with every fiber of his being that he didn't care for Isabel either.

When they stopped overnight, Isabel was ready to fall off her feet. Who would have known that being ignored by a six-year-old girl could be so exhausting?

They entered a tiny inn, and Vane had ordered rooms for

Chapter 8

all his servants and even a separate chamber for the dog, although a groom would stay with him so he wouldn't bark through the night.

Isabel found the gesture endearing. Who else would order an entire room for the dog?

Lucky for them, the inn was almost empty, and the owner was extremely pleased the marquess had booked the entire place for his family, servants, and the dog.

"Would you like to dine in the common room?" Vane asked as soon as all the arrangements were taken care of.

"Thank you. But I think I would rather dine in my room. I am too tired and would be dreadful company."

Vane nodded and turned to the innkeeper. "Please, escort my wife to her room."

Isabel smiled as the man showed her to her chambers. She entered a small, dank room with a single bed, and only then did her husband's words register in her mind. *My room.* Was he not spending the night with her?

She wasn't certain whether to be glad of that or concerned. Her parents had separate chambers, of course, but they rarely slept apart and never at an inn.

And it was their wedding night! Would he come to her room, or would she have to spend the night alone?

Neither prospect bothered her as much as not knowing. Either way, she had no choice. Her husband had a few things to deal with before he came back to his room, and she couldn't very well hunt him down and demand answers. She'd have to wait.

So she had a quiet supper, changed into her nightgown, and prepared for bed.

For now, she needed to get some rest. Her husband would

come in soon, and, hopefully, she would be one step closer to conceiving a child.

She lay in bed, biting her lip and running through all the things Evie had told her.

She needed to relax and not worry.

Well, it was easier said than done. Isabel could not lie still. Her stomach churned, and her skin felt as if she were lying on needles.

Let yourself enjoy his kisses and touches... No matter how indecent.

Isabel took a deep breath. If he kissed her the way he did in the park, then there would be nothing to worry about. And regarding his touches? Well, she'd just have to allow him all the liberties he craved, and if what Evie said was true, she would come to enjoy the act.

Isabel didn't doubt Evie's wisdom... mostly. But she doubted very much that Vane's touches would be as pleasant as St. Clare's touch was for Evie. After all, Evie was hopelessly in love, and Isabel... well, Isabel could barely stand the man.

His kisses might have been pleasant, but surely that was just because Isabel was overexcited from chasing the dog and then arguing with the man. She was in shock and did not expect to be accosted. If she were in a rational frame of mind, she would not let him kiss her at all.

Well, this train of thought did not help her at all. She needed to concentrate on enjoying Vane's ministrations and not convince herself of the contrary!

Just at that moment, there was a knock on her door.

"Mis—My lady, it's me. Vane."

Isabel swallowed, sat up, and drew the sheets over her chin. "Enter."

Chapter 8

The door to her room opened, and Vane appeared on the threshold.

He was standing in the doorway, as tall as a tree and wide as the doorframe. His face was shadowed, but she could see his mussed hair outlined by the light behind him. He had not changed for bed, Isabel noticed. In fact, he still wore his coat and boots.

Vane walked farther into the room, and once he stepped closer to the candle by her bedside, she saw that he was sporting a menacing frown. Was that man ever not frowning?

Isabel propped herself against the pillows and regarded him curiously.

"I just wanted to let you know that we'll be continuing our journey shortly after dawn on the morrow," he said.

"That is acceptable. I shall be ready."

"Good." With a nod, Vane turned away.

"Vane?" Isabel started after him but quickly realized she was in her night rail and sat back down. Vane looked at her over his shoulder. "Are you... Are you leaving?"

His scowl deepened. "That was the idea. Yes."

Isabel was tempted to just count her blessings and let it go, but her stubbornness won out. "We are sleeping in separate bedchambers, yes?"

"Yes." Vane seemed rather confused.

Oh, God. He wouldn't make her beg for it, would he? "But... Aren't you—It's our wedding night."

"I am aware," he said in the driest of tones.

The dratted man didn't even blink.

"Are you not going to spend the night with me? Are you not...?"

"I was not aware you were eager to start." Vane finally

turned fully toward her.

Isabel gritted her teeth. "The sooner we start, the sooner the heir could be conceived."

He scanned her with an unflattering gaze, then crossed his arms over his chest. "You do seem in an awful haste." He furrowed his brows, utterly perplexed by the idea.

Of course, I am in haste! I am over thirty years old. "And you seem utterly bewildered by the idea. I am your wife."

Vane scratched his chin in thought. He then stepped closer and studied her from head to toe again, making her shiver under the thin bedsheet. "You are not by any chance already with child, are you?"

"Pardon me?" It was her turn to be confused.

"Trying to pass off the babe as mine, perhaps?"

"Are you out of your mind?" Isabel puffed in indignation.

"It's not so difficult to fathom. You and your lover have a babe. To avoid a scandal, you run into me, get compromised, and force me to marry you."

"I did *not* want to marry you."

"And yet, here we are."

Isabel threw up her hands. "I am *not* with child!"

"And how am I to be certain?" The insufferable man raised his brow.

"When the babe is not born in nine months, that would be your first clue," Isabel spat irritably.

"Not unless we consummate our marriage right now."

Isabel let out a frustrated breath. "I am not looking forward to the act. Believe me! I just thought you wouldn't want to delay."

"I don't. But in case you *are* with child… Well, it could save us the unfortunate task altogether."

Chapter 8

Isabel squinted at him. What was he on about?

"We are already married. No matter if the child is mine or not, he—if it's a he—will be legally my heir."

"I am *not* with child! How many times do I need to repeat myself?"

"I need a better assurance than your word."

Isabel's mouth fell open. He didn't trust her. Not even a little. "Why would I want to spend the night with you if I were with child? Without necessity, I'd avoid it like the plague."

"Maybe you wanted to pass off the brat as mine. You can never be certain how I'd treat the babe. And I certainly cannot be sure you are not that cunning. I need to be certain. I don't mind a cuckoo in the nest. But if it removes the need to bed you, that would be just splendid."

Heat crept up Isabel's neck in utter humiliation. "You cur! I wish I were with child to forever avoid your touch!"

"Wouldn't that be lovely?" Vane grumbled under his breath and turned away. Then he added in a louder voice, "On the off chance you're telling the truth, come to me in a few weeks… with the evidence."

He walked away and closed the door behind him with a soft click.

Isabel watched after her husband with eyes wide like saucers. *With evidence?* Did he mean her bloody sheets? Well, she'd be certain to show him evidence, the pompous cad!

"Ugh!" She fell against the pillows, her mind working out a plan on how to get back at him.

How had she ever thought that beast would be gentle and accommodating in bed with her? She'd make certain to not let him into her bed at all. If he didn't trust her and sought to humiliate her, he'd have to live without an heir.

Her heart wept at the idea of never having a babe. But until the cur apologized, she would not let him into her bed. And that was that.

***

The next day's travel didn't go much better than the previous one. Isabel silently watched Millie chatter away with her nursemaid, happily bouncing around the carriage, paying Isabel little heed.

So Isabel took out her embroidery and moved closer to the window to get more sun. She moved the curtains out of the way at the same time as the marquess passed the carriage.

He sat in the saddle straight as a lance, his form impeccable as though he hadn't spent the entire day before in the saddle as well.

As good as a rider as Isabel was, she'd be hurting the next day if she spent an entire day atop a horse. Her husband didn't seem to have the same issue. He seemed relaxed and quite comfortable. The reins rested loosely in his long fingers, and he controlled the horse with barely noticeable twitches of his thigh muscles.

Isabel's gaze fell to that part of his body. She swallowed as the powerful muscles seemed to want to burst from inside the confining fabric of his breeches.

A loud thud inside the carriage startled Isabel, and she snatched her gaze from the enticing physique of her husband. She looked at the nursemaid, who looked back at her in confusion. Then Edith slowly bent down and picked Isabel's embroidery from the floor.

"Oh," Isabel exclaimed as she took it in her hands. "Apolo-

Chapter 8

gies, I got distracted. I completely forgot I was holding this in my hand."

Heat crept up Isabel's neck and up to her face. She hoped the nursemaid noticed neither her blush nor what had caught Isabel's attention outside the carriage.

Isabel turned to Millie in her attempt to break the tension and take her mind off the embarrassing incident. "Are you good at embroidering, Millie?"

The girl narrowed her eyes at Isabel before muttering, "It's Millicent."

Oh. Isabel slightly reared back. She wasn't exactly expecting an enthusiastic response. The girl had been avoiding Isabel the entire journey, but she wasn't prepared for hostility either.

"Very well, Millicent. Are you good with a needle?"

Millicent turned away and looked out the window.

Isabel took a deep breath. "Ladies are expected to answer when they are being addressed, Millicent. Since you are a marquess's daughter, you need to know those rules."

Millicent pretended not to hear a thing.

Isabel turned to the nursemaid and smiled tightly.

"Just give her time, my lady," Edith said quietly, then sent Isabel a reassuring smile.

At least one person in the household was on Isabel's side. That made her feel a little better.

"Have you been in the marquess's employ for a long time, Edith?" Isabel asked.

"Just about four years, my lady," Edith answered.

"Then you must know the house rather well. I am looking forward to—"

Isabel was rudely interrupted as Millie tugged on Edith's

sleeve and excitedly pointed out the window. "Look, Edith! A badger! It is a badger, right?"

Edith threw an apologetic look toward Isabel, and the Isabel just gave her a nod.

The nursemaid moved closer to Millicent as she proceeded to tell her all the things she knew about badgers and other animals that resided in this part of England, which ones she'd seen, and which ones she had failed to spot.

Next came a conversation about which animal Button would catch quickest. From then on, conversation moved to anything that would exclude Isabel and not let her converse with the nursemaid.

* * *

They arrived home late in the evening. Their journey had gotten delayed by a storm that started a few miles away from the manor, so they had to reduce the speed to a slow walk.

Millicent was already sleeping, so Vane swept her into his arms and led everyone inside.

"Mrs. Ainsworth, please, gather all the servants and introduce her ladyship."

An older woman in a dark brown frock scurried to follow the order.

"You are the one who—" Isabel started, but Vane shushed her and tipped his head toward the sleeping child in his arms. "Mrs. Ainsworth will show you to our quarters," he said and continued up the stairs without another word.

Isabel looked at the dog, who had just entered the hall, followed by a couple of footmen. Button barked once at Isabel and trotted after his master.

Chapter 8

Even the damned dog had abandoned her.

A few moments later, tired, but feigning good spirit, the servants had gathered in the hall.

"Bastard," Isabel muttered under her breath.

Was this his idea of welcoming his mistress to his country seat? All the servants stood, waiting—probably for their master—to be introduced to their mistress.

Isabel's cheeks heated. It was obvious to everyone that neither the master nor his daughter particularly welcomed their new marchioness to their home.

She didn't want to start her life at the mansion on the wrong footing, but the servants already studied her with distrust in their eyes. And now, she was left to introduce herself.

Isabel pulled on a cheerful smile. "Good evening, everyone," she said overly brightly. "I shall be the new marchioness and the mistress of this house."

The servants stood frozen as if rooted in place. None of them even blinked. The housekeeper, Mrs. Ainsworth, took a step forward and started introducing each servant by their name and station.

Isabel took a deep breath of relief. She studied each person avidly, trying to remember their distinct characteristics, like their hair or facial features, and associate that with their station and name so that she wouldn't forget.

For example, Mrs. Ainsworth was worthy to be a housekeeper, the head of the household. That and her particular attire made her easy to remember. Rose, the upstairs maid, had red hair, Chloe, the chambermaid, had a name starting with "C," just like her position. On and on, Isabel tried to remember everyone's name and position. It would take her a few days, but this neat little trick her mother had taught her hadn't failed her thus far.

When Mrs. Ainsworth was done introducing the household, Isabel smiled and let everyone get back to their business.

"Thank you, Mrs. Ainsworth," she said, trying not to sound overly relieved. "Would you please show me to my quarters?"

"Of course, my lady. Please, follow me."

Isabel walked through the manor in silence. It was a nice, spacious manor, if sparsely furnished and barely decorated. Now the burden of turning this place into a comfortable home fell onto her shoulders.

This was something Isabel was good at. She was glad she'd have mundane tasks to occupy herself with. Otherwise, she did not know what she'd do.

They reached the bedroom, and Mrs. Ainsworth opened the door with a flourish. "Welcome, my lady."

Isabel stepped into the spacious room and looked around. The walls were covered with extravagant wallpaper with green and golden hues. The furniture looked rich and expensive. Everything had too much grandeur for Isabel's taste. And the room especially stood out from the bare, sparsely furnished manor.

Isabel twirled, taking in the entire room. If she had a choice, she wouldn't pick this room to live in. But this was the marchioness's chamber, and it would do. At least for now.

"Anything else, my lady?" Mrs. Ainsworth intruded into her thoughts.

"Yes. Can you please spare me a maid? My lady's maid will be arriving shortly with the rest of my trunks, and I need someone to take her place in the meantime."

"Of course, my lady." Mrs. Ainsworth bowed out, leaving Isabel one on one with her thoughts in the rich, extravagant

Chapter 8

chamber, feeling extremely out of place.

Chapter 9

Isabel came down to breakfast the next morning feeling rested after the grueling journey. She was starving and looking forward to a nice, long morning meal.

She entered the dining room and immediately was immersed in a serene atmosphere.

The dining room was not as extravagantly decorated as Isabel's bedchamber, for which she was grateful. The curtains and furniture were upholstered with ocean-blue fabric with green ornamentation, making Isabel feel as though she were surrounded by blue sky and emerald waters. The sunlight streamed from the windows and illuminated the room in soft light. The rustle of paper and the smell of coffee added to the cozy feeling.

But the quiet, tranquil morning was ruined as soon as she noticed her husband, sitting at the head of the table, silently partaking in his meal. Just one glance at him reminded Isabel of all the animosity between them. The way he had treated her at the inn, the way he had abandoned her in the hall without

Chapter 9

bothering to introduce her to his staff, all of that made her blood boil all over again.

She'd had a full night to come to terms with her emotions, and she thought the anger she had felt would disappear come morning. But the memory of her humiliation did not give way.

Her husband turned the page of his paper, calmly sipping on his coffee. He was well-groomed, although his hair was still wet from a recent bath. His lips were pursed in disapproval, making Isabel wonder if he ever smiled or laughed in joy. He was so composed, damn him, and all Isabel wanted was to rip the paper out of his long fingers, tear it to pieces, and scatter it onto his head.

She smiled, the fantasy lifting her dark mood when he looked up from behind the paper.

"Good morning," he rasped, a frown lining his forehead.

Isabel composed her features and demurely sat at the table. James, the footman she'd brought with her from her household, instantly jumped to bring her breakfast from the side table and poured her the chocolate. Isabel thanked him and delighted in the hot cup, trying to ignore the formidable presence beside her. It did not work.

"Did you sleep well?" he asked.

"Like a babe." *The one you think I am carrying*, she thought irritably.

"I need to go away on business for the day," he said in an offhand manner, and her eyes rounded.

Did he mean to leave her alone? With his surly daughter and undisciplined dog? Her expression must have translated because he hastened to add, "I shall take Button and Millie with me. They quite enjoy running around the field while I attend to matters with farmers."

"Oh." Isabel expelled a breath of relief. "Then I shall familiarize myself with the manor and the villagers."

Vane grimaced and slowly put the paper down. "I think you should delay your visit to our tenants until I can accompany you."

Now he wanted to monitor her like she was a child? "Why would I? I am the mistress of this estate. I need to see them as soon as I am able."

"Because they might not be welcoming," he said calmly.

Isabel scoffed. "Similar to how you and your daughter have been?"

He straightened in his chair, throwing his vast shadow over her. "Everyone needs to get used to the fact that you are here. I just don't want any unfortunate incidents."

Isabel took a sip of chocolate to calm herself, then turned and looked him dead in the eye. "I am not about to create a scandal if that's what you are worried about. Regardless of what you think of me, I am accomplished at running estates and dealing with tenants. I have done that for my brother for over eight years."

Vane steepled his fingers. "I am not inclined to believe anything you say until I see it with my own eyes."

"Your lack of trust is tiring, my lord," Isabel said calmly, although she felt her chest fill with rage. "I shall do as I please, and if you want to accompany me, you will have to postpone your own matters."

"I am not about to change my plans because of your stubbornness," he growled. "I am certain you can find plenty of things to keep you occupied inside the manor in the meantime."

Chapter 9

"I am afraid I cannot oblige. My mother taught me that a mistress should first contact her tenants. Then, she needs to find out the villagers' needs, identify the elderly and the sick, and make certain they have all the necessary provisions. If I delay this duty, people will suffer. And that will be on your head."

Vane listened to her concerns with an air of boredom. "I shall survive the burden."

Isabel gasped. Was he truly such a heartless master? "I do not know who was helping you run the estates in the absence of a mistress, but this is not how things are done. I know my main duty, and I shall perform it whether you agree with me or not!"

"Do you have to counter everything I say? I am your husband, and you will do as I say." His voice was stony and brooked no argument.

Isabel argued still. "I am not a slave. I shall not blindly obey you just because I was forced to marry you under the most unfortunate circumstances. Our situation is as much your fault as it is mine. You have no right to act superior, especially since I have no evidence to believe that you are."

Vane's fingers fisted at his side, and for a moment, Isabel was afraid he'd lunge at her. But he relaxed and let out a deep sigh. "I didn't expect you to," he breathed.

Isabel swallowed and turned away from him. "You didn't expect me to obey, or you didn't expect me to find you superior?"

Vane took a sip of coffee and returned to his paper. "I did not expect you to be the proper wife I needed," he said, without taking his eyes off the page.

"I didn't expect you to be a fair master, either. So I suppose neither of us is disappointed."

She resolutely turned away and started on her meal again, determined to ignore him.

A few moments later, loud footsteps preceded the arrival of the giant dog, followed by Millicent, who appeared to be chasing the animal.

Vane stood, and the dog immediately ran toward him, wagging his tail.

"Millie, how many times do I have to tell you not to run inside the house?" Vane asked in a bored tone.

The girl didn't answer; she just plopped into a seat.

Isabel raised her brow. No greeting, no curtsy, in fact, not even a glance toward her parent or Isabel—this girl was absolutely mannerless. And to top it all off, she brought the giant dog to the breakfast table.

"Sit," Vane commanded, and as the dog settled next to him, he turned to Millie. "Did he have breakfast today yet?"

Millie shook her head.

"I would prefer it if you answered me verbally, dear," Vane said softly.

Millie shrugged. "I don't think so."

"Well, I'd say it's quite unfair that you get to eat, but Button doesn't."

Millie bounced her knee. "Button wanted to eat with you. That is why he came with me."

"I'm sure he did," the marquess grumbled.

Isabel raised her eyes heavenward. The stern master, the commanding marquess, just could not seem to discipline his daughter at all. However, Isabel would not start her life as the marchioness by antagonizing the girl.

She stood. "I shall inquire with Mrs. Ainsworth about

Chapter 9

Button's breakfast. I have other matters to discuss with her."

"Thank you," Vane said with a brief nod and turned back to his daughter.

Millie immediately livened up and proceeded to chat away happily. Isabel sighed and padded out of the room.

* * *

Isabel went in search of the housekeeper, still muttering under her breath. The marquess could not handle raising his own daughter the right way, and he had the gall to tell Isabel what to do and what not to do around the estate.

Not only did he think her scandalous, but apparently, he also thought her incapable of performing the simplest of her duties. Well, he would learn a thing or two about Isabel this afternoon.

She did not enjoy taking orders. Especially not about her duties. Especially not from a man who probably knew nothing of said duties, or who thought they were not as important as his.

Isabel knew the reality of the situation. She could not lounge about and let things go their own route. She would never be able to catch up.

After she found Mrs. Ainsworth and informed her of the situation with the dog, Isabel went to ask for her carriage to be prepared. She stopped halfway and turned back to the housekeeper.

"I almost forgot. I am going to the village this afternoon. And I can't as well go empty-handed. Please, have some baskets with leftover foods and medicine prepared, which I can take with me for the villagers."

"Are you certain you want to go to the village today?" Mrs. Ainsworth looked at her doubtfully.

Am I certain? What is there to think about? "Of course."

"But his lordship—"

"I am the mistress of this estate now, Mrs. Ainsworth. And as the mistress, it is my duty to visit my tenants."

"Yes, my lady." Mrs. Ainsworth hesitated. "It's just that his lordship—"

Isabel raised her hand to silence the housekeeper. She was tired of his lordship's interference. It was obvious that the manor staff was devoted to him. Well, that would need to be changed too. "Thank you for your concern, Mrs. Ainsworth. But whatever his lordship wants to say, he shall have to say it directly to me. Please, prepare the baskets."

At Mrs. Ainsworth's nod, Isabel went to her room to change for her outing.

A few minutes later, properly attired and accompanied by Anthea, Isabel set out to the village in a carriage filled with baskets of food. She was excited to see her new home and get to know the villagers. Isabel generally felt more at home surrounded by people, chatter, and busy life.

The sun was high in the sky and the weather promised no precipitation. The road had dried sufficiently for the carriage to travel without major issues. It just swayed from time to time from hitting a puddle.

As the houses came into sight, Isabel noticed a few children running after the carriage and cheering. Isabel looked out the window and waved her hand. A couple of boys stopped dead on the spot with their mouths agape while a few continued their pursuit of the vehicle.

The carriage halted by the side of the road, next to an old

Chapter 9

building, and the groom helped Isabel out. She smiled as she looked at people gathering to greet her. Finally, something she was familiar with. Something she felt confident doing.

Anthea followed her out and stood by her side as Isabel introduced herself as the new Marchioness of Vane.

Dead silence greeted her words. Her smile tensed as she looked at the crowd of people. "I brought you some goods," she said cheerfully.

People came back to life after her words. They came closer toward her, the conversation buzzing. With the help of her groom and Anthea, Isabel took out the baskets and passed the contents around.

A few people still lingered when she was done, including an old wrinkly woman. "Well?" she asked when Isabel was done. "Where are my ribbons?"

Isabel blinked. "Ribbons?"

"His lordship promised to bring me ribbons from the city. I make blankets and shawls for the entire village. I rarely decorate them with anything, but he promised."

"And the fruit, Miss—Your ladyship. His lordship promised to bring us exotic fruits."

"What about the watercolors for the school?"

Isabel blinked at the women, not certain what to say. "I—he—that's all I have… today."

The women looked at the empty baskets, forlorn.

"I shall make certain to bring all of it tomorrow," Isabel promised.

Someone tugged her on her skirt. Isabel turned to see a little blonde girl by her side. "What about my book, my lady?" the girl said in a barely audible whisper, obviously too shy to even address her. "His lordship promised to bring it to me from London."

A boulder seemed to lodge itself in Isabel's throat. She forced a smile. "I don't have it with me today... But his lordship didn't forget, I promise." She hoped she was not lying about that. "He just... He wanted to give it to you himself."

Isabel was glad she could come up with a convenient lie and prayed that the loathsome oaf didn't forget the damned book and everything else he'd promised to his people.

"Another mistress, that's what we need!" someone muttered behind her.

Isabel looked around in confusion, unsure how to react to such a statement.

Everyone started to disperse, the conversation buzzing around her. Isabel could still hear their exclamations of surprise and displeasure.

"Instead of bringing us what he promised, he brought us something we never asked for. A mistress. Huh!" an old lady exclaimed by Isabel's side.

Isabel frowned. Did the old lady not realize Isabel could hear her words?

What did Isabel do to deserve their scorn?

She wasn't about to get her answer here. Isabel picked up her skirts in frustration, climbed into her carriage, and drove away.

* * *

Rhys came down to supper that evening feeling tired. He had spent the entire morning working in the field with his farmers, as was his custom. He spoke to them daily and made sure they had everything they needed because their problems

Chapter 9

were quite literally his and his estate's problems.

The farmers were possibly the busiest people on his estates. So to have a conversation with them, Rhys needed to work alongside them.

This was an unusual activity for a marquess. However, Rhys was not a conventional lord. People already whispered atrocious rumors behind his back. What was one more thing in the scheme of things?

Besides, Rhys loved to work outdoors. He spent every afternoon locked inside his study, crouching behind his desk and looking at numbers with his solicitors, and the morning work was a reprieve from a boring existence. It also gave his highly spirited daughter freedom to roam around the estate while supervised and his massive dog a space to race freely around the fields.

Now, as he sat at the supper table, he gloomily stared at his plate, not even looking at what was being served. His mind was too occupied with the issues around the estates that needed solving. So many things needed his attention, and he couldn't quite pay enough attention to them all.

This was one of the reasons he had married, but would Lady Isabel aid him in his work or just stifle his progress?

"Ew!" Millie's exclamation of disgust was what brought him back into the present. "What is this?" she asked, her face a scrunched-up grimace. Her mouth was half-open, pieces of meat falling out as she wiped at her lips and chin.

"A duck, with beans and—" Lady Isabel started, but Millie interrupted her as she shot up from her chair.

"A duck!"

Lady Isabel blinked, and Rhys covered his face with his palm for a brief moment. "Millie, dear, there will be a second course. Please, sit back down."

"What is wrong with the duck?" Lady Isabel looked from Rhys to Millie, her gaze confused.

"Nothing, Millie doesn't like the taste, that is all."

Millie grumbled and sat back down, her face still a grimace of disgust.

Lady Isabel closed her eyes in defeat. "Nobody told me."

"That's not an issue." Rhys turned to the footmen lining the wall. "Second course, please."

"I should have asked," Lady Isabel said.

"Yes, you should have," Rhys agreed.

"No." She finally looked at him, fire behind her eyes. "No, you should have told me. I couldn't have known. You should have told me, or the chef… But the servants do not seem to respect me, and neither do tenants."

Rhys stilled. "You went to the village?"

"I did." She looked away.

"When I explicitly forbade you from doing so!"

"I don't see how you can forbid me from doing my duty!" She poked her fork at the duck, avoiding his gaze.

"And I assume it didn't go so well?"

"Of course not! Because you withheld things from me. The villagers were waiting for the items you promised to bring them from London, and naturally, they were upset. But none of it would have happened if you've been upfront with me," Lady Isabel argued.

She wasn't wrong, but Rhys felt like she went behind his back, betraying his trust, just like his late wife used to do, and it made him stubborn. "I am your husband, and you should obey my every word."

"Papa." Millie's voice sounded on the periphery of his mind.

Chapter 9

"You should trust me enough to do my duty! What were you afraid of? Did you think I'd manage to ruin your relationship with the tenants?"

"Papa!" Millie's voice sounded again.

"Wait a moment, moppet," Rhys said in an offhand manner and turned back to Lady Isabel. "Of course, I think so. Do I have any reason to believe otherwise?"

"And instead, you decided to ruin mine," Lady Isabel countered. "Now they look at me as though I am incompetent and not only that but—"

"Papa, look!"

"What?"

"What?"

Lady Isabel and Rhys turned to Millie in unison. Button—who was apparently eating off Millie's plate—slunk his head back under the table. Millie looked from Rhys to Lady Isabel with wide eyes and then burst into tears.

Rhys winced. He had argued in front of his babe, ignored her, and raised his voice to her all in the span of two minutes. *Perfect!*

Rhys quickly scooped Millie up in his arms, trying to calm his crying babe.

"Thank you for the lovely supper," he clipped toward his wife as he left the room.

Chapter 10

Isabel watched her husband disappear with Millie in his arms, and her heart sank. Was she to blame for the child's crying?

She swallowed, tears prickling at the back of her eyes. She stood slowly, her appetite forgotten, wiped her mouth with the dinner cloth, and slowly exited the room. The footmen lining the backroom wall stared ahead, pretending to see neither the argument nor their mistress's silent defection.

All the servants were mistrustful of her as it was, and now she'd frightened their favorite little mistress, although it wasn't her intention.

She left the dining room and padded toward her chamber.

Nothing had gone right since she arrived at this blasted estate. She'd wanted to make everything better, but everything had just turned out worse.

Everything had seemed to just go wrong from the moment she ran into the marquess at the ball, and she doubted anything would get better any time soon. But she needed

Chapter 10

to try. Because as much as she disliked it, this was her life now.

She entered her room and called her lady's maid to help her change into her nightgown. The usually chatty Anthea was uncharacteristically quiet. And although Isabel was thankful for that in this instance as she needed silence to clear her mind, she couldn't help but feel that Anthea was not happy in this household either. Or perhaps she'd overheard the other servants gossiping about their ne'er do well new mistress and didn't want to upset Isabel even further.

Isabel climbed into bed feeling defeated. It had been a long and difficult day, and she just wanted to close her eyes and fall asleep even though the hour was young. But as it often happened, sleep evaded her, and instead, her mind was invaded by tumultuous thoughts.

What if everything rumored about the marquess was true? Perhaps he wasn't cruel but unjust and unwelcoming, and as a result, his poor wife had no other recourse but to get away from him. What if Isabel had no one to lend her support on this cold and unfeeling estate?

Sam's residence in Bedford was close enough, and she could just take a horse and gallop away if she wanted.

But what if the marquess cut off that opportunity and wouldn't let her out of the estate? The dark thoughts wouldn't leave her, the spirit of the former lady who'd occupied this chamber crushing Isabel. Or perhaps it was the atrocious decor that was driving her mad.

Isabel sprung up from the bed and opened the curtains. It wasn't enough. The overly extravagant, cluttered room made it difficult to breathe. She started taking off the paintings one by one. Once the walls were bare save for the horrid wallpaper, Isabel cocked her head and looked over the chamber.

Somehow she could breathe easier now. Yes. She shouldn't live with the shadow of the former mistress's fate hanging over her. She was the mistress now, and she would be damned before she gave in to her fears and Vane's intimidation.

***

Millie's hysterics didn't last long. As soon as they arrived at her nursery, she wiped at her tears and demanded Rhys read to her.

It didn't matter that she'd quieted down easily and that she seemed to forgive his behavior. He did not. He had promised himself to never raise his voice to her and to never make her feel as though she was unprotected and vulnerable. He had failed.

He needed to watch his temper and not let Lady Isabel rile him up. His little daughter was the most important thing to him, and she had suffered enough in the tiny span of her life.

So he sat in her nursery, atoning for his vile behavior by reading to her and drinking imaginary tea at her imaginary tea party.

They spent a few hours together, then he asked for the maid to bring his daughter a light snack before bed since she hadn't had a proper meal at supper, and after that, he lulled her into sleep.

Rhys felt extremely guilty for being the cause of Millicent's tears, but he also felt embarrassed for the way he had treated his wife. She didn't deserve his mistrust. Deep down, he knew it.

Chapter 10

All the issues in his mind stemmed from his previous relationship rather than from his current wife, and he needed to apologize for that, too.

So he padded back to his room only to be caught off guard by a small procession moving from the family wing toward the guest wing, carrying trunks and other items.

His wife, wearing a single dressing gown over her night rail, concluded the procession, holding a small valise in her arms.

"What is going on?" Rhys barked, his good intentions vanishing like a puddle on a sunny day.

"I am moving to another chamber," Lady Isabel said, unperturbed, as she continued walking.

Rhys followed after her. "In the east wing?"

"Yes, I didn't find any other room that caught my fancy."

"But why do you need another room?"

"Because," Lady Isabel said as she reached her desired chamber, "the marchioness's room is being redecorated."

Rhys blinked. "Since when?"

Lady Isabel looked at him with an even gaze. "Since twenty minutes ago," she said with a sly smile and walked into her new bedchamber.

Rhys was so perplexed that he didn't persist further. He walked back to the family wing and padded toward his room. He paused in front of the doors to the marchioness's chambers before opening them. He hadn't entered this room for about seven years. But he remembered what it had looked like.

When Lady Isabel said the room was being redecorated, this was not what he'd imagined.

No paintings or other decorations were hanging on the walls. The wallpaper was scraped in places, the curtains on one window had been taken down, and all the furniture aside from the large pieces was collected in one corner.

Did she say it had taken her twenty minutes to do all that? Rhys gave the room a once over before walking to the adjoining room door. The bare walls made his wife's room seem different already, as though his previous wife had not occupied this chamber at all.

Well, good riddance then, he thought and entered his chamber.

* * *

Isabel woke up the next morning feeling fresh and rejuvenated. She was in a clean, bright room with no shadow of the past hanging over her. Isabel performed her morning ablutions, got dressed, and went to have breakfast.

Her husband was sitting at the table, but Millicent was not there.

"Good morning," Isabel said as she sat down.

Her husband looked up from the paper. "How are your new accommodations?"

"Perfect, thank you. And where's Millie?"

Vane cleared his throat. "She decided not to join us this morning."

Isabel's heart sank. Because of her, she was certain, but she decided not to dwell on the subject. "Can we go to the village today to rectify our mistake from yesterday?"

Vane looked up at her choice of the word "our." Well, it wasn't her mistake alone; the least he could do was share the responsibility for it.

"Yes," he said and returned to his paper.

Chapter 10

That wasn't an enthusiastic response, but at least he didn't argue. It was a start.

Isabel cleared her throat. "Since I started working on my room, I thought, why not redecorate the entire house? It is quite old, and there doesn't seem as though much improvement has been made to it for years."

Isabel needed to spring into action. The busier she was, the less likely she was to think about her abysmal marriage and all the troubles that came with it.

Vane lifted his gaze off the paper. "You're right. There hasn't been any improvement since I acquired the title. Except in the marchioness's room. That one seems to be the one that gets redecorated most often."

Isabel swallowed. So his former wife had been the one to change her room into the chaos of extravagant elements all thrown together. "So you do not mind?"

"I don't mind. Just don't touch my room." He shielded his face with the paper again.

Isabel pursed her lips. "And since we are redecorating, I was wondering"—Vane lowered the paper, his gaze annoyed—"if we perhaps should take this opportunity to host a house party once we are finished."

"You seem to want to change a lot of things at once," he noted. "I wouldn't hurry."

Well, of course, I want to make changes. Otherwise, I will lose my mind. "I am not about to turn the entire house upside down."

"That seems what you've done with the marchioness's chamber."

Ah, so you saw. "I am only talking about light redecoration, painting the walls, hanging new art, adding some more flowers. It wouldn't take me long to achieve."

Vane hummed thoughtfully. "Then perhaps my room could use some of that, too."

Isabel hid her smile. Finally, they seemed to be communicating. "And the house party?" she asked hopefully.

"I am not so certain it's a great idea."

Isabel nodded. She'd take the win where she could, and in terms of redecorating the house, she'd definitely won.

"May I return to my paper now?" He raised his brow.

Isabel nodded with a smile. "You may."

* * *

Isabel returned from their outing to the village a few hours later. She felt exhausted, although she'd ended up doing nothing. And perhaps that was the reason for her exhaustion.

When she was acting as a mistress at Gage's estate, she often went to socialize with the tenants, and she always came back feeling reinvigorated and full of life. Speaking to villagers, coming up with plans, helping people—these were the things that kept her alive. On Vane's estate, everything seemed to just suck the life out of her.

It was the same as the tiring trip from London to Vane estate when Millie had ignored Isabel the entire trip.

That was it. Being ignored and feeling invisible was entirely too soul-crushing.

When they had arrived at the village, the tenants had surrounded their master and talked to him without stopping. They had conveyed their concerns, expressed their excitement, and asked for his advice, all the while showering him with compliments and inviting him for tea.

Chapter 10

Isabel had tried to interject a couple of times, but nobody seemed interested in what she had to say. A few moments later, Isabel had found herself on the periphery of the growing crowd of people eager to talk to their master.

They loved him. At least that fact gave Isabel a tiny bit of peace. If the tenants loved him, he was a fair master. But this thought did not give her as much relief as she thought it would.

After their duty was done, Vane had left for a meeting with his manager, and Isabel sauntered toward the kitchen. She needed to come up with a new menu for the week and hoped she wouldn't commit another mistake.

She made her way to the door of the kitchen but stopped cold as she heard the conversation beyond the wall.

"Everything the new mistress does is the worst," a woman's voice said.

"Did you hear?" another woman chimed in. "She had footmen carry her things out of the mistress's bedroom in the middle of the night and moved to another wing!"

"How odd! Why move?"

There was a sound similar to a snort. "Probably away from the master after nearly poisoning his daughter."

"A duck!" the third voice intervened, and the laughter followed.

"Why move to another wing? There weren't any empty rooms in the family wing?"

"No, she just wanted to exert her power over the poor footmen as they dragged her belongings from one part of the house to another!"

Laughter sounded again, and Isabel felt sick to her stomach. She'd moved to another wing because it was the cleanest and the simplest chamber. And since she'd walked along with footmen, she hadn't thought it was a big issue. Apparently, it was.

"I wish she'd just stop trying. The first one didn't care, but at least she wasn't in the way," the first woman continued.

The matter Isabel had wanted to discuss with the housekeeper forgotten, she rushed out of the house. She wanted to be as far away from this estate as she could.

Isabel dashed through the garden and only stopped when she reached an old structure.

The stables.

Good. She needed to clear her head.

So she asked the groom to saddle a horse and galloped away, wherever the hooves of the beast would take her.

Chapter 11

After a few hours of riding, Isabel found herself roaming the woods by the side of a stream. She tied her horse to a tree and walked along the bank.

At the Gage estate, she often sat by a stream and watched the water or even swam. Running water usually had a calming effect on her. Except, this time, it didn't work. She settled on a large boulder, wrapped her arms around her knees, and placed her forehead over them.

Why was everything so difficult? Why did these people loathe her? She hadn't done them any harm. She just wanted to be a good mistress, and she'd seemed to fail in her every attempt.

She raised her head to the sky. "Oh, Mama, you always made it seem so easy. Why can't I do the same?"

The sun shined brightly in the sky, the clouds passed over her head, and the wind had carried her voice away, but there was no answer.

She sat like that, staring at the sky, tears running down her face, as she heard a scream.

Isabel looked around but didn't see a soul.

Another scream.

Isabel walked closer to the water and looked upstream. A small dark object moved downstream, carried away by the strong current. And there was a person, perhaps a woman, moving along the bank, shouting something at the bundle.

She had probably dropped something and could not get it because the current was too fast. Well, Isabel was in a perfect position to catch whatever it was.

Isabel hiked up her skirts and waded into the water. The water proved to be rather deep, almost to her waist, and the strong current had her swaying as she carefully walked, stepping on the slippery stones.

As the bundle neared her, Isabel realized in horror that it wasn't an object, it was a little boy! She didn't have time to react further as the bundle almost passed her. Isabel reached out her arms and caught the boy against her chest. She slipped and toppled over.

Isabel pushed out her arms, trying to hold the child over the water.

The strong current carried them both away, Isabel's skirts weighing her down. But she managed to push off the bottom with her feet and propel herself toward the shore. Luckily, she was an experienced swimmer. She thanked the lucky stars for growing up with brothers.

A few moments later, she came sputtering to the bank, a small child cradled to her chest. As soon as they reached the firm ground, the child coughed and started crying. Isabel's heart squeezed. Poor babe must have been so frightened.

"Jimmie!" A woman—now Isabel could clearly see it was a

Chapter 11

woman—ran toward them, took the child from Isabel's arms, and hugged him tightly. Then she pulled away from him and addressed him sternly, "I told you not to go in the water!"

As she held the boy a slight distance away from her body, Isabel could see that the woman was in the advanced stages of carrying another babe in her belly. The poor woman must have been terrified and unable to keep up with her drowning child as her rounded stomach weighed her down.

The woman embraced her child once more and then finally addressed Isabel. "Thank you. Oh, I can't thank you enough for saving my babe!"

Isabel shook her head. "Please, no need to thank me. I am just glad I happened to be here at the right time."

The woman eyed her curiously, obviously noticing her cultured accent. "You are the new lady."

Isabel scrubbed her wet hair away from her face. "I might not look like one at the moment, however," she replied with a chuckle.

She bunched her skirts in an attempt to wring some water out of the heavy gown.

"Come! You both need to dry, or you will catch your death."

"Mama, I can walk!" the boy cried, his previous mishap forgotten.

"I know you can, but you are not going to. Not until we are as far away from this stream as we can be."

Isabel turned toward the woman. "Do you want me to help you carry him?"

The woman looked at her queerly but then shook her head. "Thank you, my lady. But I am used to carrying children around. He is not my only babe."

"Please, call me Isabel." Isabel still wasn't used to being

called *my lady.* More than that, today, she did not feel entitled to wear the moniker.

The woman threw another of her odd looks. "But I can't."

"Please, I insist."

The woman nodded graciously. "In that case, my name is Lilian, and that's my son, Jimmie."

Jimmie beamed at her, and Isabel let out a breath of relief. Somehow knowing someone's name felt like it created a bond between them. And Isabel needed kinship more than anything at the moment.

"You said you have more children," Isabel noted. "How many do you have?"

Lilian rubbed her rounded belly. "This one will be the sixth."

Isabel stared at the woman in awe. Six? Lilian was a tiny little thing, and she did not look like a mother of five, with the sixth of its way. "Oh my! You must have a boisterous family!"

"Boisterous is the right word," Lilian said with a chuckle. "They barely let me attend to my duties. I have to chase after them all day."

"You don't *have* to chase after me, Mama!" Jimmie said.

"Not when you're in my arms, I don't," Lilian grumbled.

Isabel chuckled. "I grew up in a large family, too. It is a blessing." The memories of running around the estate while they were young made tears prickle at the back of her eyes. Oh, how she missed her dear siblings.

They made their way out of the woods, and Isabel saw her horse, quietly grazing nearby. She was loath to leave, but she had spent long enough feeling sorry for herself. Now was the time to get back to her life.

Lilian noticed that Isabel had slowed her pace. "You are not coming with us? I could make you a cup of tea while you dry

Chapter 11

up."

"Thank you for your gracious offer, and I would love to, but I have responsibilities of my own that I've been avoiding."

Lilian smiled. "Then perhaps you can come to the village tomorrow?"

Warmth spread inside Isabel's chest. "I would love that very much."

"Mama! We are away from the stream. Can I walk now?" Jimmie asked as he bounced in Lilian's arms.

"Oh, very well." Lilian lowered her child, and he dashed toward the village. She heaved a sigh and turned toward Isabel. "It was good to meet you, M'lady—Isabel. I shall wait for you on the morrow." Lilian bobbed a curtsy and followed her disappearing child.

Isabel turned and slowly walked to her mount, her mood suddenly lifting. This hadn't been an ideal day, but at least she had made one friend.

* * *

Rhys was almost falling off his feet by the time they made it home after a morning spent in the field. Rhys had been afraid it would rain the entire week after their gloomy journey. But the day had proved to be beautiful: sunny with a light breeze. It accommodated Rhys nicely for a good day's work. And Millie had fun running around and playing with Button.

As they entered the hall, Rhys ordered a bath to be prepared for Millie and asked the servants to clean Button as well. It had been his ritual every time he had come from the field. Clean his daughter and the dog first, and he would take care of himself later. Otherwise, the two would spread the dirt around the house, which led to more clean-up than necessary.

Once he took care of all the arrangements for Millie and Button, he walked unhurriedly up the stairs.

Rhys was not exactly an old man. In fact, he would say he was in his prime years. And yet his back hurt, and his knees creaked with every move. A long journey on horseback from London and then immediately working in the field definitely took a toll on his body. He stretched as he slowly made his way up the stairs.

As he reached the landing, the door opened in the hall, accompanied by loud cursing.

Ah, his lovely wife had arrived home. Rhys did not enter the corridor leading to his room. Instead, he leaned his shoulder against the wall and waited for his marchioness to make her way up. He was curious to find out where she had spent the day and what had prompted the unladylike expletives as she entered home.

A loud splatter accompanied the steps, and then Lady Isabel finally appeared on the landing.

She was soaked from head to toe!

Her skirts were not only wet but dirt-smudged. Her bodice was plastered to her chest. Her bonnet was missing, and her hair was just as wet as the rest of her.

Rhys's eyes widened, and he sputtered a laugh before he could control himself. Lady Isabel raised her head, only just noticing his presence. Her face took on a gloomy expression—or at least gloomier than it was before.

"Was it raining?" Rhys asked and peeked out at the window. It was as bright as it had been all day.

"No," she said and walked past him. "I took a swim."

"In your clothes?"

Chapter 11

She didn't answer and just kept walking, not paying him any heed. Rhys followed her wet footsteps into the guest wing and finally into her room.

She didn't seem to notice his presence at all. She just walked to her vanity and looked at her reflection.

"Blast it!" She chewed on her lip, still staring at the looking glass. "I am a good person. Why does this keep happening to me?"

"What exactly—?"

She started pacing, not paying him any heed. "I was an exceptional hostess. People raved about my balls and soirees. I was an example for young ladies to follow. A diamond of the *ton*! Now, look at me!" She halted and raised her hands.

She was soaked to the bone, the wet fabric of her gown outlining her curves perfectly. Rhys could see the budded nipples peeking out from under the soaked bodice. His gaze lingered there, his cock coming to attention and twitching against the confines of his breeches. When she'd said to look at her, surely she'd meant he'd see something else?

He finally forced his gaze up, but she wasn't looking at him. Her gaze was unfocused, and she was chewing on her bottom lip.

"I only try to do what's best," she continued, her voice small. "Only this place seems to suck the life out of any attempt I make."

"What happened?" Rhys asked and stepped closer.

"Does it matter? Would you even care?"

"Well, I am here. I am asking."

Lady Isabel downturned her eyes. "Your daughter dislikes me, your tenants mistrust me, you loathe me… and even servants hate me!" She ended on a hiccup.

What? "Why do you say that?"

She snorted. "Tell me I am wrong."

"Well…" He scratched his jaw. "I would at least argue that the servants don't hate you."

Her gaze turned anguished. He shouldn't have said that. He should have reassured her that he didn't loathe her. That was true, wasn't it? What he felt toward her was much too complicated to narrow down to one word.

She swallowed. "I overheard them talking… They hate me. They wish I hadn't come at all."

"What?" This time he roared the question aloud.

Lady Isabel swallowed. "Just this morning, I overheard them saying it would have been better if I just stopped trying. Is it true, Vane? Would it be better if I just left?"

Rhys stepped closer and took her by the arms. "Who said that?"

She raised her liquid eyes to him. "Does it matter? They see how you treat me. What reason do they have to treat me with respect when you don't? You didn't even introduce me to them!"

A guilty feeling started gnawing at Rhys's chest. She was right.

He hadn't introduced her. He'd treated her with contempt. What did he expect? Well, he couldn't change the past, but he could do something about the future.

He walked to the servants' bell and called for her lady's maid.

"What are you doing?" Lady Isabel asked, concerned.

"Dry yourself, change into a fresh gown, and then meet me at the base of the staircase.

"Why?"

Chapter 11

"Please, just do it?"

At her nod, he left, resolved to make it all better for his wife.

Chapter 12

Isabel took her time drying her hair and then changing into a clean and fresh day gown. After Anthea helped her arrange her hair, she looked at herself in the looking glass one more time before walking out of her chamber.

She glided softly to the base of the steps, and… froze.

Not only was Vane there, but the entire servant staff was surrounding him. Isabel's entire body flushed hot, and her hands grew clammy. Were they waiting on her this entire time?

"Ah, here you are." Vane reached out his hand and helped Isabel descend the few last steps.

"What is going on?" she asked.

Instead of answering, Vane placed her hand on his sleeve and addressed the servants. "I did not have time earlier to properly introduce my wife to you."

Isabel squirmed. It was too late. What was he doing?

"And today, I learned that some of you think it an act of disrespect, which gives you a reason to show contempt

Chapter 12

toward the new mistress."

Mrs. Ainsworth looked at the servants with furrowed brows. It gave Isabel reassurance. The head of the household did not seem to tolerate such behavior.

"Well, I am here to tell you this. Whoever speaks ill of your new mistress will need to find another household."

There was a light gasp, and Isabel tensed. She was not certain this was making things any better. In fact, she feared this would make it even worse. *Oh, why did I have to open my mouth and complain?*

"Furthermore, we are having a house party in a few weeks."

Isabel's head whipped toward her husband, but he didn't react.

"And you would do best to heed your mistress's every command toward that goal. Now that I have my wife to share the burden of looking after the estate, I shall gladly step back and let her take the reins inside the manor."

The vote of confidence gave Isabel wings. Did he truly trust her with this? She prayed he wasn't doing it out of pity. But even if he was, she would prove to be capable, so everybody could put any doubts to rest. She was a perfect mistress and an exemplary hostess, and she would earn respect on this estate no matter what she had to do to reach that goal.

* * *

The next day, Isabel sat with the housekeeper discussing the household's needs and the scope of work needed for them to host a successful house party. She decided the party would be held in two months, which would let Isabel finish decorating the manor and give her enough time to prepare the gardens and the lawn for outdoor activities.

Isabel listened to Mrs. Ainsworth patiently as the housekeeper told her about the household habits, the foods they usually made, and all the other nuances that would be helpful for Isabel to know.

"Thank you, Mrs. Ainsworth. You've been extremely helpful. I only wish I'd had this conversation with you before I crafted the dinner menu," she said with a grimace.

"Everyone makes mistakes, my lady. However, that does not define who we are. It's what we do later that counts. And by your actions, I can see that you will be a spectacular mistress."

Isabel swallowed the bulge in her throat. The words Mrs. Ainsworth had just said were very similar to what her mother used to say to her. It was as if she'd finally received her answer to the question she'd asked in the woods.

Persistence paid off, and Isabel was nothing if not persistent.

After the conversation with Mrs. Ainsworth, Isabel went into the village to visit her new friend. And since the matters with the household were moving in a positive direction, she felt confident she could do the same with the tenants.

As she descended the carriage steps, Isabel saw Jimmie running up to her. He sketched a bow on the run and skidded to a halt before her.

"Mama asked me to show you to our home," he said exuberantly. "Come!"

Isabel followed the child into a small hut. He led her into the kitchen, where Lilian stood, mixing dough.

"My lady!" she cried and bobbed a curtsy.

"Lilian," Isabel answered with a smile. "Please, call me

Chapter 12

Isabel."

Lilian wrinkled her nose. "I shall try my best. Please, sit down. I put a kettle on the stove as I saw you, but I need to finish the dough before I can sit and chat for a bit."

"Perhaps I can help?" Isabel looked around the house, truly desiring to take the load off her new friend's shoulders.

Lilian laughed, holding on to her rounded stomach. "Oh, no. I would not have a lady of the estate cleaning my kitchen. But come, sit. I shall be glad to have a bit of conversation."

Isabel perched herself on the chair and looked around the small house. It was quite cozy if one disregarded the items on the floor and other places where they did not belong. Isabel could not fault Lilian for a slight disorder. If she had five children and no servants, she'd probably be buried in unending tasks.

"How do you have enough hours in the day to cook, clean, and look after the five children?" Isabel asked as she was seated before the table.

Lilian laughed. "I am certain a mistress of the estate juggles quite a few responsibilities herself. Especially around a house party or a ball."

"Yes, that is true," Isabel said. "But I have servants who do most of the work. I have a housekeeper who helps me keep track of all my duties. You are all alone."

"Oh, no. It is not that bad. I had the most issues with my first babe, but after two or three, it starts getting easier somewhere along the way. And now I have Lizzy, my eldest daughter, helping me with the little ones while my sons are helping their father."

Isabel looked around the kitchen once more. "Are you certain you don't want me to help? Truly, I do not mind."

Lilian chuckled again. "No, no. I cannot have you baking our bread. Let me whip up the dough, and then we can have a cup of tea in peace."

"Thank you. The truth is I do not enjoy watching other people work as I idle away."

Lilian looked at her queerly before resuming mixing the ingredients. "That does not sound like a lady of leisure."

Isabel let out a chuckle. "Contrary to what most people think, you were quite right before. A lady of the estate does not get a lot of time to just sit and do nothing. I cannot compare it to what you must be doing, but it is not exactly all parties and soirees."

"It is for some," Lilian said under her breath.

"Pardon me?"

Lilian sent her an apologetic smile but didn't answer. "And do you want a large family yourself? Apologies, I do not mean to be too forward."

Isabel was taken aback by the sharp change of subject. She wasn't exactly eager to talk about the children she might never have, so she did not know what to say. "For now, I would like to establish an affectionate relationship with Millicent."

Lilian paused and looked at Isabel. "Is Millicent giving you trouble then? I can't imagine. She is a lovely little child. Very welcoming. "

"Perhaps to others. She did not take a liking to me one bit."

Lilian laughed and continued her work. "Well, I am not surprised. She thinks you are a threat to her and her papa's relationship. My little ones do not let me embrace my husband with them looking on."

"Truly?" Isabel leaned closer to Lilian, curious.

"Oh, yes, they are very possessive. They do not like

Chapter 12

newcomers arriving at their house and stealing attention away from them."

"Oh." Isabel had not thought about it this way. And after the supper incident, the girl truly did not have any reason to like her. For some reason, Isabel thought that Millie should have given her the benefit of the doubt for simply existing. But children were not logical creatures. One had to earn their trust. "How would you go about mending that relationship?"

"Well..." Lilian took the dough, placed it in the bowl, and covered it with a cloth. "I would start by spending some time with her. Give her the attention she craves."

Isabel thought on that while Lilian went to pour them each a cup of tea. Would Millie even want to spend any time with Isabel? She doubted it. The girl was intent on avoiding her. But if Isabel proposed an activity the girl could not refuse, perhaps she'd have a better chance. "You might be right, Lilian."

Lilian grinned. "I have five of those with the sixth on the way. I better be right, or else what am I doing?"

"Thank you for your kind words, Lilian. I am used to running estates, but aside from my siblings, I never dealt with children."

Lilian placed a tin with almonds on the table. "Would you like some? But I have to warn you, these are not sugared almonds. These are salty."

"How interesting." Isabel took one and crunched at the salted nut as Lilian settled in front of her with the cup of tea. "Mm, it's quite good."

Lilian grinned. "I started craving something salty when I was with my first babe and came up with the recipe. Now I can't live without them while I am increasing. Unfortunately,

I do not have much time to make them, so this is the last batch for weeks."

Isabel popped another one in her mouth. "These are very good. Even without any craving."

Lilian grinned. "Would you like the recipe?"

Isabel nodded. "Very much."

Lilian collected a jar from the windowsill. She took out a piece of paper and handed it to Isabel. "Here. And I do not think you need to worry about Millicent much. Children know a kind heart when they see one. Millicent will see it in you quite soon. I am certain."

Isabel folded the recipe and put it into her pocket. "Perhaps you can help me win the hearts of the villagers, too?"

"Oh, the villagers. Well, they too have a reason to be mistrustful."

"How so?" Isabel moved closer to the edge of her seat.

Lilian just waved a hand. "The master was young when he inherited the marquessate, inexperienced. Made a few mistakes. It took him a long time to earn back their trust. But now he spends a lot of time with the farmers and comes to visit the tenants quite often."

"He visits the tenants himself?"

Lilian gave Isabel an odd look, and Isabel realized she gave away too much with her questioning. It was evident that she and the marquess were not conversing much.

"Yes. He cares for the villagers. He brings us all the necessary supplies. He even reads to the children every other week at the book shop. The village children don't get much education, so they all treasure it."

Lilian looked at Isabel bright-eyed, but something sank inside Isabel's chest.

Chapter 12

She did not know her husband at all. And as much as she was angry at him for judging her prematurely without knowing anything about her, she realized she was doing the same thing. She needed to change that, she decided. But, in the meantime, an idea came to her that would help her with the tenants.

Isabel stood. "Thank you, Lilian, for tea and conversation. I am beyond grateful to you. But the sun is going down already. I need to return home."

"Of course." Lilian tipped her head. "You are welcome at my home anytime!"

Chapter 13

Dear Isabel,

I am glad to hear that you decided to make your chamber on that estate your own. Incidentally, my cousin, Julie, knows a perfect artist who decorated her houses a few years ago, painting the entire walls and ceilings. I have just spoken to Julie, and the artist lives not far from your residence. So, if you wish, I can send her a note, and she will come to help you decorate the place to your liking.

Evie

Isabel penned a quick reply to Evie and put it with the rest of her correspondence to be sent out. She needed all the help she could get to make the estate ready for the house party. She had written to Sam and her brothers, and all of them were excited to visit her and witness her first event as the Marchioness of Vane.

The last few days had been incredibly busy but also rewarding.

Chapter 13

The household was bustling with work, and the change was obvious. The house had already shed its gloomy look as it filled with flowers and new paintings Isabel had acquired during fairs.

The gardens were taking on a heavenly look, and the only thing that needed some polish was the walls. But if Evie's recommended artist started her work soon, then everything would be ready ahead of time.

The servants did not look at her with contempt anymore. Both James and Anthea, the servants Isabel had brought from her household, seemed happier, too. They both had made friends and went about their duty looking content.

Isabel visited the village daily. She loved checking up on her new friend Lilian and interacting with the children. People had stopped being distrustful and happily shared their woes and joys with her.

Everything seemed to be working out nicely except for her personal life. Her husband barely spoke to her during meals, and Millie continued pointedly ignoring her. And now that things were going well in the other parts of her life, she decided to pay special attention to mending the relationship with her husband and his daughter.

For one thing, her courses had come and gone, but her husband still hadn't graced her bed with his presence.

Not that he knew about her courses. She hadn't provided him the *evidence* he desired, which was a ridiculous demand.

And not that Isabel desired his presence in her bed. But she did want children, and if so, she'd have to seduce her husband somehow.

Not yet. She wasn't prepared to deal with it yet. One step at a time. Millie first, Vane second.

With that resolution in mind, Isabel headed to find her husband.

Vane wasn't in his study. He wasn't in his chamber either.

After asking Mr. Monroe, Isabel ascended the steps toward Millie's nursery.

She walked slowly, the thick carpet in the corridor swallowing her steps. The door to Millie's room was half-open, and Isabel heard the murmurs coming from within.

As she came closer, to her immense surprise, she realized that the voice she heard was not Vane speaking to his daughter. He was singing.

Isabel stalked closer to the door and stopped at the threshold, not daring to interrupt her husband's song. She leaned her shoulder and head against the doorjamb, silently absorbing the picture before her.

Millie lay in a small cot, facing away from Isabel.

A lone candle on the bedside table illuminated the room just enough for Isabel to see her husband's serene face as he quietly sang the lullaby. A bit of fur was visible by Vane's feet, and Isabel deduced it was the dog.

Button—the usually exuberant animal—breathed softly, probably soothed by his master's singing.

Vane's features were solemn as he watched his daughter's sleeping form, his throat working at the low bars of the song.

The picture before her was so intimate that Isabel felt like the worst kind of intruder, but she still couldn't step away, mesmerized by the sound of Vane's voice and by the soothing ambiance of a shadowed room.

Lost in the pleasant mood of the dimly lit chamber and her husband's low voice, Isabel's mind drifted to the carefree days she'd spent as a child. Both her mother and father had always

Chapter 13

come to say goodnight to their children. Most of the time, their mother did the singing; their father usually read them stories. These were the simplest of times when the entire family was happy and untroubled.

Isabel wished she could go back to those times, but there was no turning back.

When she was young, she wished to have the same kind of family life one day. She had wanted a brood of children. Or at least a daughter with the same blue eyes as her mother and dark hair.

Isabel had almost forgotten about those simple dreams as her life took a turn toward the unpredictable. After the death of their sibling, their entire life had changed for the worse, and they had not recovered.

Some things turned out well, though, Isabel thought as she watched her husband sing a lullaby to his daughter. She imagined her little sister Sam doing the same thing to her child. Oh, how she wished to be with her at this time. To be embraced into a loving family's bosom once more seemed like something out of a fairy tale.

A tear slid from her cheek and onto her palm, and it was only then Isabel realized that she was crying. She wiped the tear away and cleared her throat softly.

Vane—who had not noticed her presence before now—raised his head and looked at her. His expression immediately changed into a frown, and his singing ceased.

Isabel tipped her head in greeting and slid out of the room. She peeked inside a moment later, just in time to see Vane lean over his daughter and kiss her on the forehead. "Sleep well, my child," he whispered and tucked the covers tightly over her.

Vane straightened and watched his daughter sleep with a soft, beautiful smile that took ten years off his life. Isabel cocked her head. Smiling like that, calm and unburdened, he reminded her of someone. Someone Isabel once knew. But she could not remember whom.

Isabel took a few steps away from the room, not wanting to get caught spying on the pair again as she contemplated the thought. Well, she'd known quite a few people, and it was not surprising she had found Vane's features familiar.

Vane doused the candlelight in Millie's room, and the corridor was shrouded in darkness. Isabel shivered as she waited for the marquess to appear in the corridor.

Assertive steps alerted Isabel to Vane's approach, and she stepped closer to meet him. A mistake. Vane turned into the corridor at that exact moment and collided with her.

Isabel squeaked, but Vane caught her quickly and covered her mouth with his hand. "Shush. You'll wake Millie."

Isabel nodded, her eyes wide, the heat of Vane's palm searing through her skin and branding her. Vane removed his hand. "Are you just always going to be behind every corner now?" he whispered with a frown.

Isabel quickly composed herself and smiled. "For the rest of your life. In sickness and in health—"

Vane directed his eyes heavenward before walking past her. "What are you doing here?"

"I was waiting for you. I thought it was obvious."

"Very well. Why have you been waiting for me?" He was moving down the stairs now, his steps sure, making Isabel hurry after him. She picked up her skirts as she tried not to trip while she kept up with his long stride.

"Can you stop for a moment so I can actually catch up with

Chapter 13

you long enough to answer your question?"

Vane did not stop, did not even pause. He just slowed his steps. *What a cad!* She'd thought they were past his surly attitude toward her. Apparently not.

Isabel finally reached him as he turned into the corridor, heading toward his bedchamber. "I wanted to speak with you about Millicent," she said.

"What about her?" He still hadn't turned.

"I think it is imperative that she start her schooling."

"Yes. I thought we agreed that you'd find her a governess."

"I sent the notice to the papers and already received some answers, but it will take me days to sift through the letters and go through the interviews."

Vane nodded. "Send me your top picks. I shall make the final choice."

"That's all well and good. However, I think Millicent should start her schooling now."

Vane halted and turned to Isabel sharply. "And how will she receive her schooling?"

Isabel swallowed. "From me."

"You want me to leave her? With you."

He spoke as if this was something unfathomable. "Yes. She can't keep running around in the fields with you. Besides, we do not want to frighten the governess with a wild little girl, do we? Millie needs to know basic manners, she needs to learn to watercolor, and perhaps how to approach a pianoforte."

"She is quite intelligent," Vane clipped.

Isabel swallowed. She'd offended him. It was not her intention at all. "I do not doubt it. But I doubt her skills. Not because she is not capable, but because she had no opportunity to learn."

"You think I am an incompetent parent?" he barked.

Oh, Lord. "I did not say that."

"But you think that."

Isabel let out a frustrated breath. "All I think is what I say, Vane. She needs to start her education immediately. And unless you want to be the one to teach her etiquette and watercolors and pianoforte, there is no one else to do it but me."

Vane studied Isabel's resolute features, making her shift uncomfortably under his perusal. "Very well. When do you wish to start?"

Isabel licked her lips. "Immediately."

Vane sputtered a laugh. "You want me to just leave her with you tomorrow, without warning?"

Isabel shrugged. "You can warn her in the morning."

One side of Vane's mouth lifted in a smirk. "You have not spent much time with children, have you?"

"Contrary to what you might think, I am quite capable around children. I have bonded with the children from our village nicely. And I have two younger siblings to whom I was like a mother."

Vane pursed his lips. "You are this confident that you will get along with Millie. Just like that?"

"I think delaying it will do us no good. As it is, we lost a lot of time. It will take us a few moments to bond, but the sooner we do it, the better."

"And you realize that Button will be with her. She won't let him leave without her."

Isabel faltered. She could deal with a six-year-old girl, but what of the dog? "I shall have a couple of footmen around to catch him if he acts out."

Chapter 13

Vane scratched his jaw in thought. He looked at Isabel through narrowed eyes and finally said, "No."

"No?"

"I cannot in good conscience leave you three alone here. It will end in a catastrophe, whether for you or this house. And I am not willing to wait and find out which. Find her a governess, and once you've done that, I will start leaving Millie in the house."

Isabel felt that response like a slap. He did not trust her with his daughter. And he did not trust her ability to keep the house in control. Despite his brief show of trust in front of the servants, he was not willing to trust her with anything else in his life. Yet he was ready to leave his daughter in the care of a governess. "You are willing to leave your child alone with a complete stranger over your own wife?"

Vane looked at her queerly. "First off, how are you any different from a complete stranger? I do not know you at all, and neither does my daughter. At least the governess would have recommendation letters."

Isabel gasped. She wanted to smack the smug marquess so much her palm itched. But she was a lady. And ladies did not hit people. They got what they wanted by other means. So she smiled at him sweetly. "Very well. If you don't want to leave her with me, then I am coming with you tomorrow."

She turned, entered her room, and closed the door right in front of his still astonished face.

Chapter 14

Contrary to Isabel's threats, she did not join Rhys and Millicent on their outing the next morning. Instead, during breakfast, she mentioned that a crisis in the kitchen required her attention.

Rhys was not surprised by that turn of events. He'd actually expected it.

He also doubted there was any crisis. Abigail, his late wife, had often used poor excuses to spend less time with her daughter and even less time with him. Perhaps it was not fair to keep comparing Lady Isabel to his former wife, but Rhys could not help it. So far, he had not seen much difference between them. Although she was a far more apt mistress, he had to admit.

But as far as their personal relationship went and her earlier scandalous behavior, he had no reason to believe she was, in fact, different from his late wife. And seeing how limited his interactions with women were, he had no other point of comparison.

Chapter 14

Either way, he had work to do.

This day started gloomy and promising rain, but eventually, the sky cleared up, and now Millie had shed her coat and was collecting rocks by the side of the carriage. Button was running up and down the road chasing butterflies.

Vane was helping the farmer fix his fence while conversing with the man and discussing ways to make the next year's harvest better.

As a marquess, Vane had a few estates, but his country seat was the biggest and the most profitable, hence where he had spent most of his time. He ventured to his other estates twice a year, and Millie was always by his side.

It wasn't easy having the girl under his wing all this time. But the few times he had left her with somebody else had been a disaster, so he could not risk it happening again. But then, he had never had enough time to find a proper governess for his child.

Vane hoped that with Lady Isabel's help, he would have a better chance of finding someone who would be a perfect fit.

Vane looked at the sun high above the sky and then checked his pocket watch. It was an hour past noon. He wiped the sweat out of his eyes and glanced toward his daughter, who was still collecting rocks and occasionally throwing them and watching Button hunt for them in the grass. She was so innocent, so young, and so oblivious to the turmoil of this life. He had hoped to forever keep her this way.

And that brought up another worry of his. What if he failed to conceive an heir? What if he died and Millie was left with no one in this world to look after her?

The lands and her home would be seized by his cousins, and she would be forced to rely on their generosity. He hoped with his entire soul that Lady Isabel was false in her denials of being with child. Because that would almost guarantee him an heir without even having to bed his wife. However, if she was not lying, that opened the road to far more worries than Rhys was ready to face.

Just then, Vane noticed a lone rider moving in their direction. He wiped his forehead once more and tipped his head toward the farmer.

"Millie, move away from the road, please. There's someone approaching."

Millie raised her head and stared at the rider ahead. Button, noticing the rider too, barked and took off in that direction. Rhys sighed. That dog was too enthusiastic and easily excitable.

It was not an issue when they barely left the country and had no plans to have visitors. But if he wanted to return to London life and to Parliament, he'd need to train him better.

The problem was not truly in Button as he was a disciplined dog around Rhys. It was more Millie who got the dog all riled up.

Another item on his to-do list for this summer.

The rider came closer, and Rhys recognized his wife as she sat straight in her saddle. Button jumped around her, and she pulled on the reins in fright, almost making the horse rear.

"Button!" Rhys let out a short whistle, and the dog galloped back toward him. Luckily, Lady Isabel proved to be an expert horsewoman, managing to calm her horse and avoid an unfortunate incident. "Sit." Rhys raised his hand, and the dog whimpered as he sat down.

Millie moved closer to Button and stroked behind his ears, her eyes on the marchioness.

Chapter 14

"Stay here," Rhys said and walked toward his wife.

Lady Isabel sat atop the horse, straight and composed. She was wearing a beautiful, dark blue riding habit that complemented her eyes. Her bonnet framed her face perfectly, and a couple of ringlets of hair lay against her cheek.

Rhys came closer to her and tipped his hat. "Did not expect to see you here."

Lady Isabel put on a radiant smile, and Rhys caught his breath. On a bright, sunny afternoon, smiling like that, she was absolutely gorgeous. It reminded him of the days past. He tried to squash the thought.

"I did say I was going to accompany you today, did I not?"

"That you did." Rhys cocked his head toward the horse. "Do you need help getting down?"

"Yes. I would appreciate the assistance."

She was still smiling at him as though she was truly glad to join him here. Rhys took a deep breath and approached her.

As she reached for him, placing her hands on his shoulder, Rhys took her by her waist and swept her off the horse. Lady Isabel slid down his length, her limbs brushing against his body, making Rhys shiver pleasantly. When was the last time he'd felt the warmth of a woman's touch?

She was so close now, only a few inches away from him. Her hands were still on his shoulders, his on her waist. She smelled like lavender, and her heat beckoned him closer. All he needed to do was tighten his arms, and her body would crush against his. And if he dipped his head just so, he'd catch her lips in an effortless kiss.

He stepped away instead.

Rhys needed to clear the unwanted thoughts from his head. He should have known that staying away from her would not be easy.

It wasn't unexpected. After spending the last seven years like a monk, staying away from any lady would be impossible. But Lady Isabel called to him in a way no other woman ever had. His body responded to her immediately, and all logical thought flew out the window.

"Papa, come!"

Rhys blinked, collecting his scattered thoughts. He turned to Millie, who was still standing by the dog, only now her expression was that of an annoyed little girl. "Button is tired of waiting."

Rhys swallowed a smile. Of course, it was Button who was tired.

"I brought us some food," Lady Isabel said. "I thought perhaps you'd be ready for an afternoon meal."

She turned back to her horse and attempted to take a basket from behind the saddle. She was too short for the task, making the image almost comical.

Rhys pursed his lips to keep from laughing. "Let me."

Lady Isabel moved away, and Rhys swiftly collected the basket. "What do you say, Millie? Are you hungry?" he asked as he walked toward his daughter.

Curiosity shone in her eyes, and he knew she must have been truly famished. At this time, they would usually move to some farmer's house for a quick bite and a sip of tea. But since Lady Isabel had taken time to prepare the basket, Rhys would not say no to a picnic.

His daughter, however, hesitated. She was clearly unwilling to seem eager to accept a meal from a person she was determined to dislike.

"Well, I am famished," Rhys said. "And I wager Button is

Chapter 14

too. Is there food for him?" He addressed the last question toward Lady Isabel.

"Yes, I asked the housekeeper to prepare a meal for all of us."

"Well?" Rhys turned back to his daughter. "Even if you are not hungry, you cannot deny Button his meal, can you?"

Button wiggled his tail, and his black ears perked up in excitement.

"I suppose we can eat," Millie agreed gallantly.

It wasn't warm enough for a true picnic, as the ground was still wet and cold. So they walked away from the field in search of a place to sit. There was a stream not too far away, surrounded by a patch of woods. Rhys was certain they'd find a few boulders there where they'd be able to spread the blankets and eat in peace.

As they moved toward the stream, Millie immediately took off in that direction, leading the dog with her. She seemed determined to avoid Lady Isabel's company.

Rhys held the basket with their food in one hand, his coat in another as he followed Millicent at a sedate pace.

Lady Isabel matched his steps. "Beautiful weather today, isn't it?" she asked and raised her face to the sun.

The action exposed her creamy neck, and Rhys had trouble looking away. Damn his abstinent years. "Indeed," he rasped. "Why won't you take the bonnet off?"

Lady Isabel looked at him sternly. "A lady does not uncover her head in public."

Rhys looked around. There were a few farmers in the field behind them, but otherwise, not a soul who could see her up close. "Now is when you decide to be all proper?"

"I'll have you know that I am one of the most proper ladies

of the *ton*. Besides, I am to be an example to Millie, am I not?"

Rhys had nothing to say against that. He was grateful that she considered how her actions might affect his daughter.

"Besides, I do want to catch the freckles."

No, wouldn't want to mar her perfect marble complexion.

"Papa!" Millie yelled a few feet away. "Look at this beautiful rock I found!"

Rhys smiled briefly at Lady Isabel and hurried toward his daughter. He complimented Millie on a truly extraordinary rock. Then they continued on the way to finding a place to eat, with Lady Isabel lagging behind while Button galloped circles around them.

When they finally reached a bank of the stream, Lady Isabel spread a blanket on a fallen tree trunk. She and Rhys sat opposite each other on a log while Millie settled on a small boulder across from them. Button lay at Rhys's feet, begging for food with his gaze.

"I like it here," Lady Isabel said after a few moments of silence. "I used to have a favorite spot on the bank of a stream just like this at the Gage estate."

"I know," Rhys said around the bite, then raised his head, realizing that he'd said too much. "I mean, that is my favorite spot, too. I wager a lot of young people like to sit by the stream and… do whatever young people do."

Lady Isabel let out a musical laugh. "And what would that be, my lord? As ancient a marquess as you are, you certainly do not remember!"

Rhys cleared his throat. Her tone was teasing, and he wanted to keep the banter going, but all he could remember at that moment was her surfacing from under the water like a siren and forever enchanting young Rhys.

Chapter 14

He didn't care much for water, but as a young man in love, he often came to her favorite spot to seek her out. But then a darker memory clouded his happier ones, and he shook his head. "Alas, you are right. The memories of my youth are tarnished by the years passed."

"That can't be! You must have some amusing stories from your young days." Lady Isabel smiled at him and popped a sandwich into her mouth.

"I like to swim!" Millie interjected, and Rhys was glad for the interruption.

"Truly? You can swim?" Lady Isabel turned toward Millie.

"Yes, and very well. My father taught me," Millie answered proudly, and Rhys beamed at her.

Lady Isabel tapped a finger against her lush lips. "Well, it is good to know how to do it, but I would not advertise this activity to other people."

Millie puffed out her lips and narrowed her eyes on the marchioness. "Why?"

"Because the *ton* frowns upon brazen ladies who display unladylike behavior," she said.

Rhys snorted, and Lady Isabel threw him a withering glance.

"There are far more suitable activities for ladies. Such as embroidering, watercolors, oh, and playing the pianoforte. Would you like to try them sometime?"

As an attempt to entice a little girl into a boring activity, it failed miserably. Millicent grimaced. But then her face lit up, and she proclaimed proudly, "I can climb trees and sling rocks, too!"

Rhys chuckled. "Let us not shock Lady Isabel anymore. She might have conniptions."

Millicent shot up from her boulder and jumped on the log behind Rhys. She then climbed over him and settled on his lap. He bounced her on his knee as she reached for a grape and popped it into her mouth.

Lady Isabel pursed her lips in disapproval. "I do not think you should encourage your daughter's wild behavior. If we are to have guests soon, she should display proper decorum."

"I'll leave boring her out of her wits to you," Rhys said.

Isabel narrowed her eyes on him. "Boring? I thought you called me scandalous before, and now I am boring?"

Millie kept reaching for grapes, her head flashing back and forth before Vane's gaze, making it difficult to concentrate on the conversation.

"Well, you are boring with children and apparently scandalous with everyone else."

Lady Isabel gasped. "You truly do not know me enough to insist on such an assessment of my character."

Vane bowed his head. "You are right. I apologize."

Lady Isabel was taken aback, but she composed herself quickly. "As I was saying, all Millie needs is a good example and a few lessons—"

"Papa! Look!" Millie turned in his lap, her mouth full of grapes, and she kept stuffing more and more into her mouth.

Rhys swallowed a smile. "You look like a squirrel, dear."

Millie giggled, her mouth bursting, and all the grapes sputtered all over Rhys's front.

"Perhaps we'll need a lot of lessons," Lady Isabel said in defeat.

Millie shot up, giggling. Button also stood and started barking and jumping around his mistress.

"Here, let me." Lady Isabel scooted toward Vane with a

Chapter 14

handkerchief and started gently wiping the grape juice away.

"See how many grapes I can eat at once, Papa?" Millie cried, jumping in a circle with Button.

Vane chuckled. "I don't think that counts since all of your grapes are currently on my person."

Lady Isabel's hand moved down his torso, cleaning off the grapes. "As much as I hate being a bore, that behavior is unacceptable. You should know that."

She rubbed violently at his chest, then her hand moved lower toward his breeches.

"Neither is this," he croaked, then caught her hand and snatched the handkerchief out of her hand. "I can finish this myself now."

Lady Isabel blushed a pretty pink, realizing her folly. "I apologize." She turned away and started cleaning up the picnic area.

"Papa, can we go now?"

Rhys looked at Lady Isabel, and she nodded.

Millie and Button ran forward, screaming and playing while Rhys and Lady Isabel followed.

"I am certainly not an expert," Rhys said. "But it seems to me that chastising a little girl for her unladylike activities is not the best way to bond with her."

"I just wanted her to know that there are other activities worth her while."

"Well, it didn't work."

"Well, of course, it didn't! How am I supposed to entice her to sit at home and play the pianoforte when she spends most of her day running around like a little wild thing? And she needs to be interested in that before we hire a governess. Otherwise, it is bound to fail."

"Perhaps lean on your personal experience," he said, and Lady Isabel narrowed her eyes on him. "Oh, do not pretend, my dear scandalous marchioness, as if you haven't managed to fool the *ton* for years."

"I have not!" she cried.

Rhys raised a brow. "So you cannot swim or sling rocks?" He knew for a fact that she could.

"That was in the past," she grumbled.

"When you were six, perhaps? Or even sixteen?"

Lady Isabel frowned in thought. "Perhaps you are right. But you still should support me in endorsing more decorous behavior. She looks up to you."

"Papa!" Millie stopped a few feet away from them and pointed at the horizon, her eyes filled with awe. "Look how dark it is there."

Rhys disengaged from Lady Isabel and hurried toward his daughter. The patch of the horizon was dark gray, like a wall of clouds.

"Yes, it's raining there," Rhys said. "Perhaps even a storm."

"Is it far away? Is it coming toward us?"

Rhys shrugged. "It is hard to say. But it is in the direction of the Thornsby estate." Thornsby was another of Rhys's estates, the smallest and closest to Vane. "I should probably visit them once the storm passes and make sure everything is well."

"Can I go with you?" Millie looked up at Rhys in excitement.

Rhys picked up a stick from the ground to avoid Millie's expectant gaze and threw it for Button to fetch. Button galloped away, his tongue wagging out of his mouth.

"I don't know," Rhys said. "You might have to stay with Lady Isabel." He took the stick from Button's mouth as the dog returned and gave it to Millie. "Here. Now you throw."

Chapter 14

"Why?" Millicent threw the stick and watched the galloping dog, frowning.

Lady Isabel reached them at that moment.

"Because Lady Isabel is right. You need education."

Lady Isabel beamed at him. "Thank you."

"Papa! Now you throw!" Millie handed him the stick, looking as ominous as the dark cloud on the horizon.

Rhys threw it, and Button dashed after it.

"Well, I hope we can find Millicent a governess in time," Lady Isabel said.

Millicent frowned at her. Button came back just then, a stick in his mouth.

Millie took it and turned toward Lady Isabel. "Lady Isabel," she called, "Catch!" and threw the stick right at her chest.

Lady Isabel was able to catch the stick in her arms, but at that moment, Button raced after the stick and tackled her to the ground.

Chapter 15

That treacherous little fiend!

That was the last thought that ran through Isabel's mind before the world went black. When she regained consciousness, she was staring at the clear blue sky. Then Button's face appeared before her as he licked her across the face.

"Ugh!" Isabel grimaced and turned away.

"Button, off!" Vane's stern voice was able to get the dog away from her. Then the marquess himself appeared before her, his face worried. "Are you well? Can you get up?"

"I don't know." Isabel sat up and looked around.

"Did you hurt yourself badly? How is the babe? Should I ask for a doctor?"

"What babe?" Isabel was so confused. Perhaps she did hit her head badly.

"The babe," Vane said sternly. "Your babe."

"Ah, the nonexistent one." Isabel scowled. Were they back to that? "I am quite healthy. Please, help me up."

Chapter 15

Vane took her by the arms, but before she could put her weight on her feet, her right leg was pierced with pain. "Ow, my ankle."

Vane helped her back down, frowned, and reached his hands toward her skirts. "May I?"

Isabel nodded. She couldn't care about propriety at that moment. Her blasted ankle hurt like the devil.

He raised her skirts slightly to her knee, then ran his hand lightly over her calf. Goosebumps covered her leg, and the feeling of pleasure replaced the pain. Isabel whimpered.

"Does it hurt now?"

Isabel shook her head.

Vane frowned and took off her half-boot. He gently squeezed her leg around the ankle, and Isabel hissed.

"It doesn't appear to be broken, but you seem to have twisted it."

Isabel took a deep breath. "Perfect. How am I to get home?"

Vane grimaced. "Millie!"

"Yes?" The girl appeared behind the marquess, her lips pursed, but her eyes shone with glee. *Oh, the fiend!*

"Run back to the field and ask Jack to send one of the boys with Lady Isabel's horse here. And let Jack take you to his home. His wife will feed you some of those buns you like so much."

"I don't want to go," Millie pouted.

"I am sorry, moppet. Lady Isabel needs your help. Please, do as you're told. And take the dog with you."

Millie threw one last pouting gaze toward Isabel and scurried away.

Vane looked around. He took a blanket from the picnic basket and spread it on the ground. "The ground is wet and cold. You might freeze while sitting on the grass," he explained, then he unceremoniously scooped Isabel into his arms and settled her on the blanket.

"Do you mind if I take your stocking off? Might help me to ascertain the extent of your injury."

Isabel shifted uncomfortably, heat rising in her cheeks. "Um… is this necessary?"

Vane raised his brow. "It's best to take it off now before it swells even further."

"You… Well…" Isabel stumbled. "I don't know. But I don't feel comfortable with you doing this."

Vane smiled. "I am your husband. I am going to be doing far less comfortable things to you soon."

Isabel's entire body heated at his words. Did he mean marital duty? And what did that mean if he did? Had he finally acknowledged that she was not with child?

As tumultuous thoughts ran through Isabel's head, Vane reached under Isabel's skirt until he grazed the intimate skin above her stocking. Isabel's eyes closed, and she stifled a whimper.

Vane untied the garter and started slowly rolling the stocking down her leg.

Gooseflesh covered her skin, and Isabel clenched her thighs together, for a peculiar tingly feeling originated at her center.

"Doesn't seem like you hurt it terribly," he murmured. The low timbre of his voice caused Isabel to shiver again.

What is happening?

Vane sat perpendicular to Isabel and placed her leg on his thigh. "I hear it's best to keep it elevated," he said, his hand still on her shin.

Isabel looked around. Surely this was not right. She was

Chapter 15

bare from her knee down. Someone would see!

She sat up and covered her leg with her skirt. "It should be better in a few days. No need to fret. It is not the first time I have rolled my ankle."

"I am certain it isn't. You seem quite accident-prone," he said with a smirk.

"Accident?" Isabel was affronted. "First off, I have not been tackled this many times in my entire life before I met you! And secondly, this was not an accident."

Vane frowned. "You are not trying to imply that Button did this on purpose!" He gestured to her foot.

Isabel clenched her teeth. "Not Button."

"Millie?" Vane let out a laugh. "Do not be ridiculous. She isn't malicious enough to hurt somebody on purpose."

"Of course, she didn't hurt me on purpose!" Isabel threw up her hands. "That enormous monster you call a dog has never caused her injury, so how would she know what strength he truly possesses? She just wanted to divert attention away from me or perhaps the governess talk."

"By siccing Button on you?" Vane's clear skepticism grated on Isabel's nerves.

Paired with her ankle's dull pain, it made Isabel all the more irritable. "As I said, she most likely didn't think *Button* would tackle me. She just thought to stop me from speaking about the governess and didn't want you to leave her. And by the way, what person names a dog as large as a horse Button! If anything is ridiculous, it's that!"

Vane blinked. He clearly needed time to process the flurry of words. Finally, he clenched his jaw. "Millie named him." Isabel raised her brow, so he continued. "She thought his nose was shaped like a button when he was smaller. She was a tiny babe and could barely speak, so she'd tap his nose and call him Button. And that stuck."

"Why would you buy a tiny babe such a large dog?" Isabel grumbled.

"Why do you have to question everything about him? His name is Button, and he's Millie's." He threw his hands up and looked at her in frustration. She just cocked a brow. "I bought him after… after…."

"Yes?"

"After her mother left." Vane looked away as if it hurt him to remember it—much less say it aloud. "She didn't have a mother anymore, so I thought she might need a friend or a companion… a protector."

Pain flashed in his eyes before he moved her leg away and stood.

A protector. People did not refer to mothers thus. Isabel swallowed. She wanted to know more. For some odd reason, she wanted more than anything for him to confide in her, but she didn't push.

"Well, I am not stating that she wanted to hurt me on purpose. I am saying that she was trying to distract our attention during the entire picnic. She thinks I am here to disrupt your lives."

"And you aren't?" Vane grumbled under his breath.

Isabel raised her eyes heavenward, suddenly tired of sparring with the square-headed marquess.

"I don't know how you see our marriage, Vane. But I would think that your daughter getting along with your wife should be one of your priorities. You managed to make my life smoother with the servants, for which I am eternally grateful, but I would rather I had a better relationship with

Chapter 15

your daughter."

* * *

Lady Isabel did not come down to breakfast the next morning, and Rhys couldn't help but feel guilty. Did her foot ache so badly that she'd opted to stay inside? Or was she still upset that Rhys did not encourage her bonding with his daughter?

After all, Rhys had to admit she was right. Rhys treated her with mistrust, thinking she would act scandalously and inappropriately around Millicent, but the truth was he had little cause for worry.

Lady Isabel carried out her duties to perfection. At first, the servants were antagonistic toward their new mistress, but now they were in awe of her. The house had turned from a gloomy old place to a kingdom of flowers and color. The food was impeccable. Everything she set her mind to, she performed splendidly.

And this forced Rhys to accept a simple realization. His mistrust toward her about Millie had nothing to do with her *scandalous* past but everything to do with his.

He turned to Millicent, who was feeding Button bread rolls off the table. "Millie, I think we should go and visit Lady Isabel after breakfast."

Millie frowned. "Why?"

"Because Button hurt her yesterday, and he needs to apologize."

Millie chewed on her lip. "But he didn't mean to."

Rhys hid his smile. "I know that. But when we hurt someone unintentionally, we have to apologize."

Millicent grimaced, but her features cleared after a moment.

"And then can we go play outside?"

"Of course."

* * *

To Rhys's surprise, by the time they had finished breakfast and set out to find Lady Isabel, she was nowhere to be found. He had asked the butler about her whereabouts, and Mr. Monroe raised a brow.

"She went to the village, just like she always does at this hour."

Rhys felt uncomfortable. He didn't know about his wife's activities. After their last trip to the village, he had assumed she never went there again. As it turned out, this couldn't have been further from the truth.

"We are going to the village?" Millie asked, her eyes shining with excitement. She loved playing with the children whenever they went to visit.

Rhys smiled. "Yes, we are."

A few minutes later, Rhys was cantering along the road, Millicent in his lap, Button running along with his horse, toward the village.

They spotted the carriage near the bookshop, and Rhys turned his horse toward it. He handed the reins to the groom, who was waiting by the carriage, and hopped off the horse.

"Do you know where her ladyship went?" Rhys asked.

The groom blinked then slowly tipped his head toward the bookshop. "There, m'lord."

Rhys took Millie into his arms and headed toward the bookshop, Button following them. He walked inside and stopped cold.

Chapter 15

The little bookshop had a sitting area behind the bookshelves where Rhys used to read to children once every few weeks when he had spare time. Lady Isabel was sitting in his usual spot, a bevy of children surrounding her as she read. They were all so taken by her reading that nobody had paid Rhys any heed. Her melodic voice weaved around the bookshop, mesmerizing its inhabitants.

Rhys turned to Millie. "Do you want to wait outside?"

But his daughter shook her head and craned her neck, concentrating on the words coming out of Lady Isabel's mouth. Even Button moved farther into the room and settled on the floor comfortably.

Rhys set Millie down, and she immediately sat closer to other children, listening to the tale. Rhys leaned his shoulder against the wall and watched as his wife read animatedly.

Yes, he had been absolutely unfair to her, comparing her to his late wife. She was nothing like her. And whatever misconceptions he had about Lady Isabel from her past, he must have been mistaken in them too. And suddenly, he had a burning desire to learn more about the woman who was his marchioness.

* * *

Isabel noticed the marquess the moment he had entered the shop. But who wouldn't?

He was incredibly tall and broad-shouldered; the shadow he cast immediately enveloped the tiny sitting area in the book shop. Then his dog followed, just as huge and menacing, but instead of stealing attention from her, they settled on the edge of the room, listening to her read.

Isabel's voice quivered for a moment as she tried to concentrate on the page. Millie inched her way forward, and soon she was sitting in the first row, leaning her cheek against her palm and dreamily listening to Isabel's words.

Isabel finished the last sentence and flipped the book closed. "The end," she said.

Children cheered and clapped, asking for another story.

Isabel smiled. "Perhaps another time. I am afraid I need to go back to my more boring duties."

She stood, and Vane made his way toward her. "I hope you were not referring to us when you spoke of boring duties," he said.

Isabel's cheeks flushed. "I was referring to budget allocation for the next month that I need to discuss with Mrs. Ainsworth later this afternoon."

Vane raised his brow. "Well, do you have a moment to spend with Millie and me?"

Isabel's heart fluttered in her chest. "I would enjoy that immensely."

They went outside, Isabel still limping lightly. Vane took her arm and weaved it with his without asking. Isabel did not protest. She needed a strong and sturdy presence to lean on.

Before Millie could run off with Button, Vane addressed her. "Millie, was there something you wanted to say to Lady Isabel?"

The girl looked at the ground shyly. "I wanted to apologize on behalf of Button. He didn't mean to hurt you yesterday."

"And?" Vane prompted.

"And I am sorry he tackled you because of me."

Isabel smiled widely. "You are both forgiven."

Millie smiled shyly before addressing her father. "Can I go

Chapter 15

play with others now?"

Vane tipped his head, and Millie took off in the direction of the playing children, Button on her heels.

"Thank you for making Millicent accountable for what happened yesterday," Isabel said. "I wish we could spend a bit more time with her, though."

"That is easily rectifiable," her husband said.

"It is?" Isabel raised her brow. "I didn't think you wanted us to spend time together."

"I didn't," he admitted. "But I can't keep shielding my daughter from life. She enjoyed listening to you read. I think this would be a good start for you two to bond. I will bring her here every time you read. And maybe by the time your ankle heals, she will be more amenable to wanting to spend some time alone with you."

"And would you be amenable to that?" She peered into the marquess's troubled eyes.

Isabel felt his muscles tighten beneath her fingers, and that's when she realized something she should have realized all along. His mistrust toward her had nothing to do with her.

He just didn't trust anyone with Millicent.

She wanted to know why. She wanted to learn what lurked in the dark corners of his mind, but she didn't persist. Not yet.

"I shall have to learn to be," he answered hoarsely. Then cleared his throat. "In the meantime, would you like to learn how to control Button?"

Chapter 16

For the next few days, Rhys spent every morning bringing Millicent to listen to Lady Isabel read at the bookshop. It was quite ironic that they had to leave the house to spend time with the marchioness they shared a roof with.

After the reading hour, Rhys taught Lady Isabel to control Button, or at least he tried. She was completely hopeless.

The dog refused to listen to her commands, and every time he ran toward her, Lady Isabel just hid behind Vane and refused to face the dog.

The sight was hilarious because Button obviously loved his new mistress and wanted to play with her and embrace her every chance he got.

Playing outside with his dog and his wife, Rhys suddenly felt young and unburdened. And the old yearning scraped at his heart, a yearning for a real family, a loving wife…

He had to shake himself from that feeling. As long as Lady Isabel proved to be a proper mistress and a good mother to

Chapter 16

Millie, that would have to be enough.

One morning, he and Millie were sitting at the breakfast table when Lady Isabel glided into the room. She smiled brightly then twirled in place. Her skirts swooshed, the wisps of her hair flapping as she halted and looked from Vane to Millicent expectantly. "Well?"

Vane furrowed his brows. "Is that a new gown?"

Lady Isabel raised a brow.

"Her limp is gone, Papa," Millicent noted.

"You are correct. And that means that we can assume a more laborious activity before reading." She sat gracefully behind the table and turned to Millie. "What do you say we all take a ride around the estate?"

Millie visibly perked up. "Can we, Papa?"

"There's work that needs to be done," he argued.

"Surely you can take a day off to spend with your family?" his wife insisted.

Family. Something squeezed in the region of his heart. Could they one day become a real family? He wanted nothing more.

"Why not?"

"Yes!" Millie jumped up from her seat.

"Did you finish your meal?" Rhys pointedly nudged his head toward her plate.

"I am not hungry, and I need to get ready for riding!" she exclaimed, hopping in place.

Rhys let out a sigh. He popped the piece of toast into his mouth, washed it down with coffee, and stood. "Come, then. You need to change into your riding habit."

"Will I ride with you? Or my pony?" Millie asked as she skipped in excitement.

"Hmm… which one do you prefer?"

"Pony!" Sparks of joy were dancing in Millie's eyes.

"Very well." He turned toward his wife. "We'll meet you in the hall," he called and walked away.

Vane escorted his daughter to her nursery and headed toward his own bedchamber to change into his riding clothes. But before he reached his room, the footman stopped him on the stairs.

"A note for you, master!"

"Thank you." Rhys took the envelope into his hand.

"The messenger said it's quite urgent and that you open it immediately."

Rhys nodded. "Very well, thank you."

He descended to his study, grabbed the letter opener, and read the contents. He grimaced and threw the note on the table. The outing with his family would have to wait. He had urgent business to take care of.

* * *

Isabel could barely hold back her smile as Vane left the room with Millie. The little girl was so excited about the idea of riding! After spending the last week with them, Isabel realized that she'd taken the wrong approach with the girl from the beginning.

Vane was right.

Isabel had been quite a hellion as a child, and it hadn't stopped her from becoming the most sought-after debutante during her first season. Of course, she'd made mistakes. But everybody did at some point. She just had to make certain that Millicent didn't repeat hers.

Chapter 16

But as far as bonding with the girl went, she doubted she'd be able to do so by talking about manners and etiquette.

Isabel finished her breakfast and went to her room to change.

Anthea entered then and walked toward her with a frown on her face. "His lordship told me you are to go riding."

"Yes." Isabel nodded. "Please, help me into the riding habit."

"Are you certain this is the best time for you to go riding? Your foot—" She waved a hand toward Isabel's ankle.

Isabel looked down. "It is healed, I promise."

Anthea grinned. "I only worry, my lady."

"I know you do."

Anthea helped Isabel out of her day gown and brought her a midnight blue riding habit. "Would you like to wear this one today?"

"Yes." Isabel beamed.

"I am glad to see you this happy, my lady. Are things improving with the family, then? I do not mean to pry."

"Oh, please, Anthea. You are part of the family. We've grown up together. No need to watch your words. But yes. I think things are finally moving toward normal family life."

"And with the marquess, too?" Anthea did not meet her eye.

Isabel raised a brow. "What do you mean?"

Anthea worked on the buttons of the riding habit with a grimace of concentration on her face. "Well, the household is talking. They just wish—" She clamped her lips shut and frowned.

"They wish what?"

"Oh, don't pay me any heed. It's balderdash." She waved a hand and stepped back. "Do you want me to tighten your coiffure? We don't want your hair falling out of the bonnet, do we?"

"Yes, please." Isabel walked to the chair and sat in front of the vanity table.

Anthea started immediately re-pinning her hair.

Isabel watched her carefully before asking, "What were you about to say?"

Anthea let out a deep breath. "Servant talk. Nothing important."

Isabel turned toward Anthea, ruining the coiffure. "Do they still not like me?"

"Oh, no. Everyone thinks you are a sweetheart." Anthea took Isabel by her shoulders and turned her back.

"Truly?"

"Yes," she said, starting over on Isabel's coiffure. "They constantly talk about how much you care about the household and the tenants. How you remember each of their names, even the lowliest of chambermaids. They quite like you. And that's the only reason they talk."

Isabel looked at Anthea imploringly. "About what?"

"It's just that…" Anthea turned Isabel back again. She was obviously uncomfortable. "Well, it's a sensitive matter. I shouldn't have said anything."

Isabel frowned. "Please?"

Anthea placed the last pin. "All done."

Isabel turned to her, her brows raised.

Anthea let out a deep breath. "The servants are restless… The chambermaids and the master's valet all confirm something I am not privy to—"

"Anthea, please, speak freely."

Anthea looked down and visibly colored. "Well, they say

Chapter 16

you have not shared a bed with the master yet."

Isabel opened her mouth to say something but faltered. She felt the blood drain out of her face. This was the last thing she expected to hear from her maid. They gossiped about that? What else did they gossip about? Suddenly, her face heated up to her ears. "Why...? How—"

"I am sorry. I shouldn't have said anything."

"No, please. Tell me. I want to know what they say." Isabel gestured to a chair across from her. Anthea took a seat and played with the plaits of her skirt. "At first, when they did not like you—pardon, mistrusted you—they thought you were just like their previous mistress. They don't talk about her much, but what they say is not pleasant. But now that they see how wonderful you are, they want more than anything to have a little babe in the household...." Anthea looked around and dropped her voice into a conspiratorial whisper. "They even joked that they should force you two together somehow."

Isabel gasped. Well, that was beyond inappropriate. "Lord, what would they do? Lock us in a cellar?"

Anthea shrugged. "Now that I've told you... Perhaps you can tell me why the master is not sharing your bed? Does he have a condition?" She said the last in a hushed tone.

Isabel moved closer to the edge of her seat. "What condition?"

Anthea shrugged. "I don't know. I hear things I am not privy to."

Isabel frowned, still stuck on the idea that Vane indeed might have a condition that restricted him from bedding his wife. Although that was an unfounded thought. He had Millie.

She heaved a sigh. "Do not worry, Anthea. And please, tell

the others not to scheme about this. The heir will come in time." *At least I pray he will...*

There was a knock on the door, and Anthea jumped from her seat. Vane entered then, without waiting for an answer.

Anthea shot from her chair, curtsied, and hurried away.

Isabel's cheeks and ears heated. She hoped Vane had not overheard what they were discussing with Anthea. He was already dressed for the ride, but his expression was ominous.

I thought we were past his constant displeasure? What happened?

"Are we ready to go?" she asked, trying for a smile but failing abominably.

Vane grimaced. "I received a note... The black clouds we witnessed the other day at the field... Well, we were right about the location. Apparently it's been raining for days at my other estate, Thornsby. As a result, half the village is flooded. I need to go and see if I can help the villagers in any way."

Isabel hastened to stand. "Should I go with you?"

One side of Vane's mouth curled in a half-smile. "I do not think you'll be much help. And it would require a few days, so I can't take Millie with me either...."

"So she'll stay with me?" A soft smile tugged at her lips. She would get what she wanted, after all.

"She will... I just talked with her, and she is not too happy about it. So I'd approach her carefully."

Isabel stood straighter. "We shall have a great time."

Vane looked at her as if he didn't believe her. "Perhaps you shouldn't go riding either."

"Why is that? I promised Millicent we would. I don't want to break my word."

Chapter 16

"I'd be more content if you stayed indoors, where servants could help you if something happened."

Isabel smirked. "Are you worried about Millicent or me?"

Vane swallowed. "Both of you."

Warmth seeped inside Isabel in the region of her heart. Had he started to care for her? "Well, you have nothing to worry about, I promise."

Vane nodded, but his face was desolate. "I shall endeavor to come back as soon as I can."

He bowed and left the room.

Chapter 17

Isabel decided there was no reason to pout about the house just because her husband had urgent business on another estate. She had promised Millicent a ride around the estate, and she would deliver.

Before Millicent came downstairs, Isabel spoke to Mrs. Ainsworth about the workload for the day. She spoke to the artist, Emmeline, who was painting the walls, and realized that her room was done. It just needed to air out for a few days, and then Isabel would be ready to move in.

This was perfect timing. Now that Vane had left, Emmeline was free to paint his chamber, and perhaps it would be done just in time for his arrival.

As she passed the butler, Mr. Monroe, he apprised her that there were a couple of letters in her husband's study about the governess position and a few letters from her family.

Isabel smiled. It seemed like things around the Vane household were looking up. Her husband had been rather pleasant toward her lately, her servants seemed to like her,

Chapter 17

and although Millicent was still shy around her, Isabel would have a few days to win her over.

Isabel was finally not as worried about her future. And today, she would be able to write to her family and Evie that she was enjoying her life and for them not to worry. And for the first time since she had married, she wouldn't be lying to those dear to her heart.

Everything was not perfect, of course, but nothing ever was. And this was as close to perfect as she suspected it would be in this household.

Isabel was excited about the upcoming house party as well. This was something she was actually good at. She enjoyed hosting parties. She loved addressing the invitations and coming up with decorations and the menu. She quite enjoyed organizing fun games and scheduling other activities as well. And she looked forward to welcoming *ton* members to her estates. Being a hostess was something she was born to do.

Perhaps, she could get Millicent interested in the activity as well. Isabel had helped her mother from the age of eight. Millicent was younger, and she wasn't interested in ladylike activities, but perhaps Isabel would find a way to make a fun game out of it.

That would have to wait. First and foremost, she needed to bond with the girl. And if that required running around the forest and rolling in puddles, Isabel would do just that.

Millicent appeared in the hall with Mrs. Ainsworth leading her by the arm. "Are we going for a ride?" she asked, her brows furrowed. She probably thought that they would change their plans because of her father's absence. Well, she was wrong.

"Yes, we are," Isabel answered with a smile.

Millie's expression immediately cleared. "And Button?"

Isabel heaved a sigh. "And Button, too."

Isabel asked two footmen to accompany them, so they could look after Button, and a groom led both Isabel's mare and Millie's pony at a sedate pace.

They rode around the estate in companionable silence, and even Button, the usually overexcited pup who could not seem to stand still, was silently walking beside Millicent's pony. He was about the same size as Millie's mare, which Isabel found quite amusing.

Isabel decided to finally break the silence. "When I was a little girl, I did not have a dog. I think it is wonderful that you have Button."

Millicent threw her a sidelong glance. "You didn't have a dog? Ever?"

Isabel frowned in thought. "I think we had hunting dogs when I was little. But I do not remember them."

"Who did you play with?" Millicent sounded appalled.

"Well, I had five siblings."

Millie's eyes rounded. "Five?"

Isabel let out a chuckle. It seemed like Millie could not wrap her head around that many siblings. "Yes, five. And we used to play together all the time."

"What did you do?" Millicent was facing Isabel fully now, her interest peaked.

"We played games, read books, went on picnics."

"What games did you play?"

"Well, different ones. We would pretend to be pirates and build a ship in the woods. We would play pretend duels with sticks as our swords. Hide and seek was one of the popular games we played, and nobody was ever able to find me," she said proudly.

Chapter 17

Millie's eyes lit up. "What else did you play?"

"Oh, plenty. We would make tournaments and sling rocks at well... bigger rocks."

Millicent narrowed her eyes on Isabel. "You said ladies don't do that."

Ah, so she was listening. "Well, yes. But see, I grew up with four brothers, and they taught me a few unladylike activities."

"Like my papa taught me!"

"Right. And gentlemen do not always know which activities are ladylike and which are not. That is why a lady needs education from her governess."

Millicent puffed her lips. "Why do gentlemen get to do whatever they like, but ladies need to be ladylike?"

Isabel blinked. She did not have a good answer to this question. She squinted in thought. "Well, there are many things gentlemen are not allowed to do either. There are rules in this society one must follow. However, just because you are not allowed things in public doesn't mean they are completely forbidden."

"They are not?"

"No. At least not around family."

Millicent seemed to consider that idea before she turned toward Isabel again. "Does it mean that I can sling rocks, swim, and do other unladylike things around you?"

Isabel's heart swelled. Did Millicent just call her family?

"Yes," she said with a nod. "You can."

"Can we do it now?"

Isabel looked at her still tender ankle with a slight grimace. *The sacrifices one makes for family...* "Yes, let's do it now."

Isabel and Millicent spent a few hours outdoors slinging rocks and playing fetch with Button. Then they went to visit the villagers. Isabel talked to tenants and spent time with her friend, Lilian, while Millie played with the village children.

Isabel had not imagined that the day with Millicent—the pouting, quiet child, who preferred the company of a dog and servants to Isabel's—would be so pleasant.

Later, they had supper together and then spent an hour reading in Millie's nursery.

When the time came for Millie to go to bed, Isabel tucked the girl in and sat at the edge of the bed.

Millicent frowned. "Will Papa come to wish me goodnight?"

Isabel swallowed. "No, dear. Not tonight. He is still taking care of the Thornsby estate, but he shall come home soon, I promise."

"Then can you ask Edith to sing to me?" Millie asked.

"I can sing to you if you want," Isabel said softly.

Millie looked at her queerly. "I would like Edith to sing."

Isabel smiled, although a huge boulder lodged in her throat. "Of course."

She tucked the covers tightly over Millicent as her heart sank. She should not be upset over the girl's rejection. They'd only spent one day alone together. Surely it took longer than that to earn the little girl's trust.

Isabel stood and walked toward the door and pulled the servants' bell. Edith hurried in a few moments later, and Millicent smiled brightly.

"Good night," Isabel whispered as she left the room.

* * *

Vane had a difficult day. He worried about Millie his entire

Chapter 17

trip to the Thornsby estate, but all his worries were replaced with horror as soon as he got there.

The note he'd received earlier did not exaggerate. The consequences of the flooding were devastating. A few houses were affected, some livestock and food provisions.

Vane spent a few days digging people's belongings out of their cellars and making certain everyone had a roof over their head for the next few weeks. Restoring those homes would not be an easy feat.

He had sent an urgent note to his solicitor to swiftly arrange compensation for those who'd lost their belongings or homes in the flood.

This incident made him question the way he ran his estates. He had estate managers, yes. But they did not care for the lands and the tenants the way Rhys did. He needed to pay closer attention to his lands other than the Vane estate. And now that he'd had Lady Isabel to look after the manor, perhaps he could afford to leave on longer journeys and spend more time out of his family seat.

Still, he was agitated and nervous when he finally returned home a few days later.

He wanted to see Millicent before she fell asleep. He'd missed her dearly. He galloped all the way, although he was extremely tired, and still made it home quite late at night. He was also dirty, winded, and smudged with mud. But he needed to see his daughter and make sure everything was well.

He threw the reins into his groom's hands and rushed inside.

The hall was eerily dark. The ominous silence in the house heightened his anxiety. *It happened again,* his mind whispered to him with every beating of his heart.

It happened again.

The butler stepped toward him, his arms outstretched.

Anxiety rose in the form of bile up to his throat.

He swallowed. "Monroe. Where is Millie?"

"In her room, my lord. She just went to bed."

Rhys took off his gloves and hat and handed it to the butler. A part of his anxiousness abated, but he still dreaded asking the next question. "And Lady Isabel?"

"She also went to bed, my lord."

Rhys expelled a breath of relief. "I shall go and wish Millie goodnight. Please, tell my valet to bring me some clean clothes and a towel. I shall go and wash up at the stream. No need to bother maids with heating a bath at such a late hour."

Monroe nodded, and Rhys hurried up the steps to his daughter's room.

He knocked on the door and entered without waiting for her reply, as was his habit. Millie lay in her bed, and Edith sat by her side, singing. Millie looked at him under her furrowed brows as soon as he entered, her disapproval evident.

Rhys's heart swelled. He had missed her disapproving mien. How had he managed to spend so many days without seeing her?

"And how was your day, my darling?" he asked as he walked further into the room.

"Why were you away for so long?" Millie crossed her tiny arms over her chest.

"I had things to do, Millie. Important things."

Edith stood quietly, curtsied, and left the room.

Rhys walked up to Millie's bed and crouched in front of her.

Chapter 17

"I am a marquess, remember? I have a lot of people depending on me."

She pointedly looked away from him.

Rhys heaved a sigh. "You are the most important person in my life, darling girl. You know that. And I missed you dearly. But I cannot neglect my lands. "

She didn't answer.

"Was Lady Isabel fair to you while I was away?"

Still silence.

Rhys frowned, the fear in his heart growing. "What did she do?" he asked sharply.

Millie turned toward him, still frowning. "Nothing. We went for a ride every day, and then we played and slung rocks."

Rhys blinked. "Did you, now? How scandalous."

"She said it's not scandalous as long as it's with family."

Something twisted in Rhys's gut. Had his little girl just called Lady Isabel family? He only hoped his wife was worthy of that.

"She is right," he murmured and caressed his daughter's cheek.

"Why are you dirty?" Millie asked with a grimace but then erupted in giggles.

Rhys let out a chuckle. "I had to clean a lot of dirt this week, moppet."

Millie smiled and burrowed further under her covers. "Will you sing me a song?"

Rhys nodded. "Of course, my darling girl. That's what I came here for."

He tucked her tighter in her bed and started her favorite lullaby.

An Offer from the Marquess

* * *

Rhys exited the house with the bundle of clean clothing and towels that his valet prepared for him and sauntered toward the stream. He used to clean himself there all the time in the summer after a hard day of work with the farmers, but the weather was still cold in the spring, and the water was almost freezing.

Still, he had no choice if he wanted to wash off the dirt of the day and go to bed in a relatively clean state.

He took off his clothes and entered the stream. The water was so cold that he had to rush to ensure his limbs didn't fall off from the cold. Once he was done, he donned the fresh clothing and hurried back to the house, wishing for a hot cup of chocolate or milk by the fire.

Hell, forget the drink and fire. All he wanted was to burrow inside his covers and sleep in a warm and cozy room until morning, uninterrupted.

He reached the house rather quickly and ascended the stairs taking two steps at a time. He finally opened the door to his room and… froze.

If he stood there long enough, he'd freeze quite literally.

Rhys entered the cold, dark room, trying to figure out what was wrong.

He peeked into the hearth only to realize that the fire was doused!

What the devil?

Why hadn't anybody lit his hearth before his arrival? To top it off, his windows were open. He stalked toward one of his windows and tried to lock them, but the frame was too stiff. Vane shivered from either cold or irritation, possibly

Chapter 17

both, and pulled the servants' bell.

His valet showed up a moment later with a candle in his hands.

"What happened here, David? Why is my hearth dying, and the windows open?"

David, Rhys's valet, brought his candle closer to the walls. "Didn't you know? Your walls were being painted. And since it smells awful, the windows should be open for a few days after."

"And when did they finish painting my room?" Vane growled.

David swallowed. "They didn't. It should take a few more days."

A few more days and then a few more to air it out? Vane gritted his teeth. "And where am I to sleep while this atrocity is going on?"

"I am sorry, my lord, I thought you agreed to have your room decorated."

Rhys heaved a sigh. "I did, but I would still like to have somewhere I can sleep."

"Her ladyship ordered another room to be prepared for you, but we did not expect you this soon. The maids didn't have enough time to do so. Do you want to turn them away?" His lips twitched, and there was a strange glint in the servants' eye. He knew full well that Vane was not about to turn anyone away for the slight mistake.

"No, but I would like for you to find me another chamber to sleep in. Preferably one not as cold as this one."

David pursed his lips. His behavior was getting stranger and stranger by the moment. What was he up to? "Well, all the other rooms on this floor are either being painted or are not suitable for anyone to spend the night in."

He paused as if thinking through the problem, although his expression was too theatrical to be real. Vane did not care one way or another. He was frozen to the bone and just wanted the dratted valet to get to the point. Then his face brightened, and Vane expelled a breath. *Finally.*

"Yes, what is it?"

"It is not the most convenient solution but the only workable one."

Rhys rubbed his palms together to warm them up. "Yes?"

"Her ladyship's room—the one adjoining yours—has been prepared, but I believe the mistress didn't move in yet."

Vane narrowed his eyes on the cunning valet, who incidentally refused to meet Rhys's eye. Rhys would have called David on his manipulative behavior if his teeth were not chattering so loudly.

"Blast it all to hell!" Rhys muttered. "Whatever you are planning, you win. It doesn't seem like I have any choice."

So he went to the adjoining room door and walked inside.

Chapter 18

Dear Isabel,

I hope this letter finds you in good health and spirit. I know from your daily letters, which have taken a load off my shoulders, that while life at the new estate is rather pleasing, you have not yet bedded your husband.

I know that you are stubborn, and you are not interested in having the brute in your bed until he apologizes for the "evidence" remark. However, if that does happen and you decide you want him in your bed, which I know you want because you want to have a child, this gift might soften his mood.

With warmest regards,
Evie.

The note had come earlier in the day, accompanied by a beautifully wrapped package.

After tucking Millie into her bed, Isabel went to her husband's study and looked through the letters from the potential governesses. She answered them all, thinking that a few looked promising. After that, she collected her personal letters and went up to her room.

She had moved into the chamber adjoining her husband's room only two days ago, but already she felt at home there. She loved the soft colors of her walls and the sturdy but comfortable furniture. Her bedspread was new and fresh too.

So she climbed on her bed and read the letters.

Sam wrote that she and the babe were doing well, and she'd be ready to travel soon. Just in time for the house party. Gage wrote in his usual laconic style, promising hell if Vane had not treated Isabel well. And then there was the letter from Evie, which was accompanied by the package.

Isabel unwrapped the package with avid interest and took out a delicate, semi-transparent fabric.

Isabel frowned. A scarf? What was she to do with it? She took it in her hands and let it fall to the floor.

It wasn't merely a scarf, Isabel realized quickly. It was the most indecent nightgown she had ever seen. Not only was it translucent, but between the slash in the skirt and the gaping hole at her bust, she wondered how it would cover anything at all.

Isabel stared at it from every angle and came to the unlikely conclusion that the seamstress had just forgotten to sew a few pieces onto it.

Still, curiosity won out, and she decided to try the gown on.

First, there was the grueling prospect of taking off her day gown. Dressing by herself without the help of a maid did not seem like a pleasurable prospect. But she refused to call Anthea for help as she did not want anyone to witness her

Chapter 18

disgrace when she put on that piece of ribbon that Evie called a nightgown.

If that was Evie's idea of softening Vane's mood, Isabel might as well just show up in his bed completely naked.

After a few minutes of struggling with her day gown, she finally managed to take it off. By that time, however, she was all winded and warm and had to perform her nightly ablutions.

Her hair was all out of place, so she took out all the pins and spent a few minutes brushing it out.

Now that it was late enough, and there were no more chores for her to do, Isabel put away her day clothing and, in her single chemise, approached the barely-there nightgown.

Isabel realized that she had been stalling.

Why would she be reluctant to put the gown on? It's not like anybody would see her in it.

Isabel took a deep breath. She supposed putting it on was acknowledging that she indeed wanted Vane's attention. It was painful to admit—even to herself—that she wanted him to look at her with hunger in his eyes.

With a sigh of resignation, Isabel took off her chemise and unhurriedly put on the new nightgown. The cool, soft material glided against her skin, igniting her senses. Goosebumps crawled atop her skin, not from the cold but the pleasant feeling induced by the contact of the nightgown against her skin.

Isabel walked toward the looking glass and froze.

She was right! The gown did not cover anything at all!

The thing hung from her shoulders, only covering her breasts slightly over her nipples. The slash in the skirt revealed her legs every time she took a step.

Isabel had to admit that she did look rather dashing—if that was the right word to describe it. And she felt more confident than if she'd been completely naked.

She divided her hair in the middle and brought it over her shoulders, covering her body down to her waist.

There. That was better.

She liked her hair. It was thick and slightly curly. And without her breasts showing, she looked a little modest. She cocked her head to the side, surveying her reflection.

She turned sideways and studied her profile. Her bottom clearly jutted out, the soft material of the dress underlining her every curve.

No, she should never be seen like this in front of her husband. It was absolutely indecent.

The door adjoining her room to her husband's suddenly opened.

Isabel squeaked and looked around in panic. She wanted to dash toward her bed and cover herself with sheets, but before she could react, Vane had entered her room.

* * *

Hadn't David said this chamber was unoccupied? The sly little bastard. What was he trying to pull?

Isabel stood in front of the looking glass, her eyes frightened. At first, Vane ignored that little detail, as he just thought she was frightened of him entering her domain. But then his gaze swept down her length, and his eyes widened.

"What in the world are you wearing?"

Lady Isabel crossed her arms over her chest. "A nightgown. Do you not like it?"

Chapter 18

Vane blinked, completely forgetting that he had been cold a moment ago. The chattering of his teeth subsided, and now he shivered for a completely different reason. "I do not see it," he tried to say in his usual dry manner, but his voice betrayed him.

The nightgown she was wearing was a translucent piece of cloth through which he could clearly see the outline of her curves. One leg peeked out from a slash that ran down the length of the skirt, starting from her hip.

He could only imagine what view would greet him from above her waist if her dark mane of hair wasn't covering most of her body. For a moment, his imagination ran away from him as he saw the white, soft globes with tiny red peaks—

"Vane?"

He licked his lips—for he'd started salivating—before meeting her eyes. "Are you alone?"

Lady Isabel looked around, puzzled. "I was about to go to bed, so yes, I am alone."

Vane surveyed the room. Perhaps he was acting like a madman, but he wanted to ensure nobody was behind the curtains or in her dressing room. Why else would she dress so provocatively just before bed and act spooked when he entered her room unannounced?

His valet's strange behavior and insistence that Vane spent the night in his wife's room was suspect too.

Vane walked toward the window and looked out.

"What are you looking for?" Lady Isabel's voice sounded utterly confused.

Yes, I am acting absolutely crazy. "I see your windows are sound." He turned to her and crossed his arms over his chest, leaning his shoulder against the windowpane.

"Why wouldn't they be?"

"You see, apparently, my chamber is being painted, and all the windows are unlocked. Which just means that my room is freezing cold. I can't sleep there. And my valet helpfully suggested that I spend the night in this room."

Lady Isabel blinked, and her mouth opened as if to say something. She closed it and walked toward his room. He wasn't the only suspicious party in this marriage, as it turned out.

"Oh my Lord! That's how cold I imagine it is atop Mount Snowden!" Lady Isabel exclaimed from his room. "My chamber was aired out recently, but I suppose I moved in once it was already warm."

She walked back, shivering and chewing on her bottom lip. She leaned against the door, her skirt still swishing around her ankles and giving him a delicious view of her legs up to her knees.

Damn, his wife was undeniably enticing. His insides heated, and he felt a familiar jolt in his nether region. Vane shifted uncomfortably, leaning slightly forward to hide the bulge forming in his breeches. Why was she dressed like this?

"Well, I ordered the maids to prepare a room for you, didn't they?" she asked with a vague hope in her eyes.

Vane tried not to take offense to her skittishness. After all, he was the one who'd told her he would not grace her bed unless she supplied evidence of her not being with child. "My valet informed me that all other rooms—the ones not occupied by humans—are just as bloody cold as mine. And he said they won't be ready any time soon either. And I was not about to tell him that the environment in my wife's room is just as hostile."

Chapter 18

Lady Isabel frowned, then let out a sigh of defeat. "Most of the rooms are in the process of being redecorated. Perhaps the maids forgot to—" She frowned, not quite believing her own theory.

She paced back toward her vanity table, uneasiness evident on her face.

She really should not have been walking in the piece of silk she'd called a nightgown. The skirt swooshed around her ankles, baring her right leg up to her thigh every time she made a step.

She leaned against her vanity, and the pose just made the slit more pronounced. Her hair also moved away from her front, baring the low decolletage of her gown.

Vane blinked, not wanting to look away, although he knew he should. Lady Isabel sensed his uneasiness, or perhaps she noticed that nothing could save her half-clad form from revealing too much skin as she crossed her arms over her chest again.

"Did you say your valet insisted you spend the night in this room?"

"Not so much insisted that I spend the night here, merely let me know that there is no other place for me to occupy."

"Hmm… apparently, every other room is miraculously occupied or being redecorated?"

"It seems so."

Lady Isabel nodded. "You must think me a completely incompetent mistress."

Vane frowned. *Where did that come from?*

"But it's not my fault. At least not in the sense you think." She heaved a sigh and started pacing again. "I try to befriend a six-year-old and get my ankle twisted. I try to give you heirs, and you banish me until I can provide evidence that I am not with child!"

"Banish isn't exactly—"

She continued speaking, not paying him any heed. "And our servants think me incapable of luring my husband into my bed, which, let's be honest, is true." She let out a nervous laugh. "And they must have plotted to trick you into sleeping in my chamber!"

"What?" Rhys barked and took a step forward.

She was out of her mind. She had to be. Why would their servants meddle like this?

Lady Isabel nodded. "Anthea, my lady's maid, told me they were discussing the lack of nights we spend together. I am completely mortified." She covered her face with her palms.

"Were they the ones who tricked you into that poor excuse of a nightgown, too?"

"What? No!" Lady Isabel uncovered her blushing face. "No, this was a gift from a… friend."

"Which friend?" Rhys's suspicions rose to the forefront of his mind again.

Lady Isabel groaned. "I need to change now."

Rhys still didn't know why she was wearing the overly salacious attire. He couldn't imagine it being comfortable to sleep in every night. Women wore things like this for one reason only: to easily shed after exchanging a few kisses with their lovers.

The nightgown had the desired effect on Vane, too. He doubted that's what she wanted, though. Vane wasn't looking forward to spending the night with the half-clad vixen either. But he somehow enjoyed making her uncomfortable. So he said, "Why? Didn't you just don it in preparation for bed?"

Chapter 18

She cleared her throat. "I did. But I thought I'd be alone."

"Allow me to be candid. That attire is wasted without anyone being able to see it."

Lady Isabel pulled her arms tighter around herself. "I shall go change," she said testily.

Rhys let out a sigh. "Does that mean I am allowed to spend the night in your room?" he called after her as she walked toward her dressing room.

Lady Isabel nodded. "I suppose you can."

"I should probably dismiss the lot if what you say about our servants is true."

Lady Isabel shook her head. "They have good intentions. And it is your fault they acted this way."

He frowned. "Because I wouldn't bed you?"

"Because you are too familiar with them. But yes, that too," she said sadly and entered her dressing room.

Left alone in her room, Rhys looked around once more. It was completely different from how it had been before.

The formerly dark green and golden hues had been changed to warmer colors, the walls were welcoming, and the curtains calmly fell in waves to the ground. Even the scent in the room was tender and sweet. He suddenly realized that he would rather enjoy spending his nights in this chamber. He only hoped his own room would be just as charming.

He looked at the bed and was reminded of the unpleasant fact that he, too, needed to change his clothing. It was unpleasant because his nightshirt was back in his room. And he did not look forward to returning to the freezing chamber, especially since he had just warmed up.

With a sigh of resignation, he stepped back into his room and quickly changed into his nightshirt. As the cold sank its teeth into his flesh, Rhys's loins shrunk back to their original size, and his mind cleared from the lusty haze.

Now Rhys could finally contemplate the horrific realization that he wanted his wife. Previously, when he had acted rash and kissed her in the park, he had rationalized to himself that he'd been angry, and kissing her served as an outlet of his rage. He wouldn't hit a woman no matter what, but the kiss was punishment enough.

He wasn't naive or foolish, but these thoughts were easy to entertain when he'd had no more contact with her than coming across her in the hall and dining with her twice a day.

Now that he'd seen her in dishabille, he could say for certain that the picture of her, half-clad, with hair down to her waist, was forever engraved in his mind. And as long as he remembered her that way, he could never say confidently that he did not want her.

Because as soon as he entertained that lie, he would immediately reach into the hidden, dark vault in his mind and recollect her image in that blasted nightgown.

When Rhys walked back into his wife's chamber, he was blessedly frozen to the bone again. As long as his loins were not in any condition to get excited, he wouldn't do or say anything he'd regret.

Luckily for him, Lady Isabel was already in her bed. Her white, ruffled nightgown peaked out slightly from under the covers, and her hair was collected under a crime of a nightcap.

Lying like that, burrowed in the huge bed, she should have looked absolutely unappealing to him. But his mind retrieved the picture of her alluring physique out of its dark vault and flaunted it in front of Rhys's eyes.

So the only thing Rhys could see as he looked at her bundled

Chapter 18

body was her soft, white skin, her leg peeking out of the deep slash of a transparent skirt.

Rhys shook his head and walked toward the bed. He doused the lights and crawled under the sheets.

Chapter 19

Isabel lay in bed, afraid to move lest she bump into her husband's limbs. She had never slept in a bed with another human being. It was strange and slightly unnerving.

For all her thoughts and aspirations about seducing her husband, now that he lay in the same bed with her, she was absolutely mortified.

Just the idea of having his tall, broad form a few feet away from her made her heart riot in her chest, and her palms perspire. No, that would not help her in seducing him. Add to that her numbness and her fear of accidentally brushing his limbs with hers, and she was doomed.

Abandoning her plans of seduction, Isabel concentrated on evening out her breath.

What were the rules of sleeping in a bed with one's husband? Was it rude to shift too much? Should she say something before rolling to the other side? Was she overthinking this?

Isabel let out a frustrated puff of air. She had navigated the

Chapter 19

ton with absolute ease, but she had always had the rules of polite society to fall back on.

She knew when to introduce herself, what she could or could not speak about, with whom she was to attend the dinner, and even how many dances she was allowed to dance with a gentleman.

This married life was absolutely confusing.

Isabel's mother had prepared her for being a perfect hostess; she'd taught her to be a flawless member of polite society. But the one thing nobody had ever prepared her for was how to be a wife.

Evie had given her a bit of advice on how to act in bed with her husband, but that was for the marital duty. How was one to act when they were simply sleeping?

"You are allowed to move." Vane's deep voice penetrated her thoughts.

Did you just read my thoughts? Isabel turned on her side to face him. "How did you know I wasn't sleeping?"

"For one thing, you haven't moved ever since I climbed into bed. In fact, I do not think you even breathed. But you do not need to worry. I shall not touch you."

"That's not what I was worried about," Isabel grumbled.

"What were you worried about?"

The rustle of sheets and a dip in the bed indicated that Vane had turned to face her, but Isabel did not see him save for the outline of his form.

He was huge. His broad shoulders protruded from the bed, blocking her view. Heat radiated from him, warming Isabel from head to toe. Isabel's breath caught, and butterflies raced inside her stomach. Why did he have such an effect on her?

Isabel tried to remember what he had asked her just now.

Oh, what she was worried about.

Well, she couldn't very well tell him the truth. Or could she? She decided to be candid.

"I was worried about disrupting your sleep if I moved… I haven't ever slept in the same bed with anyone."

There was a grunt. "You can move."

He turned to his back again. *Is that it? Is the conversation over?*

"Wait." He turned his head toward her. "You haven't slept in a bed with anyone?"

Isabel placed her hand under her cheek and snuggled comfortably under the covers. "Why does that surprise you?"

"Because lovers usually spend nights in each other's beds."

Isabel rolled her eyes—not that he would see her. *We are back to that, are we?* "You are free to perceive that information as you please since you won't believe me anyway."

Vane let out a grunt. There was a moment of silence before he spoke again. "How were your days with Millie?"

"Quite good. I enjoyed my time with her, and I think she is warming up to me."

"I think so, too."

Isabel studied his shaded form. "Truly?"

"Yes. I just hope you won't disappoint her."

Isabel stifled a groan. How had she earned the contempt of her husband? And she had thought they'd moved past it. "I received a few replies from prospective governesses. We can expect an interview with a couple of them in the next few days."

"That was fast."

Isabel let out a breath. "I am quite competent in many things."

Chapter 19

Another grunt.

"You don't believe me," she murmured, chewing on her lower lip. She was getting frustrated by his coldness and indifference toward her. But more than that, she was tired of his contempt.

"I believe we have a lot of work ahead of us. And it will take a lot more than replies from prospective governesses to convince me of your competency when it comes to my daughter," he said.

"I do not know why trust and respect seem beyond you, but I refuse to let it affect me, my lord. You might contemplate my competency all you want. In the meantime, I have a house party to host and a girl to educate. Goodnight."

Isabel turned away from him.

Perhaps she'd been wrong when she'd thought things were looking up in the household. Her husband seemed to be as obstinate as before. No matter. She had more important things to worry about, and finding a perfect governess for Millie was at the top of the list.

* * *

"I believe that children should be disciplined strictly," the older woman in front of Isabel said as she sat straight, her hands demurely on her lap, her appearance impeccable, nary a hair out of place.

Isabel found herself trying to sit straighter just from one look at the potential governess, Mrs. Pemberley. "Yes, I agree wholeheartedly."

This was the tenth interview in over a week, and Isabel was getting extremely tired. Finding a competent governess was not an easy feat.

Every time she thought she had found someone, her husband would dismiss them.

He had called two of them too young and inexperienced. Well, he could not fault Mrs. Pemberley for that. The woman had worked in the field for over forty years.

And the third one had an inexplicable glint in the eye that Vane disliked.

Isabel had not argued with her husband, but she had not noticed any glint in anyone's eye, and she hoped Mrs. Pemberley did not possess it also.

Mrs. Pemberley was the last resort. If they didn't hire her, Isabel would have to post in the paper once more and wait weeks to gather responses and conduct more interviews.

"A lady should act as one from birth. There should be no unnecessary noise coming from the girl. She should be invisible unless called upon," Mrs. Pemberley continued.

Isabel stifled a grimace. She did not agree with that part. Children were children. They needed space to run around and play, sing and dance if they needed to. But all of this should be done away from the adults—or at least from guests. So perhaps that's what the older lady meant by invisible.

Isabel remembered her childhood fondly. Her family was large and very loud. Their household was never quiet. But this was not about her. Despite all the rambunctious fun, Isabel was raised by a lady from birth. Millicent, on the other hand, had not had that privilege.

"What are your views on female education?" Isabel asked.

"A lady should speak at least four languages, know *Debrett's* from top to bottom, pour impeccable tea, play flawlessly on the pianoforte, and be passable at two more instruments ap-

Chapter 19

propriate for a lady, such as a violin and a harp. Her stitching should be perfect, and she should be able to watercolor."

"And you can teach all of this?"

Mrs. Pemberley pursed her lips. "I am not a lady. I do not possess all the necessary knowledge. I believe a governess's main task is to teach the lady the basics. Music, dance, and art are not my forte. However, I always sit in on the lessons with other tutors to monitor my charge's behavior."

Isabel flipped her journal shut and leaned closer to Mrs. Pemberley. "I have to be quite honest with you. Millie is... She is not quite ready for music lessons and dancing. I think she needs a bit of guidance. She needs to learn manners first and foremost. And perhaps just the basics."

Isabel had spent a few hours each day in Millie's company since their first outing. And as much as she enjoyed spending time with the girl, she never managed to teach her anything useful. The moment Isabel tried to instill discipline in the girl, Millie immediately rebelled.

"Everything is interconnected, my lady. Dance teaches the lady correct posture, music teaches her persistence, and watercolors teach her patience. There is not one without the other."

"Very wise." Isabel smiled. She liked the older lady. Being around her was like being wrapped in a warm motherly embrace, although there was strictness in her voice and posture.

She was thin and tall. And even though she was probably in her late fifties, she still had a bounce in her step, although she carried a cane with her.

"Mrs. Pemberley, thank you very much for taking the time to journey here. I think you are a perfect candidate and your recommendations are exemplary. But my husband is the one who will make the final decision. Would you be willing to stay the night in the guest room and speak with him on the morrow?"

"Oh, certainly. I am too old to travel back to London right away, anyway. I appreciate your hospitality. But may I ask for one more thing before I settle in for the night?"

"Of course."

"I would like to meet the young lady."

Isabel smiled tightly. She did not think that was a good idea at all. But perhaps, she was wrong. Maybe that was exactly what they needed to do before selecting a governess. "Certainly."

They went up to Millicent's nursery a moment later. Millie sat there with Edith, flipping through her books.

"Good evening, Millicent," Isabel said with a smile. "I want you to meet Mrs. Pemberley. Mrs. Pemberley, this is Lady Millicent."

Millie raised her head to look at the older lady but did not say a word.

"The polite thing to do is greet a person to whom one is introduced," Mrs. Pemberley said softly.

Millicent just stared at her. Isabel shifted uncomfortably. "I apologize, but as I said, she isn't quite ready."

"Do not worry, my lady." Mrs. Pemberley smiled and stepped closer to Millicent. "And what are you doing, Lady Millicent?"

Millie looked down at her book. "Reading."

"And do you mind if I listen to you read?"

Millie shook her head.

Mrs. Pemberley settled next to Millicent and listened as

Chapter 19

Millie recited the passages from the book by heart, flipping the pages in all the right places.

Isabel stood in the doorway, watching the pair read. Mrs. Pemberley murmured something, and Millicent promptly straightened in her chair.

Isabel blinked in surprise. This lady was truly a miracle worker.

* * *

Isabel went in search of Vane to tell him the good news. She thought Mrs. Pemberley was a perfect candidate for the governess, but she needed to get Vane's approval before she could hire her.

The marquess was nowhere in the house, although it was rather late, and he was usually back by this time.

Isabel approached the butler. "Mr. Monroe, have you seen my husband?"

"Yes, my lady. He went to bathe in the stream."

Isabel looked out the window and instantly wrapped her arms around her. The weather was gloomy, and it couldn't have been warm. So why was he washing up in the stream instead of the house?

"Thank you, Mr. Monroe."

She put a shawl around her shoulders and went in search of her husband. The wind blew straight into her face, slowing her pace. Now that she thought about it, she should have waited inside the house. And what did she hope to accomplish by hunting him down?

Nevertheless, she wasn't one to turn back from a challenge. And perhaps the fresh country air was exactly what she needed. She raised her head to the sky, enjoying her walk and thinking about all the things she could help teach Millie once her education started.

A slight smile adorned her lips. When Isabel was younger, she loved to teach her little sister Samantha everything she knew.

With all the difficulties in their lives and all Isabel's duties, she'd completely forgotten how much she enjoyed spending time teaching Sam.

Isabel had always wanted to have a daughter. When circumstances had changed, and she was forced to embrace spinsterhood, she'd forgotten about her dreams, but they were always there at the back of her mind. And now perhaps she could finally have her dream.

Isabel approached the woods about ten minutes later. She looked around, wondering if she had missed her husband somehow. There was no one nearby, and she did not see footsteps leading back to the house.

If her husband was still at the stream, she'd go and meet him then. She stepped into the woods and proceeded toward the picnic place, hoping that would be where he chose to swim.

Only once she arrived on the spot did she understand her folly.

Her husband was bathing in the stream!

What was she supposed to do once she found him? Help him wash? She giggled, her face heating at the idea. Perhaps he was already done.

She searched the bank but did not see Vane there. Had he already left? Had she missed him?

She turned toward the water and instantly spotted him. How could she not?

Chapter 19

He stood waist-deep, splashing his face and shoulders.

Isabel's mouth went dry. Her husband was absolutely magnificent. His corded muscles glistened, his shoulders were large and powerful, and his chest was covered with dark hair that thinned at his flat, corded stomach. Her gaze followed lower, but water covered the rest of him. Isabel couldn't help but wish she could see more.

She caught herself on the wanton thought and squeezed her eyes shut. What was she doing?

She heard more splashing and opened her eyes just in time to see Vane emerging from the water. He walked toward the shore, water running down his slick body in rivulets. Her gaze slid lower to the place between his legs of its own accord. A patch of hair covered a tiny appendage.

Oh.

Isabel had only seen that part of male anatomy once, and she did not remember it too much. Somehow she thought it'd be larger.

As Vane walked further out of the water, her gaze got distracted by his thighs—the powerful thighs of an expert rider.

Isabel stood frozen in place, watching her husband in all his naked glory. A few more steps, and he reached the bank.

Oh, Lord! What am I doing?

Isabel turned away and covered her eyes with her hands. Her face felt hot to her touch, and acute embarrassment settled in her chest. She needed to leave and fast. Before Vane figured out that she was watching him like a complete wanton!

She made a step and tripped over her skirts. She caught herself against the nearby tree, but it was too late.

The noise must have caught Vane's attention because he called out, "Who's there?"

Isabel grimaced. She couldn't very well keep hiding out from him and then hope to outrun the man back home. She picked up her skirts and stepped onto the bank.

"It's just me."

To her relief, Vane had already put on his breeches and boots, although he was still naked from the waist up.

Vane looked around. "What are you doing here?"

Isabel could not take her eyes off his muscled chest. His nipples hardened into peaks from cold, and his skin was covered in goosebumps, but he looked deliciously appealing. "I needed to talk to you," she said to his chest.

Vane slowly bent down, took his shirt, and hauled it over his shoulders. Isabel mourned the loss of the sight of his slick, bare skin. She wouldn't have minded peeking a look at it again as they talked.

He put on his coat, not bothering with the waistcoat, and crossed his arms over his chest. "Well?"

Isabel tried to concentrate. "Why are you bathing in the stream? It must be uncomfortably cold." She drew the ends of her shawl closer together because just as she said so, the wind cooled her arms and heated cheeks.

"Because my room is yet to be decorated, and it is just as bloody cold there as it is here. By bathing here, I am sparing the maids from heating the water and preparing the bath."

"Oh. How considerate of you."

"Would you rather I bathed in your room?" He cocked a brow.

Yes. Very much. Isabel's cheeks heated even more. She waved a hand to dismiss the wanton ideas from her head.

Chapter 19

"Let us go back to the house. You must be freezing."

Vane silently collected his things and led the way.

"So, to what do I owe your unexpected visit?"

Right. The governess. "I think I found the perfect governess for Millie."

"Did you?"

"Yes, she is very knowledgeable and put together. She has already met Millie, and I think they bonded."

Vane raised a brow. "She met Millicent?"

"Yes."

"And Millicent was not angry or upset?"

"Well, she did not sic Button on her, so I'd call it a success."

Vane let out a chuckle. "Very well. I'd like to meet this rare individual."

"I put her in the guest house for the night. She traveled from London for this interview, and I could not very well send her away. So you shall have an opportunity to meet her tomorrow morning."

"Good."

They walked part of the way in silence.

They were almost to the house when he spoke again. "Is that all you had to say?"

"Yes. I was very excited about this new governess. I had to let you know."

"Hmm." He scratched his jaw. "And here I thought you came to ogle my bare torso. You are just lucky you arrived when you did and not earlier."

Isabel bit painfully on her lower lip. If only he knew.

Chapter 20

Something wicked glinted in Lady Isabel's eyes. She'd been quite red from the moment he'd spotted her on the bank of the stream, and her blush had deepened when Vane made the comment about his bare torso.

She looked shy, almost bashful. He'd imagined she was quite experienced if she'd been lovers with Stanhope for over a decade, and he did not expect her to blush over Vane's naked chest.

"At least we are even now," he said as they ascended the stairs to the first floor.

She glanced at him with evident confusion.

Ah, she still hadn't figured it out. He smirked and led the way to her bedchamber. He opened the door for her, and she slowly glided in.

"If you are referring to the first night we shared this room together, I am compelled to remind you that I was not nearly as disrobed as you were."

Rhys smiled, remembering the flimsy nightgown and how

Chapter 20

it hugged her womanly curves. "Thank you for the reminder. But no, that was not what I was referring to."

She walked further into the room and perched herself on the bed. "What were you referring to?"

"The first time we met," he said simply.

Lady Isabel frowned. "Do you mean tackling me at the ball?"

"First off, you tackled me. And secondly, that's not the first time we met." Vane allowed himself a slow smile.

She looked utterly confused. "No?"

"No."

Lady Isabel raised her brows. "Please, enlighten me."

Rhys leaned his hips on the edge of the vanity table. "We met at the stream. On your father's estate."

"On my—" She narrowed her eyes. "Are you telling that story you told during our wedding breakfast again?"

Rhys raised a brow. "Do you remember it?"

She looked at him queerly. "Of course, I do. And I've asked you about it."

"And I told you the truth. I said I met a girl once just like that. I meant you."

Lady Isabel looked quite confused. "I was nineteen. And I was swimming in my shift!"

"Well, I couldn't very well tell that to our wedding guests."

"And the boy I met, he was younger than me"—Rhys grimaced—"and his name was Thomas!"

Rhys let out a chuckle. *Oh, Lord.* "Do you know what my name is?"

She reared back, offended. "Of course, I know your name."

"My full name?"

"Viscount Carlton, the fifth Marquess of Vane—"

"These are my titles. What about my name?"

Lady Isabel rolled her eyes. "Thomas Rhys Townsend."

"Yes, what was that first one?"

Her eyes widened. "Thom—Thomas? But you can't be!" She raked him with her gaze.

"Yes, I've grown up a little since then."

She scoffed. "I'd say so! Look at you!" She waved a hand toward him.

Rhys stifled a smile. "You, on the other hand, have not changed at all."

"Oh, please." She didn't even smile, her entire being concentrated on finding anything familiar in him. "But… You weren't a marquess."

"No, but my uncle was. I inherited before my twentieth birthday."

She frowned in thought, then her features took on a look of horror. "You are younger than me!"

Is that all you have to say? "Well, yes."

"Significantly younger!"

"Not that sig—"

"Oh, Lord!" She started pacing the room. "What people must be saying about me?"

"Probably that you were a cunning little vixen to snatch such a handsome marquess," he said smugly.

"Oh, shush. My lord. You are… you're so much younger."

"Stop." He walked toward her and took her by her shoulders, turning her to face him. "That does not matter. We are already married. Besides, after the scandal of our betrothal, do you truly think anything else can eclipse that?"

Lady Isabel shook her head, unable to take her eyes off his.

"Good then." He let go of her shoulders and stepped away.

Chapter 20

She caressed her shoulders where he'd just held her as she looked at him. "Tell me what happened?" Her voice turned gentle.

"Where?"

"Not where, when. After... I mean, I have not seen you in a decade. What happened during those ten years?"

Rhys grimaced. "I really don't think that's necessary to rehash."

"Thomas—"

Rhys shook his head. "Nobody calls me that. They haven't since the day I—since a long time ago."

"Since what day?"

Since the day he'd walked away from her father's estate forever. Since the day his father had died. Since the day when everything had changed. He didn't answer.

After a moment of silence, she asked, "What do people call you?"

"Vane."

Lady Isabel swallowed. "What about a first name?"

"If you must... I prefer Rhys."

She cleared her throat. "I like Rhys."

His name on her tongue made his heart jolt.

She looked at him strangely now, as if learning his features anew, and Rhys felt uncomfortable under her intent gaze.

"It is late," he croaked, then cleared his throat. "Perhaps we should go to bed."

Without waiting for her answer, he walked into his bedroom. He needed a change of clothes. And perhaps a change of heart as well.

* * *

Isabel could not believe her ears. Her long-ago friend, Thomas, was indeed her husband.

Why hadn't he said anything before?

She remembered him as a gangly youth who'd followed her around for a couple of summers before disappearing. She hadn't seen him for over a decade.

He had grown into a gorgeous specimen of a man. She didn't fault herself for not recognizing him at all.

But he knew all along! He told the story of their meeting at their wedding.

Isabel called for Anthea and changed into her nightgown.

She burrowed under her covers, waiting for her husband to come back. How would she be able to look at him the same way now that she knew?

Every time she saw him, she'd see the smiling, shy youth he'd been.

What had happened to him? What had made him so stern and surly?

The door opened, and Vane—no, Rhys—entered the room. He doused the candles and settled into bed.

Isabel could not help but follow his every move with her gaze. This tall, broad-shouldered man with a constant frown on his face could not be her good-natured neighbor, could he?

"Goodnight," he murmured and turned away from her.

Isabel looked at his outlined form, still unable to believe her eyes.

"We parted friends," Isabel finally said.

"Pardon?" He still didn't turn to face her.

"As far as I remember, we parted friends," she repeated. "I am trying to figure out at what point in your life you became a

Chapter 20

surly old man because I surely remember you as a life-loving youth."

"Of course, you do." He finally turned to face her. "I was an infatuated young idiot who could not stop grinning upon seeing your face."

Isabel blinked. "You were infatuated with me?"

She could feel him frowning.

"I thought you knew."

"I knew you were attached to me. But I thought it was in a sisterly way"—He scoffed—"You were so very young!"

Rhys let out a weary sigh. "I am only four years younger than you. That is not such a huge difference."

"Perhaps it's not now, although I would argue that it is, but I was nineteen when we met! You were just fifteen!"

Rhys shrugged. "Perhaps."

Isabel took a deep breath. There was no arguing with an obstinate marquess. "Is that why you were so angry with me when we met at the ball? Because I did not return your affection over a decade ago?"

Rhys snorted. "I am not that petty."

"Then why?"

He didn't answer.

Isabel let out a weary breath. Speaking with her husband was like pulling teeth.

"Tell me this, if you were so infatuated with me, and you didn't think our age difference was a major obstacle, why didn't you say something?"

"I almost did," he said irritably. He ran a hand through his hair. "I was too young when we first met, but even during my years in Eton, I could not forget you... So when I was nineteen, I returned. I thought you would be more amenable to my courting since I was of age. I was an educated gentleman, more worthy of you."

"Why didn't you?" she asked, captivated by his growling voice.

"I came to your estate and asked to see you, but you were not at the house." He swallowed. "I thought that perhaps you were at your favorite spot at the stream, so I went to look for you. When I found you… You were not alone." There was a long pause.

"Who was I with?"

His voice turned hoarse. "You were in a heated embrace with the Earl of Stanhope."

Isabel almost choked on her tongue.

It couldn't be. *Oh, Lord, please do not let this be true.* Had he seen her with Stanhope on the exact day when they— Isabel shook her head.

"Oh, Lord."

"Yes." He nodded for emphasis.

Isabel rolled on her back and covered her heated face with her hands. It wasn't enough. She wanted to cover herself with a pillow. Or hide under the bed. Perhaps fall into oblivion.

"You witnessed that?"

"I am afraid so. At first, I thought he was forcing himself on you… I was angry and was about to intervene, but you whispered something to him. And he called you… darling." Rhys's voice broke, and he fell silent.

Isabel lay like that, her mind blank, unwilling to relive the terrifying realization that the one time she acted wanton, she'd been witnessed—and by her future husband no less!

She would never recover from the mortification she felt at that moment.

Chapter 20

Then another realization hit her. She turned toward him. "And that's the base of all your accusations? Youthful indiscretion?"

"No, it—"

"I'd like to know if you were so chaste your entire youth while you went gallivanting in clubs and—

"I was chaste!" he roared. "I was waiting for you."

"What?" Isabel's voice came out small.

"I thought—It doesn't matter what I thought. But I was chaste when I came to you that day, not that it matters. I had not thought about it or you for a long time. I left that day and found out that my uncle and father had been killed in an accident." He paused. "I became a guardian to my nephew the marquess... And then he, too, passed a few weeks later from fever. By that time, my mind was not on our courtship or anything else concerning you. I did not know what happened to you or if you married. A few months later, I met a girl from a neighboring estate and married her. I moved on."

Isabel swallowed. There was a strange feeling in the pit of her stomach. "Were you in love with her?" Her voice was weirdly high-pitched.

"I thought so at the beginning. But it doesn't matter. That youthful indiscretion, as you call it, is not—and never was—the reason for my coldness toward you. Well, perhaps a little. After all, you crushed my youthful dreams. But do not act all innocent since I saw you again with Stanhope at that ball and once again at our wedding breakfast! Do not tell me you haven't continued your liaison even though he is a married man now."

His voice turned cold, and Isabel shivered.

"For your information, that night at the ball was the first

time I'd conversed with Stanhope for longer than a ten-second greeting in years! I did not go to meet him. He accosted me in the alcove. I was hurrying away from him when I stumbled onto you. And I know you don't believe me, so you're free to think what you will." She sniffed and turned away from him.

"He did what?" Rhys's question was more of a growl.

"Oh, now you're interested! Well, I do not want to talk with you anymore."

"Turn around."

"No."

"Turn around. I want to see your face when I speak to you."

"Well, I do not want to speak to you."

Isabel squeaked as Rhys took her by the waist and turned her toward him.

"What did he do?" he growled.

"How are you any better than him, hauling me around like a brute?"

"Well, I married you, so I have the right to haul you around."

"You arrogant brute!" Isabel pushed him at his chest. He didn't budge. On the contrary, his arms tightened around her waist.

"Tell me," he soothed, his voice turning gentle.

Isabel shivered from the pleasant timbre of his voice. There in the dark room, surrounded by the heat of her husband's body, she felt the response to him deep in her soul. Instead of pushing him away, she wanted to press herself against his reassuring, hard, warm chest and tell him all her troubles.

What was he doing to her?

"I don't want to tell you," she lied, her voice curiously breathy.

Chapter 20

His arms tightened even more, bringing her body dangerously close to his. "Tell me, or I shall have to hunt him down and ask him myself."

Isabel rolled her eyes, although deep down, she enjoyed that show of protectiveness.

"He kissed me," she replied. "But I took care of it."

"How?"

Isabel smiled slyly, not that he could see. "I kicked him, and he released me."

A deep laugh shook Rhys's body, and Isabel felt it like an earthquake. Suddenly, he dipped his head and kissed her lightly on her nose. "Good girl," he whispered, then released her and turned away.

Isabel blinked, feeling cold and lonely without her husband's arms around her.

What a cad her husband was! He showed her how nice it could be to be held in his arms and then took it away from her in a matter of seconds.

* * *

Rhys was jolted awake in the middle of the night. What had woken him up?

He was used to getting up with the first light of dawn, but as his gaze traveled to the window, there was not a line of light in sight. Even the moon was hiding behind the clouds.

He shivered in the cool night air, wondering why he was not covered with sheets. He turned and immediately bumped into something—or rather someone.

His mind took a moment to process what was going on before he remembered that he was not in his own bed. He was sleeping with his wife, in her room, in her bed.

He cocked his head and squinted his eyes, trying to understand what body part he'd bumped into. As his eyes finally adjusted to the dimly lit room, he almost laughed out loud. He clamped his lips shut and shook his head.

Half of the enormous four-poster bed was completely empty while Isabel, his lovely wife, lay curled up beside him. What was even more amusing was the fact that she hogged the bedsheets, bunching them up between her legs and hugging them close to her. As a result, most of her body was uncovered, and there was not enough sheet left to warm Rhys.

Was this happening every night Rhys slept with her? No wonder he woke up most mornings feeling cold and weary.

What a selfish sleeper she was.

A few strands of her hair escaped her nightcap, and Rhys's fingers twitched to tuck them back. Instead, he lay on his side, propped himself on his elbow, and watched her sleep.

She looked so innocent.

Her night shift had hiked up, revealing her delectable calves and her feet. Vane wanted to run his fingers up her legs.

Just a touch. But he resisted.

His gaze traveled back up to her sleeping face. Her lips were puffy, her eyelashes trembling slightly.

Could it have all turned out differently?

If by some miracle she'd fancied him when they were young, and they'd married then, could they still have been happily married now? Or would their marriage have turned bitter just like his and Abigail's did? He supposed there was no way to know for sure and no reason to dwell on the past.

But was there a way to make their marriage different now? Rhys closed his eyes and lowered his head to the pillow. Those

Chapter 20

boyish dreams had not escaped him completely, it seemed. Deep down, he was still a naive young boy, dreaming of love.

But he should know better. Isabel did not love him, just like Abigail never did. And loving someone invited pain, misery, and regret. Rhys knew himself all too well. He could not let emotion into his heart. He could not go through heartbreak again.

He had Millie to love, and that should be enough. Because the last time he'd experienced heartbreak, he had neglected the only person that mattered, and he could not let that happen again.

Chapter 21

The house was bustling with preparations for the upcoming house party. Isabel had decorated the house in mild, light tones, and she also filled the entire house with flowers.

Flowers made everything better.

Everything in life was running smoothly for the first time since Isabel had married Vane. Well, almost smoothly.

Millie now regarded them coldly for hiring a governess. Isabel thought she'd be happy because she seemed to be getting on nicely with Mrs. Pemberley, but the girl said a few times that she did not like her new governess and she did not want to spend her days studying. She even pleaded with Isabel to stop the lessons, but Isabel insisted that Millie needed to know the etiquette before the guests arrived.

And truthfully, there was nothing Isabel could do. The house party was approaching, and not only did Millie need to know the etiquette rules, but she also needed someone to look after her during the party.

Chapter 21

When huge house parties took place, the children were always separated, and Isabel knew she would see Millicent even less than she did now. Isabel made certain to take Millicent out of the classroom and spend an hour or two with her every day. They usually spent the day in the garden, selecting flowers for the house. Once Isabel took Millicent to a fair, and the latter ran around, looking at all the stalls in excitement.

Now, Isabel had decided to take Millie with her while she took a jaunt to the village.

Isabel put on a bonnet. "Mrs. Ainsworth. Have you wrapped the salted almonds for the trip?"

"Yes, I did." The woman nodded.

Ever since receiving the recipe, Isabel had asked her cook to make a few batches of the salted almonds daily. Eventually, the cook perfected the recipe so that now the almonds tasted even better.

"Good."

Isabel found she was quite fond of the new concoction, and she planned to serve a few batches during the house party as well. But mostly, she asked her cook to make some every day so she could bring them with her upon her visit to Lilian.

Lilian was busy with her five children and all her duties, so the only thing Isabel could do to help was supply her with treats she enjoyed.

A moment later, Millicent walked cautiously down the stairs. Isabel could barely stifle her smile. Millie was dressed like a little lady, and now she walked like one, too. Mrs. Pemberley was working miracles with the girl!

Although, if Isabel was frank, she rather missed Millie's galloping strides down the stairs.

Most days, Vane took Button to the fields with him, so Isabel understood Millie's foul mood. Her pup was taken away, and she was forced to stay indoors when the weather had just started turning warm.

"Are you ready for our trip?" Isabel asked.

Millicent fiddled with the ties of her bonnet. "Yes."

Mrs. Pemberley appeared behind her. "Have a nice trip, my lady."

Isabel nodded and bundled Millicent into the carriage.

Millicent looked out the window during the entire trip.

Isabel felt guilty for Millie's sour mood. They had just started to bond, and now she felt like they were back to strangers.

"Did you learn anything new today?" Isabel asked.

"Yes." Millie's answer was clipped. And then, "my lady."

Isabel swallowed the uncomfortable feeling in her chest. "You don't have to call me that."

"Mrs. Pemberley says I should."

A lump formed in her throat. Isabel mourned the loss of the brief but friendly relationship she'd shared with the girl. Perhaps it was a mistake hiring a governess so soon. It felt as though Millie regarded it as a form of betrayal.

Vane had expressed his concerns, too. Apparently, Millie was just as upset with him as she was with Isabel. But at least she still allowed him to tuck her in and complained to him about the many things Mrs. Pemberley forced her to learn.

But they'd both decided to give it a few more weeks. Perhaps Millie just needed time to adjust to her new governess. And with the house party looming over them, they could not reverse their decision. They would have to discuss it after the party was over.

Chapter 21

The carriage jolted to a stop, and Isabel was glad. Millie would play with the villagers' children now, and Isabel would express all her concerns to her dear friend.

As soon as Millicent's feet hit the ground, she took off in the direction of her friends. Isabel smiled. Let her be a babe for an hour and not a lady.

She conversed with the villagers for a while, listening to their concerns and issues before walking toward Lilian's house.

Lilian must have spotted her from the window because she exited the house and waved her inside. Her friend looked much bigger than the last time Isabel saw her. Or was it her imagination?

Lilian sauntered inside and put the kettle on. "I am so glad you came for a visit!" she exclaimed. "I find myself in a constant need to complain to somebody about this enormous belly I am carrying around all day. But I can't complain to my husband, who is always just as tired as me. I cannot complain to my children since they would not understand. And especially not to any of my neighbors."

Isabel smiled and took out the box with salted almonds. "You can complain to me all you want," she said with a smile.

Lilian's eyes turned liquid. "Oh, thank you! I didn't have time to make them myself this week, and I wanted them so badly!" She covered her mouth with her palm and hiccupped.

Isabel walked toward her and patted her on the back. "Is everything well?"

Lilian nodded and wiped at her tears. "Yes, I just find myself overly emotional over every little thing."

"When is the babe due?" Isabel asked as they both settled before the table.

"A week or two. I do not know for certain. I just hope it is soon." She flipped the hair away from her face. "I can't bend down properly, I cannot walk as quickly as I did before, and this house just seems so tiny!" She took a deep breath.

The kettle whistled, and Isabel shot up. "Please, Lilian, let me get the kettle. I know how to pour tea."

"Oh!" Lilian's eyes watered again. She blew into her handkerchief. "A lady of the estate is pouring me tea! You are so exceptionally kind!"

Isabel stifled a chuckle. When Lilian said she was overly emotional, she wasn't exaggerating.

Lilian fanned her flushed cheeks. "I shall be crying all day if you let me. Please, tell me, how are things at the manor?"

"Well, actually, I came here with the hope of complaining to you, too."

"Oh, good!" Lilian instantly brightened up. "Please, tell me. I want to hear somebody else complain for a moment."

Isabel quickly told Lilian about the trouble with the governess and how her relationship with Millie had regressed in such a short time.

Lilian listened to her with avid interest.

"So, she does not like her governess? Well, it is hardly a surprise. A free-spirited young girl like Millicent is bound to dislike being cooped up in the nursery. And she was always by his lordship's side. It is nothing to worry over, I promise."

"You think so?" Isabel expelled a breath of relief.

"I had five babes, darling. I know how they can act sometimes. Just give her time to adjust."

Isabel nodded. "Thank you, I feel a tad better now."

Lilian popped an almond into her mouth. "I am glad I could ease your mind," she said around the bite.

Chapter 21

* * *

Rhys descended the steps and turned toward Isabel's room the next day, his heart heavy. He had just checked on Millicent and was disappointed to see her already sleeping. He had missed a few nights of tucking her into bed as he was working later than usual. And now, he wouldn't see her for a few days more.

He heaved a sigh, feeling extremely tired. He needed to speak with Isabel regarding the new turn of events, and he hoped she would ease his mind about Millicent.

As he ventured toward Isabel's bedchamber, he noticed that he didn't want to enter his room at all. Not even to change. Not even to check if his windows had been shut and his hearth lit. How long did it take for the walls to dry, anyhow?

He knew it was the servants' ploy to get the two of them together, and to be frank, he didn't mind at all. He'd gotten quite used to the tiny bundle of heat by his side. He'd gotten used to her tangled hair on his pillow. He'd even gotten used to her kicking him in the middle of the night.

He never wanted to go back to his chamber.

It was not only cold in that room, but it was also lonely. And he'd had enough of being lonely.

He opened the door to a dimly lit room. Isabel was already in bed, reading by the light of a lone candle. She immediately sat up straighter as she saw him and fixed the nightcap atop her head.

"Good evening," Rhys rasped. He cleared his throat and walked further into the room.

Isabel placed her book on the bedside table and cautiously watched his approach. "How was your day, husband?"

Butterflies flew around his stomach at the word husband. How easy it was to ruffle him. He sat on the bed next to her.

"It was good. Busy. How is Millicent? She fell asleep without seeing me again."

"We went to the village today, and she had a lot of fun playing with the children. Her dress was all dirty, and she lost her bonnet, but she seemed happy."

Rhys let out a laugh. "I would have liked to see that."

"Well, Mrs. Pemberley would have happily traded places with you. She was not amused."

"And is Millicent still as reserved about her governess?"

"Yes. But the fact that she was happily jumping around with the children in the village tells me that she just needs some time to get used to her. And that she still needs time to hop around in puddles."

Rhys reached out and hid a loose tendril of hair back under her nightcap. Isabel smiled shyly.

"I trust your judgment," he said.

Isabel looked at him, startled. She obviously had not expected him to say that. But he needed to say that, more for his own benefit than hers.

"Well, I shall be certain to rescue her from time to time and take her to the village. She loves it there. And it clears that customary frown off her face."

Rhys furrowed his brows. "What customary frown?"

Isabel chuckled. "The one you're wearing right now. She is her father's daughter."

Something inside Rhys squeezed. He cleared his throat.

"I received some news… I might need to travel to Thornsby again."

"Is something wrong?"

Chapter 21

"On the contrary, things seem to be progressing, and I need to keep a close eye to make certain everything is built to better withstand the floods if they come again. And... And that requires me to stay a few nights there. I shall be working till late at night, and it just doesn't make sense for me to travel back and forth."

"Oh." She looked down, her expression lost. "But the house party is in less than two weeks."

"I shall return by that time, I promise. But I need to leave now, or I won't be able to go there until the party is over." He paused. "Will you fare well by yourself?"

She looked up at him then, fire lit behind her eyes. "Do you still think me incapable? I thought you trusted me."

"I do." Rhys took her hand in his. He couldn't help it. He wanted to touch her.

When Isabel did not protest, he brought it to his lips and kissed her knuckles.

"What then?" Her question was breathy.

"I just think that I shall miss you very much," he croaked, then trapped her palm between his cheek and his hand. "And I suppose I hoped... that you'll miss me too."

Isabel blinked, her mouth falling open slightly. "I shall." Her voice came out oddly hoarse.

"Promise?" He shifted closer to her.

"I pro—"

Rhys dipped his head and took her lips in a tender kiss.

* * *

Rhys's kiss took her by surprise.

Strangely, it was not the fact that he had kissed her that was surprising. What took her off guard was the way he kissed her. Previously, he had taken her wildly, without giving her any room to object. He had kept his hands on her face, so she couldn't twist away, not that she'd wanted to.

This time, the kiss was a soft brush of lips against hers. It was slow and sensual, and it was his tenderness that undid her.

He pulled away, and Isabel grabbed onto his shirt and tugged him closer until their lips met again. He smiled before pressing his lips against hers. Isabel let out a soft moan, and then her hands were in his hair, still wet from bathing in the stream. He tugged off her nightcap and started undoing the pins in her hair.

"What—" she murmured, but he silenced her with another kiss.

Isabel's entire body hummed with anticipation. It became languid and pliant, burning for his touch.

Rhys did not hurry to touch her, though. He kept intensifying the tingling feeling deep inside her belly as he nibbled on her lips and licked the contour of her mouth.

Isabel moaned and shifted to lie flat on the bed. Vane climbed on top of her without taking his mouth off hers.

Isabel wrapped her arms around his shoulders and ran her fingers against his shirt, wishing she could feel his body, graze his skin with her fingertips, and feel the shivers on his skin. She tugged on the collar of his shirt in frustration.

Instead of obliging her plea, Rhys took her hands and held them on either side of her head. He twined their fingers, and Isabel shivered.

He kissed her deeper, his tongue seeking entrance to her mouth. Isabel opened with a sigh, and her entire body tingled

Chapter 21

at the contact of their tongues. She curled her fingers against his skin, twisting her palm, searching for more contact of bare skin against bare skin. Her hips raised on their own accord, wanting to feel him closer, as the tension built between her legs.

Isabel felt warmth unfurl inside her and… seep out of her. Something dripped onto the sheet as the familiar discomfort in her belly alerted her that something was incredibly wrong.

"Oh my God," she managed to whisper between Rhys's kisses.

"Mm, yes," he murmured, moving his mouth down her neck.

Isabel clenched her thighs together and tensed her abdomen in hopes that it would pass or that it was just her imagination, but it was no use.

She pushed at Rhys's chest and rolled from under him.

Rhys sat up and watched her with wide eyes. "I… Apologies. I went too far."

"No." Isabel grimaced. She clenched her knees together and tried to cover her shift in the most delicate places in case the liquid managed to seep through. "It's a—I have to go."

Isabel rushed into her dressing room and took a deep breath. This was the most embarrassing experience of her entire life.

She'd just let herself enjoy Rhys's ministrations, his tender kisses. Rhys's mouth had been on her skin! He had just thrown caution to the wind and was prepared to engage in his marital duty with her, she was certain.

Their relationship had finally moved from a dead spot, and this had to happen!

She took off her shift, and sure enough, there was a bloody spot on the skirt. "Blast."

Her eyes burned from unshed tears, and she took a deep breath. At least, now she had the evidence Rhys had desired all along.

She performed the necessary ablutions, fashioned some layers with strips of cloth between her legs, and leaned her back against the wall. How was she to face him after this embarrassing incident?

"Is everything well?" Rhys's voice sounded from the other side of the door.

Tears of frustration sprung to Isabel's eyes. She was always slightly more emotional during her courses, but she couldn't really blame her nerves after what had happened just now.

"Isabel, I–I did not mean to upset you—"

Isabel bit her lip. How far would this incident set their relationship back? What should she tell him? Did married people even discuss such affairs? She threw a clean shift back on and went back to her room.

Rhys paced the length of a carpet like a caged beast. He ran his fingers through his hair, looking distraught and confused.

"I did not mean to offend you," he said as she came closer. "Perhaps I was too forward, and I shouldn't have."

Isabel raised a staying hand. "Rhys?"

He stopped, his breathing still accelerated, and waited for her to speak.

"Do you remember when you demanded the evidence of me not being in a delicate condition before we could consummate the marriage?" She pursed her lips so as not to laugh.

Rhys winced. "I know. I've been an arse—"

Isabel let out a chuckle, and he blinked, halting mid-sentence. "Yes, you were, but it's not that. It's just that you have your evidence."

Chapter 21

He ran his gaze down her body, then back to her eye level, still looking confused.

Isabel bit on her lip, still holding on to her laughter. "My courses started, Rhys. I'm sorry."

Chapter 22

Rhys entered Millicent's room early in the morning. He couldn't leave without seeing her and talking with her. She was still sleeping, but as Rhys sat by her bed, she stirred and rubbed her eyes.

She blinked, her lashes fluttering. "Papa," she whispered, her voice slightly rough from sleep.

"Good morning, darling. Did you sleep well?"

She nodded and stretched in bed. "Are we going to the fields today?"

Rhys caressed her warm, red cheek. "Not today, moppet. I am leaving for Thornsby today."

Millicent puffed out her lips. "Without me?"

"Without you. But I have a lot of work to do, so I can't take you with me. Besides, you need to keep up with your studies."

"I don't like my studies," Millie grumbled. "And I don't like Mrs. Pemberley. When I grow up, I will make it so girls won't need governesses."

Rhys heaved a long-suffering sigh. "Someday, you'll change

Chapter 22

the world, my little girl. You'll be a force to be reckoned with. But until then, you need to know things. Because knowledge is your biggest weapon."

Millie seemed to contemplate his words. "Why can't I learn from Lady Isabel instead of Mrs. Pemberley? I like Lady Isabel better."

Rhys smiled, his heart warming. "I am glad you like her, moppet. But remember, you disliked her, too, at first? Perhaps you can give Mrs. Pemberley a chance."

Millie furrowed her little brows. "When will you come back?"

Rhys swept the hair out of Millie's face and kissed her forehead. "As soon as I can. I would never leave you for longer than I have to."

* * *

Days without Rhys were somehow empty. Isabel had not spent much time with him during the day when he was at the estate, but she found herself thinking of him constantly now that he was gone.

The nights were the worst.

She'd gotten used to having him in her bed as she fell asleep. She missed their conversations every night before bed. She missed his teasing smile and his ferocious frown. She missed staring at his broad shoulders outlined by the moonlight.

Quite simply, she missed him.

Isabel didn't know how she'd grown so attached to her husband and when that had started happening. She only knew that now that he was far away, she wanted him by her side.

An Offer from the Marquess

It was quite a strange feeling, missing one's husband. She had not imagined it would ever happen. Yet, here she was. He'd been away for less than seventy-two hours, and already there was a gaping hole in her heart.

To cover up the ache somehow, Isabel decided to spring Millicent from her studies and take her on an unscheduled walk. She dressed in her beautiful day gown and ascended the steps. They could pick some more flowers for the house or perhaps even go for a ride. Millicent's pony sure missed the exercise!

"What are you doing, you useless child?" Mrs. Pemberley's harsh voice sounded in the corridor.

Isabel's mouth gaped open. Was the governess chastising Millicent so rudely? She crept toward the door, not willing to believe her own ears and needing to see what was going on for herself.

"Turn around!" Another harsh command sounded from behind the closed door.

"One!" A crack sounded in the air and then whimpers.

"Two more! Stand still!"

Isabel rushed toward the room and threw the door open.

The picture before her turned her mute with horror.

Millicent was bent over her desk, her tiny bottom hanging in the air. Her dress was raised up to her back, and red marks lined her skin. Mrs. Pemberley stood over her, a cane raised above her head.

"What in the world are you doing!" Isabel cried.

Millicent immediately whipped around, her eyes filled with tears.

"I am disciplining your wild child," Mrs. Pemberley said in a calm, measured tone.

Chapter 22

Isabel clenched her teeth so hard her jaw almost snapped. "Get out of this house!" she growled and rushed toward Millicent to embrace her.

Millie stepped back but stumbled and fell to the floor. She looked up at Isabel, her gaze filled with tears of betrayal. Isabel scooped her up and pressed her tightly against her chest. Millie thumped Isabel on her arm with her tiny fist, crying in earnest now.

"You don't know how to discipline children properly. No wonder she is a wild hellion!" Mrs. Pemberley said.

"I said get out, or Lord forgive me, I shall throw you out and use your cane to aid me!" Isabel's voice broke as tears slid down her cheeks. How could she have invited this monster into her house?

"You told me to teach her discipline, and now you are ruining my work!" the old governess persisted.

Isabel sat Millie down, stood, and approached the servants' bell with sure steps. She rang with such force she nearly pulled the bell out.

Edith ran inside, her eyes wild. She saw Millicent curled up on the floor and immediately ran to embrace her. Mrs. Ainsworth was on her heels.

"Mrs. Ainsworth," Isabel said, gathering a deep breath. Her voice was hoarse, and she couldn't calm the rioting beating of her heart. "Please ask Rogers and James to throw this child-beating monster out of the house!"

Mrs. Pemberley threw her a menacing gaze. "Your ideas about childrearing are the monstrous ones. She will be a menace to society. I tried to make a lady out of her. But now I see why she is a hellion. She takes after her mother!"

Mrs. Pemberley threw her head back and walked out of the

room, her spine straight.

Mrs. Ainsworth followed her out. "I shall make certain she is gone quickly," she said quietly as she slunk out of the room.

Isabel's chest heaved with the force of her breaths. She wiped at her face and pulled her hair back.

Millicent sat on the floor, cradled by her nursemaid, her cries quieting to soft sniffs. Isabel approached her, but as Millie saw her, she cried out, burrowing her face into the crook of her nursemaid's neck.

Isabel swallowed. She deserved Millie's anger. It was all her fault. Tears slid down her cheeks again, and her lips trembled as she tried to speak. "Edith, please do not leave her side until she falls asleep."

"I wouldn't, my lady."

Isabel nodded and left the room. She needed to pen a letter to her husband. It was time for him to hurry home.

Chapter 23

I do not know what hurts more, the fact that somebody harmed Millicent or that I am to blame for the incident.

I am the one who brought the monster into our house, and I am the one who overlooked Millicent's protestations and brushed off her words as that of a spoilt child.

How can I live in this world knowing that this might happen again and that I won't be able to protect her?

How did you do it, Mother? For when you were here, I was never hurt in my life. And now that you're gone, one blow comes after another, and I do not know what to do.

What do I do, Mother?

How do I ensure that Millicent is protected? How do I ensure that I am enough? Because I fear that I am not.

I only pray that one day I become one iota of the woman that you were, and until then, I will strive to follow in your footsteps.

It is difficult to explain in words how I miss you, dear Mother. I wish you were here.

Isabel shot up, awakened by loud screaming. *What is going on? Where am I?*

Right, she had spent the night in the chair by Millie's bed.

Isabel had been upset about the incident with the governess the entire day and more upset that Millicent refused to see her and sought comfort in the arms of her nursemaid.

She wasn't her mother, Isabel had reasoned. Millicent had known Edith for a lot longer.

It hadn't worked. The pit in her stomach did not close, and she still felt just as anxious as before.

But she could not have possibly slept soundly in her bed. So she slunk inside Millicent's nursery and settled beside the bed, resolved to guard Millicent's dreams.

Isabel could not replace Millicent's mother or father. But the least she could do was be there when the girl needed her.

"Papa!"

That was the sound that woke Isabel.

She turned to see Millie sitting in bed, clutching her bedsheets, her eyes frightened.

"Papa!" she called again.

Isabel rushed toward her and sat on the bed. "Millicent, dear, what's wrong?"

Millicent's lips quivered before she climbed onto Isabel's lap.

Isabel let out a deep breath and tightened her arms around the girl.

"I had a bad dream," Millie whispered.

The door opened, and Edith peeked inside the room, her eyes wild. She noticed Isabel, and her features cleared. Isabel nodded toward the nursemaid, and the latter softly backed out of the room and closed the door.

Chapter 23

Isabel cradled Millicent closer to her heart and kissed the top of her head. "Do you want to tell me what the dream was about?"

Millicent shook her head. "I don't remember. But it was frightening."

Isabel nodded and caressed her hair. "It's all better now. It was just a dream."

There was a beat of silence. And then Millicent said against Isabel's chest, "Will you sing to me?"

The breath whooshed out of Isabel's lungs. She smiled through her tears. "Of course."

She scooped Millicent up and cradled her comfortably on her lap while rocking her to sleep and singing her a lullaby her mother used to sing to her.

* * *

Please, return home. The matter is of utmost importance.

Those cryptic words flashed before Rhys's eyes as he galloped home at a breakneck pace. What could have been so important he must return, yet could not be disclosed in a note?

Of course, his first thought was that something had happened to Millie. Was she ill? Was she hurt?

Rhys cursed the messenger, who did not find him till the morning. He cursed the horse that it couldn't gallop faster. He cursed the sun and the moon and everything in between that he could not be home, holding his little girl close to his heart.

When he finally reached home, he threw his reins at the approaching groom and rushed up the steps taking them two at a time. The butler barely opened his mouth when Rhys passed him.

"Where's Millie? Where's my wife?"

"Lady Isabel is in the breakfast room, and Lady Millicent is still sleeping."

"Good." Rhys hurried his steps and dashed into the breakfast room.

Isabel instantly stood and took a step toward him.

"What happened? Is Millie well?"

"All is well. She is sleeping."

Rhys expelled a breath of relief. "What was so urgent?"

Isabel swallowed.

Rhys waited impatiently as she chewed on her bottom lip. "What happened? Tell me?"

She finally raised her eyes to his. "I let Mrs. Pemberley go."

"Mrs. Pember—The governess?" A dark suspicion settled deep in his chest. Rhys lowered his voice. "Why?"

Isabel swallowed again. "She... She caned Millicent."

Rhys winced, his heart sinking. "I trusted you," he growled.

"I know, and as soon as—"

"No!" Rhys roared. "I trusted you to pick a nurturing governess. I trusted your judgment. But I also left my daughter—the only thing that matters in my world—to your care! Where the devil have you been?"

Isabel looked around the room uncomfortably. The footmen stood, lining the wall, pretending not to hear anything.

"Leave us!" Rhys roared, and the servants scurried away.

He started pacing the floor, unwilling to go to Millicent just yet because he knew he would frighten her in his current disposition.

Isabel stood still, following him with her gaze. "Don't you

Chapter 23

think I blame myself?" she asked quietly.

"Not enough," Rhys growled.

He was being cruel and insensitive. But deep down, he knew that all his rage was not directed at his wife. Instead, it was directed at himself.

He was the one who had the final say in the matter of a governess. He was the one who left his daughter at the manor as he went to another estate. He was the one who had failed his daughter yet again.

With a roar, he swept the dishes from the table. Isabel squeaked and jumped away from him. Her eyes were filled with terror.

After the brief episode of violence, Rhys's blood had cooled. He ran a hand through his hair. "I shall go see Millicent now."

"Rhys—"

"Not now!"

Rhys exited the room and slammed the door shut.

* * *

Isabel stood, shaking, in the aftermath of her husband's rage. She had never seen him this way, and she hoped to never see him like this ever again.

Isabel had never been a coward, but she was frightened out of her wits at the moment. She had not anticipated such a severe reaction to the news. She had not expected him to be so angry.

She took a deep breath, took in the destruction caused by her husband, and silently exited the room. Footmen stood outside, hiding their gaze.

Isabel walked past them as if nothing was the matter.

She found the housekeeper, asked her to send someone to clean up the breakfast room and load a basket with food and salted almonds, and went to her room to change.

She would not be waiting for her husband to yell at her more. She would not be cowering in the house either. She needed to get out, and she needed to do it now.

Chapter 24

Isabel left home on a beautiful and sunny afternoon.

The sun twinkled high in the sky, and there was nary a cloud on the horizon. Usually, Isabel would have been joyfully galloping, letting the breeze hit her face, but now she cantered along, glowering at animals who dared cross her path and irritably swatting at dragonflies.

It was rather annoying when the weather didn't match her mood. On the rare occasion when England decided to grace her with wonderful weather, the rest of her life seemed to be in chaos.

Her husband hated her and blamed her for all sins.

To be fair, she blamed herself, too.

Rhys had trusted her judgment. He had said that a few nights ago, warming her heart, and she had betrayed his trust in the most awful way possible.

Isabel only hoped that Millicent would forget the incident rather quickly.

Governesses had not been exactly gentle with Isabel and

her little sister Sam either. They were strict and occasionally punished them with flogging. But they used a thin stick on the rear and never with a cane.

What kind of a monster strikes a little helpless child with a thick cane?

Isabel swallowed the torrid memories. And Millicent had tried to tell her. She had told her that the governess was strict. She had said that she had disliked her. She probably could not put into words what that monster had actually done.

What more did she do?

Isabel squeezed her eyes tightly.

She made her way toward Lilian's house and expelled a breath of relief. Finally, she would be able to unburden all her worries to her good friend.

She walked toward her house and knocked on the door. Isabel heard noises from the inside, but nobody opened the door to her.

She knocked again.

When the door finally opened, a young man almost stumbled into her in his haste to leave the house. "Oh, pardon me, my lady. But I have to go! Need to find…." He was speaking as he was hurrying away, but Isabel didn't make out the last words he had said.

He needs to find what? No matter. The door was open, so Isabel stepped inside.

A light scream or a half-growl sounded from somewhere inside the house.

Isabel rushed toward the main room. "What's happening?"

She encompassed the little room with her gaze. The usually cozy chamber with lots of items in disarray looked empty save for the blankets on the floor, strips of cloth, and basins

Chapter 24

with water.

Lilian sat on a pile of blankets, her face red, her forehead glistening with sweat, holding the hand of Mary, the medicine woman of the village. Lilian's other hand was on her belly, and she was breathing erratically.

"Lilian, are you well?" Isabel looked around in shock. Mary looked at Isabel queerly, took the wet cloth, and wiped Lilian's forehead. "Sorry, I can see you're unwell. Can I help?"

Lilian looked up, and her face split in a smile. "How glad I am that you are here!" she cried. "I am having a babe! But the dratted thing wouldn't come out."

Isabel tensed at the words. What did that mean? "How can I help?" She rushed toward Lilian.

"Do you—argh!" Lilian growled again. Then blinked up at Isabel. "Do you have more almonds with you?"

* * *

Rhys had spent the entire day with Millie.

When he first entered her room, she had shot up and ran to embrace him. He stood like that, holding her close to his body, his nose burrowed in her hair until she wriggled out of his arms.

She was as exuberant and happy as ever. It was as if nothing had happened.

He had spoken to Edith while Millicent breakfasted, and the nursemaid had assured him that aside from the slight bruising, his daughter was unharmed. She'd said that his wife's reaction to witnessing the event and Millie's subsequent embarrassment were a bigger reason for Millicent's tears than the caning itself.

Rhys decided not to dwell on the matter any longer. The governess was gone, and Rhys was not about to let Millicent out of his sight again.

He took a quick bath in his wife's room, and after that, they ventured outside and spent the entire day running around the estate, slinging rocks, and playing hide and seek.

Millicent kept telling Rhys about the games Isabel had taught her and all the things they had done together. She couldn't keep silent about how much she had bonded with the lady of the house, and Rhys couldn't help but feel guilt toward the way he had treated his wife.

On the bright side, Millicent not once mentioned the old governess.

It was a good sign, wasn't it?

Rhys didn't want to be reminded about the foul old woman more than Millicent did. Perhaps less so.

Later on, Button was brought in with the carriage from the Thornsby estate. Rhys had left in the early morning on horseback, and he could not very well force his bear of a dog to keep up with the breakneck pace.

Millicent was extremely happy to have Button back, so they played with him in the field until the clouds stretched the sky, thunder rumbled above their heads, and raindrops started falling onto their heads. They needed to go back home, and Rhys needed to apologize to his wife.

He owed her more than a simple apology. Perhaps a grovel at her feet. She did not deserve his ire, and he would make sure to make her understand. He was so angry at himself. He felt so helpless and weak that that weakness had made him lash out.

He would never do that again. And if he did, she had his

Chapter 24

full permission to hit him over the head with any object by her hand.

He smiled, thinking how she would surely like to exercise that right. She had thrown a glove in his face once, and he imagined she would have loved it to be a piece of furniture.

They came upon the house, and Millicent looked at him queerly. "Why didn't Lady Isabel come with us?"

Rhys cleared his throat. *Because I yelled at her, frightened her, quite unjustly, might I add.* "She had a very important appointment to keep. But I promise you, she wanted nothing more than to spend this time with you instead."

"Will she always be with us?" Millicent asked cautiously.

Rhys looked at his daughter, trying to gauge her mood. "Do you want her to?"

Millie nodded. "Yes. I like her very much."

Rhys's heart filled with joy. *I like her very much, too.*

They entered the house, and Rhys instantly felt that something was wrong. It was colder than usual, darker. And it was not due to the storm brewing outside.

He looked at the butler. "Is Lady Isabel in her room?"

"No, my lord. She left a few hours ago."

A few hours. His heart sank.

Millie looked at him, sensing the change in his mood, and Rhys forced out a smile. "I told you, she has business to attend to. But let us go and have some supper together."

Her eyes lit up instantly.

Rhys dined with his daughter, exchanging stories and anecdotes as if nothing had happened. There was no sign of Millie's trauma. Or perhaps it wasn't as big of a trauma as Rhys made it out in his head.

Children were resilient. And one incident was not going to

break Millie's spirit. *One more incident;* his treacherous mind reminded him.

Rhys tucked Millicent into bed after dinner, and she looked at him with pleading eyes. "Will Lady Isabel come sing me a song?"

Rhys blinked. "You don't want me to sing?"

"I want Lady Isabel. I like her song."

"Lady Isabel is still not home, moppet," Rhys croaked.

"When will she be home?"

Rhys swallowed. "I do not know. I hope soon."

So Rhys sang a lullaby, watching the rain drizzle out the window and hoping that his wayward wife had returned home and just didn't ascend the steps to Millicent's room. Or perhaps she'd seen him with Millie and refused to occupy the same room with him.

Yes, that was better. Because as long as she was home, he could reason with her and beg her forgiveness. As long as she hadn't left him, there was still a chance to make her stay.

After Millicent fell asleep, Rhys slowly left her room and padded toward Isabel's room. She must have returned. It was way too late, and the storm was blazing in earnest.

But as Rhys walked through the dark corridor leading to her chamber, somehow he knew.

She was gone.

He didn't know whether it was the wilted flowers on the tables in the hall that alerted him to the fact. It might have been the change in the air that made him suffocate. The walls seemed duller, and the entire house was shrouded in darkness.

Perhaps all the beauty that Isabel brought with her to the house was not in the little silly things like paintings and

Chapter 24

accessories. Perhaps it was just her and her spirit.

He hurried down the corridor with a dim hope still present that all of that was just in his imagination. She might have just been sitting in her room, angrily stabbing at her embroidery.

The thought gave Rhys wings, and he fairly flew into her chamber. But the same dullness greeted him in her room as well.

She left me. The damned voice didn't give him a moment of peace.

She left me. And he didn't even blame her because he'd been treating her like a total arse since the moment they ran into each other outside the Duchess of Somerset's ballroom.

She left me. And the realization was like a punch to the gut.

He walked further into the room and sat on her bed, then lay down, hugging the pillow that still smelled like her.

There. A piece of her was still present in the house. She was still here.

He took a deep breath, inhaling her wonderful scent. This couldn't possibly be his life. This house did not feel like home without her.

He sat up. What in the world was he doing sniffing the pillow and walking around the house all maudlin?

She couldn't have gone far. He needed to find her and bring her back. If not for his sake, then for the sake of his daughter.

With this resolution in mind, he hurried down the stairs only to be greeted by a huge gust of wind. The cloaked figure entered the house and closed the door behind him. He took off his hat and shook the rainwater off it before raising his head.

Rhys immediately recognized their groom, George. What was he doing here?

An Offer from the Marquess

George looked up, an expression of fear shining in his eyes. "My lord!" he yelled. "Lady Isabel's horse just returned... Without her."

***

That day was quite possibly the longest in Isabel's life. She could not even imagine how it felt to Lilian.

When Isabel arrived at Lilian's house, it turned out that Lilian had already spent a few hours in painful labor. Mary had said that something was wrong, and the babe was coming out upside down.

Isabel had no earthly idea what that could have possibly meant. But Lilian's husband had rushed to a nearby village to look for an experienced midwife who could help.

When Lilian had been extremely tired and ready to give up, an old, weathered woman came into the house and did something miraculous. She put her hands on Lilian's stomach and turned the babe.

And soon after that, the babe appeared into the world.

Well, not everything was as easy as that.

Isabel learned one crucial fact during that day.

She realized why nobody ever taught ladies anything about their marital duty. Because if they knew how the birthing process took place, they would never agree to marry in their entire lives. They'd rather be a spinster than go through such a horrific experience.

Isabel doubted she would ever be able to withstand such torture and deliver a child into this world. How had Lilian done it six blasted times?

If Isabel had been split apart like this, with blood and other

Chapter 24

liquids shooting out of her, she was certain she would never be put back together. She was horrified.

Isabel had been certain she would never think of the birthing process as a miracle... until she took the babe into her arms and looked into her scrunched-up, wrinkly, pink face.

The babe was absolutely beautiful.

And perhaps it was worth reliving that pain and terror just to be able to hold her own babe in her arms.

Isabel looked at Lilian, still lying on the floor, now covered with blankets, looking tired but blissful. Her eyes were closing as she fought to stay awake.

"How does it feel?" Isabel asked, referring to the process of childbirth.

"It's the best feeling in the world," Lilian answered.

Isabel doubted Lilian had been frank with her when she had answered, but she didn't persist. Perhaps Lilian needed to believe that for the moment before all the pain left her body, which probably would take weeks or months.

Isabel glanced back at the little babe in her arms. The babe gurgled and shifted, and Isabel smiled.

Yes, she definitely wanted one of these for herself.

With Rhys?

The thought took her aback. With the miracle of birth happening right before her eyes, she had completely forgotten about her own issues. Her issues seemed quite insignificant in comparison. At least, not worthy of Lilian's attention.

Was Isabel ready to forgive Rhys for his behavior and start working on conceiving a babe? Did she even have a choice? He needed an heir, and she was his wife. It's not like she could divorce him for his rude behavior.

"May I have her back?" Lilian asked, and Isabel smiled.

"I think I'd like to keep her," she joked. "But I doubt she would be amenable to the idea."

Lilian chuckled. "I think my husband would protest too."

Isabel brought the babe to her friend and placed her on her chest. "What are you going to name her?"

Lilian smiled. "I thought I'd name her Isabel… if you don't mind."

Isabel's smile turned into a grin. "I would be honored."

Looking at Lilian, lying contentedly with her babe, Isabel had a sudden urge to see Millicent. She glanced at the window and gasped in horror. It was already dark!

She'd missed supper, and most likely, she'd missed Millicent's bedtime too!

Did Millie miss her? Was she asking for her? Her heart squeezed as she started to hurriedly collect her items and dress to leave.

"Where are you going, my lady?" Lilian's husband asked.

"I need to get home. It is late. I didn't even notice how late it had gotten!"

"But you can't go now," Lizzy, Lilian's oldest daughter, interjected. "It is raining. And the clouds are so ominous. Surely it is going to storm."

Just then, lightning split the sky, and thunder followed. The horses whinnied, and the dogs started barking, cursing at the sky.

"All the more reason for me to leave now," Isabel insisted. "Before the storm starts in earnest."

She was not about to leave her family wondering what had happened to her. And she didn't want to spend the night away from Millicent.

Chapter 24

Was Millie afraid of the storm?

She didn't even know the answer. But she knew for certain that Millie would be worried about Isabel if she did not return home. And maybe Rhys would be worried, too.

Chapter 25

Rhys rushed out of the house and into the deluge. He mounted the horse that the stable boy had prepared for him and ventured out to look for Isabel.

Where had the obstinate woman gone in such weather? How far away did she get before the horse threw her? Was she now wandering in the storm?

He did not want to think of a more horrifying possibility, but the image of her lying on the ground, her lifeless body being drummed by the rain, did not leave his mind.

Rhys had cursed himself for his behavior early in the day. He had cursed himself for not checking on her, for not telling her that he was not angry with her. He had cursed himself for not knowing who his wife would turn to in her darkest hour.

He rode toward the village at a sedate pace. He didn't want to pass Isabel if he hurried too much, but he impatiently clenched his hands on the reins because he wanted to find her as soon as he could.

Chapter 25

It seemed like an eternity passed as he scoured the road with no luck. The lightning lit the sky just then, illuminating the lone figure walking down the road toward him.

He jumped off the horse, almost falling as he slid against the wet ground and ran toward her. She looked up just then and peered under her bonnet, and Rhys's heart soared.

Isabel.

He dashed toward her and took her by her shoulders. Her bonnet was soaked, and her skirts were not only wet but covered with mud. She was wearing a strange cloak, which was also soaked to the brim. Her teeth chattered, and her lips trembled as she watched him with her wide, beautiful, blue eyes.

"Where in the devil have you been?" Rhys roared over the sound of the rain.

"I-I..."

Rhys did not let her finish. Instead, he crushed her against his body, relief coursing through his veins. She was here. She was in his arms.

Her tiny body nestled against his, her bonnet jabbing into his neck. Rhys untied the ribbons under her chin and threw the bonnet into the dirt.

Isabel blinked up at him.

"It was getting in the way," Rhys croaked. "I shall buy a new one. But let us get home now."

Isabel nodded but didn't make a move.

"Do you hear me?" Rhys's concern grew as she didn't answer.

"I am sorry," she finally said.

"Not to worry, darling. We shall get home, and everything will be well."

"No." She shook her head. "I am sorry for failing your trust, failing Millicent." Her lips trembled as she spoke, and he wasn't certain if she was crying or simply freezing cold.

It didn't matter. None of it mattered.

He bent down and hauled her into his arms. "How about we talk about all of it when we get home?"

She pressed her face against his cheek like a cat looking for more contact and warmth. Rhys turned his head and kissed her forehead.

He hoisted Isabel up onto the saddle and mounted the horse behind her. Isabel trembled in his arms, and Rhys cursed. He urged the horse into a canter as he didn't want the animal to throw them too.

Rhys took off his hat and covered Isabel's head with it.

"What happened?" he asked as they started up toward the house.

Isabel burrowed herself closer to his chest. "I went to visit my friend, Lilian. She was g-giving birth and time got away from me. But I couldn't stay there the night, so I left."

"In the storm?" Rhys growled. How did those people let Isabel leave?

Isabel nodded. "They didn't want to let me go, but I insisted. Her husband gave me his cloak, so I wouldn't freeze."

"You should have stayed inside."

"I didn't want to miss Millie's bedtime… Did I miss her bedtime?"

"No, darling," Rhys lied.

"But then my horse got scared by the thunder and threw me," she continued, her voice trembling.

Rhys nodded. "How long have you been out in the rain?"

"Not long."

Chapter 25

Rhys tightened his arms around her and prayed that she was not lying.

* * *

The relief that spread through Isabel's body when she saw the rider on the road and realized it was Rhys was a living, breathing entity. Her entire body lit with fire, and she wanted to run to him, embrace him, kiss him, and beg for forgiveness.

However, her limbs were weighted down by wet, heavy clothing, and her face had gone numb from the cold. So the most she could do was say she was sorry.

When Rhys hoisted her onto the horse and embraced her, she finally relaxed. She was home.

It was a foolish endeavor indeed to set out on the road in such weather. But in her defense, when she'd left Lilian's house, the rain had only been drizzling, and the ground was not as slippery. She had hoped to get home before the deluge started.

But to her utter aggravation, her horse threw her just a few minutes after she had started her journey.

She should have turned back then. She should have gone back to Lilian's house, had a cup of tea by the fire, and waited for morning to come and the sky to clear before she attempted her journey back home.

But Isabel was stubborn. And she knew that Millicent waited for her and worried about her. So instead of turning back, she'd marched on forward.

A chill coursed through her, and she shuddered. Rhys cursed above her head and tightened his arms around her.

"Hold on to me," he shouted over the rain. "I shall speed up the horse. Need to get you to the fire as quickly as possible."

Isabel nodded against his chest and hugged her body to his.

Rhys's clothing was just as wet and cold as hers. But his neck was bare—he wasn't wearing a cravat—so Isabel burrowed her face closer to his warm skin.

He smelled of rain, wet ground, and beneath it, all was his own masculine scent. Isabel did not realize how much she'd gotten used to this scent. It was dear to her. She associated it with safety and comfort, probably because they had shared a bed for a few nights, and now she associated his scent with her room, her bed.

Isabel slid her hands under his cloak, looking for more warmth. Rhys's arm tightened around her as he urged the horse into a gallop.

A few moments later, they reached their house. The door opened instantly, the butler and the groom rushing out into the rain.

Rhys jumped off the horse and handed the reins to the groom. "Monroe! Tell Mrs. Ainsworth to prepare a kettle of tea and bring as many blankets as she can find to Lady Isabel's room." He turned to Isabel. "Come."

She slid down the horse and into his arms. Rhys kissed her forehead as she hit the ground, then scooped her up into his arms again.

"I can walk, Rhys," she protested, but he didn't even miss a beat.

"If you think I am letting you out of my arms, you are mad," he grumbled under his breath.

Isabel relaxed against him. The servants started bustling around them, and Isabel felt ashamed she'd caused such a ruckus in the middle of the night.

Chapter 25

Rhys walked into her room and sat her down on the chair by the hearth. Isabel shivered pleasantly as the warmth of the fire chased the chills away.

Rhys took off his cloak and crouched before her. He took her leg by the ankle, and Isabel wrenched it away.

"What are you doing?"

Rhys reached for her leg again and tightened his fingers around her calf. "Sit still."

He carefully took off her boots and frowned as he saw that her stockings were soaked through. Just then, Anthea bustled in with a bundle of blankets.

"Anthea." Rhys turned to her. "Please take out a fresh pair of stockings, a couple of towels, and a chemise for her ladyship. And then bring a basin with hot water, please."

"Just a moment, my lord."

As Anthea rushed to do as she was asked, Isabel looked at her husband. "Thank you for taking care of me, but I can fare on my own from here."

Rhys ignored her, sinking his hands under her skirts and untying her garters. The ticklish feeling at her thighs had her clench her knees together. "Truly, this is unnecessary," she tried again.

Rhys scowled at her. "My dear wife," he said between his teeth as he rolled down one stocking. "I think you fared quite enough for one day. Now let me lend you a hand."

He rolled down another stocking and glowered at the wet piece of cloth.

"That's not fair. Just because I got caught in the rain—"

Rhys sat up on his knees, took Isabel's face between his palms, and kissed her soundly. Isabel went limp in his arms as Rhys swept his tongue against her mouth.

He let go of her suddenly, and Isabel had to catch herself lest she fell. She frowned at him. "If you think that your kisses are some form of a—"

She earned herself another kiss. More urgent now as Rhys's hands roamed her body. He undid the ties around her neck and took her cloak off. "I am your husband. And you shall do as I say."

Isabel frowned again. Had he just kissed her so he could do whatever he wanted without her protesting?

Anthea placed all the items that Rhys required by the feet of the chair. She blushed as she scurried away, and Isabel realized that she'd seen Rhys kissing her!

Isabel's cheeks heated from embarrassment.

"Stand up," Rhys instructed as he tugged on her arms. They both stood, and Rhys started working on releasing her from her skirts.

"Rhys, Anthea could help with my clothing. You don't have to—"

Isabel saw the annoyance in Rhys's face before he kissed her again. This time he swept his tongue inside her mouth, sending tingles along her spine. Isabel stood on tiptoes and wrapped her arms around his neck.

When Rhys finally raised his head, they were both breathing heavily.

"Turn around," Rhys whispered.

He put his hands on her shoulders and helped her do just that. Then, he started working on her buttons.

"You are not listening to me at all," Isabel grumbled. "I am trying to raise my concerns. I am trying to speak to you like a rational human being, and you—"

She felt a rip before the gown fell in a heap to the floor.

Chapter 25

Isabel carefully turned toward him, in nothing but her unmentionables, her eyes wide. "Did you just rip my gown?"

Rhys shrugged. "It was ruined anyway. The buttons won't give way, and it was soaked through."

She looked down at herself and gasped in horror. Her gown truly was soaked through to her chemise, which now proudly displayed her nipples in all their glory. Isabel covered her breasts with her arms. She was ready to cry from the embarrassment.

Rhys let out a weary sigh. He leaned down and placed his forehead against Isabel's. "I am sorry, darling," he said in a hoarse whisper. "I just want to get you dry as soon as possible. I can't let you catch ill because of me. Turn around and let me undo your stays. Then you can get dressed on your own."

Isabel was so taken aback by the gentleness mixed with anguish in his voice that she turned around without saying a word.

He took off her stays and stepped away from her. Isabel looked at him over her shoulder. "Please, turn away."

Rhys turned toward the hearth, and Isabel started ridding herself of the wet clothing. She took off her underskirts before the meaning of his words finally caught up with her.

"What do you mean because of you?" She slid her chemise off her shoulders. She was completely naked now, so she looked over her shoulder to make sure Rhys wasn't peeking at her. "None of it is your fault."

Rhys ran a hand through his hair, his back still turned to her. "How can you say that?"

Isabel put on a fresh chemise and turned fully toward him. "What exactly are you to blame for?"

Rhys rounded on her. "Everything! None of this would

have happened if I had just controlled my temper and not acted like a complete arse this morning! And if I—if I paid more attention to who I hire, perhaps that wouldn't have happened either." He said the last an octave lower.

Isabel shook her head. "You were right to be angry with me," she said quietly.

Rhys approached her and sat her back down on the chair. "I wasn't. Now let me clean you up to atone for my sins."

He poured hot water into a basin, hiked up Isabel's skirts, and proceeded to wash her feet and calves.

Isabel picked up one towel off the floor and started drying her hair. "You were quite rude," she said with a smile. "I will not deny that."

Rhys winced.

"But you were right. It was all my fault."

"No, it wasn't." Rhys shook his head. "The truth is… The truth is I blamed myself. I was too angry because… because"—he took a deep breath, for it seemed to be impossible for him to say the words—"this is not the first time something like this had happened."

Isabel paused. "What happened?"

Rhys grimaced. He lathered his hands with soap and massaged her calves, his full attention concentrated on the task.

Isabel reached down and nudged his chin with her fingers, so he would meet her eyes. "Tell me."

Rhys swallowed. He rinsed the soap off her legs and dried her with the towels in silence. Then he picked her up and deposited her onto the bed. He covered her with blankets and paced away from her.

He stood with her back to her, his stance rigid as he spoke,

Chapter 25

"Have you heard a rumor about me?"

Isabel frowned. *What is he talking about?*

He turned to her, his gaze heated. "The one that says I murdered my wife."

Chapter 26

The guilty look on Isabel's face said everything Rhys needed to know. She knew.

She'd heard about the rumor but decided not to speak to him about it for one reason or another.

It hurt.

For some unknown reason, it hurt that she had not brought up this subject. Perhaps she was trying to spare his feelings because she had married him anyway. But his rational mind refused to step in.

"I never believed it," she said, then looked down. "Well, maybe only for a moment."

Rhys let out a hoarse chuckle. "You weren't far from the truth."

Her head shot up, and her mouth fell open.

"I was very young when we married," he said and started pacing. "I had a new responsibility upon my shoulders, a responsibility I wasn't prepared for. And on top of that, I had a young, beautiful wife.

Chapter 26

"She wasn't from nobility, you see. She was a vicar's daughter. So we both were clueless about the weight on our shoulders." He shook his head. "She thought that ladies of the house lounged about all day sipping tea and exchanging gossip. I am half-convinced that was the only reason she ever married me. Because now I see as clear as day that she never loved me."

"But you loved her?"

Rhys raised his head. He'd almost forgotten he was not alone in the room. He nodded. "I thought I did. It is hard to say for certain because of what followed, but at the time, I thought I did."

"What happened?"

Rhys looked into the fire, his gaze blurring. "It took me time to learn of my responsibilities as a landowner. Too much time. I was always busy, always away. My bride grew restless. We had difficulties conceiving, and it just added pressure on our relationship.

"We started arguing every day. Abigail—that was her name—became cold and distant. When she finally started increasing, I thought things would get better, but they didn't. She became more and more irritable. But I wasn't much better either. I was rude, arrogant, bad-tempered—"

"I can't imagine," Isabel said with a smile in her voice, but Rhys didn't find it amusing.

"One night after a huge argument, she ran off, and in a fit of rage, I left that night, too." He cleared his throat. "We both left Millicent alone in the house."

Isabel sat up. "Surely she wasn't alone? Servants must have been with her."

Rhys nodded. "Yes. Abigail had hired a nursemaid for

Millie." He swallowed. "That woman slapped my daughter for every little infraction."

Isabel covered her face with her hands.

"I didn't know. Nobody knew until Mrs. Ainsworth walked in on it happening just like you did. But Millie was just a babe back then." He shook his head, tears of frustration prickling at the back of his eyes. "When I returned a few weeks later, my wife was still gone. In her place was a note, which said that she would not be coming back. And as if that wasn't bad enough, Mrs. Ainsworth told me why she had dismissed the nursemaid. She had feared I would chastise her for letting go of a servant without my approval. Apparently, Abigail was not fond of people disobeying her orders no matter how ridiculous or harmful."

"How old was Millicent?" Isabel asked, her voice small.

"A little over two years old."

"She was just a babe!" Isabel's eyes watered, and her face was red from anger.

Rhys nodded. "She had bruises on her little body. I didn't see them, but Mrs. Ainsworth told me that later. But I vowed from that moment on that I would never let Millicent out of my sight. And I haven't since…."

Isabel grimaced. "Until you trusted me to find a proper governess."

"It's not your fault. I should have been there—"

"That is not rational! You cannot possibly guard Millicent her entire life. But I was in the house, I—" Her voice broke.

There was a beat of silence as Isabel wiped her tears away, and Rhys just stood there staring at his crying wife. He'd been holding on to that pain and anger for so long, it was good to let it out.

Chapter 26

"She had other governesses after that," he said. "But the moment Millie mentioned she didn't like them, or if she looked at them with her adorable frowning little brows, I dismissed them immediately."

Isabel looked away. "Perhaps that was the right decision. My friend told me that children know a kind heart when they see it. I wish I had listened to Millie earlier."

Rhys knew how it felt to have the babe suffer because of something he'd done, and he didn't want Isabel to feel this way. "We both should have. And I hope we both will in the future."

Isabel took a deep breath. "But what of rumors about your wife?"

Rhys let out a deep sigh. "The letter came a few weeks after the incident. It said that the ship my wife had been on had sunk. There were no survivors.

"So, you see, in a way, the gossip is right. I drove my wife away with my surly moods, and she died. I then left my babe all alone, and she suffered... I have been the reason for all the misfortunes in the lives of the people I cared about. And if something had happened to you tonight—" His voice broke.

Isabel scrambled from the bed and approached him slowly as if he were a spooked animal. "Nothing happened to me," she said and put her palm against his cheek.

Rhys leaned into her touch, staring into her solemn blue eyes. "But I drove you away."

"You didn't. I would never leave you or Millicent. Not of my own free will." She stepped closer to him and snaked her arms around his waist. Rhys was so startled he didn't even respond. He just stood there with his arms limp by his sides as she hugged her body to his.

"Now, can we go see Millicent? I want to see her. I missed her so much."

Isabel's words thawed Rhys's frozen heart. He wrapped his arms around her and held her tightly against his heart. How could a woman who had met his daughter a few weeks ago care about her more than her own mother?

He disengaged Isabel's arms from his body and took her hand in his. "Yes, let's go."

* * *

Isabel walked through the dark corridor, her hand in her husband's larger one. His heat seemed to travel through their adjoined fingers and spread through her body.

The fact that he had told her about his first wife, confessed to his sins, and relived the painful memories about Millicent told her something very important.

He cared about her. He didn't want to lose her the way he'd lost his first wife. And that thought gave her wings.

Yes, he was surly and rude at times, but she was already used to the constant frown on his face. And perhaps if they agreed to be frank and open with each other, they could give one another more reasons to smile. Perhaps in time, they could become the happy family she had dreamed about as a child.

They reached Millicent's room and walked inside.

Millie lay in her little cot by the window. The storm still raged outside, but she did not seem to be bothered by it at all.

Isabel smiled. She was a resilient little child.

Isabel would make certain to always protect her from everything wicked in this world. As Isabel stepped inside,

Chapter 26

Button—who was lying at the foot of the bed—roused and let out an audible yawn.

Millie shifted in her bed and opened her eyes. "Isabel!" She shot up in bed, and Isabel dashed to her side.

Isabel sat on the bed and hugged Millicent's little body to hers. Button let out a bark and then settled back at Isabel's feet.

"Where have you been?" Millicent asked against Isabel's chest.

Isabel smiled. "I was with a friend, witnessing the miracle of birth."

"You were? Truly? Was it interesting?"

The flurry of questions out of Millicent's mouth gave Isabel comfort.

She thought awhile, remembering all the blood and the screams she'd witnessed that day. "It was… beautiful," she lied.

Well, the result had been beautiful, but the birthing process not so much. However, Millie was too young to know the details.

"Will you tell me about it?"

Isabel chuckled. "Perhaps on the morrow. It is late now. You should be sleeping."

"I was waiting for you," Millicent pouted.

Isabel caressed the top of her head, her heart swelling. "Well, now that I am here, you can sleep again."

"Will you sing me a song?"

Isabel threw a glance at her husband, who still stood at the doorway. "Of course, my dear."

Millie disengaged from Isabel and climbed back into bed. Isabel tucked her in, kissed her forehead, and started a lullaby.

By the time Isabel finished her song, both Millie and Button were fast asleep.

She stood and walked toward her husband. She ran her hands over her arms, shivering once more. She'd only managed to throw a dressing gown over her chemise when she had walked out of her room, and it was clearly not enough.

"You have a beautiful voice," Rhys said as he escorted her out of the nursery.

Isabel smiled. "I prefer it when you sing."

Rhys chuckled. "Perhaps I can tuck you in tonight."

Isabel glanced at him, startled. Playful fire lit behind his eyes. She opened her mouth to retort, and… sneezed instead.

Rhys frowned down at her. "You are cold," he said, then touched his fingers to her cheek.

Isabel shrugged. "This corridor is not well heated."

Rhys shook his head. "Let's get you back into bed."

When they reached Isabel's room, Rhys put his words to action and tucked Isabel in so that only her head peeked out of the covers.

Mrs. Ainsworth entered just then with a bowl of soup.

As she left, Isabel regarded the bowl and frowned. "How am I to eat my soup when my hands are weighed down by blankets?"

Rhys chuckled. "Not to worry. Your husband will feed you."

True to his word, he took a spoonful of soup and brought it to her lips. Isabel swallowed then sputtered a laugh. "It is rather uncomfortable eating soup when someone is feeding you."

Rhys grunted. "You shall have to get used to it."

* * *

Chapter 26

Rhys stared at the canopy above the bed a few minutes later, listening to the even staccato of raindrops beating against the window. His wife kept shifting in bed, unable to find a comfortable position.

She finally turned toward him. "Rhys?"

He grunted.

"Are you sleeping?"

Rhys let out a chuckle. "What if I say yes?"

Isabel smiled. "I won't believe you."

He turned toward her. "What's the matter?"

"I am still cold... Can you...? Perhaps if you hold me...."

Rhys hid his smile and shifted toward her. He wrapped her in his arms, her back to him, his one hand running over her body in an attempt to warm her.

She shivered instead.

"Damn. You *are* cold. Tuck your feet between my legs."

"Did you think I was lying?" Isabel let out a chuckle but did as he asked. Even through his nightshirt, he felt that her feet were like a block of ice. Why was it taking her so long to warm up?

He ran his hands over her arms and legs, and she sighed contentedly. "Do it again."

Rhys chuckled and rubbed the length of her legs and body. She started warming up, and in turn, he started getting hot.

Damn his body's response. She was suffering from the cold, but his foolish body did not seem to care. His cock stood at attention as his entire being tensed.

Isabel chose that exact moment to lean against him, her warm bottom cradling his aching erection. Rhys gritted his teeth. That was torture.

He slowly inched away from her, and Isabel turned toward

him. "What?" She blinked at him, all innocence.

"I think you're warmed up enough," he croaked.

Isabel's lips turned down in a pout. "My hands are still cold, see?"

To demonstrate, she pressed her palm against his cheek.

Her touch was warm against his skin. What was she doing?

"They seem warm to me," Rhys said, his voice hoarse.

"Perhaps if you kissed me…."

Rhys let out a hoarse chuckle. "Are you trying to seduce me, my dear wife?"

Isabel's cheeks turned dark red in the dimly lit room. "And what if I am?"

Her boldness was both arousing and unsettling. He knew she wasn't a virgin. He'd caught her with Stanhope all those years ago in the act. Perhaps she'd had more lovers since. He had no way to know, and he wasn't about to ask.

On the other hand, Rhys had only had one lover—his former wife. And his experience hadn't exactly given him confidence in his prowess. After all, his first wife had run off with her lover after months of cuckolding him.

Perhaps he was still a naive young boy deep in his heart, but he wanted his first time with Isabel to be special, magical.

But she pressed her body to his, and all his worries, intentions, and thoughts suddenly disappeared.

Rhys dipped his head and took her mouth in a sensual kiss. Isabel moaned into his mouth and raised her hips, demanding more contact. Her hand went to cradle his head, then her fingers sifted through his locks.

Rhys groaned in answer. His hand caressed her back, then traveled down to her soft and ripe bottom. He squeezed it in his hand, and Isabel gasped.

Chapter 26

Rhys rolled her onto her back, his hardened cock pointing at her belly. He kissed her jaw, her neck...

Suddenly, Isabel wretched away and... sneezed into a pillow. She covered her face with her hands, then buried her face further into the pillow, her shoulders shaking in laughter.

Rhys chuckled, then rubbed her shoulders.

"How romantic," Isabel said between fits of giggles, her voice smothered by the pillow.

"Perhaps we shouldn't do this today." Rhys's voice was still thick with passion.

Isabel shook her head. "Oh, but I just started getting warmed up."

Rhys weaved his arm around her waist and turned her on her side, hugging her, her back to his front.

"We have all the time," he said and kissed her hair. "No need to rush. Now sleep."

Chapter 27

Rhys woke up to the familiar feeling of being hugged by his wife. One leg was thrown over his thighs, and her nightgown had hiked up, baring the view of her delectable calves. Her hand was on his chest, and her head was comfortably resting just under his collarbone. Her hair was strewn about the pillow in beautiful waves, her nightcap nowhere to be seen.

And if this wasn't the most perfect image to wake up to, he didn't know what was.

Unfortunately, her heat, the feel of her soft curves, and the scent of her hair enticed him so much he wanted to throw her on her back, push her knees apart, and pound himself into her. As it was, his loins were hard and pulsing with need.

Rhys tried to slowly slide out from beneath her, but she stirred, her fingers scraping his chest through the nightshirt.

Rhys stifled the urge to groan. Lord, was his wife enticing.

His imagination got away from him as he thought about undressing her slowly, pulling down her cotton nightgown,

Chapter 27

uncovering her marble-white skin, and touching her soft breasts. He wished he could toss up her skirts and have her right there in daylight.

But his wife deserved more than such animal treatment. She deserved dim lights and the modesty of her nightclothes, especially for their first time. Perhaps later, she would be amenable to doing this in daylight.

He remembered the day he'd caught her with Stanhope out in the open and in the light of day! Rhys grimaced.

He wasn't an inconsiderate boor like the earl. He would treat his wife with the respect she was due. But what if she didn't want that respect accorded to her? She'd acted brazenly enough last night.

Rhys knew that clandestine lovers and married couples acted differently in bed. His first wife, Abigail, had been a delicate flower in his arms. She had cried the first few times they shared a bed, although he had tried to be as gentle with her as he could.

As months went by, Abigail demanded more reprieve from Rhys but went to seek fulfillment elsewhere. By the second year of their marriage, she'd barely let Rhys touch her.

Passion was not something that had existed in their marriage for long, and Rhys was afraid the same thing would happen to him and Isabel.

And he would do anything to avoid that inevitability. Because as much as he'd been hurt when Abigail left him, he didn't think he'd survive if Isabel did.

Isabel stirred and looked up at him just then. She smiled and stretched, before realizing that she was lying on top of him, with her legs bared and her rump jutting out. She smiled shyly and hid her limbs under the covers.

"How do you feel?" Rhys asked and turned toward her.

"I feel good," she said with a smile.

"You are not coming down with a cold?"

He reached out his hand and touched her cheek. It was nice and warm, but there was no fever. *Good.* So last night hadn't affected her health.

"No." She smiled, her eyes glinting with mischief. Her cheeks were flushed, and her hair disheveled. Rhys couldn't help it; he leaned down and kissed her. Her hand immediately went to cradle his cheek.

Rhys rolled over her, his knee landing between her legs, his cock pressing against her thigh. He was ready to throw away his resolve of treating her like a lady. He was ready to give up on his earlier conviction to treat her with the respect due to his wife.

Damn respect when she was so warm and open before him. He wanted to sink himself inside her heat and curse his resolutions.

There was a knock on the door.

Rhys cursed and rolled off Isabel. His engorged length pulsed with need, and he gritted his teeth.

"Just a moment!" he barked.

Isabel immediately burrowed herself under the covers, her cheeks turning a deeper hue of red. Rhys mourned the loss of her warmth and the sight of her bare skin. Damn his carnal appetites.

I really need to control myself.

He adjusted his nightshirt, stalked to the door, and peeked out.

The butler tried to hide a smile upon seeing his master answering his mistress's door but was unsuccessful.

Chapter 27

"What's wrong, Monroe?" Rhys barked.

"We have a guest, my lord."

At this hour? Rhys raised a brow. "A guest?"

"Yes, and he insisted upon seeing her ladyship right away."

"Insisted, you say? Who is this insolent fellow?" A gentleman to see his wife? Rhys bristled in indignation.

"Viscount Gage, my lord."

Rhys groaned inwardly. "Thank you, Monroe. Lead him to one of the drawing rooms. Her ladyship will be down shortly."

As the butler bowed out, Rhys closed the door and leaned his back against it.

Isabel sat up in bed, still clutching the covers to her chin. "What's wrong?"

"Your brother," Rhys said and ran his fingers through his hair. "Viscount Gage is here for a visit."

* * *

Isabel dressed hastily with the help of her maid while Rhys went to check on Millicent. He didn't want her rushing into the breakfast room with Button while guests were in residence. Isabel tried to assure him that her brother was not that kind of a guest, but he just scoffed, kissed her forehead, and went up to the nursery.

With everything going on, Isabel had almost forgotten about Rhys's apparent dislike of her family. She had hoped that would have passed with all the revelations they had shared. And perhaps it had, but there was still residue, and Isabel was certain that existed not only on Rhys's side.

Once Anthea was done with her hair, Isabel hurried down

the stairs and into the blue drawing room, where her brother was waiting for her.

Richard, Viscount Gage, stood with his back to her, his hands clasped behind him, looking out the window.

"Richard," Isabel said with a smile.

He turned, a scowl on his face. "You look healthy enough," he said, raking her body with his gaze.

"Of course, I am healthy." Isabel stepped farther into the room. "Although I was hoping for a proper greeting."

"Apologies, my sister." Richard walked toward her, took both her hands in his, and kissed her on the cheek. "You look beautiful."

"Why, thank you!" She sank into a mock curtsy. "What brings you here one week before the start of the house party?"

Isabel motioned toward the chairs by the hearth. Richard moved to sit, but his frown didn't leave his face.

"Let's just say I heard some disturbing information about your stay here," he said as he settled into a chair.

Now it was Isabel's turn to frown. "What kind of disturbing information?"

"That you are being mistreated." Richard steepled his fingers over his chest, his gaze intent.

Isabel narrowed her eyes on him. "Who did you hear it from?"

"So you *are* being mistreated?" He sprung forward, his forehead furrowed in a scowl.

"You did not answer my question," Isabel said calmly.

"Neither did you."

Isabel rolled her eyes. "Tell me what you heard, and I shall tell you whether it is true."

"Very well," Richard snapped. "I heard that your servants

Chapter 27

disliked you."

It was true, they had in the past. But what did that have to do with why Richard was here? "I also heard," Richard continued, "that you rolled your ankle. Which was supposedly an accident, but I am not so sure."

Isabel stifled a chuckle. "You think someone twisted my ankle on purpose?"

He shrugged. "Pushed you, maybe?"

Isabel pursed her lips. "What else did you hear?"

"That you had an argument with your husband yesterday so severe that you left the house with a basket of food on horseback."

Isabel shot up, forcing Richard to stand also. "You've been spying on me?"

"Well, of course, I've been spying on you! Do you think I would just let you go to the lair of a beast alone and unprotected? No way."

The meddlesome man wasn't even apologetic about it.

She narrowed her eyes on him. "And how did you hear about it so quickly?"

"I was in Bedford visiting Sam when I received—" Richard clamped his mouth shut, but it was too late.

Isabel's chest heaved, but she forced herself to calm down. "Who told you?"

"Does it matter?" Richard crossed his arms over his chest.

"It was James, wasn't it? That little traitor!"

"James is not the issue! Your husband is!"

Of course, that was the exact moment her husband decided to appear at the door. Isabel groaned.

"Good morning, Lord Gage," he snapped. "To what do we owe the pleasure of you gracing our house with your presence and insulting me behind my back?"

"As you can attest, you are the one who is behind my back."

Isabel fell into the chair with a groan. Now she had to deal with two obstinate men, as if one was not enough. Rhys stalked into the room and stood behind Isabel's chair. He grazed the skin of her arm, just below her sleeve, and Isabel looked up with a smile. He winked at her before training his gaze on her brother.

Gage was watching them with narrowed eyes. "I thought you didn't like each other."

Isabel shrugged. "I changed my mind."

She turned toward her husband and tugged on his sleeve.

He looked at her, puzzled. "I did not change my mind. I always liked you."

"You liar." Isabel swatted at his arm, but he caught her hand and kissed her knuckles.

"Lord, give me strength!" Richard shook his head and scrubbed his face with his hand. "I think I need coffee or whisky. Or both."

"I have that in my study," Rhys offered.

"Splendid!" Isabel shot up from the chair. "You two can discuss your gentlemanly business in your study, and I need to go to the village and check on my friend. I shall take Millie with me if you don't mind. I think she'll enjoy seeing a tiny babe."

Isabel was glad to escape the company of the two stubborn men. She just hoped they wouldn't shoot each other in her absence.

"You'll have to take Button, too," Rhys reminded her.

Isabel wrinkled her nose. "I'll have James look after him for me," she said and beamed at her brother.

Chapter 27

* * *

Isabel returned to the house a few hours later. Millicent had a great time playing with the village children while Isabel conversed with Lilian, who was already bustling around the house as if nothing had happened.

Millicent turned out not to be interested in the small babe. She held her for a moment, then handed her back to Isabel and dashed outdoors to play with Button and the other children her age.

Now she bounced around the carriage, telling Isabel everything she had done and seen. As the carriage rolled into the driveway, Isabel noted another carriage rolling away. Someone must have disembarked.

More guests? Or more worried family members?

She entered the hall, with Button pushing at her side and running in ahead of her, barking.

"Button, no!" A soft but firm feminine voice brought Button to a sudden halt.

Isabel opened her mouth in surprise. That treacherous fiend! He didn't listen to her commands, but he listened to... She looked up, and her face split in a smile. "Evie!" She went to embrace the duchess, then threw a side glance at her dog. "How did you do that? I can't seem to make him do anything."

Button sat at Evie's feet, happily wagging his tail. Millicent ran up to the duchess then and bobbed an uncoordinated curtsy.

Evie reciprocated, gracefully sinking to the floor. "My lady," she said with a bright smile, and Millicent giggled.

Had Millie just curtsied? On her own accord and without any reminders? Isabel's mouth fell open, and she couldn't quite close it before Evie's husband, the Viscount St. Clare, appeared behind his wife. He took off his hat and bowed with a flourish. "My ladies."

He put his hand on the small of Evie's back and smiled down at her.

Isabel sighed inwardly. That man was very much in love with his duchess.

Millicent turned her face toward Isabel and exclaimed with unconcealed awe, "She's a duchess!"

"Yes, she is." Isabel turned to her guests. "Have you just arrived? I think I saw your carriage roll away."

"Yes, we just stepped into the hall a moment before you did." Evie was smiling, but Isabel could see clear lines of fatigue on her face. And she looked slightly green in the face.

"A lovely coincidence. But you must be tired. Let me show you to your rooms!"

"If you excuse me, I shall go find Vane," St. Claire said. Then he turned to Evie. "You don't mind settling in by yourself, do you?"

"I prefer it." Evie grinned, then added at his pouting grimace, "I am rather tired, and I know you wouldn't let me rest."

"I sure wouldn't," St. Claire said in a low voice, placed a quick kiss on her cheek, bowed to Isabel and Millie, and sauntered away.

Evie turned to Isabel. "Shall we?"

Isabel led the way, Evie and Millicent following behind, and the dog closed the procession. Millicent chattered happily, telling Evie everything about her life, and Isabel couldn't help but feel jealous.

That little girl had barely said a word to her for the first

Chapter 27

few weeks of their acquaintance, yet she barely paused in her narrative to the duchess. More than that, she listened to Evie and tried to parody her in the way she walked and talked.

Even the blasted dog, who was adamant about killing Isabel, was enamored with the duchess.

They approached one of the guest rooms, and Isabel opened the door. "Welcome, Your Grace."

Evie chuckled and entered the room. She looked around in awe. "This is beautiful."

"I helped decorate," Millie said proudly. Which was true. She'd helped pick out the paintings and the flowers for the surfaces.

"You are going to be an exemplary hostess one day," Evie complimented her.

Millie beamed at first, then shyly looked away and scratched behind Button's ears.

"You must be fatigued after the journey, and I know how you feel about carriages, so I shall leave you to rest," Isabel said.

"Thank you. I wish to speak with you as soon as possible, but I wouldn't be very good company at the moment."

Isabel smiled. "I understand."

"Do we have to go, too?" Millie pouted.

"I'd say Button is the first who needs to leave," Isabel answered.

Evie sank into a deep curtsy. "It was a pleasure to see you again, my lady."

Millie tried to parody her and nearly toppled over. Isabel grabbed her by the shoulder to prevent her undignified fall. Millie chuckled and scurried away with her dog.

"Before I turn in and rest, tell me this. Is everything well with you?" Evie asked.

"Yes," Isabel answered emphatically. "And as much as I am happy to see you—I mean, I would love to have you all to myself a few days before the house party—why did you arrive early?"

Evie raised a brow. "Is that a surprise?"

"Well—" Now Isabel was confused. Had she asked the duchess to arrive earlier?

Evie crossed her arms over her chest. "When was the last time you sent me your *daily* letter?"

"Oh!" Isabel grimaced. With everything going on in the household, she had completely forgotten. She hadn't sent a single letter to anyone since the incident with the governess.

"I was worried something had happened to you, although Gabriel just rolled his eyes. But he couldn't deny me the trip a few days early."

"I am so sorry I caused you to worry."

"No matter." Evie placed a hand on her abdomen and took a deep breath. She was obviously exhausted. "But I received a letter from Sam, who said she wanted to arrive early as well. But she wanted it to be a surprise. I am sorry I ruined it."

Isabel chuckled. "I shall act surprised. Now, I shall leave you to rest. Whenever you are ready, I shall be glad to exchange gossip."

Chapter 28

Evie did not emerge from her chamber all day. St. Clare had announced that she was under the weather and would not be gracing them with her presence until morning.

Isabel understood that to mean that Evie was still suffering from the effects of the journey and hoped the rest would do her good.

Millie pouted all through supper about the fact that the duchess hadn't joined them. But then she learned that she wasn't allowed to join the adults for dinner during the house party, and her pouting was raised to another level.

She only stopped sulking long enough to ask both Rhys and Isabel to sing to her before bed. And Isabel took it as a sign that she had gotten over the betrayal of being excluded from the meals during the party.

Isabel was glad that Millie was easy to pout and just as easy to forgive. That gave Isabel room to make mistakes, of which she was certain to make plenty. Raising a six-year-old child was not something she'd ever thought she'd have to do. And she thanked the stars that the girl she had to raise was Millicent.

After tucking Millie to bed, Isabel and Rhys made their way to their respective chambers. Isabel had changed for bed and settled under the covers when her husband entered the room.

"Do you know," he said, as he approached the bed, "that the paint in my room has dried?"

Isabel smiled. "When did that happen?"

"I have no idea." Rhys climbed onto the bed and kissed her on her mouth before settling under the covers. "I keep going there every day to change, but I only just noticed that the windows are closed, and the hearth is blazing."

Isabel hid her smile. His room was once more a comfortable place of habitat, and still, he chose to spend the night with her.

He doused the candles and rolled on top of her. He kissed her slowly, and Isabel let out a deep sigh. Would they finally start their conjugal duty? Her body hummed in excitement.

Last night, when he'd turned away from her, she had worried that he simply didn't want to bed her, although his body had been hard, and she had felt the evidence of his desire against her belly.

Today, he kissed her hungrily, and his hands roamed her body, greedily gathering her against him.

She felt wanted, needed, and it was the best feeling in the world. But it had been so long since she had been intimate with a man. And the only time she was, that man had turned away from her a few days later. She hoped it wouldn't happen with Rhys, but how did she ensure it?

What was that Evie had told her?

Chapter 28

Let yourself enjoy his kisses and touches... No matter how indecent.

Well, perhaps Isabel was wanton because she didn't find anything indecent in what Rhys was doing to her.

Rhys kissed her deeply now, his tongue playing at the corners of her mouth. The taste of him dulled her senses, and all her previous worries disappeared. She was so consumed by their kiss that she didn't notice that he'd raised the skirts of her shift. He widened her knees and settled in the cradle of her thighs.

He kept kissing her as he placed the tip of his manhood at the center of her femininity, and Isabel gasped. His hot shaft jolted and pushed at her center, demanding entrance. Isabel closed her eyes and rolled her hips, wanting him inside her.

Rhys moved his hips, slowly and gently invading her heat. Isabel felt the stretching and widened her legs to better accommodate him. Rhys clenched his teeth and placed his hands on either side of her head.

"Ah, darling. You feel too good," he croaked out.

"Kiss me, Rhys," Isabel pleaded.

With a groan, he covered her mouth with his, nibbling on her lips, licking at the corners of her mouth as he rocked and seated himself inside her in one thrust. Isabel's eyes opened wide, and she gasped.

"Does it hurt?" Rhys held himself still, his face a grimace of pain.

He was hot and hard inside her, filling her deliciously. It did not hurt. On the contrary, being completely joined with him was truly the best feeling in the world.

"No," she said, her voice breathless. "Does it hurt you?"

Beads of sweat covered Rhys's forehead, and he looked truly

pained. But he shook his head. "Too good."

Rhys withdrew slightly and thrust again, the bed shaking with the force. Isabel let out a moan from the contact.

"Hold on to me," he whispered.

Isabel wrapped her arms and legs around him, holding him closer to her. As he thrust again, Isabel curled her fingers into his nightshirt.

Rhys peppered kisses onto her cheeks, her chin, before thrusting again.

Every time he seated himself inside her, he hit a spot in her body that made her jolt and leap in pleasure. If she could just savor that feeling—

He thrust again, and Isabel whimpered.

"I'm sorry, love. I can't hold on."

What? No! Don't let it end! Isabel wanted to shout her protestations, but he thrust in again, and all she could do was call out his name.

Rhys quickened his rhythm, the bed creaking with their every joining, the sounds of flesh meeting flesh blending in with their moans. Some strange tingly feeling started accumulating in the pit of her stomach, and Isabel whimpered again.

With a growl, Rhys spilled his seed, filling Isabel with hot liquid. They both breathed heavily, and Rhys had finally opened his eyes and looked at her.

"You are magnificent," Rhys breathed. He kissed her lightly on the nose and rolled away.

They lay like that for a few minutes, their labored breathing the only sound in the room. Rhys scrambled from the bed and went to her dressing room. He reemerged a few moments later, a wet towel in his hands.

Chapter 28

He tipped his head toward her. "Do you mind?"

Isabel's entire body heated in embarrassment. Did he mean to clean her? There?

Isabel shot up from the bed and took the towel from his hands. "Thank you, I-I'll do it myself."

She hurried to the dressing room to clean up after their moment of passion.

The creation of a babe sure left one in disorder. Her hair was tousled, her nightgown was rumpled, and their mutual juices were dripping down her leg.

She cleaned herself up then tried to arrange her hair back into some kind of semblance of order, but she feared she had not succeeded.

Isabel's hands shook, and she felt confused.

She'd liked their coupling; she truly had. She'd enjoyed Rhys's kisses and the moment of their joining was one of the most wonderful feelings in her life. But it was not the earth-shattering experience Evie was talking about. Had she done it wrong? Was she supposed to act differently? Should she ask Rhys about it?

She puffed a breath of air in frustration. Then, after a few minutes of fumbling in the dark dressing room, she stepped back into her room.

Rhys sat on the bed, his usual frown marring his face. His features smoothed as he saw Isabel, and he smiled.

Isabel returned the smile and climbed back into bed. Rhys helped tuck her in but didn't follow her. Instead, he sat by her side and looked into her face.

"How do you feel?" he asked.

There. This was her cue to say exactly how she felt. *Confused, conflicted, perplexed.* Anything to let him know that they should be doing something differently.

"I feel rather sleepy," she answered instead.

Rhys kissed her on the forehead and tucked the sheets over her body. "Then sleep, darling. I shall let you rest."

And for the first time since they started sharing her bed, he walked to the adjoining room door, entered his chamber, and did not come back that night.

* * *

Rhys watched Isabel quietly from the doorway the next morning as she stood in front of the window, looking out into the gardens. She had a thoughtful expression on her face, and her brows were drawn together over the bridge of her nose.

She didn't seem to notice that he had entered her chamber.

He had missed waking up next to her this morning and regretted his decision to spend the night without her. It had stemmed from the fact that he could not control himself around her.

He'd wanted to savor their first moment of joining; he'd wanted to taste her and bring her to the brink of passion, but the moment he'd entered her, he'd known he wouldn't last much longer.

It was so incredible to be inside her. She was warm and tight, soft and welcoming. She was perfect. As a result, it took him less than two minutes before he spilled his seed inside her. And it took him even less to want her again.

The moment she had cleaned herself and emerged from the dressing room, he had already been hard and aching for her. He'd wanted nothing more than to bury himself inside

Chapter 28

her heat again and have his way with her. And perhaps more than once.

But she'd had a veil of confusion over her face, and when he'd asked her how she felt, she'd said she was sleepy. That had left Rhys no choice but to leave her alone.

If he'd stayed the night with her, neither of them would have gotten any sleep.

Rhys slowly walked into Isabel's room and caught her by her waist. She shrieked and turned around, but her face split into a smile as she saw him.

"You frightened me! I didn't hear you come in."

"Apologies. I believe you were too lost in your thoughts."

"I was." Isabel smiled, stood on her tiptoes, and wrapped her arms around his neck. "But I am always happy for a distraction."

Rhys dipped his head and kissed her slowly. She moaned into his mouth and pressed her body against his.

Rhys's cock stood at attention, and he wanted nothing more than toss up her skirts and have her right there against the window.

He broke the kiss instead.

"What are your plans for the day?" he asked, hoping they could spend some time together.

"I am going riding with Millie and the duchess. And then I have a lot of work around the house. The entertainment is arriving today, too."

Rhys swallowed his disappointment. He wouldn't see her the entire day. He restrained himself from offering an interlude to his wife right then and there.

Don't be too eager.

"What did Gage tell you yesterday?" Isabel asked, running

her hands up and down his chest.

Rhys put his hands over hers to stall their movement. His nerves were overexcited, as it were. "What do you mean?"

"I forgot to ask you yesterday, but after he arrived, you two hid away in a study for a while."

Rhys smiled. "Oh, the usual. He threatened to kill me if I mistreated you. Which, I admit, is fair. But he crossed the line when he threatened my dog."

"He threatened Button?" Her eyes widened comically.

"Yes, something about sending him to Scotland to herd sheep if he didn't behave."

Isabel let out a chuckle. "What did you say?"

"I said that if he tried that, he would have to answer to Millie. And after that, our conversation turned amicable."

Isabel chuckled again. "I should remember that tactic for the next time Richard turns exasperating."

"I am certain you won't have to wait long." Rhys grinned.

"I agree."

She looked at him as though she wanted to say something. But she rose on her toes and kissed him on his chin instead. Rhys dipped his head and caught her lips, savoring the taste of her mouth.

"Will you come to me tonight?" she asked against his lips.

Rhys's body tensed. Did she want him to? Or was she dreading it? "If you want," he answered.

Isabel kissed him again, and Rhys crushed her body to his, rubbing her soft curves against his hardened length.

Isabel drew away, breathing heavily. "Until tonight then."

* * *

Chapter 28

Rhys stalked to his study and resolved not to think about his wife for the rest of the day. If only his mind was so accommodating.

Instead, he sat behind his desk, looking at his ledgers with an empty gaze, thinking about his wife.

What was it about Isabel that was so alluring?

During the day, Rhys could not get the woman out of his head. During the night, he'd lasted an embarrassingly short amount of time before losing control.

But he could not deny that it was beyond just physical attraction. He couldn't keep his thoughts away from her. He always thought about her when he was away, but he'd chalked it up to missing his home, his daughter, and everything else that he associated with them.

Now that he had spent the previous day at home, he couldn't keep fooling himself like this. All day, he had kept hoping he'd catch a glimpse of her. And the night without her was pure torture.

Rhys couldn't deny the obvious any longer. He was beginning to fall in love with his wife.

He heaved a sigh. Now he needed to ensure that she fell in love with him, too. Or at least was not inclined to leave him. And to that end, he needed to keep their passion fresh within their marriage.

Isabel had had at least one lover before Rhys. And Rhys was certain that what lovers did was different from the marital bed within polite society. He wasn't certain how different, but he had heard wild stories of shameless pursuits by many a member of society.

In fact, he'd heard most of the stories from a person who was currently residing under his roof.

Viscount St. Clare, the previously most notorious rake in the country and currently the most devoted husband to his wife, walked into Rhys's study right at that moment.

He sauntered toward Rhys's desk and plopped in the chair opposite his. "Are you busy?"

"No." Rhys eyed the viscount curiously.

"Oh, good. I find myself suffering from an uncharacteristic bout of ennui."

"Let me guess, your wife left with my marchioness and our daughter, so now you are bored."

St. Clare grinned. "You are incredibly astute. Are you going to offer me a drink or do I have to get it myself? Actually," he said, getting up, "Never mind. I shall do it myself."

True to his word, he went to the side table and poured them each a drink.

"It is truly refreshing to see you happily married after years of debauchery," Rhys noted.

"I can say the same about you. Only in your case it would be the years of being a hermit. I'd say we did a good job finding a wife for you."

Rhys scoffed. "I do not remember you doing much work at all."

"What do you mean?" St. Clare exclaimed in an offended manner. "We invited you to the ball and dropped your wife at your feet."

Rhys chuckled. "Well, whatever it was, I have to say that I am indeed content with my lot."

"Are you?" The all-too-perceptive viscount raised his brow.

Rhys cleared his throat and tugged on his cravat. "I wanted to ask you something."

"Yes?" St. Clare livened up immediately as he took a sip of

Chapter 28

whisky.

"Do you treat your wife like your mistress?"

St. Clare raised a brow. Any other man would be sputtering his drink out of his mouth in surprise at the question. Not St. Clare. "No, I treat my wife a lot better than I have ever treated any of my mistresses."

"That's not exactly what I mean…." Rhys cleared his throat again.

"Then what do you mean?"

Rhys scratched his temple. "I mean in bed."

"Oh…" Gabriel scowled. "I do not think I follow."

"Well, I mean… All the depraved things you did with your mistresses, do you do them to your wife?"

Gabriel raised his brow. "If by depraved, you mean whether I pleasure my wife in every way I have learned how, then yes. And she does the same for me."

"You let her—"

"I let her do anything she wants to do to me and then teach her to do even more," he added with a wink.

Rhys tugged on his cravat again in agitation. "What I mean is… I've heard time and time again that ladies are delicate creatures who cannot withstand arduous pursuits… There are things that are indecent—"

"Let me stop you right there, my dear, virtuous friend. Whatever you think is indecent, I do to my wife every morning before breakfast. And whatever you call degrading or embarrassing, I call Tuesday." He finished his drink and slammed the glass onto the desk. "There is no such thing as indecent between a husband and a wife. The only thing indecent is a cold marriage bed. Take it from a former rake."

Chapter 29

Isabel knocked on the door to Evie's chamber, hoping the duchess was up from her afternoon nap.

"Please, enter," Evie said from the inside, and Isabel glided into the room.

"Have you rested then?" Isabel asked as she saw Evie sitting by the window, reading.

"Yes. Thank you." Evie immediately put the book away and stood to greet Isabel.

They had both spent the morning riding with Millicent, and after a few hours of exhausting activity, Evie went up to her room to rest while Isabel continued bustling about the house. But as teatime approached, Isabel hoped she could speak with the duchess before more guests arrived, in which time one-on-one conversations would become impossible.

Isabel and Evie settled around the small tea table in the sitting room, and the maid brought biscuits and salted almonds to accompany their tea.

Isabel poured each of them a cup, and Evie popped one

Chapter 29

salted almond into her mouth.

"Oh, these almonds are magical!" she exclaimed.

"That is high praise coming from you," Isabel said. "I know it isn't easy to find something you like."

"I know! And recently, it became even worse," Evie complained. "However, I have developed quite a craving for salty treats, and these are just perfect!"

Isabel reared back and looked at the duchess more carefully. Her cheeks were flushed, her eyes were shining, and she seemed... different somehow. Isabel narrowed her eyes. "Are you—?"

Evie looked up and blinked at her. "What?"

"Pardon me for being indelicate, but... Are you with child?"

Evie's cheeks blushed furiously, and she tried to hide her smile, but it didn't work.

Isabel grinned and stood to embrace the duchess. "I am so happy for you!"

Evie bit her lip. "It's been only a few weeks, and one of the reasons Gabriel didn't want us traveling, but I could not miss your party."

"Oh, Evie." Isabel cocked her head to the side then sat back in her chair.

Despite the happiness for her friend, there was still a slight pang in her chest. Could Isabel be with child soon, too?

Evie popped another almond into her mouth. "These are quite spectacular. I shall have to write down the recipe."

"Of course, I will ask Mrs. Ainsworth to record it for you. But the original recipe came from my friend who was also *enceinte*," she said with a chuckle.

"Thank you." Evie popped another almond into her mouth, savoring every crunch. "You must have a lot to do for the upcoming house party. Do you need any help from me?"

Isabel shook her head. "This household is very competent. I have everything ready. And the entertainment should arrive today, too. They wanted to see the place beforehand and set up their things and properties."

"Oh, how interesting! Who did you hire for entertainment?"

"A theater troupe," Isabel said proudly. "This is the first time I am using them for a party, but I've seen them play before."

"That sounds intriguing. So you are certain you don't need help?" Evie insisted.

"I am. But if you feel like you need something to occupy yourself with, you are free to spend some time with Millie. Do not feel obligated, it's—"

"I would enjoy that very much!" Evie interrupted.

Isabel smiled. "I would be so grateful. Millie has a nursemaid, but without a governess, she doesn't get much of a ladylike education, which she seems to copy from you. Not to say that you should act as her governess—"

"Oh, please, Isabel, stop rambling. I love the girl and would love to spend more time with her. And I promise I shall find enough energy to occupy Millie and then dance at your balls."

Isabel chuckled. "I don't know. Millie is a very exuberant child."

"It works out well because so am I!" Evie said excitedly.

"Just don't overexert yourself, please. But Millie seems quite taken with you. I have to say I am a little bit jealous," Isabel confessed.

Evie raised a brow. "Oh?"

"Yes. She seems to have warmed up to me, but she looks at you with such awe in her eyes. And she copies everything you do and wants to be just like you. I suppose I should be

Chapter 29

glad she picked you as a role model because you're perfect."

Evie waved a dismissing hand, then popped another almond into her mouth. "I am a novelty for Millie. Someone who appears once in a while and dazzles her with pretty dresses and shiny red hair. At the end of the day, she will always choose you."

"How do you know that?" Isabel bit on her lip.

Evie put the teacup down and looked Isabel squarely in the eye. "Because you might see how she looks at me, but I see the way she looks at you. You might not have given birth to her, Isabel, but you *are* her mother. And that's exactly how she sees you."

Isabel's eyes filled with tears. "Oh, my, Evie. You know how to make a lady teary-eyed." Both ladies laughed and dabbed at their tears with a handkerchief. "But that's exactly what I needed to hear. Thank you."

"It is true." Evie grinned.

Isabel shook her head. "I never thought when I first met the wild child that I would love her this much."

"It is rather odd how complete strangers can become the most important people in your life in a span of a few weeks, isn't it? After all, this is how quickly I became friends with you lot!"

Isabel chuckled. That was true. Evie became close friends with Isabel's sister Sam in a matter of days. After that, she became a part of the Lewis family.

They sipped the tea in silence for a moment before Evie spoke again. "Now that we sorted out your relationship with your child, how about you tell me about your relationship with your husband?"

Isabel's cheeks heated, and she fought to keep her smile at

bay.

"Ah! So he is no longer evading his marital duty, I assume, by the shy look on your face?"

"He is not," Isabel said and pursed her lips again lest her smile broke out.

"And is everything—how do I say this without being crude?—ah, satisfactory on that end?"

Isabel hesitated before nodding.

It was satisfactory, wasn't it? And either way, she didn't feel like it was something to be discussed with third parties. Especially since she hadn't discussed it with her husband.

"Yes, it is," she finally said.

* * *

Isabel came to her room later that evening feeling tired. Everything seemed ready for the house party, and all she needed was to wait for the guests to arrive. Richard didn't cause any trouble. He seemed amicable enough, although he had that look like he had something on his mind.

Isabel would ask him later. She had too many problems of her own. And perhaps that made her a selfish sister, but today, she decided to be a little selfish. It didn't hurt to prioritize oneself once in a while, did it?

She called for Anthea before she noticed the wrapped package on her bed. The maid entered just then and started preparing Isabel's nighttime clothes.

"Anthea, do you know who this package on my bed is from?" Isabel asked.

Anthea looked at the package and shook her head.

Isabel shrugged. She would find out soon enough. She

Chapter 29

slipped into her nightgown with the help of her maid before dismissing her. Then she sat on the bed and looked at the package and the note accompanying it.

Dear Isabel,

From our conversation today, I gathered that the marital bed is not as pleasant as it can be. I might be wrong, and if I am, please, excuse my meddling. But I know how nervous you were about this, and I only wish you the best. So, I am enclosing a deck of cards.

These are not a usual deck of cards. I found them in my husband's library, and this should tell you that they are not for showing to strangers. But they might help you in your endeavor to seduce your husband.

Sincerely,
Evie.

Isabel put away the note and unwrapped the package.

Sure enough, inside, there was a deck of cards. The cards were slightly larger than the ones people used for playing, and they had words written on them. Without reading, she turned one card around and gasped.

It was a picture of a man standing erect, completely naked. A woman, dressed in a delicate, pink gown that was falling off her shoulders and showcasing her breasts, was crouching before him, and... she had the male part of his anatomy inside her mouth!

Isabel turned the card again and closed her eyes. Her cheeks were flushed, and she felt decidedly uncomfortable. Did Evie mean for Isabel to do *that*?

She picked another card. The image on that one was similarly indecent. Only this time, a woman was straddling a man while he fondled her breasts. Isabel quickly flipped through the deck's contents and realized all of them had lurid images depicted on them.

In all of them, a man and a woman were in some state of dishabille, and in more than one of them, a woman or a man had the other's genitals in their mouths.

That was beyond indecent. Isabel couldn't help but peek at the cards again. Isabel's skin felt hot and clammy. She shifted uncomfortably, feeling liquid gather between her thighs.

Isabel picked up the first card again and turned it to read the text. As it turned out, these were instructions on how to perform the task that was pictured on the other side. Isabel's eyes rounded as she read the words, but she couldn't quite look away. Her breaths turned shallow, and she kept flipping her hair away from her warm face.

The handle on her door scraped and turned as the door to her room creaked open.

Isabel jumped guiltily, collected the cards, and threw them under the pillows. It wouldn't do to be caught ogling the lurid images. The door opened, and her husband entered the room.

* * *

As Rhys entered the room, his wife gasped and jumped guiltily. What was she doing?

"Is everything well?" he asked, moving deeper into the room.

"Yes." Isabel looked rather flushed.

There was a beat of silence.

"Are you ready for bed?" he asked.

Chapter 29

Isabel shook her head. "Not quite."

"No?"

"I didn't... I haven't performed my nightly ablutions yet." She hid the loose lock of hair behind her ear and licked her lips. She was acting strange.

"Very well," he said. "I shall do the same then."

He turned to leave the room, but Isabel stopped him.

"Rhys, wait..."

"Yes?" He turned back to her.

"You will spend the night with me, yes?"

Rhys blinked, startled. "Of course. Don't you want me to?"

"Oh, yes, I want you to." Her voice was curiously breathy.

Rhys hurried into his chamber, performed his nightly ablutions, and changed into his nightshirt. He entered Isabel's chamber just as she emerged from her dressing room... in her indecent semi-transparent nightgown that he'd seen on her before.

I suppose I shouldn't call it indecent.

Whatever he should call it, Rhys couldn't take his eyes off his wife. His mouth went dry, and his cock sprung in attention. Damn. He wouldn't be able to last long again.

Isabel walked toward him, her hips swaying from side to side, her legs bared with her every step. Finally, she stopped just a few inches away from him and looked into his eyes.

Rhys slowly reached out and swept her hair behind her back. Isabel swallowed, a ripple in her throat drawing his attention before his gaze slid lower and stopped at the peaks of her full, round breasts.

"I wanted to speak to you," she said, her voice breathy.

The conversation was the last thing on Rhys's mind. He raised his eyes to her face, and Isabel licked her lips. Rhys's restless eyes fell to her mouth.

Such a plump, beautiful mouth. He'd rather suckle on her lips than have this conversation, but he resisted. If she needed to say something, he would listen. Although perhaps she shouldn't have dressed so provocatively if she wanted him to pay attention.

"Yes?" he croaked.

"About last night."

"What about it?" Rhys's eyes could not help but roam her body.

She chewed on her bottom lip nervously. "Do you plan on doing that every night?"

Rhys's gaze snapped back to her face. "Do you... Do you not want me to?"

Isabel grimaced, and his heart sank.

What was going on? Had she worn the most seductive gown she could find to tell him she didn't want him to share her bed anymore?

"Of course not!" she exclaimed and stalked away from him, her bottom swaying with each step. "I'd rather you stayed here."

Rhys blinked. *Did I miss something?* "Apologies, darling, can you clarify? What do you want me *not* to do?"

"You left me last night after... after... Well, you know."

"After we shared a brief but passionate interlude. Yes."

"And I had to sleep alone... And I did not like that."

Rhys's lips twitched in a smile. *Thank God!* "Darling," he said as he stalked toward her. "You said you were tired. I did not want to bother you."

"Oh." Isabel blinked. Had she thought he actually wanted to sleep away from her? "I don't mind you being here at all,

Chapter 29

even if I'm tired."

Rhys hid a smile. "As you wish, my lady. Anything else?"

"Yes." She sat on the bed and looked at her hands, folded demurely on her lap.

"I am waiting in trepidation for your next request, my lady," he said, his voice low.

"I was thinking that maybe, perhaps, if you would oblige me in—"

He took a large step and appeared right before her. Isabel raised her shining, blue eyes.

"I was hoping the next time we shared a bed you would... you would spend a little more time just kissing me."

Rhys blinked. He had not anticipated this request either. He crouched before her and took her hands in his. "I am so glad you feel comfortable enough to tell me of your wants and needs. I want you to continue doing that."

A shy smile appeared on her lips. "Then I want you to kiss me. And I don't want you to stop."

Rhys dipped his head. "I am happy to oblige," he said against her lips and kissed her deeply.

Isabel moaned and plunged her fingers into his hair. Rhys couldn't help his answering moan. It felt so good to feel her fingers sifting through his locks, her nails scraping his scalp.

More than that, it felt incredibly good to feel wanted. Needed.

He swept his tongue into her, tasting the corners of her mouth. She shyly touched his tongue with hers, and he was lost in their sensual dance. Rhys gently moved her knees apart and settled between them. The heat from her thighs rubbing against his body and the sensual rhythm of her breaths fanning against his face made him mad with lust.

He ran his hands down her back, then circled her delicate waist. His hands inched up her sides, and he was dying to touch her breasts. Would she allow it? He moved his hands higher, and in a moment's time, her soft globes were resting in his palms. Isabel gasped, but instead of moving away, she pressed herself firmer into him.

He brushed his thumbs over her nipples, and she gasped again.

"Do you like that?" he whispered, looking into her lust-hazed eyes.

"Yes," she breathed.

He brushed the tips of her breasts once more. They turned into hardened peaks, and Rhys's entire body went stiff with want. God, she was magnificent.

Her head fell back in bliss, and Rhys brushed his mouth against her neck. He sucked on her silky skin, then grazed the spot with his teeth.

"Rhys!" His name was a breathy moan.

Rhys's hands went to the ribbons on her shoulders. He hooked them with his fingers and looked into her dark, passion-filled eyes.

"May I?" he asked.

Isabel swallowed the tiny ripple in her throat, doing unconscionable things to his already painful erection. Then Isabel nodded, and it was all he could do not rip her nightgown to shreds.

Instead, he slowly lowered the ribbons down her marble-white shoulders until her bodice sagged at her waist.

He kissed her just at the juncture between her neck and shoulder, and she whimpered.

"Do you want more?"

Chapter 29

"Yes... So much more."

Rhys chuckled and bit her there, then soothed the spot with his tongue. Isabel sank her fingers into his hair and tugged lightly.

"Mm... yes, guide me, my love," he whispered against her skin.

She tugged again, and Rhys followed her instructions, licking down her shoulder, then her collarbone, until finally, he was face to nipple with her breasts. He licked around the dark areola, and Isabel whimpered again.

He licked just below her breast, and she tugged on his hair in frustration.

"Hmm... It seems like you want something else," he murmured. "Perhaps I should go back to the start."

Rhys moved to raise his head, but Isabel tightened her fingers around his head. "No! Oh, please no," she cried, and Rhys chuckled.

"Are you certain?"

"Please, Rhys... Please, don't make me beg anymore."

"Mm, but I do like hearing you beg," he murmured before taking her hardened peak into his mouth.

The jolt of pleasure that originated deep inside his stomach grew as his tongue made contact with her nipple.

Lord, if heaven was real, then this was it, in the arms of this woman, on his knees before her, with his mouth on her.

He continued licking her skin with renewed vigor, holding her close to him, feeding off her every moan.

Kiss me and don't ever stop, she'd said.

Well, he couldn't stop even if he tried.

Isabel wriggled in his hold, and he raised his head.

"I am so hot, Rhys. I can't...." She didn't finish her sentence, but she was pleading with him with her gaze.

"Do you want to take this off?" Rhys fingered the fabric bunched up at her waist.

She nodded.

Rhys stood and tugged her up. The nightgown slid from her curves and settled on the floor in a heap. Rhys studied Isabel's naked body, his gaze settling on the dark patch of curls at the juncture of her thighs.

"Rhys?"

He hated that there was a note of uncertainty in her voice. He wanted her to know that she was the most beautiful thing he had ever seen.

He raised his gaze to her eyes. "You are magnificent." His voice came out hoarse, almost a whisper. He cleared his throat and kissed her soundly on her mouth.

Without breaking the kiss, he took Isabel into his arms and laid her down on the bed.

Chapter 30

Rhys climbed on top of her and kissed her on the mouth again. His hands went back to her breasts, weighing the soft globes in his palms, his thumbs playing with her nipples.

Isabel whimpered, and Rhys looked down at her.

"Tell me what you want," he whispered.

"Touch me," she said on a whimper.

"Here?" He ran a thumb over her nipple again.

Isabel arched against him, shooting off the bed. "Lower."

Rhys's cock jolted at her request. He took his index finger and slid it down her body.

Isabel moaned.

Rhys dipped his finger into her belly button. "Here?"

Another moan. "Lower."

Rhys chuckled and moved his hand lower. He reached the patch of hair at the juncture of her thighs, and Isabel raised her hips.

"Here?"

"Lower! A little more... Ah!" she ended on a cry as Rhys dipped his finger lower into a wet patch of hair.

He split her feminine lips then circled her center before withdrawing his hand and bringing his fingers to his lips.

Isabel watched him lick the evidence of her desire off his fingers, her eyes wide.

She tasted so damn good, her scent driving him mad with lust.

Rhys returned his hand to her center and kissed her deeply as he kept playing with her wet petals.

Isabel moved her thighs, drawing his fingers in deeper. Rhys plunged his digits inside her, and she moaned into his mouth. Rhys placed his forehead against hers.

His body was covered in sweat as he plunged his finger in and out of her depths while trying to control his own need. His cock was painfully hard, and every time he accidentally brushed her skin, it threatened to erupt.

Isabel wrapped her arms around his shoulders and bunched the fabric of his nightshirt tightly in her arms. Isabel writhed beneath him, her face a grimace of unfulfilled tension. She bucked her hips, and his thumb brushed the tiny bud above her center.

Isabel cried out and bucked her hips again. "Again," she cried. "Do it again."

Rhys circled her swollen bud with his thumb, his fingers still inside her. Isabel's fingers curled into his shoulders, and her head fell back. He continued his ministrations, watching every minute feature of her face until she cried out and fell limp in his arms.

Rhys sat up, discarded his nightshirt, and fell back on the bed. He closed his eyes, took his erection in his hand, and

Chapter 30

squeezed. God, he wanted her.

But if she needed a reprieve from him after a moment of passion, he'd give it to her. She shifted on the bed, and Rhys opened his eyes just to see her face over his.

She smiled at him and ran her finger down his torso. "Now it's my turn."

* * *

Isabel crawled on top of Rhys and took his mouth in a kiss. After the incredible heights of pleasure he'd taken her to, she wanted to do the same for him. She licked his lips, then plunged her tongue into his mouth. He tasted like tea with sugar, sweet with a bit of spice.

Her hair fell on either side of them in thick cascades, covering them like curtains in an intimate setting.

Rhys sifted his fingers through her locks, then caressed her shoulders. Her skin shivered under his touch, and he smiled. Isabel broke the kiss and looked down at him.

He was absolutely gorgeous, this husband of hers.

Isabel stared at his naked chest, then ran her fingers against the small patch of coarse hairs in the center before scrubbing her fingertips over his skin.

Yes. This was what she was dying to feel all along. Skin on skin.

Her heart thumped loudly in her chest as she kept exploring his body. She kissed his neck, then the hollow at the base of his throat.

Rhys took her backside in his hands and squeezed. Isabel moaned, and her head fell back. Rhys took that opportunity to sink his mouth into her neck, then down to her breasts.

Isabel moaned, her hips moving in a sensual rhythm.

Suddenly, she remembered the cards she'd been perusing and was curious to try something out. Her hand slid lower, and she touched his engorged length.

"Wait," Rhys said on a hiss and caught her fingers in his. "If you touch me there, I am not going to last more than two minutes."

She didn't care if it took him two minutes or two seconds. She wanted him to come to completion, and she wanted to be the one to cause it.

Isabel smiled slyly and, without breaking eye contact, slid down his body.

Rhys's breathing accelerated, and he fell back with a groan.

Isabel reached his shaft and licked her lips. It was quite large, dark red, and covered with tiny veins. It was pulsing and seemed like it was about to burst. Isabel remembered how tiny it was that day at the stream and how she naively thought that was how it was going to stay.

Well, she couldn't say she was upset to learn the truth. Isabel giggled.

Rhys raised his head. "A woman's laugh is not something a gentleman likes to hear when he's exposed to her in all his manly glory."

Isabel covered her mouth with her hand and giggled again. "I am sorry. I think you are gorgeous."

Rhys smirked. "It doesn't appear so."

"Oh, no. I do." She tentatively touched his length with her fingertips, and it jumped in reaction. "It's just… when I saw you naked for the first time, I thought it was rather tiny."

Rhys sat up again, a familiar scowl adorning his beautiful face. "When was this?"

Chapter 30

Isabel licked her lips. "I didn't tell you this, but I saw you that day at the stream."

"That—" Rhys's eyes widened. "You saw?"

"I did." Her cheeks heated.

"And you thought—"

"I did."

Rhys fell back down with a groan again. "It was cold. My nether regions do not respond well to the cold."

Isabel giggled again and touched his length, then enveloped him with her hand at the base. It was smooth and silky to her touch. It jumped in her hold, and Isabel smiled.

"But it does respond well to warmth?" Her voice came out thick and breathy with passion.

"Yes, very well." Rhys's answer was a pained groan.

Isabel tried to remember the instruction on the cards as she crouched before him and took the tip of his length into her mouth.

His hips bucked, and his hand immediately went to cover her head. "What—"

Isabel swirled her tongue, tasting him, and took him in deeper. Rhys wrapped her hair around his fist and pulled.

"What are you doing, vixen?" he croaked.

Isabel licked her lips. "Do you want me to stop?"

With a groan of surrender, Rhys loosened his hold, although he didn't let go of her fully. Isabel took it as encouragement, lowered her head, and licked him from the base to his tip.

"Isabel," Rhys growled. "Whatever you are doing there, you have less than a minute."

Isabel chuckled and took him into her mouth again. Recalling more of the instructions from the back of the cards, she started pumping his length with her hand while taking him deeper. She swirled her tongue, tasting him, sucking on his length.

Her insides quivered, and hot liquid seeped out of her. She clenched her thighs together while not letting go of his length.

Isabel ran her tongue over his tip, tasting his salty essence. Rhys guided her lower down his length, and she obliged, taking him deeper once more.

Rhys groaned, and his hold on her tightened as he dragged her face away from his length. She still held him in her hand when the hot liquid spilled out and covered her fingers.

"Damn you," Rhys growled as he lay prostrate on the bed, his chest heaving.

Isabel blinked up at him. "Did I—Is something wrong?"

"Wrong?" Rhys frowned. "No… I would have preferred to last a little longer, but you make it impossible."

He closed his eyes, his face still a grimace.

Isabel rolled off the bed and moved to the dressing room on shaking legs. She still didn't know what she'd done to earn his displeasure. She was quite certain he'd enjoyed her ministrations.

She washed her hands and cleaned up the moisture between her legs. She was extremely wet, and she felt an acute discomfort between her legs.

She took another towel, dipped it in water, and brought it to Rhys.

He sat on the bed, watching her curiously. Isabel handed him the towel, her entire body flushing in embarrassment. She'd almost forgotten that she was completely naked.

Rhys cleaned himself, discarded the towel, and went to help her into bed.

He pulled the covers from under the pillows, and the cards

Chapter 30

Isabel had been perusing earlier fell out to the floor. Isabel squeaked as she saw them, but it was too late. Rhys had already picked them up and studied them with an unblinking stare.

"What are these?" he asked, still looking through the cards.

Isabel climbed into bed and covered herself with sheets. There really was no good way to explain these cards to her husband.

"Isabel…" He was frowning again.

She wanted to reach up and smooth the wrinkles on his forehead. He sat next to her, still completely naked. Isabel's gaze couldn't help but roam along his slick, muscled body. "Did you… You do not have to answer if you don't want to. You do not owe me your past, but… Are these yours? Did you… use these with Stanhope?"

Isabel's mouth opened and closed, but no sound emerged. What did Stanhope have to do with anything? She sat up, still clutching the bedsheet to her chest. "The cards?"

Rhys nodded, and Isabel couldn't help but spill into laughter. She shook her head emphatically. "No. It is a gift from a friend for our honeymoon."

Rhys raised a brow. "A friend?"

Isabel let out an exasperated breath. "From Evie."

"Oh." Rhys's features immediately cleared, the relief evident on his face. "That explains a lot. And did you learn all that you did from those cards?"

Isabel gave a tiny nod. "Did you not like it?"

"Not like it? It was the most blissful experience of my life!"

"Oh!" Isabel's mouth split into a grin. "You were frowning, but now I realize you always do that."

Rhys frowned again. "I don't always frown!"

Isabel raised a brow. "No. Sometimes you scowl or glare."

Rhys caught her by the waist, and she giggled. "Isabel," he rasped. "What you did just now. It was lovely but… if you didn't like it—"

"I did." Her smile gentled, and she cradled his cheek.

"Are you certain? Because I wouldn't want you to do it if you didn't enjoy it."

"I did."

She slid her hand lower and caressed his arm. Oh, what a strong and beautiful arm it was. She could look at Rhys's naked form forever. Her gaze moved down, and her mouth formed a silent 'O' as she saw the appendage between his legs start growing again.

Rhys noticed her distractedness and smiled. "You know what we did just now… It wouldn't result in a babe. And if you're not feeling tired yet, we can—"

Isabel wrapped her arms around his neck. Perhaps it made her a wanton, but she did not care. She was, and would forever be, her husband's wanton. "I am not tired," she said and covered his mouth in a kiss.

* * *

The next day, more carriages rolled down the driveway as Isabel's sister Sam arrived with her husband and their babe. And only a few minutes behind, two more visitors graced their doorstep, their brothers Adam and Alan.

The exuberant greeting in the hall surprised even the reserved butler, but now that the entire Lewis family was reunited under the same roof, quiet was not something that would be observed in the house for a long time.

Chapter 30

They moved to the drawing room, as everyone continued chattering away.

Rhys and Sam's husband, Ashbury, immediately bonded over the subject of reconstructing housing at their estates. They quickly disengaged from the Lewis family, giving siblings space to catch up.

"When did you arrive from the Continent?" Isabel asked as she embraced her brother, Alan, for the first time in years.

"A few days ago. I've missed enough family events, it seems," he said, looking pointedly at Sam's babe gurgling in her arms. "I didn't want to miss anymore."

Richard clapped him on the shoulder. "We had to marry both our sisters without you."

"And I regret that immensely," Alan answered solemnly.

"Why didn't you tell me Alan had returned?" Isabel threw an accusing gaze toward Richard.

He just shrugged. "I wanted it to be a surprise."

Adam guffawed. "Right, a surprise! You should have seen him gallop away in rage as he received the latest correspondence from James."

"He is getting dismissed. You should know this," Isabel grumbled.

Everyone laughed.

"I shall take him if you don't want him," Alan said with a smile. "I need to set up my townhouse now that I am back. And James seems like a nice chap."

"Yes, if you want Richard to know about your every step!" Isabel scoffed.

"Oh, don't act all innocent!" Sam intervened. "I remember a time when James was spying on me and spilling everything to you."

Isabel pursed her lips. "You were unmarried, and I was justifiably worried about your activities!"

"Since when does a family stop worrying about their sisters just because they got married?" Richard barked out.

"I would rather you worried like normal people. You know, actually asking instead of spying," Sam said as she rocked her babe in her arms.

"Give her to me! Poor Angel will have vertigo if you keep rocking her like that." Adam reached out his arms.

"As if you know how to care for a babe!" Sam exclaimed with a chuckle but still handed the child to her brother.

Sam's nursemaid stood quietly in the corner, waiting for her lady to hand over the babe. Isabel doubted that would happen anytime soon now that there were so many people to carry her in their arms.

Adam took the child and walked away, murmuring something as he did so.

"I think Adam just needed an excuse to leave us," Isabel noted.

Sam stretched out her arms. "Well, he can have both the excuse and the babe. My arms feel like they might fall off soon."

"Why don't you let your nursemaid care for her if you are tired?"

"I am not tired," Sam protested, then added with a soft smile, "Well, at least not enough to hand her over for long. You will understand soon enough."

Isabel's entire face heated, and she was certain she was blushing furiously. She looked away. "Oh, I am being a terrible hostess! I shall order us some tea and then show you all to your rooms. Adam, if you want to—"

Chapter 30

Adam shushed her. "Angela's falling asleep," he whispered loudly and turned away.

Sam blinked. "Well, looks like he worked a miracle on that child!"

Isabel shrugged. "Seems so. Well, let him bond with the babe while we have some tea."

"Yes, and you can put Adam in the room closest to ours, so he can lull Angela when she has trouble falling asleep," Sam added exuberantly.

Isabel chuckled. "I shall be certain to do just that." She pulled the bell and had just instructed the housekeeper to prepare them some sandwiches and tea when Rhys approached her.

"Ashbury wants to see Thornsby," he said. "Perhaps he can help with advice."

Ashbury was a new baron, and only recently, he and Sam had brought the entire village from ruin. He and his fellow villagers worked day and night building housing for the new inhabitants, and it wasn't surprising that he wished to see Vane's progress and was willing to help if needed.

"Today?" Isabel stepped closer to Rhys and placed her hand on his sleeve.

"Yes, unless you want me to stay."

Isabel looked at her family members lounging about the room. "Perhaps right now is the best time. I shall have my family to keep me company. Besides, I am glad that you're getting along with Sam's husband. You need to stick together if you want to survive my obstinate brothers."

Rhys chuckled, lowered his head, and kissed her on the cheek. "We shall be back before nightfall."

Isabel turned toward her family as soon as Rhys left, her

cheeks burning. All eyes were on her as her brothers raised their brows, and Samantha openly grinned at her.

"They do that a lot," Richard supplied. "Kiss that is."

"I thought you didn't like him?" Sam asked with a chuckle.

"Apparently, she changed her mind," Richard answered again.

Isabel rolled her eyes with a groan. She was glad to have her family back with her, truly. No matter how much teasing she was about to endure.

Chapter 31

Carriages were rolling in every few minutes. Rhys stood in the hall, his wife's arm on his sleeve, and it was the best feeling in the world.

When he was younger, he had dreamed of having Isabel on his arm or claiming her as his own for the entire world to see. And now, that dream had finally become a reality.

He'd never truly thought it would, and the fact that it had still felt unreal to him.

Every moment of their time together, he expected something to go wrong, something to happen that would drive Isabel away from him. And with every moment that it didn't happen, instead of relaxing into his pleasant new reality, he became even more anxious.

The fear of losing Isabel was so intense that sometimes he dreamed about it. He'd wake up in a cold sweat only to feel the warm bundle that was his wife's body by his side.

He loved waking up next to her. It was probably his favorite part of the day.

He let his mind wander as they greeted yet another couple.

Isabel smiled up at him as the couple left. "Are you tired yet?"

Rhys shook his head. He took her hand in his hand and kissed her knuckles. "I could never tire of being next to you."

Isabel's gaze gentled, and Rhys was lost in the depth of her deep blue eyes. Another carriage rolled up, and their footmen helped two elderly ladies out of the vehicle.

Rhys let out a deep sigh. "Although I would enjoy it more if we were alone. And preferably naked."

Isabel let out a burst of choked laughter. Rhys caught her by her waist and placed a quick kiss on her lips before promptly letting her go as the pair of older women entered the hall.

Isabel stumbled but caught herself against his arm. She threw him a sidelong gaze before turning a sweet smile toward the approaching ladies.

Rhys turned to them, and his mouth set into a grim line. He sketched a shallow bow. "My ladies."

Isabel sank into a perfect curtsy by his side.

"Lovely to see you two again," Lady Crosby said, watching them with narrowed eyes.

"A pleasure, indeed," the Dowager Marchioness of Somerville echoed.

"Please, enjoy the party," Isabel said sweetly. "Mrs. Ainsworth will show you to your quarters."

"Why did you invite them?" Rhys growled in a low voice as the women walked past them.

Isabel chuckled. "And why wouldn't I? They are the ones who brought us together."

"Hmm... I suppose you are right. I better go and thank them for the best gift in my life." He turned away as if to leave,

Chapter 31

but Isabel caught him by his arm.

"Stay!" Isabel tugged him back with a giggle. "More carriages are approaching."

"See, I told you they were in love!" the Dowager Marchioness of Somerville said to Lady Crosby as they ascended the stairs.

Rhys glanced at his wife, but she shyly looked away, pretending she hadn't heard the older woman's words.

Well, the old marchioness was not wrong about Rhys. He was completely and utterly in love with his wife.

Isabel's fingers tightened on Rhys's arm as the next couple entered the hall. Rhys pulled his gaze away from his wife just in time to meet them. The Stanhopes.

Rhys sketched a bow. "Lord Stanhope. My Lady."

Isabel sank into a curtsy. "Lovely to see you," she said between her teeth.

Rhys covered her hand that rested on his sleeve, and Stanhope's gaze followed the action.

"What a lovely home," Lady Stanhope exclaimed. "It's so fresh with so many flowers!"

"I can't take any credit for that, unfortunately," Rhys answered. "The merit goes to my lovely wife."

Lady Stanhope eyed Isabel queerly, and her husband seemed equally unable to take his eyes off Rhys's wife.

Anger bubbled up inside Rhys. He didn't want to stand there exchanging pleasantries with the man who had once betrayed Isabel and then accosted her on two separate occasions. He wanted to throw him out on his arse and lock the door.

"I hope you enjoy your stay," Isabel said. "Our footmen will show you to your rooms."

Stanhope tipped his hat. "I shall be looking forward to seeing you again during the party."

Isabel's fingers tightened on Rhys's arm even further. As the couple left, Isabel turned to Rhys. "I had to invite them. My betrothal to Stanhope was public, and if I didn't, there would be gossip," she said in a flurry of words.

Rhys silenced her with a finger to her lips. "Isabel, I am not worried about that. I do not give a fig if they are here as long as you don't feel threatened by him."

"By Stanhope?" Isabel frowned. "I do not care about him one whit. I just worried that you—"

Rhys shook his head. "I'll admit, it is not pleasant to see a man my wife used to be intimate with. But you're mine. I won. And as much as I feel sorry for the chap, I am glad it turned out the way it did."

Isabel didn't say anything, but her eyes shone as she turned back to the doors to greet more guests.

* * *

Isabel glided from one group of guests to another the entire day. More carriages were bound to arrive during the night and on the morrow, but for now, she had to make certain everyone was comfortable and relaxed.

The acting troupe was performing short skits in the parlor. The play they were to perform was scheduled for the third day of the party, but they were invited to stay for the entire duration, and they did not mind entertaining people before and after their play.

She looked at the clock. The dinner would be soon, and before that, she wanted to see Millicent. Isabel hadn't seen

Chapter 31

the girl the entire day, and she had missed her terribly. Millie was spending her day with Edith, so Isabel did not worry for the most part. They were supposed to be playing in the garden, and Isabel allowed them to go into the village if James accompanied them.

Still, Isabel wanted to know how Millie's day went and if, perchance, she had met some of the guests' children. It would be lovely if Millie could make friends with some children of her own station, but Isabel also feared that she would be teased.

Either way, so many thoughts about Millie swirled around her mind that she could not concentrate on her tasks.

She walked toward her husband, who was in a heated argument with some gentlemen by the hearth. They seemed to be discussing some important parliamentary issue, so Isabel hesitated before turning away. This could wait. The entire point of the house party was for Rhys to make connections.

"Isabel," he called her back, and Isabel turned toward him.

"Vane, this is important," one of the gentlemen barked.

"Yes," Rhys agreed. "So is my wife."

He sketched a bow and walked toward Isabel, his brows furrowed. "Is something wrong?"

Isabel's cheeks were afire. "You didn't need to…." She cleared her throat. "I didn't mean to interrupt."

Rhys took her hands in his. "You looked worried. Did something happen?"

Isabel shook her head. "No, but dinner is approaching, and we need to change. I need to check in with the cook before that. But we didn't have time to check on Millie yet."

Rhys's face softened in a smile. "It's a good thing you interrupted then."

"But your discussion...." Isabel peeked at the scowling men by the hearth. "It seemed important."

"Isabel," Rhys said emphatically. "Nothing is more important to me than you and Millie."

Isabel's heart soared, and she was suddenly weak in the knees. He offered his arm, and Isabel gratefully placed her hand on his sleeve as they moved out of the parlor.

She was grinning like a simpleton.

She was the most important thing in her husband's life aside from his daughter. And if that wasn't an admission of love, she did not know what was.

Isabel was still walking with her head in the clouds as they passed the hall. At that moment, the doors opened, and one more couple entered their house. Isabel tugged on her husband's arm. They might as well greet the new arrivals.

They turned toward the middle-aged man of average height, with a slight belly pouch, accompanied by a gorgeous, tall, blonde woman in a demure gown.

Rhys tensed as the couple made their way toward them.

Isabel knew the gentleman. He was the Baron of Mowbray from a neighboring estate. The lady, she assumed, was his wife, but she had never seen her before. They exchanged pleasantries, but Rhys had not taken his eyes off the woman, and Isabel started feeling rather uncomfortable. What was going on?

The woman eyed Rhys with a strange glint in her eyes, too. Isabel could not help but feel jealousy bubble up inside her. Did they know each other? Did they share a past? Was there more Isabel didn't know about her husband?

As she sent Mrs. Ainsworth to show the guests to their rooms, she turned to Rhys. "Who was that?"

Chapter 31

Rhys clenched his jaw. "The man was the Baron of Mowbray. And the lady... she is my late wife's sister."

* * *

The moment Rhys saw Abigail's sister, Beatrice, walking into his main hall, somehow he knew. This was how his nightmares would come true.

He didn't know why and how, but he felt that she was not there just to enjoy the party. The woman with such open hatred in her eyes could not have possibly come to his residence to enjoy a couple of balls and share gossip during the game of cards. She was there to ruin him.

Beatrice had always openly disliked Rhys, even when her sister was still alive. After Abigail's death, she was one of the women who fanned the flames of gossip, insinuating that Rhys had murdered her sister. Furthermore, Beatrice claimed that Abigail had never left Rhys and that he had concocted the shipwreck story to cover up his crimes, although she was one of the very few people who knew for certain that it wasn't so.

He had not seen her in years, and he would have loved not seeing her at all, but here she was. Of course, it did not help that she looked exceedingly like his late wife, and that alone was enough to drive him to distraction.

Isabel tugged on his sleeve. "Are you ready to go see Millicent?" She had concern shining in her eyes, and he hated that he was once again the cause for her worry.

"Yes, darling. Let's go."

They ascended the steps in silence, but all Rhys's troubles disappeared once they entered Millie's room. Millie was the light of his life, and she had always made him smile no matter the circumstances.

Of course, Millicent was rather upset that she had been neglected most of the day by both her parents, but she quickly forgot about that as she started recounting all of the day's adventures.

After a few minutes, Rhys tucked Millie into bed, taking turns singing a lullaby with his wife. It was almost time to leave for dinner, so they exited the room, pausing by the doorframe to take one last look at their sleeping daughter.

Rhys turned to his wife. "Today was perfect," he rasped.

Isabel smiled. "I agree."

"Every day with you is perfect."

Isabel giggled. "You, liar."

"I love you," he whispered, and before she had a chance to answer, he covered her mouth with his.

Chapter 32

Isabel sat in front of her vanity, brushing out her hair later that night. Rhys had still been playing whist with the gentlemen below stairs when she turned in for the night, and Isabel had come to terms with the inevitability that she just might have to go to bed without her husband that night.

She knew he'd come to her later, but the cold, empty bed did not look enticing in the least. And after seeing his late wife's gorgeous sister, she felt rather intimidated by her.

Rhys had acted strangely for the entire night, throwing glances toward the woman, and Isabel wondered if she had reminded him of his late wife and perhaps reminded him of feelings he had for her.

He had said he loved Isabel, and instead of feeling overjoyed, Isabel was concerned that he had said that during his moment of desperation after seeing his wife's sister. Especially since he had not allowed Isabel to react and had avoided her for the rest of the night.

An Offer from the Marquess

It was irrational, wasn't it? Rhys had never remembered his late wife fondly. But jealousy was quite an irrational feeling.

Jealousy? Since when had Isabel been jealous of Rhys? She did not know the answer to the question, but the fact was undeniable. He was hers, and she was not about to share him with anyone. Even the memory of his late wife.

Isabel took her time with her nightly ablutions, brushed her hair with two hundred strokes, and still, she stalled going to sleep.

Just when she was about to douse the candlelight, there was a knock on the door. Isabel waited a beat for her husband to enter without waiting for her permission as he always did, only to hear another knock. And it wasn't coming from the adjoining room door either.

Who could it be?

She put on her dressing gown and wrapped it tightly around herself before walking to answer the door. She cracked it open and beheld the tall form of her husband.

He leaned one hand on the doorjamb, his head hung, his hair disheveled, and his cravat hung loosely around his neck.

Isabel chuckled. "Can I assume your state of attire to mean that you've lost our money in whist?"

He raised his head then, mischief lurking in deep brown depth. "No, ma'am. We are still rich."

Isabel opened the door wider. "Would you care to come in?"

He shook his head. "I am here to ask a lady out on an assignation."

Isabel's lips split in a smile. "Then why wouldn't you come in, my lord?"

He raised a brow. "I am afraid your dear husband might

Chapter 32

come and catch us in a compromising position."

Isabel let out a giggle. "What are you doing, Rhys?"

Rhys took her by the wrist and tugged her out of her room. Then he wrapped her arms around his neck. His face was perilously close to hers as he whispered, "Don't you know, my lady, that house parties are the most scandalous events of the *ton*? Ladies are expected to be caught, either in bed with another woman's husband or out in the open."

Isabel licked her lips, her gaze falling to Rhys's mouth. "Well, my lord, then you've come to the right door. Did I ever tell you that being compromised out in the open is my favorite pastime?"

"Mm?"

"Yes, this is what landed me a husband once."

Rhys let out a hoarse chuckle. "You don't seem to regret that."

Isabel bit on her lip and shook her head. "Not in the least."

Their lips were a hair's breadth away now. Their breaths mingled, Isabel's breasts rubbing against Rhys's waistcoat with every inhale. She stood on her tiptoes, and their lips would have met, but Rhys suddenly pulled away. He took her hand in his and tugged on her arm again.

They dashed through the house and toward the servants' exit.

"Wouldn't want to be caught prematurely," Rhys reasoned.

Isabel just giggled like the silly girl she was, running through the house with her husband, in her nightclothes.

He opened the door, and only then did Isabel realize that she wasn't wearing any slippers.

"Rhys!" She halted on the doorstep. "I am barefoot."

"Hmm..." Rhys let out a slight growl, then bent down and

swooped her into his arms.

He moved through the garden, easily carrying Isabel as if she weighed nothing. She held on to his neck and placed her head against his shoulder. Being held so tightly by the man she loved was a dream come true.

The man she loved?

The thought caught her off guard. But as she looked at his face so close to hers, the stern determination in his eyes, his square jaw covered with midnight shadow, his enticing lips, and more importantly, his deep dark brown eyes, she could not deny it any longer.

She loved him.

She loved him with his customary frown on his face. She loved him when he smiled at her. She loved him dressed impeccably and in any state of dishabille. She loved when he barked and growled like a beast when something was not to his liking, but she loved, even more, his low beautiful voice when he spoke gently or sang to Millie.

She loved him. And the realization was so freeing she wanted to sing.

Rhys entered the gazebo at the center of their garden and perched Isabel against the pillar.

Isabel didn't have time to catch her breath when his mouth was on hers. He kissed her hungrily, eating at her lips, running his tongue over every corner of her mouth. Isabel threaded her fingers through his hair, bringing him closer to her. Rhys weaved his hand through her hair, then wrapped it around his fist and tugged, angling her for better access.

Isabel moaned and wrapped her legs around his hips.

Rhys broke the kiss and trailed his mouth down her chin, her neck. He swirled his tongue over the hollow at the base

Chapter 32

of her throat, and Isabel whimpered.

"Rhys..." she breathed.

She wanted him closer, so much closer.

Rhys ripped his mouth away from her skin, and Isabel cried from frustration.

She wasn't ready for it to stop. She felt like her heart would bust out of her chest if he didn't resume kissing her. She felt vulnerable in the light of her new revelation.

She loved him.

And it made her want to weep in joy.

Rhys placed his forehead against hers, his breathing labored. He kissed her lightly on the mouth, then ran his thumbs over her nipples. Isabel arched against his touch.

"Do you know," he spoke to her breasts, "that lately I've been rather bored during the day while working. I found myself staring at the ledgers with a vacant gaze, and my mind keeps being diverted by one enticing vixen."

"Oh?" Her heart leaped.

Rhys untied her dressing gown and pulled the corners away from her body. He then lowered his head and licked her nipple through the fabric of her shift. Isabel whimpered.

"So instead of working, I decided to dedicate some time to studying."

Another lick.

"Ah!" Isabel arched again. "What d-did you study?"

"The cards," Rhys said with a grin.

It took her a moment before she realized what cards he was talking about. By that time, he had lowered himself on his knees before her and raised her night rail over his head. Isabel's head fell back.

Rhys ran his hands up her thighs, and goosebumps covered

her skin.

"Let me show you what I learned." Rhys's voice was thick with passion.

He took one of her legs and threw it over his shoulder, then caught her bottom in his firm hold and split her feminine lips with his tongue.

The sound that ripped from Isabel's throat was animal. It was a sound of pure pleasure.

Isabel leaned back against the pillar, her hands grabbing at the edges of its base. Her knee gave out, and she was afraid she'd crumble on the ground, but Rhys held her tight and fast in his arms. He licked again, and then his tongue traveled higher to the sensitive bud above her center, and Isabel was lost.

She couldn't control the bucking of her hips or the sounds coming out of her mouth. Stars burst behind her eyelids, and she was flying somewhere in the sky, looking down upon the picture of Rhys eating at her center.

Isabel came down to earth only to have the feeling of complete bliss build inside her again… and again as Rhys refused to stop his ministrations.

When she finally fell limp in his arms, he emerged from under her skirts and licked his lips. His mouth and his chin were still covered by her juices.

Rhys took Isabel into his arms and settled her on his lap as he sat on the stone floor. He cradled her close to his heart as her breathing returned to normal.

"How was that?" he finally asked.

Isabel let out a satisfied sigh. "You are an exemplary student, my lord."

Rhys chuckled and kissed her mouth, the taste of her release

Chapter 32

still lingering on his lips. He nuzzled her neck, his hand roaming her body. As Isabel relaxed, she noticed the hard, hot bulge poking at her bottom. Right, she might have achieved the height of pleasure, but Rhys hadn't had his release yet. She was looking forward to rectifying that mistake.

"Anything you wish me to do for you, my lord?" she asked and fluttered her lashes.

Rhys let out a hoarse chuckle. "No, my lady. But I have a few things I would love to do to you."

"Oh?"

Rhys raised his brow in a flirtatious manner. "I promise you, my lady, I have studied a very long time."

Isabel giggled, and he caught her mouth in another lingering kiss. He kissed her deeper and threw her dressing gown off her shoulders.

"I want to see you," he rasped.

And if her mind was in order, she might have protested, but Isabel didn't care about anything at the moment except for Rhys's kisses, his hands on her, his tongue against her bare skin, so she took off her nightgown in one smooth motion.

Rhys stared at her breasts for one long moment. Her peaks hardened either from his intent gaze or the cool air or perhaps both. He then lowered his mouth and sucked her nipple into his mouth. He ministered to her breasts while his hand went to her center, and he worked on her little sensitive bud until he brought her to completion again.

He tugged her to her feet, and she tried to stand tall, although she swayed and her legs refused to hold her.

"Turn around," he whispered, then propped her hands against the beam of the gazebo. "Hold on, darling. Now it's my turn."

Isabel moaned from anticipation. Her juices flowed down her leg, and she was beyond ready to take him in. Then she felt it, his heat, his steel-hard shaft poking at her buttocks. He slowly guided himself to her center, and Isabel gasped at the contact.

Rhys plunged inside her in one hard thrust, pressing Isabel against the beam. His hands snaked around her, and he squeezed her breasts. Her peaks rubbed against his palms as he withdrew and drove himself inside again.

He continued the unrelenting rhythm, his grunts and her moans punctuating each thrust. The sound of their flesh meeting echoed through the gardens. Rhys bit on her shoulder and growled.

"Rhys…" Isabel moaned his name, unable to keep silent. She was close, so-so close again. Rhys lowered one of his hands and pressed his finger lightly against her swollen bud.

Fireworks lit up behind her eyelids again, and she let out a guttural moan.

Rhys growled against her skin, and then his seed filled her womb.

They stood there, still joined, their breathing accelerated, their bodies cooling with the light breeze.

"Well," Isabel said, wiping sweat off her forehead. "This was a bit longer than two minutes."

* * *

Isabel lay in Rhys's arms, watching the stars. Rhys had cleaned them up with her night rail, bundled her into her dressing gown, and now they lay on the grass, staring at the sky.

"Did you dream a year ago that—" Isabel started.

Chapter 32

"No," Rhys interrupted her.

"But I didn't even finish my question."

Rhys smiled against her shoulder. "Whatever you were going to ask, no. I had given up on dreaming about anything involving myself before I ran into you during that ball. The best ball of my life, by the way."

Isabel chuckled. She turned and looked at him, the dearest man on earth, and she couldn't hold it in any longer. "I love you," she said, pouring every feeling she had inside her into the words.

He just smiled and kissed her hair. "Thank God."

Chapter 33

The weather was beautiful the next day, so the party moved outdoors. Men played lawn games while women sat with children by the sidelines, watching their gentlemen in their masculine pursuits.

Isabel was especially glad that day because she'd gotten to spend some time with Millie, and Millie had gotten to see her parents interact with the members of the *haute ton*.

Isabel and Rhys had agreed that Millie would not have a governess for a while, and Isabel thought it imperative for Millie to learn etiquette by observing and copying others. And to have so many people interacting at once worked for her benefit.

But there was another reason she was enjoying that day. She loved watching Rhys in any kind of strenuous activity. That man was incredibly gorgeous. The wind in his hair and the sun on his skin only improved his overall appeal. Isabel watched as his muscles bunched beneath his clothes and fanned herself.

Chapter 33

"Isabel." Millicent tugged on her sleeve.

"Yes, dear?" Isabel turned to her.

"Can I go play over there?" Millie pointed to a lone tree a few feet away, where a few children laughed as Josephine Claremont, the troupe's lead actress, seemed to be performing some overly dramatic skit.

Isabel smiled. "Of course."

She stood to accompany Millicent, but before she could take a step, Millie had already taken off in the direction of the laughing children and entertaining actress.

Isabel followed her slowly, occasionally turning back to look at her handsome husband. She basked in the feeling of happiness, wondering how everything had turned out so perfect when somebody called her name. She stopped in her tracks and looked in the direction of the sound. Isabel shielded her eyes from the sun and squinted at the approaching lady.

As the woman caught up with her, Isabel finally recognized her. It was Lady Mowbray, Rhys's late wife's sister.

"Can I help you, Lady Mowbray?" Isabel asked with a sweet smile.

"On the contrary, my lady. I might be able to help you," the woman answered and looked around.

"Oh?"

"May we take a walk? I won't take much of your time, I promise," the woman insisted.

Isabel threw one more glance toward Millicent. She was surrounded by children and laughing uproariously at something the actress had done. Isabel looked toward her husband, who didn't seem to notice her disappearance from the sidelines, then turned back to Lady Mowbray and nodded.

"Very well, let's walk."

They moved away from the house with unhurried steps.

"What did you want to speak to me about?" Isabel asked after a moment of silence.

Lady Mowbray looked around again as if afraid of something or someone. "I've wanted to talk with you since the moment I arrived. Actually, since the moment I heard the news of your wedding."

"Well, in that case, I am very curious to hear what you have to say," Isabel said with a tight smile.

Lady Mowbray fiddled uncomfortably with the tips of her gloves. "I am usually not one to meddle, you see. But the marquess was married to my sister. I don't know if he told you—"

"He did," Isabel interrupted.

"Oh… Well, then you know who I am. And you know that my sister died because of him."

Isabel stopped sharply in her tracks and clenched her jaw. "Lady Mowbray, I do not mean disrespect, but I am not certain you know all the facts involving your sister's death, and you are not clear-headed enough about this."

"And are you the one clear-headed?" Lady Mowbray countered.

"I know you must have loved your sister very much," Isabel tried to say softly.

"And I saw the way you look at the marquess. You love him," Lady Mowbray insisted. "And perhaps that love is impairing your judgment."

Isabel let out an impatient breath. "What it is you wanted to say to me, Lady Mowbray?"

Tears appeared at the corners of her eyes. "I loved my sister.

Chapter 33

I still miss her immensely." She swallowed and dabbed the corners of her eyes with a handkerchief. "And she wasn't an angel, I shall be the first to admit, but she did not deserve to die."

"I am very sorry for your loss," Isabel said, slightly confused.

"When I just heard about your hasty marriage, I was horrified that you would repeat my sister's fate, you see," Lady Mowbray continued. "But I couldn't get to you at the wedding, and I didn't risk sending you a missive."

Isabel frowned. "What is so important you wanted to tell me?"

Lady Mowbray swallowed and looked around again. Then she dipped her hand into her pocket and took out a bundle of letters. "I have the way out for you."

Isabel took the bundle and rotated them in her hands. "The way out of what?"

"Of this marriage." At Isabel's startled look, she added, "See, I thought you were forced into this marriage. I heard as much. And I wanted to help you, but as I said, I was unable to reach you earlier. Now you seem content, perhaps even in love, but my sister was in love with the marquess, too, albeit not for long. She wrote me letters describing his misconduct and, yes, her own indiscretions, but perhaps reading these letters will help you understand who your husband truly is. And why my sister wanted to leave him."

"Whatever you say is in these letters seems too personal for me to read. I do not have the right to rummage through your late sister's personal missives. And whatever I need to know about my husband, I trust him to share with me."

Lady Mowbray nodded. "Then burn them. I do not need to hold on to the memories of my sister's painful past. But you might change your mind. If in a few years, you are still childless and your marriage is growing cold… Perhaps you'll want some answers or a way out. Understand that I wish you no harm. I just want to help you, if my help is appreciated. If not… well, you can discard those letters and go back to your life. I shall not bother you any longer."

* * *

Isabel had disappeared from the sidelines while Rhys was too concentrated on his lawn bowling match. Neither Isabel nor Millicent were watching him play, and he tried not to let that affect his ego, although his main goal was to show off especially for them.

He scanned the field with his gaze and finally saw Millicent sitting on the grass, watching an actress hop around the tree, laughing merrily.

Isabel was not there, however.

"Not bad," Gage said as he passed Rhys and clapped him on the shoulder.

"Thank you," Rhys said absently. Still unable to find his wife, Rhys stopped the viscount in his tracks. "Gage, do you mind keeping a close eye on Millicent for a while? Isabel has disappeared somewhere, and I wish to find her."

"Of course." Gage shrugged and walked toward the tree occupied by the children.

Rhys rushed in the other direction and, in a few moments, finally saw Isabel slightly to the side talking with some lady. The lady looked around then, and Rhys could clearly see her face. *Beatrice.*

What could the two possibly be discussing?

Chapter 33

He hurried toward them, but before he could reach them, Beatrice turned and hurried away. Rhys walked to Isabel with ground-eating strides while she stood there fiddling with something in her hands.

"Isabel," he called as he reached her side. "What did she want?"

Isabel turned toward him, a frown of confusion on her face. She licked her lips. "I don't know…."

Rhys nudged his chin toward the bundle in her hands. "And what are these?"

Isabel looked at the letters. "She said these are letters from your late wife to her."

An unpleasant shiver ran down Rhys's spine. "Why did she give them to you?"

"She said they were a way out for me."

"Way out of what?" Rhys's voice was oddly hoarse.

"Out of this marriage."

Rhys froze. "Did she describe the contents to you? Do you know what's in them?"

Isabel shook her head. "No. And I am not going to read them."

Rhys shifted from one foot to another. "Why not?"

Isabel looked at him queerly. "Because I do not need a way out."

"But… Aren't you curious?"

Isabel shook her head resolutely, and Rhys let out a breath of relief. She trusted him.

But what if the contents of those letters would change Isabel's mind? He wanted to know what kind of compromising evidence Beatrice had on him. It was probably all lies. Rhys might have been rude and arrogant, but he had never acted in a way that Isabel would find repulsive enough to leave him. Or at least he hoped he hadn't.

Still, he wanted to see what lies Beatrice had gathered about him.

"Whatever is in there, Beatrice wanted you to know," Rhys insisted.

"Well, I don't want to know. I do not want to read what your former wife had to say about you." She lifted the bundle in her hands. "And these are probably lies."

"What if they're not?"

She bit her lip and studied his face carefully. "You are curious. It is understandable. Perhaps if I was in your place, I would want to know as well. But it isn't my place to read them." She held out the letters. "You can if you want."

There was a pause as Rhys stood watching the bundle in her hands with an empty gaze.

"And after you're done, you can tell me if you still want me to know what's in them. I mean, truth or lies, these are intimate details about your life with your former wife. And I do not want to intrude unless you read the contents first."

She nudged the bundle toward him. Rhys took a deep breath and accepted the letters. *Do I really want to know?*

Something told him that he needed to.

* * *

Isabel entered her room to prepare for the opening ball. She hadn't seen Rhys since this morning when she'd nudged the bundle of letters his way. He'd left to read them in peace. Part of Isabel wished she had gone with him, held his hand, or just sat by his side.

Chapter 33

Where was he? What was written in those atrocious letters to make him disappear? And if he didn't return soon, what would Isabel do? How would she host the opening ball of the house party without him?

Surely he did not mean to leave her all alone!

She walked farther into the room and was about to call Anthea to help her change for the ball when she noticed the letters scattered on her bed. She walked toward them with quick steps and gathered them into her hands. A note enclosed with them was scribbled in Rhys's hand, and it only said two words:

Read them.

Isabel looked at the clock on the mantelpiece. "I'll read them later," she whispered. First, she needed to prepare for the ball. If she didn't, she might not have the strength after she'd read whatever those letters had to say.

So Isabel called for Anthea, got dressed, and pretended nothing was amiss until her maid left the room. She settled on the bed, took a deep breath, and started reading.

The letters started about a year into Abigail and Rhys's marriage. At first, they didn't seem that important. Abigail had complained that she did not enjoy her lot in life, calling Rhys cruel for not buying her more dresses or staying a long time in the country while she wanted to be in London. She was bored in the country home and unhappy with her husband. More than once, she mentioned she wished she could conceive an heir so Vane would be able to finally leave her alone, and she'd be free to carry out her liaisons in public, without fear.

Isabel swallowed. So she'd already had her liaisons at that time. Isabel's heart squeezed for Rhys. The woman had never loved him, and Rhys seemed unable to please her no matter what he did. But her letters were also full of fear.

What if I am barren as people whisper in the shadows? I shall have to stay with him forever.

Isabel's heart squeezed because she was afraid of a similar fate but for different reasons. What if she never conceived an heir for Rhys?

Isabel made it to the last letter, not quite comprehending which information from the woman's scattered thoughts would help her escape her marriage if need be. Or what Rhys thought was so imperative for her to know.

She picked up the last envelope and read the contents.

Dear Beatrice,

I am finally with child, though with no help from my husband. The ease with which I conceived makes me realize that I have not been the problem all along. Nobody would believe me that the marquess is the one who can't give me children. The poor bastard tied me to him and wasn't able to carry out his main duty—to sire a son.

If I am carrying a girl, pray for me because I shall attempt to run off with Marcus.

Much love,
Abigail

Isabel blinked, then reread the letter a few times to make sure she'd understood it correctly. The date of the letter corresponded with the date of Millicent's birth. Abigail spoke of Millicent in the letter.

Millie was not Rhys's.

Isabel's fingers shook as she placed the letter on the bed,

Chapter 33

her heart hurting for Rhys.

"Did you read them?" Rhys said from the doorway, and Isabel jumped.

"Rhys! Where have you been?" She hopped to her feet and hurried toward him, but he stepped away from her.

He was impeccably dressed for the ball, but his eyes were red as if he'd been crying. Isabel took a tentative step toward him. "Rhys—"

"Did you?"

Isabel nodded. "I did."

"And do you still want to stay married to me?"

Isabel blinked. "Of course. Why wouldn't I?"

"Even if I can't give you children?"

There was a knock on the door, and then Mr. Monroe stepped in with the flourish. "It is time for your first dance, my lord, my lady."

Isabel looked at Rhys. He stood silently for a moment before offering his arm. Isabel took it, her fingers shaking as she rested her hand on a steel-hard arm.

They walked through the house and into the ballroom in silence. As the lord and lady of the house, it was a tradition for them to start the ball with the first waltz. So they glided to the center of the ballroom, Rhys took Isabel into his arms, and the moment the music started, he swept her into a dance.

Rhys was a perfect dancer. His form was impeccable, his movements soft and smooth, and Isabel would have enjoyed the dance under any other circumstances, but her thoughts were not on the dance floor.

"Have you thought about it?" Rhys asked.

"About what?"

"A divorce," he said nonchalantly as he whirled her around

the dance floor. Other couples started joining them, and Isabel smiled at them as their eyes met.

"Are you out of your mind?" Isabel said to Rhys. "Why would I think of divorce?"

"You said you read the letters."

"And they told me nothing except that your late wife—may God rest her soul—was a selfish, vile woman. And I don't know how Lady Mowbray thought any of those ramblings would help me escape the marriage if I wanted to."

"By declaring me unfit to give you a son."

"Ramblings of a departed, lost soul do not constitute evidence, Rhys. You are physically capable. People would sooner think me barren than believe that you—"

"That's not the point," Rhys interrupted sternly.

"Then what is the point?" Isabel cried, then composed her features as they passed yet another couple. "Because I do not understand."

"The point is *you* can get a divorce. I can grant it to you. We can say I sustained an injury and am unable to perform my marital duty."

"But you can perform—"

"It doesn't matter if it doesn't result in a babe." He looked away.

Isabel's head was beginning to spin. "Rhys, I can't discuss this while we are spinning around the ballroom."

Rhys nodded and, after a few beats, glided out of the circle of dancers and seamlessly whirled Isabel from out of the ballroom and onto the patio.

"Here, now we are not spinning," he said as they came to a stop.

"Rhys, you are mad," she said as she disengaged from him.

Chapter 33

"Your wife could have been wrong. Millie could still be yours. You don't know—"

"But I do know!" Rhys turned away and raked his hand through his hair. "I do know," he repeated quieter.

He turned back to her, his eyes anguished. "The math didn't add up. I hadn't been intimate with Abigail for over ten months before Millie was born." He shook his head. "I always knew, although I preferred not to believe."

Isabel stood there watching the play of emotion on her husband's face. Regret. Anguish. Pain. Her eyes watered, and she took a step toward him.

"And do you love her less because of it?"

Rhys turned on her sharply. "Of course not!"

"Then how can I love you less just because you can't give me a babe?"

"You're not thinking clearly. If you stay married to me… You will *never* have a babe of your own. And I know you want to."

Isabel cleared her throat. "I have a babe. I have a wonderful six-year-old daughter who is as free-spirited and stubborn as her father. She is my daughter, Rhys, and you are my husband. My family. And I wouldn't wish for another one."

"You might regret it later," he croaked.

Isabel looked into the ballroom at the swirling couples. Most married couples there did not share affection or even respect toward one another. When the night fell, they went to another chamber to seek solace in someone else's arms. The only happy couples she knew were her sister Samantha and her husband, who could not share a bed because of his violent dreams, and Evie and her husband, the notorious rake whom scandal awaited behind every corner.

They were all scarred, but they were happy. And she would rather have an imperfect but happy marriage than what others perceived to be perfect but miserable for her. Because any other marriage, any other relationship that did not involve Rhys and Millicent, would never bring her happiness.

She took his hand in hers. "I might regret many things, Rhys. But the only thing I will never regret is marrying you."

Rhys squeezed her fingers. "I hope you won't come to regret these words either."

Isabel smiled. "You know that before I ran into you in Evie's ballroom, I was content being a spinster. No children, no husband, nothing but me and my quiet, peaceful life. Since I met you, I haven't had a moment's peace," she said with a laugh. "And yes, I thought I wanted a babe, someone to love and give me solace in an unwanted marriage. But I gained so much more. You gave me so much more." Her eyes started to tear up, and she licked her lips.

Rhys tugged her closer and placed his forehead against hers. Isabel took a deep breath, inhaling the lovely, calming scent of her husband.

"And I don't know if you truly can't give me a babe. I am not a young maiden, Rhys. Perhaps I wouldn't be able to birth a child as it is. But I know one thing."

"What is that?" His voice was hoarse.

"We can spend a lot of nights trying anyway."

Rhys let out a chuckle and kissed her on the lips.

The music ceased in the ballroom, the waltz ending.

Isabel heaved a sigh. "I don't want to go back to that ballroom. I don't want to go back to those suffocating walls."

Rhys looked at her, mischief glinting in his eyes. "We can leave. We don't have to go back."

Chapter 33

Isabel let out a giggle. "It is our ball. If we don't return, there will be a grand scandal."

Rhys chuckled, then cupped her face in his palm. "I spent the last seven years avoiding scandal. But it turned out that a scandal with you was the best thing that's ever happened to me."

Isabel's smile turned into a grin. "Then…" She looked back at the ballroom, remembering how she'd tried to be a perfect hostess, a perfect mistress her entire life. Rhys was right. The best thing had happened to her when she finally became the most scandalous lady of the *ton*. She looked into Rhys's eyes. "Then take me away, my lord."

"I know just the place." Rhys grinned before tugging on her arm and taking off in the direction of the gazebo.

Chapter 34

"You should have seen people's faces when they started realizing that you'd disappeared," Samantha said the next morning as they picnicked on the lawn.

All the guests were scattered around in small groups. Isabel sat next to Sam and Evie, hiding in the shade, while their brothers and husbands sat a few feet away under the harsh sun. Children once again gathered in the shadow of the tree to watch Josephine perform.

"Yes, they might have expected it from me—having a former unscrupulous rake for a husband gives one leeway for scandalous activity—but nobody had expected you two to disappear from your own ball!" Evie exclaimed with a giggle.

"You are just lucky you had us to pick up the mantle of hostess in your stead," Sam said.

Isabel pursed her lips. "I expected to be scolded by Richard, but I hoped you two would be understanding."

"Oh, we are very understanding." Evie waggled her brows and laughed.

Chapter 34

"Richard would be scolding you, too, if he hadn't spent the entire evening flirting with Josephine, therefore too busy to notice," Sam said.

Isabel rolled her eyes. She didn't want to know about her brother's shameless pursuits.

"I don't think I can blame your brother," Evie said. "The actress is gorgeous."

Isabel turned to look at the chestnut-haired beauty. She didn't disagree. But she was happier with her attitude rather than beauty. She kept the children occupied every day, and in the absence of the governess, she was the perfect distraction Millicent needed.

Nevertheless, Isabel could not ignore the fact that Josephine turned men's heads. Isabel turned to see if the actress had the same effect on her husband but instead collided with his heated gaze.

Isabel smiled, and Rhys winked at her.

"Vane? Did you hear a word I said?" Adam called. He then turned to see what had him distracted and groaned. "Stop staring at my sister. You're making me uncomfortable."

Everybody laughed.

"For shame," St. Clare called. "She is your wife. It's indecent to ogle her like that." And then he turned toward Evie.

Adam covered his face with his palms.

Isabel chuckled and fanned her burning cheeks.

"I am glad to see you so happy," Samantha noted. "I don't think I've seen you like this in the last ten years."

"I feel like it's the first time in years that I am." Isabel could not stop herself from grinning.

"And what about Millicent?" Evie asked. "How will you fare without a governess?"

Isabel straightened at the word governess. "I decided she is too young for one."

"You think so?" Sam asked.

"Yes. I was too worried that she was a wild little child, considering she wasn't raised by a lady, but I am not worried anymore. She has me to look up to, she has you, and I am certain both of you will visit often. And once she is about ten or twelve, we can start thinking of hiring a governess to prepare her for her debut."

"Or sooner if you have a brood of children to steal your attention," Sam teased.

Isabel thought she'd feel tightness around her chest at the words, but she didn't. She was not so certain she wanted a brood anymore. She had Millie, and that was enough.

Ashbury, Samantha's husband, padded over to his wife. "Our Angel needs you. Or at least, our nursemaid asked for a wet nurse," he said with a chuckle.

"Oh!" Sam laughed. "Well, that is me. Thank you, Isabel, for the lovely picnic. We shall see you at dinner, shall we not?"

Isabel chuckled. "I have no plans to avoid it so far."

Evie stood also. "I think I need a nap before dinner, too. Besides, my husband keeps looking at me and irritating your brother," she added with a giggle.

Isabel kissed Sam and Evie on their cheeks. She went to join Millicent under the tree, but Richard caught up with her and stopped her with his hand on her arm.

"Can I speak with you?"

Isabel blinked. "Of course."

He steered her away from the crowd.

"Is something amiss?" Isabel asked, watching the scowl on her brother's face.

Chapter 34

"No," he said. "Everything is perfect."

"That's good to hear," Isabel said slowly, unconvinced of the sincerity of her brother's words.

They stopped a few feet away, and Richard turned toward her. "I need a favor from you."

"Of course," Isabel answered readily. "Anything."

"I invited another family to come to your house party. I hope you do not mind."

Isabel wrapped her arms around herself against the light afternoon breeze. "Of course, I do not mind. I have a few spare rooms. Is that the favor?"

Richard shook his head. "No."

Isabel raised her brow. "Richard, please. You are making me nervous."

Richard let out a deep breath. "I want to...." He cleared his throat. "I'd like to make an announcement during the closing ball of your party."

Isabel blinked. "Of course, but what is the announcement?"

Richard cleared his throat, then looked at some point beyond Isabel's head. "My betrothal."

The End

Keep flipping for the epilogue!

If you are curious to know whom Richard, Viscount Gage, chose as a bride, get book 5 of the Necessary Arrangement series, An Affair with the Viscount
Release date: 23 August 2022

Sign-up to my newsletter to get a bonus novelette:
https://sendfox.com/sadiebosque

An Offer from the Marquess

By signing-up, you'll also get new release alerts, bonus content such as extra epilogues, deleted scenes and other.

After The End

Isabel stood in the garden, taking in the beauty of the flowers and enjoying the lovely floral scent.

"I saw you coming here. I thought you wanted me to follow," a familiar masculine voice said, and Isabel turned.

She groaned inwardly as she saw Stanhope approaching her. When would the man learn?

"No," Isabel said tightly. "I am actually waiting for someone else."

"I am not so certain you are," he countered.

Isabel was tempted to roll her eyes. Just then, loud steps sounded, and it felt as if the ground shook. Stanhope turned toward the sound, perplexed, before Button appeared behind a rose bush. The exuberant pup saw his mistress and, as was his custom, lunged at her.

Isabel slunk behind Stanhope and hurried to the other side of the garden just as Button tackled the poor man to the ground.

Millicent appeared from behind the bushes, followed by Rhys.

"What happened here?" Rhys barked as he saw Stanhope

lying on the ground as Button licked his face.

Isabel giggled. "Seems like Button made a new friend."

She walked toward her husband and kissed him on the lips.

"Ew!" Millie turned away with a grimace. "Button, come!"

The dog sprinted toward his little mistress, and the entire family walked out of the garden and toward the stream for their own little picnic.

* * *

Dear Mother,

Although this entire situation started as a disaster, now I am a very proud mother of a vivacious soon-to-be seven-year-old girl and a wife to the most attentive husband on earth.

You were right, sometimes mistakes catch up to us and make us pay, but sometimes it's a blessing in disguise. After all, we wouldn't have ices without a blizzard.

I hope you are resting in peace,
Until the time we meet again,
Isabel

Epilogue

Eleven years later...

Isabel wrung her hands in front of her, feeling as nervous as if it was her debut. *But, no.* At her debut, she was not nervous at all. She was delighted, bright-eyed, and absolutely excited for the next chapter of her life.

But today, Isabel had butterflies rioting in her stomach. She had been preparing for this night for two long months. The invitations, menus, decor, and everything else had taken a great deal of effort. The night seemed like a success, and still, Isabel felt as though she'd forgotten something.

Had she?

"You're beautiful," a low voice of her husband announced just behind her ear.

His warm breath moved the wisps of her hair, and shivers ran down her spine. He stepped closer then, his arm snaking around her waist. His hand burned through the layers of her clothes, tipping her off balance and anchoring her at the same time.

Isabel looked around at the crowd surrounding them. The open display of affection would once again get them in trouble. It wasn't proper, Isabel knew. But at the moment, she was too nervous to care.

So she accepted the embrace and leaned her back against Rhys's hard chest. She covered his hand on her waist with hers, her breaths evening out, her heartbeat slowing to the regular rhythm.

"How is she?" Isabel asked.

"Just like she was five minutes ago when you checked on her. Fearless." His voice held a note of pride.

Isabel smiled. "She gets that from you."

"I am confident everything good in her is from you." Rhys kissed the top of her head.

Isabel let out a nervous chuckle and was about to wriggle away from his arms, but Rhys tightened his hold on her.

"Stay awhile," he whispered.

"I can't." Isabel let out a deep sigh. "People will start gossiping again. And that's the last thing Millie needs. We must behave with decorum."

"Then why did you lean against me?" His low voice caused goosebumps to rise on her skin and a tingle low in her belly. Even after more than a decade, he still made her heart race.

"Because I needed your strength," she said, her voice oddly breathless.

Another kiss to the top of her head, and then he let go of her and stepped away.

Isabel reeled, not quite ready for him to leave, although she was the one who'd asked for it. Rhys stepped forward and placed his hand on the small of her back.

She looked up at him with a smile, love shining through her eyes.

"Lady Millicent Townsend," Mr. Monroe announced from

Epilogue

the top of the stairs, and all eyes moved to the lone figure making her way down.

Millicent glided gracefully in a shimmering blue gown, her eyes shining with happiness and a smile on her face. She was breathtakingly beautiful.

Tears burned at the back of Isabel's eyes as she remembered the small, uncoordinated little girl who tripped with her every attempt at a curtsy. She certainly had grown.

Rhys offered his arm to Isabel, and they both stepped forward to meet their daughter at the bottom of the stairs.

She sank into a deep curtsy before them, and Isabel placed a hand to her heart lest it escaped the confines of her body.

"You are the most beautiful debutante I've ever seen," she said.

"You are gorgeous," Rhys echoed. "How do you feel?"

Millicent smiled as she took her father's proffered arm. "Like I am ready to conquer the world."

Salted Almonds

In the novel, Lilian enjoys, and even craves, salted almonds.

When I wrote about Lilian's pregnancy, I knew she was going to need some sort of craving. And like many women in my life who had been pregnant, I assumed she'd want something crunchy and salty.

In my research, I came upon a lot of sweets and desserts, including sugary almonds, which were popular in Regency times, but nothing salty. At least, nothing that I thought would fit Lilian.

So I decided that as a working woman, she would just make up a recipe of her own.

Salted almonds actually became popular during Victorian times, and more variety of recipes were invented during Edwardian times. Not to say that people did not make them during the Regency times; they were just not popular.

Who is to say that Lilian wasn't the one to invent the very first recipe for salted almond?

Printed in Great Britain
by Amazon